PRAISE FOR
THE HOUSE IMMORTAL NOVELS

Infinity Bell

"Grit and adrenaline drive the action-filled, romance-tinged second novel in Monk's House Immortal SF/fantasy series.... Continuous action makes for a roller-coaster effect as the myriad twists and turns of politics and time travel slam together. Each sentence is crafted for maximum impact with exquisite storytelling and relatable, emotional characters."
—*Publishers Weekly*

House Immortal

"Like Monk's Allie Beckstrom, Matilda has the misfortune to be sought after by powerful immoral men; she has been dealt a no-win hand, and the entertainment is in watching how she plays it out." —*Publishers Weekly*

"I love Devon Monk's books. There is something about each story that sucks the reader in completely and doesn't let go ... an excellent story. Devon Monk is incredible at weaving a tale that makes the reader excited, crazy, and astonished all at the same time." —Fiction Vixen

"Original and intriguing ... [a] kick-ass heroine, powerful, near-immortal beings, fun sidekicks, and [an] original world."
—All Things Urban Fantasy

"I didn't want to stop reading. *House Immortal* kept my interest every second." —Yummy Men & Kick Ass Chicks

"A fresh and unique world.... Devon Monk once again proves she's a powerhouse in the genre." —A Book Obsession

"*House Immortal* brings *Frankenstein* into a new world, and Devon Monk puts it together excellently!" —Drey's Library

continued ...

"Beautifully written and brilliantly imagined."
— *New York Times* bestselling author Rachel Vincent

"Action and romance combine with a deft precision that will keep readers turning pages—and anxiously awaiting the next volume." — *Publishers Weekly*

"Monk flawlessly blends fantasy, steampunk, and Western in this fantastic series." — SciFiChick.com

"An exhilarating adventure-thriller that grips the audience."
— Genre Go Round Reviews

"Monk's entrance into steampunk is a tour de force."
— *RT Book Reviews* (top pick)

PRAISE FOR THE ALLIE BECKSTROM NOVELS

"Loved it. Fiendishly original and a stay-up-all-night read. We're going to be hearing a lot more of Devon Monk."
— #1 *New York Times* bestselling author Patricia Briggs

"Gritty setting, compelling, fully realized characters, and a frightening system of magic-with-a-price that left me awed. Devon Monk's writing is addictive."
— *New York Times* bestselling author Rachel Vincent

"Highly original and compulsively readable."
— Jenna Black, author of *Resistance*

"Breathtaking. . . . Monk is a storyteller extraordinaire!"
— *RT Book Reviews*

"Urban fantasy at its finest. . . . Every book is packed with action, adventure, humor, battles, romance, drama, and suspense."
— *Sacramento Book Review*

"Dark and delicious. . . . Allie is one of urban fantasy's most entertaining heroines." — *Publishers Weekly* (starred review)

BOOKS BY DEVON MONK

The House Immortal Series

House Immortal
Infinity Bell
Crucible Zero

The Broken Magic Series

Hell Bent
Stone Cold

The Allie Beckstrom Series

Magic to the Bone
Magic in the Blood
Magic in the Shadows
Magic on the Storm
Magic at the Gate
Magic on the Hunt
Magic on the Line
Magic Without Mercy
Magic for a Price

The Age of Steam

Dead Iron
Tin Swift
Cold Copper

CRUCIBLE ZERO

A HOUSE IMMORTAL NOVEL

DEVON MONK

A ROC BOOK

ROC
Published by New American Library,
an imprint of Penguin Random House LLC
375 Hudson Street, New York, New York 10014

This book is an original publication of New American Library.

First Printing, September 2015

Copyright © Devon Monk, 2015

For more information about Penguin Random House, visit penguin.com.

ISBN 978-0-451-46738-6

Printed in the United States of America
10 9 8 7 6 5 4 3 2 1

Penguin
Random
House

For my family

ACKNOWLEDGMENTS

This book wouldn't be nearly as shiny and strong without the excellent guidance from my editor, Anne Sowards. My gratitude to her, and all the many talented, hardworking people at Penguin who helped bring this book to fruition, knows no bounds. Thank you also and always to my agent, Miriam Kriss. To the wonderful artist Eric Williams—thank you for bringing Matilda to life and for giving her that great jacket.

An especially big thank-you to my wonderful first reader, Dean Woods, who not only helped me navigate the logic holes inherent in adding a component of time travel to a story, but also read through many, many drafts of the trilogy as a whole. Thank you also to Dejsha Knight, first reader and best friend extraordinaire, for all your support along the way. To my big, fabulous family— I love you. Thank you for sharing in the fun with me. And to my husband, Russ, and my sons, Kameron and Konner, thank you for being such great people. You are the best part of my life. I love you all dearly.

Finally, and most importantly, thank you, dear readers, for letting me share this twisty-turny adventure with you. I hope you have enjoyed this world, these people, and their stories.

1

I'm not one to write my thoughts down. But the doctors say a journal is good for my mental state. So from this ruined and dying body, I cast my hello. If you're out there, Matilda, I'll find you.

—W.Y.

"This is a bad idea, Evelyn. A bad idea." My brother, Quinten Case, paced the dirt patch just outside our farmhouse door, one hand stuck stiff-fingered in his dark, curled hair. His other hand kept drifting toward the gun holstered on his thigh, while his gaze flicked constantly toward the kitchen window. The flannel shirt and work boots he wore didn't disguise who I knew he really was: a restless genius and a brilliant stitcher of living things.

I should know. After all, I was one of the living things he'd stitched together.

"Matilda," I corrected him gently. I was sitting on the top edge of a rain barrel, *thunk*ing my bootheels absently against the hollow side of it, and wondering what else about my farm and my world had changed since the Wings of Mercury experiment had broken and then mended time. "I'm not Evelyn anymore, Quinten."

He pulled his fingers out of his hair and waved impatiently at me. I guess he was still trying to get used to the changes in his world too.

I understood why he was calling me Evelyn.

I was born his sister, and named Matilda Case. But when I was a little girl, I'd become deathly ill. Quinten and his genius mind had found a way to transfer my thoughts, my personality, my mind into the comatose body of a girl named Evelyn. A girl who had been asleep for more than three hundred years.

He stitched everything that made me *me* into her. It had been a desperate, risky thing to try. But he had succeeded. In my world, in my time, I'd woken up in her body as Matilda, and lived until I was twenty-six.

That was when we'd done something even more desperate: Quinten had sent me back in time to change the Wings of Mercury experiment. We didn't have much choice, really. If I hadn't gone back in time, billions of people would have died.

That was how I remembered it. That was what had happened in my time.

But in this world, in this time line, Evelyn had been the one who had woken up when my brother had tried to transfer my mind into her body.

She'd lived until today, just a few minutes ago when I'd found myself standing in the kitchen. I'd felt Evelyn in my mind with me for a moment. Then she had lifted, all her memories and thoughts fading like smoke on the wind.

My going back in time was supposed to save the world. And it had.

But it had also changed it in massive, chaotic ways.

So far, I'd been told there was a war going on between the Houses who ruled the resources in the world. House Brown, or House Earth, as Quinten had told me it was referred to now, was the house that used to be made up of a loosely connected network of people, each living on their own piece of land. Those people had rejected servitude to the other Houses to live free, and were now living in several walled strongholds scattered across the world.

Another huge change I was still trying to wrap my mind around was that the galvanized, people like me who had survived the original Wings of Mercury experiment and whose brains and bodies were more than three hundred years old and stitched, were some kind of wanted criminals.

Back in my time, the galvanized had done a lot of good for the world, and for people and human rights.

"You have a price on your head," Quinten said, back to pulling at his hair again. "They—those killers in our kitchen—shouldn't even be here."

"I know." In my time, I'd had a price on my head too. That, unfortunately, hadn't changed. One of these days I'd figure out how to avoid such trouble in my life.

"How can that even be possible?" he demanded. "No one, except Neds and Grandma, knows you exist."

"Someone knows," I said, waiting for him to turn and start pacing back the other way.

"No. You can't be a wanted criminal if no one knows you're alive."

"I take it you registered my death when I was young?" It was a weird thing to ask, but, then, I'd led a weird life.

He nodded, his palm resting on the top of his head so his elbow jutted out. "We never registered Evelyn as alive, since she wasn't technically or medically supposed to be alive. She was just a forgotten medical experiment

Dad got his hands on before things really went to hell. There is no Matilda Case alive on record."

"Still, you couldn't have kept Evelyn in the basement all her life," I said, hoping to lighten things up a bit. "We must have neighbors or friends who saw her and maybe thought she was me."

"Yes, we have friends. But they think Matilda died. And we told them Evelyn was a child our parents took in after the One-three plague killed her parents."

"One-three plague?"

He stopped, lowering his hand finally. Stared at me, his eyes flicking across my face as if looking for a lie there. "It's . . . eerie," he said. "Knowing you're not you."

"I am me," I said softly. "I'm just not her."

He nodded, and sorrow darkened his eyes. "For the past fifty years, we've had a plague hit each decade. One-three spread widely enough, it wiped out millions."

"Oh," I said. "Oh." There had been no widespread plague in my time. I was still reeling with the changes of this world, and I knew Quinten had his own things to get his brain around.

But in my time, Quinten had died from a terrible explosion. We had been hunted by the Houses who chased us to our farmhouse. The House soldiers had killed Quinten; our farmhand, Neds Harris; and the galvanized Abraham and Foster. They'd killed the others who had helped us too—Welton, who was head of House Yellow, and House Brown's doctor, Gloria.

Even though this news of plague wasn't exactly welcome, so far I preferred this time and this world, in which my brother and the people I loved were alive.

Whatever else was wrong here, we'd make right. This was the only world left to us. That time-travel trick had been a one-shot deal.

"Could it be the stitching?" I asked. "If someone had seen my stitching, they'd know I was galvanized, right? And galvanized are . . . criminals?"

He pulled up the sleeve of his flannel, his eyes locked on mine.

I glanced down at his tanned forearm. Muscular, a few lines of scars that had healed too white against his tanned skin. A row of neat, small stitches ran at an angle below his elbow.

Everything in me chilled.

"Everyone is stitched, Ev— Matilda," he said. "At most times, anyway."

I couldn't take my eyes off that tidy row of thin gray thread piercing my brother's arm. "Why?"

"The One-one plague made healing slower and more difficult. Things go necrotic more often than not. Especially open wounds. If you want a cut to heal, you need to stitch and keep it as clean as possible."

"So those stitches aren't permanent?"

He shook his head and rolled his sleeve back down. "I'll take them out at the end of the month if everything looks okay."

"Are mine permanent?" I asked, a small hope catching in my heart.

"Yes. You are galvanized. But since nearly everyone goes around with stitches, spotting a galvanized isn't easy. And no one I know thinks you are a galvanized."

"So people just assume I'm recovering from injuries," I said.

He nodded. "You— I mean, Evelyn keeps her stitches covered when anyone from House Earth stops by."

"I thought you said no one knew I was alive."

"No one except the people in House Earth whom I trust implicitly. Well, and the Grubens."

I shook my head. "The what?"

"Family down a ways. Closest we Cases have to relatives. They're an . . . energetic bunch, but loyal to the grave."

"So stitches aren't rare, and my being galvanized isn't why someone wants me dead. That's different."

"Are the galvanized the only stitched where— I mean, *when* you came from?" he asked.

"Yes. Twelve of them, plus me. They were owned by the Houses. They were celebrities, in a way. World changers. Heroes. They did a lot of good, Quinten. We did a lot of good. I knew Abraham. I knew Foster." I pointed toward our house, where both Abraham and Foster were drinking tea at our kitchen table, probably at gunpoint. "We trusted them then with our lives, and they died trying to protect us."

"What's your point, Ev?" he asked.

"Matilda," I said. "We should trust them now."

"That would be suicide."

"Because they're galvanized?"

"Because they are here to collect on that price on your head," he said.

"Abraham said he came to warn us that there was a price on our heads."

The crease between his lowered eyebrows deepened. "They're mercenaries, Matilda. All galvanized are mercenaries. Guns for hire. No loyalties to anything other than money. No loyalties to Houses, people, or each other. It's what they do."

Oh.

"Well, that's not what they're going to do here. We should at least get as much information out of them as we can, don't you think?"

"There's nothing they know that I want or will pay for," he said flatly. "I do not do business with galvanized."

"Well, I do." I hopped down off the water barrel, my boots landing with a crunchy *thud* in the dirt and gravel. I dusted my hands.

"They came to our farm looking for me and for *you*," I said. "I'm not the only one someone wants dead. We don't know why someone wants me dead, since no one should know I'm alive. But from the way you're acting all nervous and hair-pully, I think you know exactly why your head is worth hunting."

"It's a mistake," he scoffed.

"No, I don't think it is. What did you do that has made someone want to kill you, Quinten?"

He pulled his shoulders back and tipped his head up, as if I'd just punched him in the chest. It took him a moment or two before he answered.

"You are not at all like Evelyn," he said slowly. "Do you know that? She was kind. Trusting. She was the sweetest girl I'd ever known. And she would never have accused me of doing something worth being killed over."

His words stung. Quinten and I had been close. Hell, I practically worshiped the ground his boots trod upon. It hurt to hear him tell me I wasn't as good as the sister he loved more than me. A girl I could never live up to. A girl I could never be.

But I knew him. He had a habit of striking out when people got too close to the things he didn't want to talk about. I refused to back down on this.

I lifted my chin and stared him in the eyes. "I'm sorry I'm not her. Really, I am. I'm sorry you've lost her. I'm sorry she's gone. But you haven't answered the question I asked," I said calmly. "Tell me what you did, Quinten. If I don't know why someone wants to kill you, I can't help you stay alive."

"No."

It was my turn to study him, looking for clues. His body language said he wasn't going to budge on his silence. His eyes had gone all sharp and judgy. Closed off.

Fine. He wasn't the only person on the property who had information.

There were three mercenaries at my kitchen table. They must know who had put the hit out on us. Someone had to be paying them. Maybe they'd have a clue as to why we had suddenly become such hot property.

"I may not be as sweet as Evelyn," I said, unable to be angry at him. "But you, brother, haven't changed a bit. You are just as stubborn, smart, and insufferably righteous as you've always been. And I wouldn't want you any other way." I took a few steps and dropped a quick kiss on his cheek. "I missed you." I patted his arm. "But you're being an idiot."

I strode off toward the corner of the house, and the kitchen door beyond.

The twisting sensation of an elevator suddenly plunging down flights of a building hit me. I stumbled, but caught myself before I fell. The sharp scent of roses filled my nose and mouth as I gasped, and my ears rang with the distance echo of a bell.

My vision blurred, and I blinked hard to clear it. The house in front of me dissolved into nothing but a pile of rubble, as if an explosion had reduced it to smoldering dirt and timbers. Men in black uniforms milled around it.

My heart raced. Something was wrong. Something was very wrong. I looked behind me, and Quinten was no longer there. But it wasn't just Quinten that was missing. This world had changed.

No. The world had shifted. This world, this property

with the broken, burning house, was the property and world from my original time.

But I didn't want to be in my time. In my time, my brother was dead.

I must have made a sound.

One of the men looked over at me. "Hey. What are you doing? This location is under House Black lockdown. There's been an explosion. It isn't safe to be here."

I heard him—honestly I did. But all I could see was the destroyed farmhouse on the very familiar land where I had grown up. All of it exactly as I remembered, and not the different world I'd woken up in recently.

If this was the time I remembered and had grown up in, that meant my brother was currently dead, buried under that pile of rubble that used to be our home.

"Matilda?"

I turned to that familiar voice. John Black, head of House Black, wore a black uniform like the other men, but carried himself with a manner of authority and bulldog strength. He had just come around the corner of the rubble field and looked as startled as I felt.

"Were you in the explosion?" he asked striding my way. "Were there any other survivors? Welton Yellow, or your brother, Quinten? Have you seen Abraham?"

I shook my head and pressed my hand over my mouth, words stuck somewhere in the clot of panicked silence filling my brain.

He stopped in front of me. "You're shaking," he said, not unkindly for a man who had been sent to bring me in as a fugitive accused of murder. "Matilda, tell me what happened here."

And then the world twisted again, filling with that dizzy rose scent. John Black reached out for me. I reached back. I felt the warm pressure of his fingers on my wrist, and then he was gone—whisked away as if he were a curtain that had been pushed aside to show the open window behind it.

I was holding my breath, my hand cupped over my mouth.

The house was standing in front of me, whole. The day was quiet and still. In the distance, I heard a bird warble, and a sleepy lizard answer with a rumble.

"Ev— Matilda?" Quinten said from behind me.

Relief washed over me, and I finally exhaled. He was alive. Quinten was alive, and I was back in the time where I belonged.

I turned and dropped my hand from my mouth. The faint ringing in my ears was gone, the flower scent faded.

A very alive Quinten strode my way, wearing flannel, jeans, and boots, an irritated scowl on his face. "Where do you think you're going?"

"Did you feel that?" I asked. "Just now, did you get dizzy or smell roses or see . . . anything?"

He paused and gave me a look. "No. Why, did you?"

I took in the scenery behind him. This was still the property I'd always known, but the familiar pear orchard wasn't in sight, and a flock of six pocket-sized sheep of various pastel shades shambled along a fence line, stopping to nibble on weeds there.

We had only three pocket-sized sheep in the time I was from.

I must have been back to the time where Evelyn had grown up.

"I felt something. I . . . saw someone," I said. "Do you know John Black?"

He shook his head. "Matilda . . ."

"He must have been an echo," I said. "No, it was more

than that. I saw what this place used to be. What I knew it as. He was real. He felt real."

"You're telling me you saw something from your own time?"

"Or I somehow stepped into my time. Is that possible? Did I just disappear and reappear?"

He camped back on one foot and stuck his hands in his pockets. "No. You were walking toward the house, and I was walking after you."

"Maybe it was just a second for you, but longer for me. Why would that happen? What would make that happen?"

"Don't look at me," he said. "Until today, I would have told you time travel—of any kind—was impossible, and now you're telling me you've experienced it twice. Maybe you're just tired, and your brain can't sort through what's happened. Maybe it's old memories surfacing. Some glitch in the switch between what Evelyn knew and remembered and what you know and remember."

It wasn't a hallucination. That had been John Black. That had been his touch. And that had been our demolished house. I was sure of it. But I had no way to prove it to Quinten.

"Okay." I swallowed and nodded. "Okay. Maybe it's just a onetime thing. I can deal with that." I set my shoulders and turned back toward the house. Sometimes experiments had unintended consequences. Maybe seeing into my old time stream was that consequence.

Or maybe it was a fluke of the Wings of Mercury mending time. A wrinkle that hadn't been ironed out yet.

Whatever it was, I would handle it if it came up again. Right now, here in this time—the real time—I needed to save our lives.

"Where are you going?" he asked.

"To get the information I need to save both our heads."

I heard the sound of his boots as he did a short jog to catch up with me. "Does *no* mean something else in your time?" he asked.

"No."

That, finally, got a chuckle out of him. "Just— Please. Listen to me on this. Trust me on this. I know the way the world works, with or without time travel."

"I am listening. I am also going to get us some information."

"We do not do business with mercenaries."

"Is that the family motto?"

"It is now."

"Well, I'm still following the other family motto: do whatever necessary to keep the people you love alive."

Quinten swore softly.

We'd rounded the house. The big barn was behind us now, a worn wooden structure two stories high with odd creatures slipping or winging in and out of the windows, doors, and other cracks of it. I hadn't had time to get acquainted with the stitched beasties my brother was keeping, but from the glimpses I'd caught, Quinten had a full-blown menagerie here.

However, I had not missed the half-dozen winged lizards of various impressive sizes that skulked a little farther out by the trees and filled up the dirt road, belly-flat soaking up the sun.

"Sure are a lot of dragons around the place," I noted.

"Lizards," he automatically corrected me, just like I corrected everyone else who had met our single stitched, winged monstrosity back in my time.

"Do you use them for scale jelly?"

"Of course. Other than stitching, it's the jelly that keeps this place running," he said. "But mostly the lizards patrol the property and make sure the things and people we don't want here never make it to the house."

"How many do you have?"

"Thirty-six."

I shot him a grin. "We had only one. Big as a barn."

"Still do," he said. "And, well, a lot of others, the size of other buildings."

"As soon as I get the three killers in our kitchen sorted away, I want to see all the critters. We had a unicorn. Well, sort of a unicorn."

Quinten picked up the pace enough that he reached the door at the same time I did. He straight-armed it, his palm smacking flat in the middle of the wood. "Listen to me, Matilda."

I stopped, folded my arms over my chest. Waited.

His face was a little sweaty from the jog, but also pale. "We are not on their side. They are not on ours. They want us dead, and they plan to make a profit on our deaths. Anything they say, any information they give us, is suspect."

"I don't see that we have a choice," I said. "Good idea, bad idea—doesn't matter. We need to know who wants us dead and why. They can tell us."

The door opened, swinging inward.

Quinten moved back and took hold of one of the guns under his overshirt so quick, you'd think he was on fire.

I stood my ground but didn't draw the gun strapped to my thigh.

In that doorway, filling most of it with all six foot six of his height and muscle, was the galvanized Abraham Seventh. The man I'd loved.

In a different world.

In a time that I didn't think existed.

The man who was now a stranger to me.

2

*The only problem with dying is it takes so
damn long. Of course, the same could be said
of living.*

—W.Y.

Abraham was powerfully built in my time. But here
everything about him was harder, carved, chiseled,
as if there had never been a day of easy living to soften
him. His hair was long, pulled back off his tanned face
with a band, revealing grim scars on his face and thick
black threads tacking a line down one cheek to the edge
of his mouth. Another row of stitches slashed up away
from the opposite eyebrow to his hairline.

His eyes were still his: hazel flecked with red. The red
was a result of him either being angry or in pain, though
all galvanized were numb to physical sensation, including pain.

And he was handsome—gods, he was good-looking.

His wide forehead, lined with too much worry, held
eyebrows that were darker than his brown hair. His nose
was arrow straight, giving his angled cheeks a hard edge,
even though scruff covered cheeks and jaw.

I knew that face was capable of great joy and laughter. I'd seen him laugh so hard, his entire body radiated joy. I knew his eyes softened with kindness, compassion, and human goodness.

Or, at least, those were the things he had been. Now he was all edges and intensity.

A hammer looking for an anvil to strike.

I couldn't see the muscles under his layers of clothing, but his movements had a tension and fluidity that made it clear he had often, and would at any moment, fight.

My stomach tightened with electric tingles that made it hard to keep a needful gasp from escaping my mouth. I wanted him to be mine again.

I had loved him. I still loved him.

I searched for some recognition of that connection in his stern expression.

Nothing.

"Decided to kill us yet?" he asked, his voice low.

"We're keeping our options open," I said.

He didn't smile. I guess he hadn't been joking.

Abraham wore sturdy, loose leather pants, a layering of cotton and wool shirts under his jacket, and an arsenal of weapons. Over his shoulder jutted the butt of a long gun and an ax. A bandolier of bullets crossed his chest, giving me just a hint on the hard muscles beneath his shirts and making me wish I could see more. Handguns were holstered at both hips.

That was a lot of weapons for a galvanized to carry, considering he didn't need weapons to kill a man dead. A galvanized is so strong, all we need is our bare hands to end a life, bloody and quick.

And while Quinten and Abraham hadn't drawn weapons on each other, they were doing that man thing: squared off and glaring, just waiting for an excuse to start a fight.

So I stepped up between them to make it clear that neither of them had time for this.

"Back it up, stud," I said, pointing toward the kitchen behind Abraham.

Quinten choked on the inhale of whatever he'd been about to say.

Abraham's mouth twitched upward on the unstitched side for a second, and that familiar flash of wicked humor flickered in his eyes, then was gone.

"Stud?" he repeated, tipping his head down and narrowing his gaze.

I stepped toward him, as if I were going to walk right through him. "You heard me. Move it back, good-looking."

Abraham paced backward, still squared off to me as I strolled into my kitchen, the look on his face a mix of curiosity and caution.

It was like a dance, his movements and mine, and we were in perfect sync. Memories, hot and suddenly intense, flashed through me. My body tingled with the sensation of his wide hands against my skin, his mouth pressed to mine, his tongue exploring me.

We had been good together.

Really good.

Back in my time, I'd regretted waiting to sleep with him. I'd promised if I had a chance to do it all over again, I'd put sex with Abraham as number one on my to-do list.

But now? I didn't think he wanted anything to do with me. I found myself wanting to move forward with some caution. Just because he had been a man I loved before didn't mean I would love him now.

"Problem?" Abraham asked.

I realized I'd lost a few seconds to my thoughts. My hand was raised toward him midreach, the other pressed against my stomach. He hadn't moved, but Quinten had stepped into the room and closed the door.

Everyone in the kitchen was looking at me.

This was not the time to appear crazier than they already thought I was.

"Matilda?" Quinten said.

"I'm fine," I said.

"Move away from her, stitch," Left Ned said, breaking the mood and scrambling up a new one.

I glanced over to where he was standing near the icebox, a sawed-off shotgun tucked against his shoulder.

Neds Harris was our farmhand. He was all one body, with extra width to his shoulders so his two blond-and-blue-eyed heads could rest side by side in a pleasing, if unusual, arrangement of parts. In my time, Right Ned was always the kinder, more thoughtful of the two, while his brother, Left Ned, had a more suspicious, blunt nature.

Looked like they weren't any different in this time. They'd told me once that Right Ned controlled the left side of their body, and Left Ned controlled the other. So that meant Left Ned was the one ready to do the shooting.

Typical.

"Neds Harris," I said. "I said I was fine, and these are our guests."

"So?" Left Ned said.

"So we do not bring guns to the kitchen table. Set it aside. We all know we can kill each other if we're of the mind to. Waving it around isn't making a point. It's just being rude."

Sallyo, a woman whom I'd only met once, chuckled. She sat at the table, a cup of tea in one hand, and looked as relaxed as could be. Sallyo was pale and pretty, her eyes snake-pupiled, which indicated she was born a bit like

Neds: mutated. Her dark hair was shaved off above her ears, leaving the rest pulled into a heavy braid down her back. Hard and lean, the sleek and deadly woman had run the biggest, most feared smuggling ring in the world.

I knew zilch about her in this time, though. Well, I knew she had just showed up on my doorstep with Abraham and Foster First, the latter of whom was also galvanized, and albino pale, white-haired, huge, and silent.

Sallyo lifted her fingers. "I wouldn't say no to food, if you have any."

"Tea's customary," Left Ned said. "But you'll pay for food."

"You know I'm good for it, Harris," she said.

"I know you're good for nothing, Sallyo." That was the coldest, hardest thing I'd ever heard out of Right Ned's mouth.

"I'm sure we have plenty to share," I said into the weighted silence. "Foster?" I asked the seven-foot-tall gravedigger, who stood next to Abraham, silently scanning the people in the room. "Would you like some tea? Or cocoa?"

His red eyes lit up. "Cocoa?" His voice was low and gravelly, as if left unused for so long, it had gone to dust.

"Let me see what we have." I pointed at the table. "Go ahead and sit down. Make yourself comfortable." I gave Abraham a look. "You too."

Abraham waited to see what Quinten was going to do.

Quinten stared at me a moment longer, then holstered the gun he'd drawn.

Abraham strolled over to the table and sat down, his long legs taking up a lot of space.

"You too, Quinten," I said as I turned to the cupboards. "We'll all feel better after a bit to eat. So," I said, "there's a price for killing my brother and me?" I opened the cupboard where we usually kept baking goods and was tearfully relieved to find the cocoa there.

I'm not going to lie. Coming back to a world that was not quite the same world I'd lived in all my life was spooky on so many levels, it was overwhelming. If I thought about it for too long, if I lingered on the consequences of having both gained and lost everything I loved, I was going to be asking for a panic attack.

And that little time twitch outside I'd just experienced wasn't helping my nerves any.

Better to stay busy, keep everyone talking, and find out how to remove myself and my brother from the wanted list.

"There is a reward for finding you," Abraham said. "But that is not why we came here."

"Now, now," Quinten said. "No need to lie. We know what you do. We know what you are."

"Tell me, Mr. Case," Abraham said. "What are we?"

"Mercenaries. Bounty hunters. Galvanized," Quinten said.

"Not to mention murderous, thieving bastards," Left Ned muttered.

Foster growled softly.

"The only reason you are here is to collect on that price," Quinten said.

"Well, that's good news!" I said.

"The price on our heads?" Quinten asked.

I turned with a jar in my hand. "No. We have cocoa."

Left Ned sucked a little air between his teeth with a *snick* sound. Right Ned shook his head as if he still hadn't gotten used to words coming out of my mouth.

"Anyone else want some?" I shook the jar. "We have plenty."

"We came," Abraham said, completely ignoring me

and instead leaning forward toward Quinten, his legs pulled back so he was in a better position to spring into a fight, if need be, "to warn you. To warn her." He nodded toward me. "Nothing more."

Sallyo shifted a bit too, and I noticed one of her hands had disappeared under the table. Probably to draw her gun.

Damn it. We did not need a shoot-out.

"Good," I said. "Great. Then my brother, Neds, and I will take you at your word, Abraham."

"You don't speak for me," Left Ned said.

"Matilda," Quinten admonished, as if I were a child who had interrupted while the adults were handling business.

"We welcomed them into our home," I said. "No one gets shot. Understand?"

The tension in Abraham, the coil of anger, shifted to a hard sort of caution. It was like watching someone close all the shutters on a glass house. Everything about him went dark, flat, but there was still a lot of emotion leaking through his walls.

"Also?" I pointed at the gun Left Ned still had in his hand. "I asked you once to please put that down. This is the last time I'm going to ask you. Next up, I'll make you put it down."

He looked over at Quinten, and to my surprise, my brother nodded.

"Might as well," he said to Neds. "She has questions she isn't going to let go unanswered. And, frankly, so do I." Quinten took the time to make eye contact with each of the strangers in the room. "You are welcome to a meal. But I would advise you not to pick a fight. This is our land, and that makes us the law here. We don't have to stand up in any court and tell them where we buried the bodies. Do we have an understanding?"

"We have an understanding," Sallyo said, placing both

hands on the table. "And you have my curiosity. Ask your questions."

Abraham still hadn't moved. His eyes flicked and dismissed Neds, then settled on me, tracking my every movement as if I were the dangerous one here.

That was interesting.

"Hold on. Let me get cocoa for Foster, because I promised." I put some milk on the stove to warm, then opened a few cupboards and checked the bread box and icebox for food. "It looks like we'll be having a cold lunch." I pulled out cheese, pickled eggs, meat, and rolls.

Quinten paced over to the table, and Abraham's attention switched to him.

"There are some sauces on the lower shelf," Quinten said as he pulled out a chair and sat, purposely putting his back to Foster. It was a very clear sign that he was in the mood to be trusting.

Thank you, brother.

Foster First locked gazes with Abraham. If I didn't know better, I'd think they could read each other's thoughts. But galvanized weren't telekinetic or magical. At least, they weren't in my time.

Abraham nodded, and Foster walked across the kitchen, his steps betraying just how heavy of a creature he was.

Sallyo used her foot to scoot out a chair for Foster to sit next to her.

"Shee-it," Left Ned said. Then he finally pushed away from the wall and took a seat at the table, resting the shotgun at his knee.

A genius, a smuggler, a two-headed man, and three stitched monsters sit down for tea, I thought to myself.

"So, who wants us dead?" I asked as I pulled out the jars of sauces, then the meat and cheese, and set them all on the table. I added an empty plate for each person.

"We don't have details," Sallyo said.

Okay, so she was the boss of this party. Good to know.

"Are you sure about that?" Left Ned asked. "It's not like you to take a job without them."

She shrugged. "I have a contact. Who has a contact. Who has a contact. It goes back to House Fire. I know that much."

I poured the warmed milk, cocoa, and sugar into a big mug. "What's House Fire?"

Quinten cleared his throat into the silence. "You know House Fire, Matilda," he said slowly. "Half of all the Houses that rule the world joined under that name. The other half joined under House Water, remember?"

"Right," I lied. I did not remember that, because it was not how things were in my time. "Fire, Water. Must be all the excitement has my mind slipping. Sorry." I dug through our pantry for marshmallows, but couldn't find any, so I dropped a stick of cinnamon candy into the mug.

"Here we go." I handed the mug to Foster.

His face lit up like a kid at a fair, and he very carefully took the cup into both his huge hands. "Thank you, Matilda," he said in that rolling rumble of his.

"You are very welcome."

He closed his eyes and inhaled the steam rising off the cocoa. When he opened his eyes, he took a sip and savored it like fine wine.

I sat between Quinten and Neds, and put some cheese, bread, and sauces on my plate because, seriously? Time travel and being a wanted criminal were hungry business.

The room filled with the scents of a picnic lunch, rich chocolate wafting through the air mixing with the tang of pickling spices and the buttery warmth of bread, invoking—for me, at least—warm, safe feelings.

Quinten spoke up. "So, you're working for House Fire, but don't intend to collect the ransom money? I haven't met any mercenaries who go out of their way for free."

"Especially you, Sallyo," Right Ned added. I noted neither of the Harris boys were eating. They were watching Sallyo like she was a snake ready to strike.

"Oh, I'll get paid. Even mercenaries go out of their way if the job is worth it. And since this job is half finding you and half delivering something to you, I'll make out just fine."

He scowled, but didn't say anything more.

"What delivery?" Quinten asked, his hands away from his plate so he could draw his gun quickly if he needed to.

Yeah, I'd stopped eating too. For all I knew, they had bombs strapped to their chests, and their answer to Quinten's question would be *explosions*.

Please don't let it be explosions.

"A letter," Sallyo said.

"Takes three killers to deliver a letter?" Left Ned asked.

"It does when the price for delivering it is so . . . generous. No one pays top credit for the safe jobs." She reached toward her jacket, and I heard the clack of hammers jacking back as both Quinten and Right Ned pulled guns under the table.

Sallyo stilled, but she was still smiling. It was almost like she enjoyed her line of work. "And I believe I've just made my point. The letter is in my jacket. I'm going to pull it out now."

"Slowly," Quinten said.

Sallyo slipped her long fingers into the fold in her

jacket, her eyes on Neds alone. There was something heated in the way she looked at him. Something almost sensual and daring.

Had they been lovers in this time too?

She drew out an envelope and placed it in the center of the table, turned so the red wax seal that was intact across the back of it was clear to see.

Pressed into that red wax was the symbol of a sun.

"House Fire," Quinten said, probably for my benefit.

"I was told to deliver it to you, Quinten Case, and if not you, to Matilda Case," Sallyo said, settling back in her chair and watching my brother's expression. "I was also told I would make a lot more money if I could drag you back with me."

Quinten had not moved. His eyes were focused on that letter. "Who sent you?"

She shook her head. "All I know is a contact had a contact who had a contact who wanted this letter delivered."

Quinten's gaze flicked up off the envelope to me. I probably looked as tense and sweaty as he did. No one should know Matilda Case was alive. And certainly no one in House Fire.

Foster slurped the last of his cocoa and set the mug down with a satisfied sigh. He plucked the candy out of the cup and slipped it into his mouth.

"Open the letter," Abraham said.

I reached for it, but Quinten pulled it toward himself. He already had a pocket knife open in his hand and sliced through the top edge of the brittle paper.

Yes, we were all terribly curious about what the letter contained. But I knew Quinten; he wasn't going to let anyone see it until he'd had a chance to read it first.

True to form, he stood and paced across the room, far

enough away that none of us could see anything that was written on the single piece of paper he unfolded.

I couldn't look away from him. But I felt someone watching me. I glanced over and into Abraham's hazel gaze.

"Why did you want me to find you?" he asked.

I took a few seconds to sort through all the things that had happened and all the things that he knew had happened, and finally realized what he was asking. "You mean all those years ago when you were in jail?"

Right Ned frowned my way. He didn't know I'd gone back in time, riding this body to when she was really only eight years old, and sharing the body and mind with Evelyn. He didn't know I had to do it to save the world, to mend time.

"Yes," Abraham said. "You knew the Wings of Mercury experiment was about to happen, didn't you?"

"Yes."

He sat back, as if giving me room to prove my statement was true. "You told me if I didn't find you, the world would end."

"Maybe it already did," I said softly, "and we just didn't notice."

He bit his bottom lip, his eyes narrowing. "I searched the world for you, Matilda Case."

"You searched the world?" That was probably the most romantic thing I'd ever heard in my life. "For me?" And *that* was probably the dumbest thing I'd ever said in my life.

"Son of a bitch," Quinten said, interrupting my stupidity.

He pulled his handgun in a smooth, swift motion and aimed it at Sallyo's head.

Abraham turned his gun on me under the table and grabbed my wrist above the table.

He jerked his hand back as if he'd just touched fire. He fisted and unfisted his hand, a scowl darkening his face.

I gave him a steady look. I knew what had happened. When he touched me, his ability to feel, to have full sensation, returned.

I could make him feel. Pleasure or pain.

Quinten didn't notice our little exchange, since he was too busy threatening to blow Sallyo's brains out. Or if he did notice, he didn't care. "Who is Slater Orange?" he demanded.

That name shot ice through my veins. My heart started beating too hard, and a wash of heat raced over my skin so quick, I was left shivering after it.

"I don't know him," Sallyo said, avoiding a direct answer. "That isn't the name of any of my contacts."

"You have five seconds to tell me the truth," Quinten said.

"He's the head of House Fire," Sallyo said.

"Bullshit," Left Ned said.

"Rumors say he took over last month when Ina died of the One-five plague."

"Sure are a lot of heads of sub-Houses specifically dying of the newest plague," Left Ned said.

Quinten shot him a "shut up" look.

"Rumors?" Quinten demanded of Sallyo. "What else do you know?"

"Nothing else." She shrugged. "Although I'm interested in what you know about those deaths, Neds Harris."

"No," Quinten said. "We're asking the questions. Who is Slater Orange?"

"I told you I don't know him."

"Slater Orange is a galvanized," I said. "Like us. Like me."

"Not even close," Abraham said. "He is nothing like us."

"Quinten," I said, "you really need to listen to me. I know him. I've always known Slater Orange."

That seemed to sink down through his anger and reach the parts of his mind that were still capable of reason.

"How long is always?" he said to me, even though he hadn't moved the gun away from Sallyo's head.

"All *my* life," I said, hoping he understood what that meant. "And he is a very, very dangerous man."

Quinten took a breath, then lowered his gun.

Abraham still had the gun pointed at me under the table, but I didn't care. I'd been shot before and survived it. We galvanized could really be killed only by several bullets through our brains.

"What does the letter say?" I asked.

"That if we don't turn ourselves in—you and me, Matilda—with the cure for the plague, Slater Orange will begin bombing one House Earth compound a day, starting ten days from now. He was certainly confident you'd find us in time," he said to Sallyo, his voice low with anger.

"I am the best at what I do," she said.

"Can he do that?" I asked. "Can a head of a House bomb House Brown—I mean, House Earth? He has the um . . . technology, weaponry, and resources?"

"Yes," Right Ned said.

"All right. Then we need to warn them," I said. "We need to warn House Earth. Now."

"Is it true?" Abraham asked Quinten.

"What?"

"Do you have the cure for the plague?"

"No."

Good God. Quinten was lying. I'd known him long enough to catch the subtle hints of when he wasn't telling the truth.

"Then why would House Fire think you did?" Sallyo asked. "Accusing someone of hiding the cure for the plague is a rather specific charge, don't you think?"

Quinten still hadn't holstered his gun. "I have no idea what the Houses think. Nor do I care."

"It appears they care about you. Expensively so," she said.

Quinten stiffened, his head high, and looked down his nose at all of us still sitting at the table. I knew that brilliant mind of his was sifting through possibilities, connections, solutions. I just didn't know which problem he was trying to solve, since he seemed to have gathered a kitchen full of them.

"We need to warn House Earth," I said again. That was the most important problem we needed to solve, and fast. I stood. Abraham stood with me, his gun still aimed at me.

That got Neds on his feet. Sallyo too.

"There are people out there," I said, "a lot of people who are going to be killed if we don't figure out why Slater thinks Quinten has the cure. We need to warn House Earth about the bombings. We need a plan for them to escape or survive the attacks. And right now we need to either trust each other or go our separate directions. This isn't just about the prices on our heads or the money we can make. This is about the loss of innocent human lives."

"Lives won't need to be lost if you turn yourself in," Sallyo said.

"That's not happening," Right Ned said flatly. "We're

not coming with you to whomever you're really working for in House Fire. So you'll just have to hope that Slater fellow believes you delivered the letter, and get on out of here."

"Put the gun down, Abraham," Quinten said.

I'd forgotten Abraham's gun was still aimed at me. I raised one eyebrow. "Do you really think I'm afraid of a gun?"

He bit at the inside of his lip.

"Would you be?" I asked.

He twitched one eyebrow and tipped his head in a sort of shrug.

Then a strange growl rose outside. All the hair on my arms stood up as that guttural hum rattled through the air. I knew that sound. That was the sound Lizard made right before it started killing things.

The single growl was joined by another higher growl and a lower growl, echoed in the distance by more and more lizards, until the air was a painful clash of vibrating snarls.

Cutting through it all was a man's scream.

3

Good news: I've found a reason for living: re-
venge. I plan to destroy him before he destroys
everything and everyone who is left. I'm still
looking for you, Matilda.

—W.Y.

"**W**ho's out there?" I said.

"No one important." Quinten didn't seem at all worried, even though the screaming suddenly stopped.

"There were other bounty hunters headed this way," Abraham said.

"You didn't want to mention that before now?" I asked.

He shrugged his right shoulder and holstered his gun. "We killed three on the way here. I assumed you knew they were out there."

Everyone else was handling this like screaming bounty hunters and howling lizards were normal.

I hurried to the window over the kitchen sink and looked out.

I could see four lizards, the smallest about the size of a German shepherd, and the largest bigger than a rhino.

They were made up of an oddly sleek hodgepodge of different animal parts—all reptilian—some with heavy bodies, some stretched out longer and more snakelike, and others bunched up and armored like a crocodile. Two of the lizards had enormous bat wings tipped with wicked hooked claws. The wings lifted and dropped in a predatory rhythm.

The lizards all surrounded one man. He wasn't screaming. He had a gun in his hand and looked like he'd been on the road for a bit, dressed in worn but sturdy pants, jacket, and boots. The gun in his hand was a huge lump of a thing. He eyed the lizards slowly closing in on him.

At his feet was a lot of blood. Since I didn't see anyone else out there screaming and he wasn't bloody, I could only guess that the puddle was all that remained of his companion.

Lizards were uncommonly fast when they got going, so I saw the crux of his situation. If he shot at one lizard, the rest would take him out in a snap. And that gun in his hand wasn't enough firepower to destroy one stitched lizard, much less four.

The largest lizard saved him the trouble of wasting bullets. It whipped its head forward and bit right through the middle of him like a hot knife through pudding. The gun fired once, uselessly, from his dead hand. And then he was gone, scooped up in big chunks and sent down the lizard's gullet. Eaten, so whole and completely, that between two blinks, it was as if there'd never been a man standing there at all.

"The lizards ate him," I said.

Yes, I'd seen the one huge lizard in my time do some terrible damage—tear down trees, destroy our barn, throw cars around like they were toys. And that lizard had done its fair share of eating people and things with the same quick scoops.

But these four had swallowed two men—or so I assumed—in the matter of a minute.

"Are we sure he was a bounty hunter?" I asked.

"People know not to come knocking around our place if they haven't contacted us first," Quinten said. "Which makes the three of you a question. How did you get past the lizards?"

Abraham shrugged. "They liked Foster."

All eyes turned to Foster.

"I like them too," he said as if that explained it all.

"How many mercs are after us, Sallyo?" Left Ned asked.

"Us? No one's after you, Harris," she said.

"How many are headed to this property?"

She looked up at the ceiling as if working out a list. "Just to be safe, I'd assume everyone. It was a *very* generous reward."

"Shit," Right Ned breathed. "If we have every damn merc in the country looking for us . . ."

"You're screwed," Abraham said.

"Better to turn yourselves in. Come with us," Sallyo said. "That will shut down the mercs. Shut down the bombing of House Earth. And we have a decent chance of keeping you alive until we reach House Fire."

"Or Slater will just bomb House Earth anyway," I said.

"We don't know if he's serious about that," Quinten said.

"Slater is serious about everything he threatens," I said. "She's right, Quinten. The best move would be to turn ourselves in."

"No. You just pointed out that there would be nothing

to keep him from bombing the compounds," he said. "House Fire and House Water have been looking for a reason to wipe out House Earth for years. But when Slater finds out I don't have the cure, he'll kill us and blame House Earth, and we'll all be dead."

"I think he'll just kill us to kill us," I said, "cure or not."

"How much history *do* you have with Slater?" Abraham asked.

"Too much," I said. "He's tried to kill me. A lot."

He frowned. "When? We galvanized knew each other from our reawakenings, and I've never met you after my reawakening, Matilda Case."

"I've just recently awakened."

"Then how exactly do you know Slater?" His voice was low and measured. "How could you have spent time with him, enough that he would try to kill you?"

I glanced at Quinten. The only way to explain it all was to tell the truth. Which I was pretty sure no one would believe.

Quinten shook his head just slightly. He didn't want them to know what I was. I didn't blame him. Finding out that Quinten could transfer a modern person's thoughts, memories, and personality into a galvanized body was exactly how Slater had ended up taking over the galvanized body he was currently inhabiting.

"Let me ask you a question," I said. "Why are you here, Abraham? I thought Sallyo was the one who took the delivery job."

"I was looking for you."

"Right. Searching the whole world. So you could turn me in to Slater?"

He tipped his head down just a bit, and the stitches at the corner of his mouth pulled hard against his scowl, stretching the skin there into white creases.

"I will never help that vile, soul-rotted filth of a man," he said.

Good to know we had similar opinions of him.

"Why did you come out here with Sallyo?"

"When I heard she was looking for Matilda Case, I volunteered."

"For a cut of her fee?"

"Volunteered, Matilda," he said very plainly.

"You aren't intending to take us in to Slater?"

"No."

"So you're on our side."

"I am on my own side."

"But you're not on Sallyo's side?"

Sallyo chuckled.

"Not exactly. No," he said.

I looked over at Sallyo. She was staring at her nails like she might want to get them done soon. "Do you really think you can drag both my brother and me in on your own?" I asked.

My long-sleeved shirt did not hide the stitches across the back of my hands, nor the line of thread tracing the edge of my neck like a grim necklace.

I was galvanized, and I was not hiding it.

Sallyo had made herself a person to be feared in my time. Her name was whispered amid furtive glances over shoulders. She hadn't been a smuggler, she had been *the* smuggler, the queen of all black-market deals who had undermined the Houses to establish her own underground rules of commerce.

But as proven by the Neds and my brother, it didn't look like the personalities of the people I'd known from my time had changed much in this time. If Sallyo had been a ruthless, clever, brutal woman in my time, she was all those things here too.

But she would be sorely wrong to underestimate me.

"I, of course, didn't have full information on the Case family," she said. "Dragging you all in would take more effort than anyone's paying me for. Letter's delivered. I made my dime."

"Will your contact believe you delivered the letter?" I asked.

"My contact doesn't have to believe anything. I know how to stand aside until the bullets are spent."

"Then you should leave," Quinten said. "Now. Night's only a few hours off."

I thought the night thing was an odd detail to bring up, but Sallyo pursed her lips. "I suppose. I suppose I should. You coming, Bram?" she asked Abraham.

"No, I don't think I am."

That surprised me. I think it surprised Sallyo too.

Quinten shifted the barrel of his gun toward Abraham.

These people sure did seem comfortable standing around a kitchen table, waving loaded firearms at each other.

"Foster will also stay with me," Abraham added.

"I didn't invite either of you to stay, as I recall," Quinten said.

"Then consider this an offer of my services." Abraham held his wide hands out to either side of him. "I was not hired to bring you in. I came here looking for Matilda. And now that I've found her, and you, I offer— I *volunteer*—my services."

"For what?" Left Ned said. "We don't need a farmhand."

Abraham ignored him. "I will help you warn House Earth. If you travel, I offer protection."

"Still not seeing your play in this," Quinten said. "What do you want?"

"Do I need an ulterior motive for wanting to help people who are in the firing line of a fight they didn't bring upon themselves, Mr. Case?"

Oh. There. That was the man I knew and loved. The man who would stand up for what was right even if it meant doing the hardest thing. A man who would stand for those who couldn't stand for themselves.

"Yes," I said into the silence. "Yes. You can help, Abraham. We accept your offer. Don't we, Quinten? And Foster too."

I stared at Quinten, begging him to trust me on this. Begging him to trust his not-sister who knew zero about this world and the workings of it. Willed him to let the mercenary we'd just met be a part of our plan to keep the people of House Brown—I mean, Earth—alive.

"Agreed," he said, after what felt like a very long pause.

My heart went back to a more normal beat.

"Well, then," Sallyo said, "isn't this cozy? Maybe I should stay as well."

"Nope." Neds advanced on her. He'd secured his weapon too. "You'll be leaving right about now, Sallyo."

"With all those hungry dragons out there?" she said.

"And plenty of other ferals that will eat your skin off your bones. So you'd best be going now, before dark."

She narrowed her eyes, but there was a small smile playing on her lips. "You're not at all concerned that I might die?"

Neds hesitated. And when Right Ned spoke, it was with the evenness of old pain. "You don't need my help, remember?"

That, finally, seemed to get through her devil-may-care exterior.

"Isn't it sad how two men with one body don't even have a single heart between them?" she said.

"Good-bye, Sallyo," Right Ned said.

"Oh, we'll see each other again. I still owe you on that promise. And I am a woman of my word."

"Looking forward to it." Left Ned opened the door and held it for her.

She searched his face, as if she expected him to change his mind. But if she knew him enough to say he was two men with one body—which he was—instead of one body with two heads, she must know he never unmade his mind once it was made.

She glanced over at my brother. "You'd do yourself a favor if you'd just surrender to Slater, Quinten Case. A head of a House is the worst enemy a man can have, and denying his orders is just an invitation to an early death."

"There might be a death," Quinten agreed. "But it won't be mine."

That made her smile, a quick flash of teeth and delight that softened her features and made her already lovely face come alive. "Well, then, good luck to you. Good luck to all of you."

She stepped through the door, and Neds strolled out after her.

"Is she going to get eaten?" I asked Quinten. "Because I don't think she deserves that for delivering a letter."

"No. Neds will tell the lizards not to eat her. This time."

He started pacing slowly, the unfolded paper in his hand. "I want you to know that I do not share my sister's trust in you, Abraham," he said, not looking away from the paper. "But we could use some information and contacts, and I imagine a person in your position, who knows who you know, could be very helpful."

"As long as our goals remain in agreement," Abraham said, "I will tell you anything you need to know."

"Good," Quinten said, as if they'd just given a verbal handshake. "We have a lot of things to take care of and not a lot of time. Evelyn, would you check on Grandma, please? Tell her I'm going to call the Grubens to come stay with her for a bit. She's probably in her room."

Grandma! I'd almost forgotten she was here. I glanced in the corner where I'd last seen her knitting and her chair was empty, the little light blue pocket sheep that followed her around nowhere to be seen.

I didn't know exactly who the Grubens were, but hopefully Grandma would.

"Sure. I'll be right back."

The kitchen had two doors, one to the outside, and one leading to the hall that stretched between the two wings of the house that contained the bedrooms, and the stairs leading down to the basement and up to the attic. Through the hallway was the living room, sitting room, and door to the front porch.

I hoped.

I walked down the hall to where Grandma's room used to be and paused with my hand on the latch.

Dizziness swept over me again. A rush of roses filled my nose and lungs as a distant bell toned.

The door in front of me was gone, replaced by what I'd seen before—a pile of rubble instead of a house. The explosive blast that had sent me back in time and the bullets and whatever bombs the Houses had set upon our property to try to bring me, Abraham, Foster, and Quinten in to justice had destroyed our home.

"This is a surprise," a familiar voice said behind me. "Evelyn."

I spun.

Slater Orange stood there in Robert's galvanized

body. He wore a fine dark suit. The stitching that had run across his shaved skull was now covered with light brown hair kept short and combed back from his high forehead. His other visible stitches were carefully covered in flesh-colored makeup. Robert's bird-sharp features twisted with Slater's disdain.

"Slater," I said.

His eyebrows slipped upward. "Ah. I see. Perhaps you are no longer the innocent." He tipped his head down, fixing me with his brittle blue gaze. "Is that finally you behind those pretty brown eyes, Matilda Case?"

"What are you doing here? How are you doing this?"

"This?" He raised his hand to indicate the world around us. "Surely you aren't so conceited as to think you made no mistakes in your attempt to change the Wings of Mercury experiment? Your brother and Welton may have been brilliant, but time is a very delicate and contrary thing. Any slight adjustment, and worlds collide. Man was not meant to play with the toys of the gods, dear Matilda." He *tsk*ed. "Look at the mess you've made."

"This isn't real," I said.

"But it is. This is the timeway you and I were born into. The timeway you nearly destroyed. Well, you and your brother. Here, the Houses rule as they have always meant to rule. Here, the galvanized are rotting away in prison for breaking treaty and murdering a head of House."

"You were the one who murdered Oscar," I said. "Not the galvanized. You tried to kill Abraham. You killed Robert and took over his body, and framed the galvanized. You have destroyed the world."

"I repaired a broken and flawed world," he snarled. "A world you never belonged to, Matilda. You should have died young, like all weak things."

"No," I said. "I should have killed you when I had the chance."

"Ah, but you didn't. You and I are locked in this struggle. Until only one of us remains. And I shall rule. No matter who I have to kill. No matter which timeway I decide will become the set reality."

I still had my gun on me. I pulled it from the holster.

The world went dizzy and I couldn't move, couldn't squeeze the trigger, as Slater was whisked away. The strong scent of roses lingered, and a ringing filled my ears.

I was in the hallway, still in front of Grandma's door. The gun was in my hand.

Holy crap.

I holstered the gun and pressed my fingers over my eyes, breathing until I could push the mix of panic, anger, and fear away.

Slater was alive. And he knew I was alive too. Or at least he knew I was alive in that . . . What had he called it? A timeway.

Too many questions crowded my head. How had he known about the timeway? What did he mean about choosing which one became a set reality? And why were he and I locked together in this?

I had no answers. And here, I didn't even know if anyone would believe me if I told them about it. Quinten thought I was hallucinating.

So I'd need to figure this out on my own. There had to be records left behind. There had to be information on the Wings of Mercury experiment that could give me clues.

Or maybe Abraham knew about the experiment. Maybe he knew someone—another galvanized—who had information.

It was worth a shot.

I took a deep breath to push away my nerves and knocked on Grandma's door.

"Grandma, it's Matilda . . . I mean, Evelyn. I'm coming in, okay?" I pushed open the door.

She was sitting in her rocking chair by the window, two little sheep—pink and blue—sleeping at her feet, a creamy white one cradled in her lap.

"Grandma," I said, "how are you feeling?"

She was a small woman, her long hair white as bleached bones, her eyes wide and watery in her narrow face. She wore a faded blue dress with tiny, bright yellow flowers on it. In her hands was a cream-colored scarf that she was methodically knitting.

I remembered her arms around me, comforting my childhood bruises and scrapes, listening to my silly childhood dreams. She had always been there for me. Even after Mom and Dad died. Even after Quinten took to leaving me here on the farm for months at a time.

I knew her mind had been slipping for years. In many ways, it had become my turn to comfort her pains and listen to the silly dreams she chased between the sunshine and shadows of her memories.

"Evelyn?" she asked.

"Yes, Grandma?" She wouldn't understand I wasn't the sweet girl she'd raised in this body. She wouldn't ever understand I was someone else who had loved her dearly as she'd loved me.

I'd done everything I could to save this world. To save my family. But my family didn't know me. I'd become a stranger in their midst, an intruder in my own life. The life that was supposed to be mine.

I didn't expect them to instantly love me. But that didn't stop me from wanting them to.

She smiled, her eyes holding that hollow glitter of nonrecognition. "Is it time for us to go?" she asked.

"No, Grandma. It's not time to go." I walked over, sat on the end of her bed, and petted the pocket-sized woolly sheep in her lap. It flicked its little sticky-out ears, and I scratched softly behind one.

"Quinten wanted me to tell you the Grubens are coming over."

"Oh, my." She chuckled. "They are fun. So fun. Are they bringing Floyd?"

"I don't know. Maybe."

"They must. They must bring Floyd," she insisted.

"I'll tell Quinten. I'm sure Floyd will be here." I had no idea who Floyd was and hoped I hadn't just promised her something impossible.

"Good," she said. "Good. Such a sweet girl. Sweet Matilda."

I paused, surprised that she had spoken my name. Then I pressed my hand gently on the back of hers. "You remember Matilda?"

"Oh yes. Things were so different then. Poor thing. Poor thing gone away."

"When she was little, right?" I asked. I knew she must mean she still remembered Matilda's death. I wanted to tell her I was Matilda and I was happy, I was alive and fine, but her mind was fragile and forgetful. I never knew what might worry or upset her.

"Aren't you Matilda?" she asked.

I held my breath, my heart thumping hard in my chest. "Yes." I breathed.

"I thought so, dear. I thought so. Are you sure it's not time for us to go?"

"I'm sure," I said.

"Promise you will tell me. When it's time to take care of it all."

"I promise." I had no idea what she was talking about.

"Good," she said, patting my hand fondly. "Case women must stick together. To the very end."

"Yes," I said. "And we will." But she had already drifted off, her eyes unfocused, her hands reaching for her knitting needles.

I leaned forward to kiss her on her forehead.

"Thank you," I whispered. "I love you." I didn't really think she thought I was Matilda. But it was nice to hear it anyway.

"Yes, dear. Yes," she said thinly. "Is Floyd here?"

"I'll find out. Do you need anything? Tea? A nap?"

"Oh, I'm just fine. Fine."

I gave her hand an extra squeeze, then left her room, pausing a minute outside the door.

What had I gotten myself into? What had I done? Saving the world had tipped the frying pan of my life right into the fire.

So many people's lives were on the line. Even if we did turn ourselves in to Slater, like his letter told us to, I knew he'd show us no mercy.

He'd just told me he wanted me dead so that he could rule the world.

Which meant I needed to warn House Earth that he intended to bomb them. And then I would find a way to get to Slater and kill him before he made that threat a reality.

4

*The trials have concluded. The madman walks
free while the others pay for it with their lives.
The galvanized should not die this way. They
should not die at all. If there is a place or time
out there for them, I'll find it. And I'll find you,
Matilda.*

— W.Y.

Neds were taking Foster and Abraham to the old
nursery down the hall, where I remembered tending Abraham's wounds when he'd first come knocking
on my kitchen door, telling me people were out to kill
my father and me. I guessed they were going to be staying with us tonight.

Quinten saw me walking out of Grandma's room and
waved a hand my way. "In here."

I followed him into his room.

His room was big—really, two smaller bedrooms that
had been opened up to make a larger space. It was as
neat as I ever remembered it to be, though the items that
filled it were a little more worn, scuffed at edges, or me-
ticulously repaired.

"There's only one person who knew what I was doing," Quinten said in a loud whisper as soon as I shut the door.

"Who? Doing what?" I asked, not following his train of thought. The time twitch with Slater was still rolling through my brain and making it hard to concentrate. And so was Grandma's odd insistence that she and I had something to do. To the very end, whatever that meant.

"This." He held up the letter that was crumpled a bit from his fist. "There is only one person who knew what I was doing. One."

"What were you doing?" I asked, taking the letter out of his hand and scanning it.

"Mining information and medical reports out of House Fire and House Water so I could find a cure for the damn plague."

Oh, hell. I knew he'd been lying.

"And did you?" I gave the letter back and walked through his room. It was set up a little differently. The bed was on the wrong side, blocking a clear shot line from the open doorway. The chest of drawers was a different style. Stacks of books lined wooden shelves around the room and his closet, which was open only a small crack, seemed to contain a lot more flannel and sturdy work clothes than the white dress shirts and tweed vests I remembered him preferring.

There were other things here. Not knickknacks, exactly, but things he had collected. Several jars of bones that probably belonged to rodents and birds; a human skeleton the size of a doll, carved out of fine balsa wood; metal clamps of various sizes, many broken and laid out as if for parts; and the most delicate set of brass crochet hooks I'd ever seen, carved in the shape of birds and carefully wrapped in a velvet case.

Quinten hadn't said anything while I wandered. I finally looked away from the stack of books overflowing the chair and side table, all of them medical journals.

"Quinten," I said. "Did you find a cure for the plague?"

He nodded.

That was bad.

"That's good, right?" I said. "Why are you worried? People need a cure, and you've found one."

"This cure will change the world," he said.

"Well, we're Cases. We apparently are all about changing the world."

A wan smile shadowed his lips as he paced over to his bed. He folded down, suddenly all the restless, angry energy gone, the letter still gripped in his hand.

"You don't let insurmountable troubles worry you, do you, Matilda?" he asked.

"Oh, I don't know," I said, trying to sound upbeat. "When we have some, I'll let you know."

I thought about telling him that I'd slipped into the other timeway, but he was picking at his fingers, staring at the floor.

"Do you know . . . do you know what happened to Evelyn?" he asked, his eyes still on the floor. "Was she hurt? Afraid? You said you went back in time to change the Wings of Mercury experiment. Does that have something to do with Evelyn not being with us anymore?"

I leaned against the chest of drawers, pressing my palms into the edge of it, my elbows out. He still wasn't over the loss of her. I didn't blame him for that, even though it meant I was probably on my own with the timeway thing.

"From how I experienced it, I was back in 1910, trying to keep Slater from killing Abraham and all the other galvanized, and then the Wings of Mercury device was set off.

"A ... bell rang out, only it was a huge, world-smashing sound. Physical and alive. I felt it ringing in my bones and rushing over my body like I was caught in a wave and trampled to death. I thought I was dying. I didn't feel Evelyn in pain. I didn't feel her fear. There was just the dying. And then I was standing here, in our kitchen, washing dishes. I was so happy to see you and Neds alive...." I stopped. I hadn't meant to tell him that part.

He tipped his head up, though he still leaned arms on his knees. "We died in your time?"

I nodded. Maybe he did need to hear the truth. "Soldiers from the Houses overpowered us. They had weapons. Bombs. Everyone died. Neds, Grandma, Foster. You died too." I held my breath against tears as the memory of my brother being ripped in two flashed behind my eyes. If that's what existed in the other timeway, I didn't want it to come true.

"I thought I'd never see you again." The words came out a little shaky, but I cleared my throat. "But here I am. And I don't want to waste that. What day is today?"

He lifted his hand and pulled at his hair again. "September thirteenth, 2210."

"That's the day I went back in time. That's the day the Wings of Mercury experiment triggered. Evelyn leaving this body must have something to do with that moment. I am sorry, Quinten. I really am. I would have told her to stay if I knew what was happening."

"It's not ... it's not any of our faults," he said. "Things happen. I was the one who tried to transfer your mind into Evelyn's body. If I hadn't done that, I would never have known her. If the experiment had been successful, I would never have known her."

"The experiment was successful." I shrugged. "I'm in here now."

He nodded. "Tell me how you know Slater."

I paused. Wondered if I should tell him everything.

"He was the head of House Orange in my . . . um . . . timeway."

"Timeway?"

"That's what I think it's called."

"Is this a timeway?"

I nodded.

"Go on."

"The Houses were separate of the others, working for their own interests. Slater was human, not galvanized."

"Abraham said he's galvanized."

"He wasn't born that way. But he is that way. Now."

My brother was smart; he could put the two and two together. "I did it, didn't I?" he said. "I transferred his personality into a galvanized body."

"Robert's body. Yes. Under the threat of death—mine and your own. Slater was here when I went back in time, his mind in Robert's body, just like mine was in Evelyn's. Slater was thrown back in time, just like I was thrown back in time. Or, rather, he was inside Robert's mind and body, just like I was inside Evelyn's mind and body, and we sort of woke up back in time. In them."

"Are you sure it was him? Slater?"

I remembered the boy's cold gaze as he held the gun on Abraham, intending to kill him and as many galvanized as he could find.

"Yes," I said. "I'm sure it was Slater in Robert's body."

I waited. Didn't have to wait long.

"He remembers your time . . . timeway," he said. "He remembers what I did in that timeway, what you did in that timeway. I take it we were not his friends?"

"He imprisoned you. He killed our parents. He murdered heads of Houses and killed galvanized. We were not friends."

"So he knows I have a medical and stitching background. If one of my contacts mentioned my name, I could see how it might draw his attention. It makes a little more sense as to why he focused on me. I was very careful."

"Taking data from the Houses is illegal?"

"Very. Which means I trusted the wrong people."

"Someone in House Brown—shoot. Earth—betrayed you?"

"I think so."

"How much of the plague cure have you manufactured?" I asked.

"Only one dose. I have the formula. I think it's right. But I haven't had a chance to test it."

"Do you have the supplies to make more?"

"No. But House Earth should."

"What will it take to make the cure available to all the Houses?"

"I'd need to partner with House Earth. Pool resources, medical equipment, staff."

"I suppose whoever has the cure could gain a lot of power in this world," I said.

"I wasn't doing it for power."

"I know." I wasn't thinking about Quinten trying to rule. I was thinking about Slater. "But Slater wants power. He always has. He wants to rule the Houses, rule the world. And he knows as long as I'm alive, I'm not going to let that happen. Do you know anyone in House Earth you trust to help manufacture the cure?"

"I think so. But from my previous judgment?" He held up the paper. "I don't know."

"Well, it's a risk we have to take, isn't it? Putting the cure for the plague in Slater's hand won't do anyone any good."

"He could claim it as his own, deliver it to the masses as if he were their savior," Quinten said.

"No. He doesn't save people. He breaks them and forces them to serve him. If he allowed the cure to be released, it would be given only to the people whom he decided deserved it. And he loves no one except himself."

"Which rules out House Earth and all of House Water," Quinten said.

"Okay. Plan. You take the cure to House Earth, get busy producing it so we can distribute it through House Earth, and maybe House Water, if they'll work with us. While you do that, I'll take the fight to Slater and remove him from the equation."

"Not the plan," Quinten said. "We travel to House Earth together—end of story. I'm not going to let you stand alone against a head of House."

"It's not like I haven't done it before. Besides, Slater is a personal problem I intend to personally solve."

"Why?"

"He killed people I care about. Friends. Family. I know he'll do so again, given the chance. So I'm going to make sure he's dead and buried before he gets that chance."

Quinten just stared at me and shook his head. "Evelyn would have never said such a thing."

"I know," I said.

I was getting tired of apologizing for being alive.

"I think," I said, "the best thing you can do right now is warn House Earth that they're about to be bombed so they can take necessary actions. Do we have a communications system of any kind? Computer, network, satellite?"

He scoffed, on the edge of a laugh. "Things haven't been like that for a hundred years. Computers—the ones that work—are House based and are a closed network in the major cities. Satellites went down disastrously in the meteor shower of 2100 . . ."

I shook my head.

". . . which devastated two-thirds of the communication and energy resources in the world, including most of the World Wide Web, and very quickly led to the mismanagement of resources and to wars, a downfall of borders, countries, and powers."

Things had certainly played out differently in this timeway.

"We must have some way to reach House Earth. Telephone? Telegraph? Smoke signals?" I asked. "People always find a way to communicate. What do we have, Quinten? How can we contact House Earth?"

"Radio. Did we have that in your time?"

"We had everything in my time. We ran the communication hub for House Brown and did our best to keep one step ahead of the Houses trying to take away homes, land, and freedoms."

"Huh."

"We don't do that now, do we?"

"No. Well, the compounds all look after each other, and we do our part."

"House Earth people are living in compounds?" That didn't sound good.

"Strong walls make for safe cities," he said. "I need to pack a few things anyway. Come with me."

We left the room.

Neds stood leaning in the doorway to the kitchen. "I

let the rest of the lizards out, so we shouldn't have any more people showing up at our door," he said. "But the pump house is still down. Want me to take a look at it or keep my eye on the stitched?"

"Watch the galvs while I contact the Grubens," Quinten said. "Then I'll take over guard duties."

"I can fix the pump house," I said.

They both gave me an odd look.

Right Ned shook his head. "You got handyman skills, Matilda?"

"I ran this farm on my own for three years," I said. "Well, I hired you after a year, but there was nothing on this farm I couldn't handle."

"You hired me?" Left Ned asked with a grin. He nudged his chin toward Quinten. "You figured her out yet?"

"It's a time-travel thing," he said.

"Those things exist?" Right Ned asked.

"They apparently did," Quinten said. "Watch the galvs. We'll be right back."

Quinten slid a key into the basement-door lock, then stepped through into darkness. I was right behind him.

The familiar cool and dusty smell of the basement reached me and triggered a parade of memories. But when Quinten pulled the chain on the single lightbulb, I knew this basement wasn't anything I'd ever seen before.

"I'll call the Grubens from here." He started down the wooden stairs.

The room was much more rudimentary in makeup. Basic dirt floor; wooden tables and shelves. But in the center of it all were two metal operating tables, scrubbed and clean and shining like knives in the dull light.

And while the tables were eye-catching, what really drew my attention were the shelves that covered the walls, and what was on those shelves.

Jars of clean cloth squares, cotton rolls, needles, blankets, and an array of medical hardware, all of it neatly hand labeled, filled half of the room's shelves, while the other half was stuffed with jars of animal parts and bits floating in gel. Wooden crates stacked up in an organized jumble, holding, I assumed larger parts.

"Stitching," I said.

"That's right."

"You do a *lot* of it?"

"I am the most-sought-after stitcher on the continent."

"So you're famous for this for making . . . beasts?"

He shrugged and pushed his way back into the shadows, where an old shortwave radio station was set up. "I guess."

I walked that way with him, drawn by the familiarity of it. We used to have all our other, much higher-tech communication equipment back here.

"How many people come out here to get stuff stitched?"

"Not many. I work through middlemen and only supply the House Earth people, who pay in trade. Fire and Water want a stitched, they can do it their own damn selves."

"And what kind of things do you make?"

He pulled out the wooden chair, sat, then flipped the toggles and adjusted the dials in the faces of the heavy gray metal boxes.

"Work beasts for fields, guard beasts for the ferals, egg-laying beasts, herder beasts, and whimsies."

"Anything else?"

"Medicines," he said. "I put up a fair share of medicines. Scale jelly, especially. Our soil has some unique properties and makes strong compounds."

"Devilry in our dirt."

He smiled. "Something like that." He turned the dial and thumbed the microphone. "CQ, CQ, CQ, this is W-three-QNT, standing by for a call."

"W-three-QNT, this is W-three-GBR, Gruben family. This is Todd Gruben. What can I do you for, W-three-QNT?"

"Todd, I wonder if a few of the Grubens have any free time. I need to handle some things away from home, and Grandma will need watching over."

"Of course! You know we love stomping the dirt off our heels. Need us before sundown?"

"Tomorrow morning, bright, should do it," he said.

"We will be there."

"With Floyd?" I asked. "Grandma wanted to see Floyd."

Quinten thumbed the toggle. "Todd, can you see if Floyd can come along too? Grandma would love to see him."

"Hi-hi that, my friend. We'll bring Floyd and all the fixin's."

"Thanks, Todd. Seven-three. This is W-three-QNT clear and QRT."

"Seven-three. This is W-three-GBR clear and monitoring."

Quinten sat back from the microphone, then rubbed his palm over his mouth.

"So, are you going to go to House Earth to warn them?" I asked.

"No." He turned the dial, pulling up a different frequency. "We can warn them from here."

"Then why are the Grubens coming over?"

"Because I'm going to go to House Fire with you to kill Slater."

That surprised me. "That's . . . reckless," I said.

"That's direct," he replied. "And it's the best way to handle him wanting us dead. CQ, CQ, CQ. This is W-three-QNT, standing by for a call."

"W-three-QNT, this is W-three-TAN, Earth Compound Five, returning. Name's Jamie," a man said in a pleasant bass. "Back to you W-three-QNT."

"Jamie, it's Quinten," he said. "Is Paxton around?"

"Hey, Quinten. He's . . . he's on watch. You need something?"

Quinten flicked his gaze my way at the man's pause, and frowned. "Is Riva there?"

"She's busy too."

"I need to talk to one of them, Jamie. If not Paxton, get me Riva."

Again the pause. "There's someone else who needs to talk to you. Give me a second."

"Who's Riva?" I asked.

"Paxton's wife."

"Who's Paxton?"

"Second in command, House Earth, Compound Five."

"Why aren't you talking to the first in command?"

"Because he and I don't really get along. And Paxton will be the one who takes care of getting this information out anyway."

We waited a little while longer before a woman's voice came over the line, which sounded farther away and static laced.

"Hello, Quin. Is everything okay out there?" she asked.

Everything in Quinten went tense. Even I recognized her voice.

"Gloria?" he said. "What are you doing there? What's wrong?"

"There's been an outbreak," she said. "I'm doing what I can to make the infected comfortable."

"Is it One-five?" he asked.

"Yes. It's been resistant to everything we've thrown at it."

"What does One-five do?" I asked.

His thumb hovered over the toggle. "The infected go through all the other stages of One-one through One-four plagues, and then they fall asleep. When they wake up, they aren't human anymore."

"What? What are they?"

He ignored me and toggled the mic again.

"How many people are infected?"

"In this compound? Six."

He took a breath, and I knew what he was thinking. He didn't have nearly enough of the cure made yet.

"What do you mean, not human?" I asked.

"After the One-five puts you to sleep, you wake up hungry, mindless, feral. And violently strong."

Does he mean zombies? That's just stuff of old horror stories, isn't it?

Yeah, well, so is time travel.

While I tried to wrap my head around the idea of feral living dead, he hit the toggle again.

"How quickly is it spreading?"

"We've kept it contained so far," she said. "But, Quin . . . Listen, this isn't good news. I've been infected."

Quinten sat there, silent for a long stretch.

Finally, he licked his lips. When he spoke, his voice was calm, belying the grief that pressed his face into grim lines. "How long ago?"

"Today. If I follow the same progression rate as the others, I have only five days left to live. I'm sorry, Quinten. I'm so very sorry."

After a few minutes of Quinten doing nothing but

staring at the wall in a daze, I took the microphone out of his numb hand. He didn't seem to notice.

"Gloria?" I said. "We'll be there as soon as we can."

"Who is this?" she asked.

"A friend."

"Is Quinten still there?" she asked.

He seemed to rouse at his name. Anger shifted across his face when he saw I'd taken over the communication.

He held his hand out, palm up, and gave me a stern scowl.

I dropped the microphone in his hand and mouthed, *Fine*.

"I'm here," he said, his voice rough.

"Under no circumstances should you come out to this compound," Gloria said. "The chance of the plague spreading is too high."

I folded my arms across my chest and gave my brother an expectant look. He had his thumb off the microphone, so Gloria wouldn't be able to hear us.

"If she is close enough to you that you blanked out from the grief just hearing that she's sick, then there's no choice," I said. "You have to take the cure to House Earth. You have to take it to Gloria."

"It's untested."

"Then we'll test it."

"We?"

"I'm going with you. You aren't thinking straight, Quinten. Not with Gloria at risk. I'll help make sure nothing goes wrong. I'll help you get this cure to her in time."

"The compound is a bomb target," he said. "You are staying right here, where you're safe."

"Where I'm sure Sallyo or Slater will send people to try to drag me in? It's not safe here. Not anymore. No.

I'm done hiding. I go with you to that compound and try to save Gloria. Then I'll find a way to stop Slater. What are the armaments at the compound?"

"Jesus, Matilda," he said. "Just stop! Stop . . . being that. Stop being *you*. I have enough problems on my hands not to have to deal with some stubborn girl who won't do what I tell her to do."

I knew my cheeks were reddening up from that scolding, and I had to bite my tongue not to yell back at him. How dare he tell me I wasn't worth listening to. How dare he imply that Evelyn was just a sweet, obedient child he could do all the thinking for. He had just insulted both of us. And I was in a mood for a fight.

But we had a bigger battle to deal with, and very little time. People were going to die. A lot of people, either by bombing or plague. And us arguing about it wouldn't save a single damn soul.

"Quinten? Do you copy?" Gloria asked. "You will not approach this compound."

"I heard you," he said, his words still tight with all the yelling he was holding back. "But I am coming your way, Gloria. Tell the watch to look for me before sundown tomorrow."

"Quin. Don't. Please don't."

"There's something else you need to know," he said. "What I originally called for. We got news, Gloria. Bad news. House Fire is going to start bombing House Earth compounds."

There was a stretch of silence. Then she asked, "Do you know who and when?"

Just like in my time, when I'd known her as a doctor and Quinten's ex-girlfriend, she took terrible news with level calm. She didn't even ask why; she just got down to dealing with the situation.

"Ten days from now should be the first attack," he said. "Unless we can stop it. I don't know which compound will be hit. It could be any of them."

"All right," she said. "All right. We'll spread the word, keep our eyes out, and hunker down. You need to stay where you are. Promise me."

"I'm headed your way early tomorrow. Sorry, Gloria. I have to. W-three-TAN, seven-three. This is W-three-QNT clear and QRT."

Another long pause interrupted by the static of a mic switching on, then off again. Then Jamie's voice came on the line. "W-three-3QNT, seven-three. This is W-three-TAN clear and monitoring."

Quinten set the equipment aside.

"I'm going with you," I stated. "And after that, I'm going to kill Slater."

"Then you'd better pack," he said, not looking at me.

I nodded and stared at the ceiling a minute. He was angry. He wanted some space. I understood that.

But it didn't give him any right to be an ass.

"That's two, Quinten," I said. "Two times you've treated me like a child or worse. I'll give you one more; then I'm not going to be quiet and take that kind of condescension from you. Do you understand? I know Evelyn was sweet and kind and perfect, and I'm none of those things, but I think even she would be disappointed in how you're treating me."

"Don't talk about her," he said. "You didn't know her. You'll never know her."

He was still sitting. Not looking at me, his hands fisted.

I started toward the stairs. Paused at the bottom. "You lost a sister, and I'm sorry. But I lost my entire world. Everything I knew is gone or so different, it's unrecognizable. If I can deal with that, and, believe me, I can, then you are just going to have to deal with me being me."

I walked up the stairs. Before I closed the door behind me, I heard him swear and throw something against the wall.

So far I was doing just a bang-up job of fitting into this world.

Neds were where we'd left him, down the hall, leaning in the doorway, where he could keep an eye on every wing of the house. I didn't think he could hear what Quinten and I had been talking about. The basement was too well insulated.

"I'll take over not doing anything useful in the hallway for you," I said. "You can go fix the pump now."

Right Ned grinned. "What I'm doing is all kinds of useful. I'm guarding us from the mercs in the nursery, since our life has just turned into crazy town."

"Thanks for bringing the crazy, by the way," Left Ned added.

I could tell from the curious glint in their eyes that they were just joking. "Anytime." I leaned on the wall across from him. "Just so you know, this"—I waved one finger around in the air—"is going exactly to plan."

"Which part?" He settled to better face me, his hip propped against the wall.

There was something pleasing about those boys. Sure, he wasn't built like your average man, but those blue eyes of his, the breadth of his shoulders, the way Right Ned was almost always smiling while Left Ned rolled his eyes or scowled at him, made him approachable and interesting.

And I knew how very kind and loyal they could be.

They'd saved my life. They'd done so at great risk to their own.

"The whole I'm Not the Sister My Brother Wants Me to Be and the World Is a Thousand Times Weirder Than What I Remember thing," I said.

"Weirder?"

"Plagues. Bombs. Mercenaries. Time troubles."

"They didn't have those things in your world?"

I pulled my hands back through my hair and tried to tuck it behind my ears. First chance I got, I was going to either cut it short or braid it to get it out of my way.

"Sure, we had those things. But there were technology and medicine and plenty of resources to deal with it all."

"Sounds like easy living."

"Not at all, really."

"Quinten coming back up here?" he asked.

"I think he needs a little time. He just found out Gloria is infected with One-five."

"Well, shit," Right Ned said. He eyed the basement door, looked me over again. "That pump needs to be fixed before nightfall. You've got a piece in your holster."

"I know."

"Do you know how to use it?" Left Ned asked. "Have you ever fired a weapon before?"

"Yes and yes. Ran the farm, remember?"

"Thought you said your time was filled with rainbows and rabbit's feet," Left Ned said.

"You know how you get a lucky rabbit's foot, right? You cut off the rest of the rabbit."

Right Ned chuckled. "So, you're comfortable shooting those two clanks if you have to?"

"Shooting them wouldn't do much good." Then, at their looks: "I can hold my own if they get out of hand."

They both glanced down at the basement door again, and from how they held themselves, I had a moment to wonder if they could hear each other's thoughts.

In my time, the Harris boys had a knack of touching a person and being able to see a vision or two of their past, or sometimes of their future. It made skin-to-skin contact distasteful to them, but it had come in handy more than once.

"I know this won't make any sense to you," I said. "But I want to thank you. For everything. I don't think I said that before. When I had the chance."

They both leveled those blues at me. I could tell what they were thinking with that heated look. "What kind of everything did we do for you?" Right Ned asked, his eyebrow ticking upward.

"Not that kind of everything," I said. "You were the most loyal friend I've ever had."

Left Ned rolled his eyes.

"You risked your life to save me, to save Abraham. And you . . ." I took a breath and pushed away the memory of Left Ned bleeding, dead, as Right Ned stumbled brokenly down the basement stairs.

". . . you gave everything, did everything to try to save the world. To help me and Quinten and Grandma and Abraham."

"Ain't nothing but fairy tales to us," Left Ned said.

"You say you remember these things, Matilda, but they never happened," Right Ned said.

"Except they did. I know. I still want to thank you. You're a good man, Neds Harris."

They both shrugged. "We do in a pinch," Left Ned said.

Right Ned looked thoughtful. "I notice Abraham keeps coming up in your list of thank-yous, right there next to your brother and grandmother. What was he to you?"

"It doesn't matter now. We have bombs to stop, a killer to kill, and a plague to cure. No time for fairy tales."

"Well then," Left Ned said. "We should tell you something about your brother."

"Quinten?"

"He's a driven man," Left Ned said. "Don't get me wrong—he has a good heart and most often stays in touch with it. But sometimes he sees priorities in a manner that leaves no room for any kind of living while he's getting the results he wants. He tends toward the trigger, if you see what I'm saying."

"He has always been focused," I said. "And brilliant. I'm not surprised he has a short temper."

"Was he ... was the Quinten you knew the same?" Right Ned asked.

"Mostly. It's strange. The whole world changes, and all of us are still mostly who we would be anyway."

"Is that why you're standing up for those two patchworks back there?" Left Ned asked.

I nodded. "Abraham tried to save my family. Foster tried to save us and the world. Twice."

"It is an interesting life you have lived, Matilda Case."

I sighed. "You know what I really want?"

Right Ned shrugged.

"Life to be a little less interesting and a lot more happy. I want to settle down here or on a farm of my own. I want my family and friends happy and safe, and for the galvanized to be counted as human beings, with all the rights a person should have. I want House Earth free from the other House rules and threats. And I want Slater dead."

Left Ned shook his head. "Hearing that sort of thing out of your mouth is strange, strange, strange."

I shifted how I was leaning against the wall and dragged my heavy curls back. "Quinten said Evelyn was very kind. I don't suppose she would ever want to do harm to anyone."

"She was kind," Right Ned said. "Very much so. But she had a spine. Quinten . . ." He frowned, glancing at the basement door. "He took it on himself to be her protector."

"Overprotector," Left Ned muttered.

"He couldn't see that she wasn't helpless," Right Ned said. "She might not like shooting a gun, but she knew how to. Given the chance, I think she would have done whatever it took to defend herself and her family."

"Well, I'm not going to let Quinten stop me from doing what I know has to be done to defend my family either."

They pushed off the wall and took a step or two. Right Ned held out his hand. "It's a pleasure to meet you, Matilda Case."

I shook his hand. "You too."

Left Ned held out his hand. We shook.

"So," Right Ned said. "Don't let those galvs talk you into anything, you hear? Just because they look like the people you knew doesn't mean they are."

"And when your brother flips his shit over our leaving you alone," Left Ned said, "tell him you're not six years old anymore and he needs to stop mothering you."

"Can do," I said.

"We'll get that pump patched up." He walked through the kitchen. I knew when he opened the door because I could hear the warbling hum from one of the lizards, who must have been napping right outside the door.

"Go on," Right Ned said softly. "Back it up, Petunia. That a girl."

The door shut, leaving me in the quiet of the house, with only the steady dripping *tick* of the clock in the living room marking the rhythm of time sliding away.

5

*Finally, a breakthrough. I have in my hands
Grandma Case's journal. The footnotes are
fascinating tidbits on a particular experiment:
the Wings of Mercury. Still looking for you.*
                                    — *W. Y.*

I stood there in the hall, the living room to my back,
soaking up the silence. Soaking up the reality that I
was alive. I was me, and I was in my home with my family, who were still alive and breathing.

So this was the outcome of our crazy, untested plan to
try to change the results of the Wings of Mercury experiment.

We'd done it. We'd changed time. And we'd messed it
up too.

Figures.

I leaned my head against the wall and closed my eyes
for a moment. So much had happened, and all of it too
quickly. I felt like I'd been running for years and could
sleep for centuries.

Slater was out to kill us. In more than one timeway.
Telling Sallyo we didn't want to come with her wouldn't

stop him from bombing House Earth or sending more guns to drag us in. Or finding another way to destroy us.

To destroy me.

Locked in this struggle until only one of us remains.

Slater was after Quinten and the cure for the plague, and I knew he wouldn't stop until he had both. He was going to kill me. He thought he could choose which time-way became reality.

My head hurt. I didn't understand the reality-decision thing. But I didn't need to understand it to know he should not be alive when his only goal was to destroy lives and worlds. In any time.

That was something I could not abide. He was right to send mercenaries to take us down.

Abraham didn't remember me in this time. Didn't know who we had been together, what we had.

I'd gained so much—the lives of my family and my friends.

And I'd lost just as much.

I didn't know how long I stood there. Long enough my feet were going a little numb from not moving them.

It was just nice to not have to worry about anything for a minute or two, to not have to fight or flee.

I was aware of the sound and vibration of footsteps coming down the hall's wooden floor, coming toward me.

Since it was from my left and didn't sound like a herd of oxen, I knew it had to be Abraham.

He stopped. I waited with my eyes still closed to see if he'd say something. Decided that was a dumb idea, since the man was a mercenary who carried multiple weapons.

I rolled my head toward him and opened my eyes.

*   *   *

The dizziness slid over me again, and everything around me went blurry, then shuddered, as if I were looking through a pair of glasses with rapidly changing lenses.

The scent of roses faded, overpowered by rich, warm coffee.

Abraham stood there, holding two cups in his hands and wearing nothing but a pair of jeans, which were unbuttoned. His chest had more stitching than I remembered, and a few bullet-hole scars. Over the curve of his left pectoral muscle was a tattoo of the face of a clock with keys for hands, and the words *in somnis veritas* written below it. He was muscled and lean but not thin, stitched but not wounded, and his dark hair was pulled back in a band.

He was also giving me a full come-hither grin, three lines of stitching beginning at the corner of his left eye and fanning out to beneath his hair.

"What are you doing out of bed, love?" he asked. "I was bringing you coffee."

"Bed?" I said.

Love? I thought.

He nodded. "The thing we sleep in, and do other things to each other in? It's back there," he said, twisting to look over his shoulder. "We keep it in the bedroom, with our pillows."

He turned back to me and took a drink of one of the coffees.

I couldn't stop staring at him. He was relaxed, happy, smiling.

And I had never been happier to see him in my life. Whichever, *whenever* this him he was. This couldn't be the same timeway where the house was destroyed, because it appeared to be perfectly sturdy around us. How many wrinkles in time had we created?

That question would have to wait for a much more pressing one.

"Our bedroom?" I said.

His eyebrows twitched down over hazel eyes devoid of the red of pain. He was still smiling. "Are you sleep-walking? Because I think I could do something to wake you up."

He closed the distance between us, the coffee still in his hands, and stepped into my space.

Oh.

Every inch of my body felt like it was on fire. And not in a bad way.

"Good morning, Tilly," he murmured. "Wake up, love." He slanted his mouth to mine and kissed me so deeply and lovingly that I went hot and tingly down to my toes.

I went a little light-headed too. The scent of roses mixed with the taste of coffee and the rich taste of him on my tongue.

And then Abraham wasn't kissing me anymore. He stood, halfway down the hall, in the shadows, watching me with some amount of caution.

Except for having removed his jacket and bandolier of bullets, he was still fully clothed and had all his weapons strapped to his body.

This was not the same Abraham who had been kissing the breath out of me.

Which, I'll admit, was a little disappointing.

This Abraham didn't have the lines of stitching fanning out from his eye. This Abraham looked exactly like the Abraham who was a part of the timeway where my brother was alive.

"Hey," I said softly. "Are you okay?"

He seemed to make up his mind and walk closer to

me. The deeper shadows of evening softened his features and carved tantalizing lines along the stitches that stopped at the corner of his mouth, as if to draw attention to his lips. His red-specked hazel eyes caught the light just enough, they glowed.

I'd be lying if I said he wasn't the sexiest man I'd ever seen. I'd be lying if I said I didn't want to pick up where we'd left off. That I would be very happy to, right this moment, fold myself against him and let his arms wrap around me.

But I couldn't throw myself into his arms. I remembered a life with him he hadn't lived.

He wasn't the same man I'd loved.

Except that he was. Also, apparently, in some timeway, we shared a bedroom—and a lot more.

He glanced into the rooms as he passed the open doorways, a hunter searching shadows, and finally settled across from me, where Neds had been leaning in the kitchen doorway.

"Where's your brother?" he asked.

"Dealing with things. Is the room all right?"

He quirked his eyebrow. "It needed some rearranging. But it's fine."

Lord. How many times would he rearrange that room when he stayed in it?

"Feng shui?" I asked.

"Do you know it?"

"Not at all. You are terribly predictable, Abraham."

"Am I?"

I shrugged.

"You aren't, Matilda Case. It was generous of you to offer us the room."

"Didn't seem right for you to sleep in the barn when we have a perfectly good, empty room in the house."

He shook his head slightly, then leaned back a bit, crossing his arms over his wide chest. I noticed his left shoulder hitched a bit lower than the right, as if catching on an old wound. I wondered if this Abraham was the same Abraham with the tattoo.

"I've met all kinds of people in my long life," he said. "No one like you."

"Thanks?"

"You trust too easily for someone raised House Earth."

"I don't trust too easily. I just know whom I can trust."

"And you think you can trust me. Why?"

"We're both galvanized. . . ." I started.

"No," he said softly. "The truth. Tell me the truth, Matilda."

"You won't believe it. No one would."

He released one hand from where it was tucked against his crossed arms and spread his fingers, indicating I had the floor. "I'd like to hear it anyway."

"All right. Here's the truth: I've met you. Before I ever came running into that jail, before Robert shot the sheriff and tried to kill you, I knew you. This body?" I drew my hand down to sort of wave at all of me. "Not mine. She was born a girl named Evelyn Douglas. I was born Matilda Case. When I was eight years old, I got sick. I underwent an experimental procedure and was implanted into Evelyn's mind."

"That's impossible."

I nodded. "Yes, it is. Except it's not."

I waited. So did he.

"I, Matilda, was born in 2184. When I was twenty-six, we realized exactly what the Wings of Mercury experiment had done back in 1910. It had broken time, temporarily granting those who survived the experiment's blast zone—galvanized—long lives. You are more than three hundred years old. So is Evelyn's body, but she woke up only eighteen years ago, when I was eight."

"She woke up when you were sick and transplanted into her mind?"

"Yes." I took a breath, and dragged my hand through my hair again, twisting it to make it stay behind my ear. "We realized the Wings of Mercury experiment was about to mend the piece of time it had broken in 1910. So we set out to fix it."

"Why?"

"The consequences of time mending would have killed all the galvanized. And the resulting blast zone of that mending . . ." I shook my head and swallowed back the fear that rose with the memories. "It would have killed billions."

"This is . . ." He reached up, scratched at the stubble on his jaw, then bit his lower lip and let it go.

My mouth watered with the need to kiss him, to feel the rough edges of his skin against mine. I wanted to trace that unfamiliar line of stitches down to the corner of his mouth with my finger, my lips, my tongue. I wanted to know the taste of him. This him.

"Go ahead. Finish your story," he said.

I dragged my gaze away from his mouth and pressed my hand on my stomach, trying to settle the butterflies there. Hadn't I just decided not to throw myself into his arms?

I glanced away to compose myself. "So, I went back in time. To 1910. We didn't have all the calculations figured out for how a person would actually travel through time, but since I was a modern-born person in a three-hundred-year-old body, I rode this body back in time. I was me, but Evelyn was still in her mind, in her body, which we shared."

"You went back in time." He didn't believe me.

"You should know," I said reasonably. "You saw me. You heard me tell you to find Matilda Case in the future. In 2210. I told you the Wings of Mercury experiment was going to happen, because it already had."

"Then why aren't all the galvanized dead?"

"I found the scientist behind the experiment and gave him the calculations that we thought would change it enough that time didn't break. It worked. Mostly. Enough that billions didn't die."

"Mostly?"

"It's complicated. Have you ever heard of timeways?"

"No."

"Complicated," I repeated.

He bit his bottom lip again, then released his arms and tucked one thumb into his belt. "You know there's no way to corroborate your story."

"I don't suppose there is."

"Then why should I believe you?"

"I didn't say you should. It doesn't matter if you do. We have bigger problems to deal with."

He watched me for a moment. I didn't know what was going through his mind.

"When you were in the jail in 1910, why did you call the boy who tried to shoot me Robert?"

"He was Robert—the body was Robert. But Slater was in there too, implanted into Robert's mind. Slater wanted you dead, but Robert . . ." I nodded. "Robert was a nice kid. A good man."

I waited to see if he followed the logic of what I'd just said through to the ultimate outcome.

"Slater traveled back in time with you. The same way you traveled through time?"

"Yes."

"And you knew Robert before Slater was implanted in his mind."

"Yes. So did you. He was your friend."

"Then why was he trying to kill me?"

"Slater was trying to kill you because you got in his way. You organized the galvanized, negotiated a peace treaty between the Houses, and could prove he was a murderer who should be removed as the head of his House."

"Why would anyone believe me?" he said. "I am galvanized."

"You were a hero. Respected. You led people out of servitude and helped establish House Brown—Earth; whatever—as a safe and legitimate place for people to live free. You did great things, Abraham. You were a great man."

"I can assure you," he said, "I have never been a great man."

For a moment, the anger and violence that he wore like a second skin faded away, revealing something that looked suspiciously like regret.

Then that sparse emotion was brushed away. Gone. "Slater," he said, snapping back into mercenary mode. "Does he want you dead because you know how to time travel?"

"No. He wants me dead because I know what he is, and there's nothing I won't do to stop him."

"Including time travel?"

"I don't know how to time travel willingly. I wish I did. I went back on purpose only once."

"And?"

"Things didn't go exactly how I expected. How any of us expected."

"Then why did he put a price on your head?"

"Well," I said, "I know what he's done, and I intend to kill him. As long as I'm alive, he's wise to be afraid of me."

"Have you ever killed a man, Matilda Case?"

"No."

"Maybe you shouldn't start with the head of a House."

"That monster put my family through hell," I said. "He's still after my family. And I intend to put an end to that."

Abraham's eyes were hooded in shadow, but he made a little *hm* sound. "Then we have more than one goal in common. I'd love to see his head on a platter."

"That won't be enough to kill him."

"I know. But after I get done, there won't be anything left of him to kill."

Well, there we had it. We'd found something to bond over: revenge.

"I'd like to know one other thing," he said, moving away from the wall and taking the few steps toward me. He halted just shy of my personal space, then took one step closer. He towered over me. "What did you do to me when I touched you?"

I tried to figure out what he was talking about, the kiss we had just not-shared still ghosting my lips and making me too warm. It finally came to me.

"You mean in the kitchen, when you grabbed my wrist and pulled a gun on me?"

"Yes."

"I don't think I owe explanations to anyone who likes to point guns my way."

"It wasn't my best moment."

"You owe me an apology."

"I'm sorry your brother was being an ass and I had to use you to make my point."

"Worst apology I've ever heard. Want to try that again?"

He shifted that left shoulder again, and it made me curious as to why he favored it. "People don't say no to me," he said.

"You might want to get used to it," I said. "I'm not intimidated by you."

"I can see that."

"And?"

"I like it."

I narrowed my eyes. "This tough-guy thing you're trying to pull off? Not really doing anything for me."

I was lying. Tough Abraham was all kinds of hot. It was making my knees wobbly just watching him move, listening to his low, rumbling voice, imagining his hands stroking over my skin.

"Well then, maybe I'll try a different approach."

"Try approaching an apology."

"I'm sorry I grabbed you. It was . . . ungentlemanly." That slash of a smile was a little rakish, the stitches at the side of his mouth pulling and not allowing the corner of his mouth to lift completely.

"So, we're clear that my personal space is my own?" I said. "Because you're all over it right now."

He stepped just a fraction of an inch closer, and I couldn't help it: my breathing got a little tight and quick.

"If I ask you kindly," he said, "would you please explain why touching you made everything in my body come alive?"

The soft burr of his voice washed me in sensual memories. I wanted to make those memories a reality again; needed him. But a part of me, the smart part of me, realized what he'd just said could also be taken as a threat.

Sorry, memories. Survival comes first.

"No, I will not," I said. "But I will point out to you that

if I can make you feel, I can make you hurt. Just so we're both clear about where we stand on the whole touching-without-permission thing."

The smile was back. It looked good on him.

"If I ask you nicely—*very* nicely—will you give me permission to touch you?"

"No." That would have sounded more assured if my voice hadn't cracked.

His eyes flashed with heat and amusement. "If you've lived a life before, if you've known me before, then I must have been something very special to you."

"Not really."

"You did go back in time to save me from Slater."

"I went back in time for other reasons. But since I was there, it seemed polite to warn you about Slater."

"You tackled him when he tried to shoot me. You were definitely trying to save me. And I'm asking myself why a woman would do such a thing for a man she didn't hold in high regard."

"Maybe I thought you'd live your three hundred years and actually do some good for the world instead of hiring yourself out to kill people for money."

"Doesn't sound a lot like me."

"And that, Mr. Vail, is so very disappointing."

He frowned, stilled by my cold tone.

"What was I to you?" he asked, genuinely puzzled.

"It doesn't matter. Things are different now."

"They don't have to be."

Ah, gods, there it was. The words I most wanted to hear from him. The promise that we could be together again. We could make it right again.

My heart thumped hard with need for that, even though I knew he didn't mean it. Even though I knew he didn't know what he was saying.

He was just looking for my weakness, a way to get what he wanted out of me: information.

"Don't do that," I said, too much emotion coming out with the words. "Don't be so cruel as to make promises you won't keep."

The calculating look in his eyes faded, replaced by concern that made me forget for a moment that he was a different man and this was a different time. A time I wasn't all that sure I'd get to keep.

"Matilda," he said. "I'm sorry—"

"Is there a problem here?" Quinten asked from the end of the hall.

Abraham immediately stepped back, and I realized he'd been leaning so close to me, I'd been wrapped in his heat, lost in his presence, my world filled by the sensation of him.

A sharp knife of loneliness twisted through my heart. I missed him, even though he was standing right next to me.

I straightened knees that had buckled despite my best intentions.

"No problem, Quinten," I said, my voice steady. Good thing too.

Quinten was covered in shadows there at the end of the hall, but as he walked our way, the light caught the gleam of an ax in his clenched hand.

Where is he going with an ax?

In his other hand was a bottle of something that smelled like moonshine.

"Why are you out of your room, Abraham?" Quinten asked.

"Am I a prisoner here?" Abraham squared off toward him, but hadn't quite declared a fight. Yet.

"You are to stay where I tell you to stay. My property and my rules," Quinten said. "Or do I need to make that point clear? The only reason you're still here and not tossed out on your ass like your friend Sallyo is because I thought you might be useful. Don't make me change my mind."

I knew how this was going to end. In a fight. That bottle in Quinten's hand was down a couple inches. I didn't know how full it had been when he'd started drinking it.

Maybe it would be good for both of them to get a little of their anger out on each other. Although my brother was at a distinct disadvantage, since, one, he could feel, and, two, he had only human strength.

"Are we leaving when it gets dark?" I asked.

"Not now, Matilda," Quinten said. His breath smelled of booze, but he sounded stone-cold sober.

"Where are we going?" Abraham asked.

"House Earth," I said. "We need to handle some things there before we go kill Slater. And if you two are going to be snarling at each other all night, we might as well be traveling while you do it."

"We'll wait until morning," Quinten said.

"No one travels at night." Abraham turned his attention fully to me, a frown on his face. It was perhaps a ploy to think he didn't have his guard up, thus tempting Quinten into swinging that ax, but I didn't think so.

Abraham wasn't afraid of a man with an ax. It took more than that to kill him.

"I travel at night," I said with a shrug.

"No one travels at night, because they'd spend more time fighting off ferals than getting anywhere, and that's if they were lucky. If they weren't lucky, they'd just be dead."

Ferals. Right. Quinten had mentioned those.

"Are they that bad?" I asked. "I mean, we had croc-boar and other roving mutants in my time. They weren't too hard to put down if you weren't afraid of getting bloody. I'd take out one or two a week on my own and feed them to the lizard."

Abraham shook his head slowly, then looked over at Quinten. "Do you believe she traveled back in time?"

I answered before Quinten could. "We haven't had much of a chance to talk about it," I said. "How long does it take to get to Compound Five?"

"On foot? A few days," Quinten said. "But we can take the truck. If we start early enough, we should get there before sundown."

"After we stop by House Earth, we're going to kill Slater?" Abraham asked.

Quinten nodded.

"Do we have a plan for how, exactly, we're going to do that?" Abraham asked. "You have every mercenary in this hemisphere looking for you, and unless you turn yourselves in or issue a challenge, we have no idea where Slater really is. You need intelligence on his movements. Reliable intelligence."

"I know," Quinten said. "Let me handle the details."

"I don't see that to be in my best interest," Abraham said. "Or yours. If we're going to take down a man as powerful as Slater, a head of a House, we will need to work together with at least a modicum of trust between us."

I waited. Abraham was being more than reasonable, especially considering Quinten had just been threatening him with an ax.

And I thought Quinten had been mostly reasonable to admit that having Abraham and Foster on our side was only to our advantage.

I just didn't know why there was so much hatred between them. It wasn't like my brother was above the law.

He'd admitted to smuggling information out of House Fire to work on the cure that had put us in all this trouble anyway.

No, whatever Quinten was angry at the galvanized about, it was personal.

"You are armed and in my home," Quinten said. "I would be a foolish man indeed to give you more trust than I have. But it is getting late. You and Foster are welcome to a meal or a bath." He paused, pressing his lips together. When he next spoke, the words came out in a measured drone. "Matilda can show you where the bath is."

He glanced at me, and I nodded.

Quinten turned and walked back down the hall to his room. "Get some sleep," he said without looking back. "We'll go over the route to Compound Five in the morning before sunrise."

He took a long swallow from the bottle, stepped into his room, and shut the door behind him.

"He's a cheerful man," Abraham said, nodding after Quinten. "Who died?"

"Most recently? His sister," I said.

He frowned.

I walked down the hall to the bathroom I hoped would be there.

"Neds should be in soon," I said when his footsteps sounded behind me. "Don't get in his way, okay? He's more than happy to mess a person up, and keeps enough guns on him to arm a battalion. And don't count on me riding to your rescue again. I'm done playing referee between the menfolk."

I put my hand on the latch, held my breath, and turned it, opening the door. Bathroom. Decorated a little differently, but there was still indoor plumbing with a shower and a tub. I exhaled and nodded.

"So, that's the bathroom," I said. "Help yourself if you want a scrub."

"You walk through this house, your home, like you've never seen it before," he said. "Why is that, Matilda?"

He was waiting for me to fill in the last piece of the puzzle. Waiting for me to tell him I had woken in this body and found Evelyn on the way out of this mind just hours ago, when he'd knocked on the door.

I gave him a small smile. "It's been a long day. I'm going to get some rest. I'll see you in the morning, Abraham."

I turned to walk past him down the hall. Close enough he could reach out and touch me if he wanted. Close enough I could reach out and touch him. In my mind's eye, I took his hand and drew him with me back to my room, where I could lay him in my bed and fill myself with comfort that would only be lies.

I walked past him, without a brush of contact.

"Good night, Matilda," he said, his voice so gentle, so familiar, so *him*, I wanted to cry.

Instead, I kept walking, not daring to look back.

6

*Time is killing me. Killing us all, I suppose.
And it's giving me a terrible headache the
more I try to unwind the puzzle of it.*

—W.Y.

I opened my eyes, my head heavy with a confusion of dreams. I tried to remember where I was, what time I was in, and what had happened.

I lay in bed, dressed down to my underwear and a T-shirt. A quick glance at the crocheted-lace-curtained window showed it wasn't yet true light outside.

I was home.

For several beats of my heart, I just reveled in that truth. No matter what happened from here forward, I had survived going back in time. My brother was still alive. So were Grandma, Neds, and Abraham. That was good. A win.

But we had people to save and a man to kill. Today was the day we got down to it.

Someone was laughing in the kitchen. Several some-ones, actually. Low voices, high voices, a babble and crash of tones and demands and laughter, as if the whole house had been suddenly filled with people having one big party.

Why hadn't Quinten woken me? Had he already left? Or was I in another timeway, filled with people?

I threw the heavy blankets off and crossed the cold wooden floor to my chest of drawers. I didn't feel dizzy, didn't smell roses. Both those things seemed to announce the timeway shifts. So maybe I was still in the right timeway.

I changed into new undergarments—which were a lot more lacy than anything I'd ever owned—Evelyn's, I assumed. Then I shrugged into a tank top and layered on a lighter shirt. I was delighted to see that Evelyn had also commandeered Quinten's old sleeveless jacket. I slipped that on with a smile. The pants selection consisted of supple leather or denim. I chose leather, then pulled on a pair of hand-knitted socks and stuffed my feet into sturdy boots.

Evelyn might have more feminine taste in clothing, judging by her undergarments, and in decorating, judging by the lace doilies and crocheted frills that set a soft edge to every clear surface of her room, but when it came to her outerwear, she went all out for practicality.

I approved.

Last night when I came into my room, I hadn't expected to fall asleep. But now it was almost daylight, and I hadn't even packed for the trip.

I pulled a duffel out of the closet, threw in a spare pair of clothing, and, remembering my travels from last time, added in anything I could carry that was lightweight but could be used for barter or trade. I snooped through Evelyn's things and found a little wooden case with a handle.

Inside that was the finest set of sewing needles, hooks, clamps, and other accouterments that I'd ever seen. The items looked like they'd gotten some use, but were well oiled and sharpened.

A small, fine square of cloth held tiny silver stitches across it—different loops and crosses and staggers. It was like an embroidery sampler, except I knew what these stitches were used for.

I glanced down at my arm, where the neat row of X's marched around my elbow.

"You were quite the hand at stitching, weren't you, Evelyn?"

The bottom of the box was filled with thread of different thicknesses, and beneath that was a small packet of powder I assumed was medicine.

Everything in that tidy case seemed useful, so I tucked it in my duffel, along with the spare knives, bullets, and the two small hatchets I found hanging on the back of her closet door.

There was a palm-sized mirror propped on her nightstand, so I took that too. I couldn't help but catch a look at my hair as I packed the mirror away.

An annoyed growl escaped my throat. The wild, maple-colored waves would only get in the way.

I took the time to braid my hair loosely in one plait that fell to the middle of my back and to bind it off with a tie.

Then I hefted the duffel over one shoulder and walked out into the rest of the house. Most of the noise was coming from the living room.

There must have been twenty people gathered there, little children who were only waist high running around, six men of various heights and widths, and several woman with tanned or freckled skin and hair cut short or pulled back in buns or braids.

Everyone was in clean, work-ready clothing, including boots and trousers, though the jackets and hats had been piled up in one corner of the room.

In the middle of them all, sitting in her rocker with a huge grin on her face, was Grandma. She looked like she had just woken up inside a dream come true.

I noticed something odd rooting around at her feet. At first I thought it was a pig, but then one of the smaller children threw a ball of Grandma's yarn and the creature waddled off after it, little bat wings pumping as it ran on its stubby reptilian legs.

It wasn't a pig. It was a stitched pig. A dragon-pig.

Aw. Cute.

"Come on back now, Floyd," Grandma called. It trotted around, pushing the ball with its ridiculous scaly pink head.

So that was Floyd. Well, one mystery solved.

"Evelyn!" one of the men hollered when he caught sight of me standing in the doorway. He was the tallest of the lot, maybe about six foot, his skin a smoky brown, his eyes even darker. "How's my favorite stitcher?"

The room filled with a tide of greetings and waves, while one of the kids tripped over the charging dragon-pig and fell down, crying.

I waved and smiled and hoped I was acting like Evelyn to them.

"Come on in the kitchen. Let's get you some food." A woman whose black hair was shot through with silver put a toddler down on his feet and took me by the hand. Her grip was strong and warm and friendly, and I got the feeling she'd taken my hand more than once when I was younger.

It wasn't a memory, but more of a tactile response to her. I had known her, or, rather, Evelyn had known her. Maybe even been under her care for a good long while.

"We got in a little early because Peter just couldn't wait. He had us all packed up and ready to leave an hour after your brother called. I swear he would have gone charging into a pack of ferals if it meant getting away from the homestead. The old man has itchy feet."

We were in the kitchen now. Quinten sat at the table with a man who looked several decades older than him, his gray hair receding away from a square, dark face made memorable by his short, crooked nose.

A younger man and woman were expertly cooking up a breakfast of ham and eggs and thick sliced bread that made my mouth water.

Abraham and Foster stood on the far side of the room, their backs to the wall, eyes shifting between the doors and people. They did not look comfortable, but other than the man at the table occasionally tossing a glance over at the galvanized, the other people in the room didn't seem to notice them.

Abraham nodded slightly as I entered. I didn't have a chance to respond.

"Evelyn," Quinten said, standing up from the table and making direct eye contact with me. His expression was asking me to play along, to be Evelyn for him and for the people around us. "I told you the Grubens would be here before sunrise, didn't I?" He gave me a cheery smile, and I smiled back.

"You sure did," I said nicely.

"Why don't you just sit down and have some breakfast with Pete and me?" he said. "We've almost finished planning for our trip."

"Sure," I said. I knew he was trying to guide me through how I was expected to behave in front of these people, but it was annoying to be talked to as if I were a child who always minded her manners.

I really wish you would have stood your ground more, Evelyn.

"Everything okay in the other room, Jacinta?" he asked the woman who had led me into the kitchen.

Now I had a name for her.

"Oh, it's fine. You know how they get when there's a day ahead of them and no particular chores. Think they're going to do nothing but waste the hours away, chasing your beasties around."

"Who thinks that?" Right Ned asked as he walked in from outside.

"Mike, Ace, and all the rest of the kids in there," Jacinta said. "You're looking well, Neds."

"I'll be looking even better after a plate of Dolly's amazing cooking."

The girl at the stove glanced over her shoulder. She had the most amazing green-gold eyes framed by orange freckles. "Well then, sit down, Mr. Harris, and be prepared to be amazed."

I walked over to the cupboard and pulled out a plate for myself and one for Neds. Dolly filled Neds' plate with eggs and a generous slab of ham, two hunks of bread, and a muddle of undetermined greens.

"Hey, Evelyn." The man at the stove next to Dolly could be her twin, with the same eyes and freckling. "I brought along a couple spools of mercerized cotton, if you have anything interesting to swap for them."

"What kind of interesting?" I asked.

"You know the kinds of things I like." He lowered his head and gave me a direct stare that made me blush.

"I don't think I'll be here for very long," I said, trying to make it sound like I regretted not taking him up on the offer.

"Oh, we don't need much time," he said a little quieter.

His sister smacked his arm with the spatula. "Leave her be, Tom. She's been turning you down for years. A couple skeins of cotton aren't going to make her change her mind."

"Can't blame a man for trying," he said with a grin.

I gave them both a quick smile and beat a hasty retreat with the full plates in my hands.

Neds were standing right behind me. "Thank you, Evelyn. Now be a dear and pour me some coffee, won't you?" Left Ned asked while Right Ned waggled his eyebrows.

"Sure," I said through my teeth. These Evelyn-like manners were not going to last if he pushed it. "I'd be happy to."

I set my plate aside on the counter, then scrounged for mugs while he sat down and started eating. Poured coffee for Neds and myself, then hooked the mugs in one hand and my plate in the other.

"Here you go." I set the coffee in front of Neds and put my plate down in front of one of the empty chairs at the end of the table.

Abraham and Foster hadn't moved. They still stood at the end of the kitchen like forgotten statues. It was creepy. "Can I get you anything?" I asked them.

Quinten and Pete stopped talking, and both looked over at me like I'd just lost my mind.

Abraham blinked, his hazel eyes flecked with a little more red than yesterday. "Coffee would be nice."

"Sure thing. You can have mine. I'm of the mood for tea anyway," I walked over, handed him the cup.

He took it, his fingers brushing mine, and the look of curiosity and need flared in his eyes.

Oh, don't go starting that now.

"Thank you ... *Evelyn*," he said quietly, holding his fingers all to himself.

Yeah, I heard his unspoken question: *Why are these*

people calling you Evelyn? So there was another thing I'd have to explain. But not now.

"Foster?" I said. "Would you like tea or coffee?"

"Water. Thank you."

I poured him a tall glass of water and took it to him, aware that all eyes in the room were on me. He accepted it with a grateful nod.

"Evelyn," Quinten said. "Please join us."

I walked back over to the table. Tom and Dolly were staring at me like I'd just snatched my head out of a lion's mouth.

"As we were saying," Quinten continued, "we'll be heading out as soon as we've eaten. Is the truck in order, Neds?"

"All set," Left Ned said while Right Ned took a big bite of bread and ham.

"I still don't think little Evelyn should have to go along with you," Pete said. "Might as well leave her here with us. We can keep an eye on her."

Little Evelyn?

"I'll be fine," I said. "I know how to take care of myself. It's not like I've never fired a gun."

Neds kicked me under the table. "Plus," I added, "Quinten might need me for, um . . . stitching, and all that . . . womanly stuff I do."

Left Ned rolled his eyes, and Right Ned choked on his food.

I shoveled some eggs and toast into my mouth to keep from screwing this up any worse.

Good choice. The food was delicious.

Dolly set a mug of water and tea leaves in front of me. She shook her head, as if telling me she couldn't believe what I'd just said. I guess I wasn't very good at being Evelyn.

"All right," Pete said cautiously. "You're set on this, Quinten?"

"It'd be best for her to come with us. But I sure do appreciate you and yours keeping an eye on Grandma and the beasts."

"It is our pleasure," Pete said. "Always, always happy to help out a Case. Why, your grandmother practically raised me and my brothers. You're family."

"You certainly are," Jacinta said, and sat down next to Pete. She reached across the table to pat Quinten's arm. "But are you sure it's wise to hire those . . . gentlemen?"

She was talking about Abraham and Foster.

Quinten nodded. "I believe they will be very helpful to us in attaining our goals."

"Be sure to send a call once you reach the compound," Pete said.

"I will."

"Well, then, give Paxton our love," Jacinta said. "And tell him I expect him home for a visit before the weather goes bad."

Quinten nodded and hid his frown by drinking down the last of his coffee. "I'll be sure to tell him."

Neds sat back from the table, then stood and drank coffee while returning their plate to the sink.

Tom lost a game of rock-paper-scissors with Dolly and started up a sink full of soapy water for washing.

"Daylight is just about upon us," Quinten said. "I still can't believe you got out here so quickly."

"Ferals weren't too bad, since we traveled quiet and most of them were denning up for the day. I think it's going to be a hot one."

Both men rose from the table, and then there was a general hubbub of putting dishes away, and good-byes and handshakes and hugs.

The rest of the crew in the living room must have heard the commotion. They came pouring into the kitchen, and in an instant there was no place to stand in the room that wasn't filled with a Gruben looking to say farewell or jostling for seats at the table, while fussy children were being soothed by mothers and fathers alike.

I tried to slip out onto the porch without being noticed, but Evelyn must have been a favorite among the family members. Each and every one of them gave me a hug and made me promise to stay safe and keep that brother of mine out of trouble.

The sea of faces all blurred into each other, and I felt bad that I didn't remember their names. It was overwhelming to be cared for by so many people. I'd never had a big family, since all of my life I'd lived on this farm, hiding from the world with just Neds, Grandma, and Quinten.

But this comfortable chaos put a real smile on my face. It might be a hard life these people were living; it might be a hard life I was living. But it was a good life, with joy and good people in it. And these Grubens were good people.

I finally escaped the kitchen and hugs and stepped outside. During the good-byes, I had been handed a cloth-wrapped wedge of chocolate; the cotton thread Tom had teased me about and a few other good-luck charms, buttons, and stones. I tucked them all away in my duffel, but pocketed the good-luck stones.

I figured I could use as much luck as I could get.

Abraham and Foster had long ago exited the kitchen. They stood a short distance from the house.

Morning light was just edging the sky with a pink blush, and the occasional birdsong peppered with the other stitched beasts' warbles and growls.

I walked over to the two men. "Sorry about my brother's lack of manners in there. Did you two get something to eat?"

Foster smiled and made a little grunting noise, then looked over at Abraham expectantly.

"We were up before the Grubens arrived," he said. "We ate. Evelyn, is it now?"

"Thank you for going along with that."

"Your brother called you that yesterday. Why do all those people think you are Evelyn?"

"Because I was. I guess. Up until yesterday."

Abraham was not a dumb man. He seemed to put the pieces of the puzzle together. "She's been alive in that body up until recently?"

I nodded.

"When?"

"Just before you showed up. For me, just after the Wings of Mercury experiment exploded and the infinity bell rang out."

"September thirteenth, 1910," he said.

"And yesterday was September thirteenth, 2210."

"So, when you said your brother had lost a sister . . ."

"He did. And she was a sister he very much loved."

He was silent a moment. I wondered, in his three hundred years, how many people close to him he had lost.

Abraham shifted his gaze to the horizon, and the specter of pain fell over him briefly.

"So, you're not seeing him at his best," I said. "I mean, he's smart—a genius, really. Runs a little hot on the temper side, but he's a good man. He's done a lot to help people, even when he didn't get anything back from it.

"And there's one more thing you should know. The plague hit Compound Five. There are six people infected, as far as we know. I'd understand it if you don't want to go there with us."

"Why?" he asked, turning back to me, his left hand tucked in his belt, his shoulder lowered.

"Well, it's a plague. A bad one," I said.

"And?"

"And if you don't want to be exposed . . ."

"It is the small details like that, Matilda, that makes me want to believe your outlandish tales."

"True tales, outlandish or not," I corrected. "What details?"

"Galvanized aren't affected by the plagues."

"We aren't?"

"No."

"None of the plagues?"

"No. We've been through all of them, and all of us are standing."

"Oh. So that's good."

"Seems to be." He was smiling, the stitched corner of his mouth lower than the other. I liked that smile on him. Especially when it was aimed at me.

"Well, Quinten has a friend there who's infected," I said.

"That makes sense. I couldn't fathom why we'd have to go out there in person, when you have a radio in the basement."

"How do you know about the radio?"

"Every 'steader has a radio."

"Okay."

"You might not want to do that."

"Do what?"

"Believe everything I say. I could be lying, you know, and have just found out you have a radio."

"Don't worry. There's something I haven't told you about me."

"Oh?"

"I can tell when anyone lies. It's a gift." I was lying through my teeth.

His eyebrows ticked down, and he bit his lip.

Okay, the lip thing was totally becoming a distraction. It made me want to kiss him, to taste him, to run my tongue along that curve of him and see what he'd do to me in return.

"Evelyn?" Quinten called out from the kitchen door, where I was sure the Grubens could still hear him. "Do you want to say good-bye to Grandma?"

I knew I should. "Sure. Be right in."

I left Abraham and made my way back through the noise and laughter, which was layered with comments about how quickly I'd made it to Compound Five and back. Grandma was at the table, as excited to be there among the noise as I'd ever seen her.

"I wanted to give you a hug," I told her, doing just that.

"Are you going somewhere, dear?" she asked.

"Just for a little while. I'll see you soon."

"Shouldn't I go? I should go. It's time to go. Always time. I'll bring the sheep." She patted her lap, looking for the sheep, which were not there.

"It's time to stay. I'll be home before you know it." I gave her a peck on the cheek. "In the meantime, the Grubens will be here with Floyd, and that's going to be fun, isn't it?"

"Oh yes." She brightened a little, then gave me a very clear look. "I will see you in time, Matilda. Be safe, my child."

I glanced up, and a couple of the people looked uncomfortably at me or at her with concern in their eyes.

"I will be careful," I said. "Don't worry a bit."

The people around us seemed to relax when I took

the name change in stride. I said one final farewell and got the heck out of there.

They were good people, loving people. I could see that. But the longer I stayed with them, the easier it would be for me or Quinten to slip up and reveal that I wasn't who they thought I was. And explaining what I was, who I was, had quickly become tiresome.

I strode outside again, and found Neds had brought what must be the "truck" out of the barn.

It was not now, nor had it ever been, a truck.

It looked more like an armored bus and a Conestoga wagon had had unprotected sex. The engine was running strong and smooth, a deep, chugging growl, but I didn't smell gasoline. I wondered what it used for fuel.

Quinten walked out of the kitchen, waving his hand behind him one last time. He wore a backpack slung over one shoulder and a duffel that looked like it weighed something in his hand.

Peter and Jacinta were in the doorway, his arm around her shoulder. "Bye, now!" Jacinta called out. "Safe travels."

I gave them a wave too.

"Let's go," Quinten said as he passed me.

I followed him into the vehicle, which was separated with seats up front and benches that looked like they could break down into beds in the back. The rear of the vehicle was also fitted with cupboards and a small table.

Neds sat the driver's seat, and Quinten made himself comfortable in the middle of the bus.

Foster and Abraham stepped into the vehicle and paused just inside, as if committing the space to memory. Then Foster moved silently down to the back and chose a seat, while Abraham took the seat in the front, nearest the door and Neds. He reached over and slid the door closed.

"The direct route?" Right Ned asked, glancing in the rearview mirror at Quinten.

"To begin with," Quinten said. "Once we make Copple's Rise, we'll decide which road looks best."

Neds slipped the beast of a vehicle into gear and put his foot down. The vehicle lunged forward, then smoothed out, taking us down the dirt road of the farm, past lizards of various sizes.

I stared out the window, hungrily taking in the view. The farm was beautiful in the pale beginnings of the day. Fields neatly tacked down by split-wood fences; orchards of pear and also plum, peach, and apple; and generous acreage set aside for vegetables and grain.

"Just the three of us work the land?" I asked.

Quinten was watching out the window too, but he was much more subdued. "We bring in the Grubens during harvest when we need it. Trade our grain for their meat."

I noticed a clump of cream-colored sheep, small but not as tiny as the pocket sheep Grandma kept around. They were normal-looking except for their ridiculous rabbit ears that stood tall off their heads.

"Bunny sheep?"

He smiled. "Shabbits. They were a fluke. I stitched some bits together, wondering if it would affect the wool they produced."

"Did it?"

"Yes. They are also the only stitched I've made that breed. So there's quite a few of them now."

"And does their wool, um . . . hold bits of time?"

He frowned. "No. Why would you even assume. . . . Wait. Did they before?"

"I don't know how it worked. Grandma could do it. She knitted up spare bits of time in their wool somehow—

the tiny-sheep wool; she didn't have shabbits. She never told me how, and I've only used it twice."

"She knits," he said. "But she's never mentioned she's knitting time. Not even when she was of a clearer mind. It isn't something I think is possible."

"There's a lot of impossible going around these days." Maybe the wool did hold time. More likely, it didn't. When I saw Grandma again, I'd ask her.

The fields rolled past, and I caught a glimpse of more lizards, trundling along the edges of trees and slinking through tall grasses. They were built like patchwork dragons made of crocodiles and a hodgepodge of iguana, monitor, and turtle.

"Did you try to make any of them the same?" I asked.

"Why bother?" he said. "Better to use what I have on hand and try to make the most viable creature. Reptiles are particularly hearty in all their shapes and forms."

"And they don't eat the sheep—I mean, shabbits?"

"They don't have a taste for stitched things."

"Well, I, for one, am happy to hear that," I said.

His eyes strayed to Abraham, who was slouched back in his seat, his arms crossed over his chest, looking as relaxed and unconcerned as a man could be.

"Most of them, anyway," Quinten said.

I could have asked him why he hated galvanized. Over the rumble and jostle of the vehicle, I doubted Abraham or Foster would have heard his answer. But this conversation between us about the sheep had been the first time he hadn't been looking at me like I was an unwelcome stranger behind his sister's eyes. And my questions—things Evelyn already knew—didn't seem to make him angry.

I liked the hint of trust that might be growing between

us. We'd need it if we were going to take on Slater. So instead of pushing him for answers, I contented myself with watching the sunlight warm the edges of the world, happy here in the small peace of this moment before the storm I knew was coming.

7

I think something went terribly wrong for you, Matilda, back in our time. I am running out of time to find you. Are you alive?

— W.Y.

After all the talk about ferals, I expected the country-side to be filled with teeth and claws. Instead, it was a serene landscape made mostly of the occasional walled farm separated by wide, hilly fields and forests.

The road we'd been rumbling along for a couple hours took us up past Pock cabin, and on past the small out-cropping of House Brown families that used to live in what was now an empty field.

We made it up a rise that offered a horizon-to-horizon view of the valley, roads, and hills beyond. Neds pulled to a stop just off the side of the road, where a little brook glittered a few yards away.

"Good enough place to fill up," Neds said, "and pick our trail into Compound Five."

Quinten took a deep breath and nodded. "Let's stretch our legs."

"How much farther to the compound?" I stood. My

legs were still vibrating from the miles we'd put in so far today.

"Depends on which route looks open," Quinten said.

Abraham and Neds had already exited the vehicle. Quinten was next, and I glanced behind me to make sure Foster was coming.

He was already on his feet, ducking a little for the ceiling height. He offered me a small smile and a wink.

"You're enjoying this, aren't you?"

"I am happy. You were lost. We found you."

From his perspective, he'd lost me back in 1910. Three hundred years thinking a child you'd only just met was missing was a long time to hold out hope of finding her.

"I'm happy you found me too," I said.

"I never lost you," he said quietly.

I wondered what he meant by that, but we stepped out of the bus thing and into clean, cool air, with sunlight slipping between clouds. He walked past me and down the road without another word.

There were no sounds of distant engines, no airplane rumbles or whistle of trains. It was as silent as I'd ever heard it be. Only the birdsong, broken by the rattling of grasshopper wings, and the burble of a nearby brook filled the air.

Near enough I could hit it with a rock rose a two-hundred-foot radio tower built on the other side of the road. It speared through the view across the low hills and fields ahead of us.

If Abraham was right and everyone out here in the scratch communicated by shortwave radio, then this tower was a good bounce station that probably serviced a hundred-mile radius.

"I thought you said ferals were out here." I scanned the landscape separated by only a few two-lane roads, and with a disturbing lack of speed tubes to be found. From here, I couldn't even make out any of the small, walled-off farms we'd come across as we'd traveled.

"Only at night," Quinten said.

"What do they eat?" I asked.

"Other nocturnal beasts and each other. Farm animals, if they can get them."

"I don't see any farms."

"Not in this valley. Too many ferals to risk it," Quinten said. "They move in packs of ten or twelve, but the scent of blood will set them into a feeding frenzy. They give off a pheromone, and then all the other ferals in a hundred miles will come for the feed.

"House Brown does some planting and harvesting out here. If it's in a day's driving distance, they'll work the land. Sometimes a little farther if there's a bolt cabin. Orchards and such."

"Where did the ferals come from?" I asked. "Are they stitched?"

"You said you had crocboar back in your time?"

"Yes."

"Was it stitched?"

"No. Just a mash-up of critters that evolved or mutated, I suppose."

"Ferals are the same," he said. "Never have gotten the straight story, but when all the power grids and communication systems went down, a lot of things collapsed. Things in cages and science labs broke out. Escaped to the wild. Thrived in a lot of zones too contaminated for humans. And eventually they bred. A lot."

"So there's a lot of them?"

He stared at me a moment. "Far, far too many. But since they are all nocturnal, we won't have to worry about them until sunset. We should be at the compound by then."

Neds swung back into the bus and walked out with something that looked suspiciously like a picnic basket.

"Jacinta made sure we had a lunch," Left Ned said. "Since you're the girl here . . ." He handed me the basket.

I gave him a withering glare. "What? Only a girl knows how to unpack food?"

"No," Left Ned said. "I meant, since you're the girl here, you should have first choice."

The wicked twinkle in his innocent eyes told me otherwise.

"Don't give me those doe eyes, Harris," I said. "I have matches, and I know where you keep your porn."

He inhaled, shocked by my response. Probably Evelyn wouldn't have said something like that. Then he laughed so hard, both of him were howling.

Quinten just shook his head and sighed at me.

"Good God, Matilda," Right Ned said, catching his breath, "remind me not to get your dander up."

"Here's an idea," I said. "Try being nice, and your smut might survive the week." I gave him a sweet grin, then started unpacking the basket onto the grass.

"Think I'll fill the tanks," Left Ned said. "Try not to spit in my sandwich."

"Too late," I said without looking up.

He was still chuckling as he walked over to the back of the vehicle. He pulled a long hose out of a small door in the back and dragged it behind him as he trudged down to the creek.

Abraham and Foster were out of hearing range, walking down both directions of the road, guns in their hands.

"Where do you suppose they're going?" I asked Quinten.

"To see if the mercs who have been following us are

going to start a fight." He pulled out a pair of binoculars and scanned the horizon.

"Mercs? We've been followed?" I glanced around, looking for any sign of movement in the grasses or trees.

"Since just after we left our property."

"I didn't see them."

"They stayed a good distance behind us."

"How?"

"Motorcycles."

"I didn't hear engines."

"Like I said, they stayed a distance back."

He pivoted north, his eyes still behind the binoculars.

The basket contained sliced bread, plump green apples, cheese, and cured meat.

"Hungry?" I asked him.

He *hmm*ed, still scanning the horizons. I cut a hunk of cheese with my pocket knife, pressed it and an apple into his hand. "Eat something."

Then I cut up the rest of the cheese—a pale, buttery yellow—and split it five ways. Jacinta had included cloth napkins in the basket, so I spread out five and filled each one with a serving of everything.

I held one of the napkins in my hand and paced a bit while I bit into the tart, juicy apple. "Did you bring everything you needed for the cure?" I asked.

"Of course I did. Why would you even ask me that?"

He finally pulled the binoculars away from his eyes and noticed he had a hunk of cheese in his hand. He took a bite. "Why are you pacing?"

I shrugged. "Other than there are mercenaries after us and ferals in the shadows and we're out in the open like sitting ducks for flybys?"

"Flybys?"

"Aircraft? Jet, helios?"

"Airplanes?" he said. "Trust me—no one is going to waste fuel flying over the countryside, looking for us."

"I should be comforted by the fact that they'll just put mercenaries after us instead?"

"No, but you can stop pacing. We're safe here. We'll see them coming if they make a move."

Three quick blasts of gunshot rang out. A flock of birds rattled up out of the trees.

I grabbed the gun at my thigh, drew it.

Quinten and Ned had done the same, though they didn't look nearly as twitchy as I felt.

Abraham came walking up the road. I half expected to see him dragging a dead body behind him.

"Did you talk them out of following us?" Quinten asked.

"For now." Abraham scanned us and the space around us, his eyes flicking down the opposite end of the road, where Foster had disappeared.

"Were there more?" Quinten asked.

Foster strode up the road, his pace steady, looking like a tank that could break through any barrier set in front of it.

Abraham flicked a few fingers his way, and Foster responded with a gesture.

"There was one other," Abraham said. "He has been encouraged to report to Coal and Ice and tell them that killing us is not a job worth the pay."

Quinten made the *hmm* sound again.

"Coal and Ice?" I handed Neds his portion of the meal and then gave Abraham his share.

"It's the center of criminal activity and information," Left Ned said. "Abraham and Foster here probably frequent the place quite a lot."

"We do," Abraham said, not rising to Ned's taunt. "All jobs come and go through Coal and Ice; all information is gathered there."

"So it's like a House?"

"No," Quinten said.

"House of villainy," Right Ned said.

"It is efficient," Abraham took a bite of the meat and bread together. "And if it were not exactly what it was, Quinten would not be interested in either Foster or me."

"Why?" I asked.

"They're my ticket in," Quinten admitted.

Abraham nodded.

If they had come to some kind of an agreement, it must have been when I wasn't around.

"Into Coal and Ice?"

"Exactly," Quinten said.

"I thought we were going to House Brown. I mean Earth. House Earth."

"We are," Quinten said. "Then we are going to Coal and Ice. For information. And to hire a few people."

So, Coal and Ice was a hub of mercs and spies. Killer central. "To take out Slater?" I asked. "I mean, telling people you want to storm House Fire sounds a little crazy, don't you think?"

"Crazy doesn't matter," Abraham said. "All that matters is what it pays." He was giving Quinten a look, studying him while they both ate. Foster stepped up beside us, and Abraham handed him the remaining share of food.

"I am curious as to what you will be paying for the job," Abraham said.

"Do not concern yourself with that," Quinten said. "Concern yourself with the business at hand."

"It's all the same business," Abraham said.

Neds scoffed. "All you care about is getting paid," Left Ned said. "Stitch."

Abraham finished his bread and cheese. "Mostly. But if that was all I cared about, shortlife, I would have dragged Quinten and Matilda in for the reward."

"Like Sallyo would let you do that," Left Ned said.

"Sallyo couldn't stop me."

That resonated with the Neds. It was true, after all. Galvanized were built stronger than humans, even mutants like Sallyo and Neds. If Abraham, Foster, or, hell, I got it in our heads that we should make a stand or take someone down, those who stood against us would be quickly stopped or killed.

Which reminded me.

"What kind of bomb?" I asked.

Quinten brushed the crumbs off his fingertips. "What kind of a bomb what?"

"Slater said he'd begin bombing House Earth compounds in ten days . . . well, nine days now. You told me he had the weaponry and technology to do that. So, what kind of bombs can he lob at the compounds?"

"It depends on which compound he targets," he said.

"Are they all on this continent, or are they around the world?"

"Most are on this continent." Quinten settled into the history-teacher tone he always used when he knew more about a subject than I did. "After the cataclysm, cities and countries fell as the power complexes fell. The disasters that followed made many places untenable, though a few roughs and stragglers scratch out a sort of living even in those zones.

"The richest soil, the cleanest water, drew the major cities of House Fire and House Water. Between those cities, where the water isn't always as plentiful or the soil as sweet—"

"Don't forget the ferals roaming free," Left Ned added.

"—and the ferals are out killing every night is where House Earth built their strongholds."

"How many?"

"Twenty-three."

Twenty-three was an awful lot of targets; nearly a month's worth of killing, if Slater wasn't stopped.

"The other thing I don't understand," I said, "is why the Houses are at war with House Earth. Self-sufficient people shouldn't have any reason to get in the way of the more powerful Houses."

"Who said the Houses were at war with Earth?" Right Ned asked.

"Aren't they?"

Quinten shook his head, then went back to peering through the binoculars. "There are disagreements, skirmishes, fights, and accusations. So far there haven't been any wars."

"Except for fifty years ago," Abraham said quietly.

Every muscle in Quinten's body tensed.

"What happened fifty years ago?" I asked.

"The One-one plague hit," Abraham said.

They were quiet, as if expecting me to pick up on some important detail.

"And?" I asked.

"It brought new scarcity and disagreements between Houses," Abraham said. "There were raids on House Earth. A lot of people were angry."

"A lot of people were killed," Quinten said flatly. "And not just fifty years ago. Much more recently. Much more."

"Unintentionally."

Quinten shook his head. "You will never convince me of that."

"Who did the killing?" I asked. But just as I said it, it came to me. "Galvanized?"

"It was a time of upheaval," Abraham said. "Galvanized were the only people who weren't falling to the disease. Some made regrettable choices."

"Some never stopped making regrettable choices. Do you know who killed your parents, Matilda?" Quinten asked.

Everything in me went sick and hot. "Did you?" I whispered to Abraham.

"No."

Quinten didn't say anything, but the hatred radiating off him was a heat wave. "Only the galvanized attacked that road. Only the galvanized dragged the living off to House Fire and House Water. Who else would you like me to blame, Abraham?"

"Those who are responsible," Abraham said. "Those who ordered the caravan to be stopped and seized. Those who ordered the innocent people brought in for experimental treatment."

"You killed innocent people."

"*I*," Abraham said, "was not there. There was only one galvanized on the road that day, and he belonged to House Fire."

Quinten stood at his full height, his hand cocked back in a fist. The brother I knew would ask who was that galvanized. The brother I knew would put his anger aside and deal with facts before he took action.

This brother, this Quinten, swung and hit Abraham square in the jaw, knocking the bigger man back a step.

Quinten pulled his gun before Abraham had a chance to return the blow.

I jumped in between them, pushing them apart, my back to Abraham as I shoved on Quinten's chest, forcing him to walk back and back.

"Lying stitch!" he spat over my shoulder.

"That's enough," I said.

Quinten made a move to push past me, but I grabbed his arm and pulled, halting him in his tracks.

Like I said, I am a very strong girl.

He half spun on his foot and squared to me, and I yanked the gun out of his hand.

Out of the corner of my eye, I could see Abraham was standing, arms crossed over his chest, head tipped down, eyeing Quinten over Neds, who was standing in front of him.

Foster stood to one side and behind Abraham, chewing on his apple and looking positively unconcerned about the entire situation.

"Let go of me now," Quinten snapped.

"So you can get yourself killed?" I said. "I don't think so. You are picking a fight with a galvanized, Quinten. If Abraham wanted to, he could crush you with one hand."

"He killed them!"

"He said he wasn't there."

"You believe him? You believe *that* monster over me?"

"I don't think any one of us is a monster here. They died years ago, Quinten. Instead of blaming the first stitched who walks into our house, I'd like to find out who really did it."

I kept my hand around his wrist. He wasn't pulling against me, but that was no guarantee that he wouldn't lunge at Abraham the first chance he got.

"Who killed them?" I asked Abraham. "Do you know?"

"The order to stop that caravan didn't go through Coal and Ice," he said. "The roadside attacks were never vetted with Binek."

"Who's Binek?" At this rate, even I was getting tired of how many questions I still didn't have answers to.

"The man who runs Coal and Ice," Abraham said.

"The man who sends mercenaries out on jobs for the Houses?"

"Jobs for anyone who can pay," Abraham said. "Yes."

"Then who do you think was staging the road attacks?"

"Slater," Foster breathed.

"Bullshit," Quinten said. "How convenient that the man who wants our head—the man you were recently working for, I'll remind you—is the one you want us to think killed our parents. Our friends."

"Do you have proof?" I asked.

Abraham took a breath. The look he gave Foster was pointed. I didn't think he had wanted Foster to call Slater out by name.

Interesting. So Abraham and Foster might have another angle on this game, maybe even another reason for wanting to go with Quinten and me to House Earth.

It was starting to be very difficult to decide just who I should really trust in this world.

But my gut said Abraham wasn't playing us, or at least he wasn't playing us with an intent to harm us. Of course, that could just be old love getting in the way of my logical mind.

"Proof?" I asked again.

Abraham shook his head. "Nothing you'd believe. Nothing on me. But it is true. I give you my word, Matilda

Case. Slater culled those caravans, and the people he pulled out of them have never been heard from again."

"Only House Earth people?"

He hesitated just slightly. "Yes."

Something wasn't lining up, but I didn't know what it was. "Okay, here's the deal. I still want Slater dead. More dead if he really was the one who killed my parents and the people in House Earth. You," I said to Quinten, "need to decide how you're going to deal with this. Either we travel with Abraham and Foster and use their connections, like you told me you wanted to, or we cut here and go our separate ways."

"I don't have to do what you—"

"You do," I interrupted. "You have to do what I tell you to do. This is not a democracy, brother. I'm taking over. At least until we get to House Earth. You need to tell me if you can keep your fists and bullets to yourself for the rest of this trip."

"Why," he bit off, "should I?"

I shook my head. "I don't know. Is it worth the information you want them to give to you?"

Quinten's eyes narrowed. I watched as the gloss of rage slipped sideways into something that might not quite be sanity, but could be sanity adjacent.

He nodded. "There are ... things that only a galvanized connected to Coal and Ice would know. Things that would help us destroy Slater."

I held eye contact with him, watching to see if the crazy came creeping back. "Then we travel together. And leave the past in the past."

"I can't do that. I won't."

"I don't care. You have to, at least temporarily." I released his arm, then walked toward Abraham.

Neds, who had been uncharacteristically quiet through this exchange, his back toward me and Quinten as he stood in front of Abraham, had a gun in his hand.

"Neds," I said. "I appreciate you not firing on them while I worked this out. Am I going to get flak from you about me calling the shots?"

"Near as I can tell, you're just doing what we'd planned on anyway," Right Ned said. "Isn't that right, Quinten Case?" he called back over his shoulder.

Quinten dragged his hand up into his hair and tugged on it. Then he walked stiffly toward us. "That is correct. We have a long way to go," he said, looking only at me. "We should leave."

"Abraham, Foster," I said, "are we settled, then? Or would you like us to drop you off somewhere suitable between here and House Earth?"

"There is no place suitable," Abraham said. He was watching me again, like he thought I might not be someone he should trust, which was weird, since I'd just stood up to my brother to keep him from being accused of something he said he didn't do.

"What I told your brother is the truth," Abraham said. "I didn't kill your parents."

"I'm willing to let that question lay fallow for a while, if you don't mind," I said.

"Thank you."

"I didn't say I believed you."

"You didn't say you didn't."

"Then it's settled. You're with us for the ride. Please keep your hands to yourself. Both of you," I said, with a nod toward Foster.

Foster lifted his chin. He jerked his head to scan the road down the way we'd come.

Abraham sucked in a quick breath, gaze intent in the

same direction. Both men stood as if someone had just cranked their spines tight as catgut on a guitar.

"What?" I asked.

"Engines," Foster breathed.

I held my breath. Listened. Heard nothing. "I thought you said the mercenaries would return to Coal and Ice and stop hunting us."

"One thing you should know about mercenaries, Matilda," Abraham said. "None of us follow rules."

"Get on the bus," I said. "Neds, are we fueled up?"

"We're good to go. Backup tanks too."

"Then let's get moving." I got three steps toward the bus.

My gut twisted. Dizziness washed over me, bringing the stench of roses. *No. Not now.* I didn't have time for this now.

The world whisked away, taking the bus, my brother, farmhand, and galvanized with it.

I stood in front of a concrete building that looked like a storage shed. There was no road, though I could hear the hum of cars moving along a highway in the distance, and saw the glint of the local speed tube in the sunlight.

"Where is it?" Slater demanded.

I turned on my bootheel.

He wore the same dark blue suit with a black shirt beneath that he'd been wearing the last time the world had spun and he'd threatened me. He strode my way, a gun in his hand, pointed at me.

Holy shit.

I backed up, my hands out to the side.

"Where is the machine?"

"I don't know what you're talking about," I said.

"The Wings of Mercury. You have it. You've hidden

it," he shouted. "You or your brother. You *Cases*," he spat, "will not control time. Only I will live forever. Not you. Not any of you!"

Raging madman with a gun. Apparently, Slater was an asshole in every timeway.

"Slater," I said, "listen to me. I don't control time. I don't have the machine. It was destroyed back in the 1900s. I don't know what the hell you're talking about."

"Time," Slater said as if that explained everything. "These timeways are not random. And you are in every one of them. Something must be controlling it. A piece of the machine . . . It's impossible, but the Wings of Mercury must still exist. What part of it did you keep? How did you keep it?" he yelled. "Is it your brother? Does he have a piece of the machine? I can kill him, you know. In every timeway. And I will."

"We don't have anything," I said. "I'm not controlling this. Quinten doesn't even know about the machine. You can't kill him in this timeway. He's already dead."

He shook the gun to include the world around us. "I will stop this. I will break this. I will crush you into dust, Matilda Case."

He squeezed the trigger.

I screamed as the red-hot pain of a bullet slammed through me just below my left collarbone.

Pain flashed through my muscles and nerves, hitting so hard, I couldn't breathe.

Then the world stuttered and swirled away from beneath my feet into the scent of roses and the distant hum of a bell.

I inhaled on a sharp breath, swallowing air against a second scream.

Slater was gone. The storage shed was gone. I drew

my fingers up to my chest. There was no blood, no hole, no bullet.

I wasn't in that timeway, and I wasn't wounded.

Shit. Shitshitshit.

I bit my lip to keep the panic behind my teeth. Switching times wasn't making any of this easier.

"Hurry." Left Ned jogged past me and quickly climbed behind the driver's seat.

I looked around, trying to ground myself in this now. Still on the rise. Still outside our vehicle. Still had mercenaries coming after us.

Foster and Abraham strode up and into the vehicle, Foster pressing his huge hand on my shoulder in comfort as he passed.

We had to get going. Now.

I glanced back, suddenly afraid my brother wouldn't be there behind me.

My heart thumped hard, then settled into a more normal rhythm. He stood there, whole and alive.

"Quinten," I said, finally getting my brain in the right gear. "We need to go. Right now."

He dropped the binoculars and strode toward the bus, not looking at me. "Take the south fork," he said to Neds. "There should be decent cover if we're followed. Unless you'd rather pick our way across the countryside too, Matilda?"

What was his problem? Oh, right. I'd just told him I was making the decisions.

"We don't have time for your hurt feelings," I said, following him into the bus. "If you say the south fork is the way to go, then that's good enough for me. Neds, go."

I closed the side door behind me. Neds started the engine, which coughed and died and sputtered, and made me wonder if I should take up praying.

Then the engine caught and smoothed out. He released the clutch and got us back on the road, rolling down the other side of Cooper's Ridge.

"Can we tap into the radio towers?" I asked.

I sat a couple seats behind Neds, and Quinten sat across from me. Abraham had walked into the back of the vehicle and was standing there, watching the road behind us out the small double windows. Foster was sitting near the back. He had pulled a heavy leather duffel out from under one of the seats and was methodically withdrawing weapons from it.

I was pretty sure he was humming a song about the harvest moon shining on a pair of young lovers.

"Tap in?" Quinten asked.

"Do you have a battery? A mobile radio unit that can tap the towers?"

"If we had to, yes," he said. "But there's no one out here. Not for the next hundred miles."

"But if we needed help?"

"Matilda," he said, and tugged his hair, then wiped his hand down his face. "Right now if we called for help, the only folk who would answer are the Grubens. And by the time they got out here, whatever we needed help with would be over."

"They've made us," Abraham said.

The pop of gunfire was echoed by the sharp pinging of the metal siding of our vehicle taking the hit.

"Get down! Get down!" I waved at Quinten, but he was not getting down.

So much for me being the boss.

"How many?" he yelled back to Abraham.

"Four I can see."

"Weapons?" I asked.

Another rattle of bullets peppered the vehicle.

"Guns," Abraham said unnecessarily.

I strode back to where Abraham was assembling a long-range rifle and scope that Foster had handed him.

"Are there rules about mercenaries not killing their fellow mercenaries?" I asked.

A spatter of bullet popped out again, and Abraham turned his back toward the fire. He simultaneously reached out and pulled me closer to his chest, using the width of his body to block the bullets.

I breathed in the scent of him, copper and smoke and leather. His arms tightened against my back; the rifle pressed down my spine, a cold counter to his heat. For a moment, no longer than a heartbeat, I turned my cheek against his chest and closed my eyes tight, wishing I could hold him forever.

The bullets paused and I released Abraham, though his arms were slow to loosen from around me.

I was trying to step away when the bus jerked. I grabbed hold of his waist and shoulder to keep my footing, my fingers curving around his neck, brushing stitches and skin . . .

He inhaled sharply and exhaled on a slight moan.

My touch, skin to skin, made him feel. And right now he felt me, the curve of my thigh braced inside his, my hips pressed against his groin. And I knew he wasn't feeling pain.

"Sorry," I said, stepping back. I wasn't sorry for touching him. Wasn't sorry he wanted me physically, just like I wanted him. But there wasn't any time for that. There wasn't any time for us.

His hazel eyes searched my face, burning with a hunger that plunged into deep shadow. He licked his lips and briefly closed his eyes. When he opened them again, they were flat, cold, and empty of emotion.

"Mercenaries don't follow rules," he said, answering my previous question. He released me and drew his gun, turning to tug open the hinged window, the rifle tucked against his shoulder. He set his stance wide to take the buck and sway of the vehicle. The back of his jacket was ripped. Bullets, or maybe just shrapnel from the shots. He'd been shot. While trying to protect me. That hadn't just been pleasure he'd felt at my touch.

"Matilda," Quinten called out. "Get down!"

I crouched. Quinten bent low between the seats, his gun out the side window, returning fire. Which meant the mercenaries weren't just behind us anymore. Foster strode up the length of the bus to the door. He shoved it open, then hung on to an overhead bar with one hand and leaned out. The ammunition belt was draped over his shoulder as he held a machine gun that must weigh a hundred pounds in one hand.

Left Ned swore up a storm over the noise, gripping the wheel tight, while Right Ned kept one eye on the rearview mirrors.

I drew my gun and slid on my knees into the seat behind Quinten, just as Foster let loose a deafening spray of bullets.

Quinten and I ducked as casings littered the floor of the bus, rolling and clattering between the seats.

My quick glance out the window had given me a glimpse of two men and a woman on motorcycles, driving through the scrub and rough of the rise to our left, while we careened down the twists and turns of the ragged concrete and dirt road.

Foster leaned back inside to reload, and I sat up and popped open the window.

"Matilda," Quinten said, "don't!"

I took aim and fired on the rider nearest us, who was

about half a car length to the rear. Hit something— maybe his leg, maybe the tire—sending him veering off to the right. His bike bucked and flipped end over end, taking him along with it in a tangle of metal and bones.

The other riders didn't pause to worry about their buddy. They fired at us.

I ducked back in and down between seats again.

"Nothing laser guided?" I asked Quinten.

"What?"

"Their guns? Do they have trackers? Laser-guidance systems?"

"They have anger and skill and want to get paid. They don't need anything else."

"Shit!" Left Ned yelled. "Hold on."

The vehicle leaned hard, throwing me out from between the seats. I thumped my head into the seat across the aisle, and everything lurched the other way. Then an explosion pounded through the bus, knocking the world sideways hard.

Too much happened at once. The world went upside down. I was thrown like laundry in a washing machine, hit everything, and tasted blood as the vehicle lurched and flipped, rolling with an enormous amount of noise down the hillside.

It took forever.

It took an instant that never ended.

And then the crashing, grinding, tumbling pain stopped.

8

*There's something causing these rifts in time.
If I can find that, track these ripples, maybe I
can find you, Matilda. Before he kills you.*
                                        —W.Y.

The first thought that ran through my head was that I
was alive. The bus had fallen off the side of a cliff,
and yet I was still breathing.

I inhaled, moaned a little at all the parts of me that
hurt. My head especially. I could feel the matted, sticky
warmth of blood in my hair, and yet a corresponding
cold on the rest of my skin, like someone had just dunked
me in freezing water.

The second thought that went through my head was
Quinten.

Was he alive? Neds, Abraham, Foster? I opened my
mouth to say something, but the only thing that came
out was a choked cough.

"I've got you," Abraham's voice filtered down from
the light spearing through shadows above me. I blinked
to try to make sense of . . . well, everything. Didn't do me
any good.

His hand stretched toward me, and I reached up for him. He grunted a little at the impact, but carefully, and gently, considering the circumstances, lifted me up out from where I'd landed behind a set of seats that had come unbolted from the floor.

He pulled me against him, and I could feel his muscles bunching as he wrapped his arms down beneath my butt and carried me across a space that I still couldn't piece together, his breathing a little hard, his body warm against mine.

"I'm going to lift you up to Foster," he said.

"Quinten?"

"Haven't found him yet. But I will."

Then he pushed me upward, extending his arms with a grunt. A new set of hands reached down around me, even wider and larger than Abraham's hands.

"Relax," Foster said. "You are safe." He pulled me up out of the vehicle, and the world spun so hard, I thought I was going to lose my lunch.

I didn't want to go into another timeway. I was in no shape to face crazy, gun-wielding Slater or anyone else who might be waiting for me there.

I tucked my head against Foster's chest and waited for the scent of roses. But the scent never came and the world never shifted. Maybe the dizziness was just a head wound.

What kind of a life was I living that a head wound was the preferable option?

Foster carried me to wherever safety might be, and when he stopped, he lowered me to sit with my back against a tree.

"This is loaded." He handed me a handgun. "The mercs are still out here."

The mercs! That fear brought a shot of clarity through

my veins, and I took the gun with one hand and wiped the blood out of my eyes with the other. *Definitely head wound.*

"Just go get Quinten and Neds," I said. "I'm all right."

Foster pressed his big hand on the side of my face in such a kind gesture, I was surprised by it. Then he turned and walked away.

I took stock of where, exactly, I'd landed. Tree above me; brush around. I could make out the spindly radio tower to my right.

I didn't see the road, and since I was too dizzy to stand, I didn't bother looking for it.

Instead I controlled my breathing, working hard to use my ears and eyes to sense if anyone was coming my way.

Soon I heard footsteps, heavy and steady. Foster. He worked his way up out of the ravine to my left, his arm around Neds.

Neds both looked a little banged up, and I noted his left arm was tucked up against his chest, as if moving it would cause him great pain, but they were both conscious. A massive bruise had already spread across Right Ned's face. "Wait here." Foster handed Neds his other gun, glanced at me, and then walked back down to where the vehicle must have come to rest.

Neds were standing, though both of them were pale as sun-bleached sheets.

"What happened?" I asked, squinting up at him.

"They shot out the tire." Right Ned's voice was strained. "I couldn't keep it on the road, and when we came around the curve, we rolled down the hillside."

"Did you see Quinten?" I asked.

"Woke up to Foster slapping my face, then dragging me up here to you," Right Ned said. "Abraham still alive?"

"Yes."

"Figures," Right Ned said without any heat.

Left Ned was being uncommonly quiet. I glanced over at him. His eyes were a little dazed.

"Are you okay?" I asked. "Both of you?"

"We'll live," Right Ned said.

"If we don't get shot," Left Ned whispered. "Or eaten."

"We're going to be fine." I placed my palm against the tree and pushed myself up carefully, as if I were balancing on a trapeze in a high wind. It was slow and not very graceful, but I managed to stand without vertigo pushing me over.

"Are you okay, Matilda?" Right Ned asked.

"Knock on the head is making me dizzy," I said. "I'm fine. Keep your eyes and ears open for mercs. They must have seen us go over."

"They might think we're dead and leave," Right Ned said.

"Are they that sloppy?" I asked.

"No," he admitted.

We waited. The road was above us. Foster had climbed about three-quarters of the way up the hillside and left us on a ridge that jutted out a bit, with plenty of bushes to offer us some camouflage. The wind through the bushes and trees rattled and hissed, and a distant bird or two called out, but I didn't hear the buzz of the motorcycles. Why weren't they coming toward us to finish the job?

An unsettling answer came to me. "Did any of them have scopes? Sniper rifles?" I asked.

"Don't know," Right Ned said. "I was too busy crashing a bus."

I gave him a wan smile.

The wrenching sound of metal twisting rang out from below us. I hazarded a glance that way, but looking down the hillside made my head swim.

"Are they okay?' I asked.

Right Ned looked down, while Left Ned kept an eye on the horizon.

"Foster is braced on a broken tree outside the bus," Right Ned said. "I don't see Abraham or Quinten. Wait— there's Abraham. He has him. I don't think he's conscious."

The wind shifted, bringing with it the low rattle of engines approaching.

"Shit," Left Ned whispered. He shifted the gun in his hand, but still wasn't using his left arm.

I scanned the rise, which was probably about twenty feet above us. The angle of the overhang might be enough to keep us hidden from the casual glance, but the mercenaries were hunting us.

There was nothing casual about this.

Foster was making a bit of noise getting Quinten up the rise. He finally made it to the little outcropping where we were standing.

Quinten was draped over Foster's shoulder in a fireman's carry. Unconscious. There was a lot of blood on what I could see of him, and a lot of blood covering Foster's hand, which held him secure.

"Is he alive?" I said, horror twisting my stomach.

"Yes," Foster rumbled. "We must treat him."

My duffel had, miraculously, remained draped over my shoulder. I had Evelyn's little sewing box in there and some bindings, but no other medication.

"He said we have to do it fast," I said. "That wounds go bad quick nowadays. You need to let me stitch him up. Put him down, Foster. I need to look at him right now." I was talking too fast, my voice rising with each word.

Panic. Even though a small, reasonable part of my

mind knew panic would not help anything, I was shaking, my heart racing.

Foster kept walking up the ridge, carrying Quinten, right on past us.

"Foster," I said. "Don't. They're coming!"

Abraham powered up the cliffside, resting a moment on the outcropping. Quinten's heavy trunk and bag were in one hand, and more gear was strapped across his back and chest and in his other hand.

He glanced up after Foster, then at both of us. "Stay here. I'll put this down and come back for both of you."

"Quinten's hurt," I said, rather unnecessarily, since Abraham was the one who had pulled him out of the wreckage.

"Mercs are on the way," Right Ned said.

"I know," he answered, starting up the hill. "We'll take care of that too."

I watched the path Foster chose up the hill—a diagonal that sent rock and dirt shifting and rolling down the hillside with each step. I could do that. I could make that climb. There were small bushes I'd be able to use as handholds, and it wasn't far.

"Let's go help Quinten," I said to Neds.

"He'll come back for you, Matilda," Right Ned said. "No need for you to fall down the cliff going after him."

"I'm not going after him. I'm going to help Quinten," I said, securing the gun. Climbing might not be a good idea, but climbing with a loaded weapon in my hand was clearly a stupid idea.

"All right," Left Ned said. "Show us what you can do, Tilly."

I met his challenging gaze, and couldn't help it. I smiled. "I like that name, and I like you using it. Also, be prepared to be impressed."

I took a step, holding my breath against the sway of the world, then took another, following Abraham's route.

It was not easy. My head rushed with heat and pain; my arms and legs shook; and, if I wasn't very, very careful about how I shifted my gaze, how I turned my head, everything rocked and reeled.

I heard Neds starting up after me, and one time when I miscalculated a grab for the branch in front of me, I felt his hand press against my back to steady me.

"You got this," he said.

I would have thanked him, but all my air was currently being used to feed my starving lungs and racing heart.

I couldn't hear the engines over the pounding in my head. But when I took the last step up the hill onto the level shoulder of the street, I wanted to fall down on my knees and not move for a week.

Instead, I took stock of our situation.

Foster and Abraham had set everything they were carrying down the road a ways, off to one side under a fir tree. Foster knelt next to Quinten, and had amazingly produced a blanket of some sort to drape over him.

I started that way.

Abraham turned, saw me. His eyes went wide, and then he shook his head, walking toward me.

"I told you I'd come back for you," he said once he was near enough. His eyes took in my face, flicking up to my head, where I knew blood matted my hair. The blood down the side of my face was dry, so I assumed the bleeding had slowed or stopped.

"You're injured," he said.

"I know. I can feel it."

"You . . . feel?"

Oh, right. He didn't know that about me. "I'm just full of surprises," I said.

The rumble of engines finally registered. They were coming our way. Close now.

I pulled my gun and turned my back toward Abraham, expecting the mercenaries to round the bend in the road and be on top of us any second.

Abraham reached out from behind me. His hand slid down my arm, and he wrapped his fingers gently around my wrist, lowering the gun slightly. He had stepped so close, I unconsciously leaned back into him to steady my stance.

"Take care of your brother," he said, his voice low and intimate, his mouth tipped down by my cheek so that he might kiss me if I turned even just a fraction of an inch. "I'll take care of our company."

I nodded, felt the rough of his stubble interrupted by the silky smoothness of his stitches against my cheek, the scent of him bringing back memories of things I wanted so badly, I ached.

"Go," he said gently.

I lowered the gun and he stepped back an inch. I turned and made my way to Quinten as quickly as my unsteady head would allow.

Foster was standing off the side of the road over Quinten, but had taken the time to unpack a couple of items: an ax and a wicked-looking machete.

He shifted his grip on both, gave me a short nod, and strode over to where Abraham stood in the middle of the road about thirty yards or so from me. Neds had just made the rise in the hill and he hesitated, then chose to walk my way, pulling the gun from where he'd had it tucked in his belt.

The engines were growing louder. I knelt next to Quinten and assessed the damage. Broken nose, scrapes on his face, and bruising. His cheek was split. I ran my fingers over his head. Deep cut there. That wasn't good.

Then I checked his neck, which seemed okay, and pulled off the blanket to get his jacket and shirt open enough that I could look for breaks and cuts on his torso. Torso looked relatively fine—bruised, though. Most of the blood I'd seen on Foster probably came from the gash on Quinten's thigh.

"Okay," I said, watching his breathing, which was even and clear. "This isn't too bad. We can take care of you, Quinten," I said. "You're going to be fine."

I pulled the duffel over my head and held still while a wave of nausea rolled over me, then unzipped the duffel and pulled out the sewing kit. "Do we have any antibacterial?" I asked Neds. "Anything to coat those scrapes to keep them from getting infected?"

Neds crouched down, opened Quinten's bag, and handed me a metal can with a screw-on lid. "Use it sparingly," he said. "It's strong."

"Got it." I used one of the cotton wraps as a rag, retrieved a canteen of water, and cleaned Quinten's head wound as best I could. I'd always been competent at stitching up the beasts on the property, and Grandma and Neds and myself back in the day. But right now, even with my hands shaking, they were more than competent. They were brilliant, practiced, knowledgeable.

It was like I'd somehow become even better at tending wounds overnight.

Which I supposed was partially true. Evelyn had had a fine hand with stitching, and I was certain she had used her skills to look after the injured. She must have been downright amazing at it, and the muscle memory remained with me.

Thank you, Evelyn, I thought as I unscrewed the lid on the container and sniffed at the pearly blue contents. It smelled of licorice and lemons—a lot like the scale jelly I remembered.

I used the clean cloth to scoop up a bit of it and spread that over Quinten's wounds. I also dragged the thread through it before sewing up his cuts with quick, even stitches, leaving room for some swelling.

A gunshot cracked the relative silence. I jerked and looked over my shoulder.

Abraham had just shot a man on a motorcycle right through the head and was stepping to the side as the vehicle wobbled, fell, and skidded down the road.

He took aim at the next rider—a woman—and fired; missed. Foster rushed forward, brandishing the machete. He swung for her head.

I turned away, my stomach and nerves not up to watching the grisly deaths. The other mercenaries must have realized we weren't yet over-the-side-of-the-cliff dead. They pulled guns and started shooting.

Abraham and Foster stood their ground and returned fire.

"Shit," Left Ned breathed. "If those two ever decide to kill us . . ."

"Not going to happen," I said.

"But if they do . . ." The sound of another crash, and then an engine shifting gears to turn and retreat filled the air as I finished binding first Quinten's head, then his leg.

I glanced over my shoulder again. Abraham and Foster were running—and those two big men were *fast*—after the remaining two mercenaries, one who was on foot, and one who still had his motorcycle beneath him. The road was strewn with blood, gore, and motorcycle wreckage.

Foster tackled the man on foot and then commenced to pound the guy's head into the concrete until he no longer moved.

The remaining merc fired at Abraham over his shoulder. He didn't miss. But Abraham was still running toward him. He lifted his gun, took aim, and shot the tires of the motorcycle out from under the man.

Man and machine went flying, twisting and tumbling, and landed in a mess of metal and flesh. Abraham slowed his pace, and calmly walked up to what was left of the man and shot him in the head. He stared at him a moment, then walked off to the motorcycle to see if it could be salvaged.

Galvanized are mercenaries. Dangerous. Quinten's comments rang through my mind. *No loyalties to anything.*

No kidding. There was no hint of mercy in that man, nor in Foster, even though they might have just killed people they knew.

My brain was trying to grasp the cold-blooded actions I'd witnessed and match it up to the gentle and kind people I'd known them as before. Although they had been gentle and kind to me, even in my time they had once been killing machines—super soldiers who had been deployed by governments seeking control.

Abraham and Foster were no strangers to destruction, chaos, killing. Not in that time, and, certainly, not in this.

Abraham had asked me if I'd ever killed a man before. He had told me I might not want to walk that path.

Right now, in this crappy moment beside this crappy

road, dealing with my wounded, unconscious brother, I didn't think I wanted to see anyone die ever again.

"Okay," I said, finishing putting some of the goo on every tiny scrape I could find on Quinten's body. "You're next, Neds. Where are you hurt?"

"That," Left Ned said, pointing at Right Ned's face. "And the shoulder."

"Anything else?" I asked as I did my balancing trick to stand on the ground that seemed to be swaying side to side.

"You're pale as a bone, Matilda," Right Ned said. "I think we need to get a look at your head."

"I'm fine, and stop stalling," I said. "But it would help if you were sitting. You're a little taller than me."

He glanced over at the road, and I followed his gaze. Abraham and Foster were dragging the bodies to the side of the road and sorting through the vehicles.

"We can't stay here, can we?" I asked.

"Dead bodies will draw the ferals within a hundred miles." Right Ned sat down with a groan. "And we have only a few hours until it gets dark."

Crap. I pressed at the bruise to see if Right Ned's cheek was broken. He hissed in pain and his eyes got watery.

"Jesus, Matilda."

"Sorry," I said. "I don't think it's broken." I checked the pupils of his eyes, then Left Ned's. "No concussions. Let's look at that shoulder."

"It's dislocated," Left Ned said.

I ran my fingers gently along the joint, and Right Ned cussed.

"You're right," I said. "It's dislocated. I'm going to set it into place. Ready?"

They both nodded, inhaled, and held their breath.

"One . . . two . . ." I pushed his shoulder with a sharp, abrupt punch.

"Whoreson," Left Ned seethed.

"Sorry," I said. "Sorry. Let's get that in a sling."

"No time," Left Ned said.

"Wrong. We'll make the time." I dug around in the duffel, then looked through Quinten's stuff and was surprised and happy to find a sling folded in a small canvas bag. I pulled it out, looked over the buckles, and helped Neds into it, adjusting the straps for his wider shoulders and chest.

"How's that?" I asked.

"Hurts like hell," Left Ned said.

"Better," Right Ned corrected. "It's better."

"Can you take pain pills?"

"Let's save them for later," Right Ned said. "We need to get to shelter before nightfall."

"How are we going to do that? Our bus went over the cliff, and Quinten is unconscious."

"I think the clanks have a solution," Left Ned said.

I turned to get a look at Abraham and Foster, overshot how fast my head could handle my moving, and ungracefully fell forward, away from Neds.

Crap.

"Matilda?" Right Ned said, startled.

"I'm fine." I pushed back up while the world did a hard spin and made me want to puke. "Just a second."

"You're injured and stupid," Left Ned said. "Hold still."

He helped me roll onto my back, my head near Quinten's knees, the tree we'd been deposited by spinning lazily around the edges of my vision.

I closed my eyes. "Spinning. But no roses. Never thought I'd hate the smell of roses."

"You're babbling," Right Ned said. "Just rest. Let me see how bad that hole in your head is." He paused. "Well, I'm not gonna lie. This is going to sting."

He was wrong. It didn't sting. The cloth he pressed against my scalp burned like a thousand angry bees had nested in my head.

"Ow. Sonofa— That really hurts," I said.

"Baby," Left Ned said. "You've had worse."

"I know I have." I opened my eyes, because I always dealt with pain better with my eyes wide open.

Right Ned frowned a little. "You have?"

"Bullets hurt more than this. Getting chewed up in an explosion while time smashes you apart hurts a lot more than this."

Left Ned sucked air through his teeth. "You sure did come up odd, didn't you, Tilly?"

"More than you know. How's Quinten?" Talking was helping me keep my mind off their fingers poking and prodding at my head. How could a man with only one hand suddenly have a hundred poking fingers?

"Still out. We'll get smelling salts after we get this cleaned." Right Ned frowned, and then his pretty blue eyes flicked downward to hold my gaze.

"You have a cut and it's swelling. I don't think stitching it is going to do you any good. So I'm going to pack it with the medicine, then wrap your head. I might need to cut some hair."

"Shave it—I don't care."

Right Ned shook his head. "No, I just need to make sure I can get enough medicine on the wound. I am sorry."

"It's okay. It will grow back. And I've always thought going really short would be fun."

He pulled out Evelyn's small, sharp sewing scissors;

cut away some of my hair, trying not to pull too hard on it, which was sweet but mostly unnecessary; and then spread a thick layer of the tin-can balm on it.

To my great relief, the medicine numbed and soothed. I sighed.

Then he pulled out a pad of cotton and the binding. "I'll need your fingers. Think you can manage?" Left Ned asked.

"I just set your shoulder," I said. "I can manage a square knot."

He got to work placing the cotton, which I helped hold in place, since he was one-handed right now. Even one-handed, it didn't take him long to wrap my head to his satisfaction.

I felt like a mummy, but he'd stretched the bandage around my head a couple times, careful to make it tight enough to hold the medicine and pad in place and to not slip into my eyes.

"Good?" I asked.

"Enough," Right Ned said. "I'll see if I can wake Quinten. Rest a minute."

He moved away from my line of vision, and even though I knew we had to get moving before the ferals showed up, and we needed to be either somewhere safe or at least in a defensible position before nightfall, I was more than happy to lie there for a moment and pull myself together.

We'd traveled only half a day outside our property and had already been shot at, driven off a cliff, and almost killed.

Slater had shot me.

I suddenly understood how comforting a nice, walled fortress might actually be.

"Matilda?" Abraham said.

I rocked my head so I could see him, standing to one side of me. Wisely, he crouched.

"Thanks for, um . . . dragging us all out of the crash," I said. "And killing the mercs."

"We need to get to cover before nightfall," he said.

"You're not one to stand on gratitude, are you?" I tucked my elbows under me and rolled a bit to one side so I could prop myself up.

Ouch. My pulse hammered against the inside of my skull, and that bandage felt much too tight.

I thought I had been doing a fairly good job, but when Abraham reached over and helped me sit, his hand resting beneath both of my elbows in case I tipped over, I was grateful for it.

"You have a concussion," he said.

"I know. I'll be fine. But my brother's unconscious. How are we going to get him" — I pointed, and was pretty proud that I didn't topple over — "on that?" I shifted my finger to indicate the motorcycle.

"One of the vehicles is a four-wheeler. We should be able to transport him that way. Can you stand?"

"You have no idea how good I am on my feet," I held my hand out for him, getting ready to shove up onto my feet.

He smiled. "Love to see it," he said. "But maybe at a later time."

Oh. The look he was giving me was sharp with curiosity and something else: he found me fascinating. And from the way he took my hand and smoothly straightened up to standing, his arm reaching around to wrap me in an embrace as he stepped into me, so that our bodies were pressed together, thighs, hips, stomach, and chest, I knew clearly that he was intently interested in more than a dance with me.

I should not fall in love with a killer. Should I?

With my head tipped back so I could look at him, the world was a little fluttery and dizzy around the edges, but, blessedly, without any scent of roses.

Or maybe that wasn't the world. Maybe that was just me and my wants and needs. Because even though my brain knew Abraham was not the man I had loved, my heart refused to listen. I loved him. Still. I thought I always would.

His smile was soft; his gaze unrelenting. Asking me, without words, if I understood what he was offering me. What he wanted from me. What he was willing to give.

I wanted to tell him yes. To give in to what my heart knew was true. But there was a world to save. A plague to end. My brother was wounded, and even though I had done the best I could with the supplies we had on hand, his best chance for survival would be to get him to a real doctor: Gloria.

Who would die if we didn't get to her in time.

That was a lot to do and not a lot of time left for love.

I took in a breath, and it was too shaky.

He frowned slightly and lifted one hand, his thumb wiping away a tear that I hadn't realized was there at the edge of my cheek.

"We have time," he said softly, strangely guessing my fear.

Or did he? Was he telling me he and I had time, or that we all had time to try to save Gloria and kill Slater? Either way, I didn't think we did have time. Not as long as Slater was alive. Not as long as there was a bomb ready to take out innocent people. Not as long as galvanized were considered criminals in this world.

"Then we should spend that time on something important. Like finding a safe place for the night," I said.

He relaxed his grip on me, held my arms to make sure I was steady, his expression closed, but his brow furrowed, as if confused at my response.

I was confused at my response too. Had I just told him my feelings for him—and his for me—weren't important? Weren't worth taking time for? I didn't mean that. The head injury was making it hard to think. Not that it mattered. All that mattered was that we get to safe ground before nightfall, before ferals and more mercenaries showed up.

I walked over to Neds. Quinten was moaning softly, semiconscious. He was trying to push away the smelling salts Neds held under his nose.

"It's going to be okay," I said to him. "We have to leave now. We'll help you up. You're going to be fine."

Between the four of us—Abraham and Foster being the least injured, or the least hampered by their injuries—we got Quinten on the four-wheeler, with Foster carefully holding on to him.

I wasn't sure I could handle driving a motorcycle, what with my jumpy vision and dizziness, but Neds had only one good arm, and I wasn't sure he could handle a bike on his own.

In the end we decided that Foster and Quinten would take the lead, Neds would follow on his own bike, and Abraham would drive another bike that I'd be passenger on.

It wasn't the best solution, but it was the best we had. And so we pulled the vehicles together, loaded them and ourselves with as much of our gear as we could carry, then started off at a careful pace, down the hill and across the valley to House Earth Compound Five.

9

Slater knows you're out to kill him. He's tearing the world apart looking for the key for how to kill you. If you read this, Matilda, don't get close to him; don't fight him. You can't win.
—W.Y.

Even though I had my head tucked against Abraham's wide back, my arms locked around him and legs straddling his sides, riding a motorcycle when one is concussed is all kinds of painful.

I found the best thing I could do was keep my eyes closed and concentrate on the shifting of his muscles beneath the layers of clothing he wore, trying to make myself useful—or at least not a hindrance in the turns and switchbacks of the road.

Unfortunately, none of the vehicles had survived the crash well, and we had to take it even slower than the vehicles might manage, because Quinten was semiconscious and Foster had to compensate for his nearly dead weight.

What would have taken us an hour in the bus took more than two. It was late afternoon, and when I did risk a quick look out to the goal horizon, it felt like we hadn't even crossed half the distance.

When Neds' motorcycle started sending out an alarming amount of smoke, we decided to pull off the road under some trees to let the engine cool down.

I groaned as I tried to get feeling into my butt and legs, and walked stiffly over to where Foster was still straddling the four-wheeler, Quinten facing him in his arms.

"How's he doing?" I asked.

"He needs rest," Foster said. "Shelter."

"I know." I glanced down the road, then back at Neds, who were strolling off a distance to pee.

Abraham had pulled out his canteen and taken a drink, and handed it to me.

I swallowed until I cleared the dirt in my throat, then took the canteen over to Foster.

"We're not going to make it to House Earth before nightfall," I said to Abraham.

"Mmm," he replied.

"Do you know of a place we can hole up until morning?"

Foster took a swig of water, then, without having to say anything, we both worked on waking Quinten enough to take a drink.

Quinten's eyes were swollen almost shut, but he opened them a slit. We tipped the canteen to his mouth, and he managed to down three or four gulps.

"Where?" he croaked.

"Still on our way to House Earth. Almost there," I lied. "We fell off the road. Last time I let Neds drive."

He grunted, which I think was supposed to pass as a laugh.

"The ferals . . ." he said.

"I know. You don't have to worry about them either. We've got that all taken care of."

That either satisfied him or it was all the strength he had. He closed his eyes and slumped forward into Foster again.

Foster wrapped his left arm around him, holding him steady as easily as if he were a child.

"Do you want me to trade with you, Foster?" I asked.

He shook his head. "We should go soon. Abraham. Shelter."

It wasn't quite a command. I glanced over at Abraham. He stood near his bike, eyes set on a point to the northwest. "There's a cabin. It's not large, but it should have fire lines, and it might have other provisions."

"How far away?" I asked.

"Two hours. In the right direction. We'll be able to make the compound in the early morning tomorrow."

"Should we just push through the early hours of the night instead?" I asked.

"No," Abraham and both Neds said.

"We'll go to the cabin," Abraham continued. "Foster, I'll take lead; you follow. Mr. Harris, you take the rear."

Neds rolled his good shoulder and shook out his hand. "Let's do it," Right Ned said.

I glanced at the motorcycle. My legs were already feeling the past couple hours. But two more wouldn't be so bad. Besides, we still had good weather, and so far no other signs of mercenaries.

"Is there a reason no one else has come out to kill us?" I asked Abraham as he mounted the bike and steadied it for me to get on.

"It's getting late," he said. "Whoever is out here is looking for their own place to hole up."

"Do they know about the cabin?"

"Probably."

"And we're just going to ride up to a cabin full of mercenaries and knock on the door?" I wrapped my arms around his waist.

"I wasn't going to knock." He started the engine, checked to make sure Neds and Foster were set, and started down the road again.

Evening was draining down quickly, shadows growing under the brush thick beside the road. Old, abandoned fences threw stripes of darkness across our path.

It was cold, and getting colder fast. I glanced up, trying to get a bead on the sunset. I couldn't see the sun, and even the cool gold light that had poured through the trees fifteen minutes ago was gone.

There would be no more light until morning.

Abraham had turned off a side road about an hour ago. It was little more than a rutted path in the dirt that we had to take slowly, because of the winter washouts that had cut deep wallows in the road. Brush and brambles reached out from either side of the path, and at one point were so dense, we had to stop for Abraham to hack away at them with a machete.

Every time we stopped, I could feel the shifting in the shadows. I'd been around ferals at the edges of our property my whole life. Crocboar and the like. I knew what they sounded like; I knew how they hunted.

And I knew they were hunting us.

The only good thing about us having to go so slowly was the possibility that other people—people who wanted us dead—hadn't been out this way recently. The disadvantage?

Well, those were lurking between the trees, flashes of teeth and fur I caught out of the corner of my eye.

If anyone was following us, we had left obvious tracks in the dusty soil, and hacking back the brush would be a clear indication that we'd turned this way.

Every inch of my skin was tight with goose bumps, my senses sharp, heartbeat pounding. There was danger here. We were in danger.

"How much farther?" I asked as Abraham rolled to a stop so he could hack back another bramble of blackberries.

"Half a mile?" he said between swings.

I glanced at the forest around us. "Give me your knife." I swung off the bike, pulling the one blade I had with me. Why hadn't I packed my usual weapons?

Maybe because I didn't have any usual weapons, seeing as how I'd been mostly dead in this world and Evelyn had been living this life instead of me.

Abraham pulled his knife—a long, wicked-looking thing—and flipped it, offering me the hilt.

"Why?" he asked.

"Ferals. Close."

He swore in a language I didn't recognize—maybe Russian—and redoubled his efforts to clear a hole we could drive through out of the thicket.

I stepped away, walking several yards back the way we'd come so I had some maneuvering room to fight. Foster was sitting on the quad, Quinten strapped on in front of him and leaning into him. Since Quinten was unconscious, Foster's hands were full. He couldn't help fight if the ferals attacked.

Neds were half asleep, Right Ned's head resting against Left Ned's. They had only one working arm, and needed that for the bike.

Only Abraham and I were well enough and unencumbered enough to deal with the beasts.

And if Abraham didn't clear that trail, we were in for a hell of a time. I didn't think we had enough knives or bullets between us to put the ferals down if they were as blood hungry as I'd been told they were.

"Matilda," Left Ned said softly.

He didn't have to. I saw it.

The feral slunk out from behind the tree, three more behind it. They weren't as ugly as the crocboar we had on our property, but they looked intent on the same thing: killing.

Mottled fur covered their heavy heads and blocky torsos, and spindly hips were tucked down low over short, wolflike back legs. Their front legs weren't legs, but more like monkey arms. They moved forward on all fours, lips pulled back from hooked yellow teeth, pointed ears flattened against their wide heads.

There was only one way to make sure a crocboar went down and stayed down: stab it through the eye and into the brain.

Since these ferals were mutated too, I figured that would work with these beasties.

I shifted my grip on the knife in my right hand. And bent my knees.

The beasts rushed. A storm of teeth, muscle, and claw.

I dodged the first two, and sank my knife into the third one's eye. It howled and squealed. I worked to pull the knife free, but it was thrashing too hard for me to get leverage. It kicked and bucked at the knife, then swung its front arms wildly, grabbing for me.

I grabbed it back, holding its arms and pivoting. I threw my weight to force the beast in front of me.

The other two slammed into me. I swore and braced my back leg and hips. They clawed and bit at their fallen pack mate, who was my temporary shield. I wrenched the knife free and stuck it in one eye, two. The ferals fell off, writhing and shrieking.

I threw the dead feral on top of the other two. Ducked as another bolted out of the shadows at me.

It practically bent in half to turn back on me. I slashed, missing the eye, my knife wedging into its shoulder.

Shit.

It backed off before I could withdraw the knife, snarling off into the shadows, tugging at the knife.

Terrific. I'd just armed my possibly opposable-thumbed enemy.

Three more ferals galloped out of the shadows. Two came straight at me while one waited. That one appeared to have spotted the pile of dead I had left in the middle of the road and seemed to be reconsidering the direct attack.

They were feral, and they were smart. It was probably how they'd survived out here this long: quick adaptation.

That could be a problem.

I pulled the revolver; didn't know how many bullets I had left, and didn't have time to look.

Aimed for the eyes. One feral jerked, went down. Aimed for the next. Two shots. Hit, but not clean.

I swore again, rushed to meet its attack, stuck the knife in its eye, and danced back out of arm's length. It fell, rolled, and howled, then was still.

I scanned the shadows. Didn't see any more ferals.

"Matilda!" Abraham said. I glanced his way, expecting a swarm of ferals to have slipped around behind me.

He was jogging to the bike. The road was clear.

"Wait!" I yelled.

"Now," he said. "There will be more. Many more."

I hurried over to where the feral had retreated with the knife and searched the forest floor for the blade.

"Matilda!" Abraham said again.

I heard the engines. "A minute!"

Weapons weren't exactly plentiful. We'd lost most of what we had in the tumble over the cliff. I wasn't going to leave a perfectly good knife behind.

Something shifted in the shadows. Brittle timber snapped. They were out there. They were coming.

Crap.

I pushed aside needles and leaves.

Found it! I picked up the knife and ran back to the road, stumbling once but catching myself before I fell.

Abraham was already driving my way, his gun drawn. He fired at whatever was in range behind me. Pulled the bike to a stop and fired again as I got on.

"Told you to come," he said.

"I was looking for your knife," I said as he handed me the gun.

"Don't care about the damn knife. I care about you." He turned the bike, barreling down the road at speed.

"You're welcome," I yelled over the growl of the engine. I twisted to get a look at how close the ferals were.

Close. Too close. And it wasn't just three or four. It was a dozen. More than a dozen.

I didn't have enough bullets to take them all down, so I held fire unless one of them got within a couple yards of the bike.

And they did. They might look like top-heavy wild-dog things, but they could put on bursts of speed.

I fired, and the closest feral tumbled. The rest leaped right over its body, galloping after us. I took down another. Missed as Abraham swerved, fired again. Hit.

I turned to look ahead. No ferals outpacing us yet, but it couldn't be long. The cabin was in sight. Larger than I expected, maybe a thousand square feet or so inside it.

The roof was peaked and relatively moss-free. A good hundred yards around it was cleared of trees and brush.

Foster and Neds had already made it to the cabin and had dismounted their bikes. Foster kicked in the door, carrying a still-unconscious Quinten in his arms. Neds lifted his rifle one-handed, tucked it against his good shoulder, and fired.

Abraham pulled up under the cover of Neds' fire, stopped the bike, and killed the engine.

"Go!" I yelled at Neds.

I hopped off the back. Assessed the situation.

A wave of fur, fangs, and claws was closing in on us. Twice as many as I'd seen before.

We didn't need bullets. We needed flamethrowers. This was no time to take a stand.

I ran for the cabin door. Neds were already ahead of me.

Abraham was on my heels. "Go, go, go!" he shouted.

We rushed into the cabin, and Abraham slammed the door shut.

The only problem? Foster had broken the latch, and our pursuers had opposable thumbs.

"The door won't hold," I said, leaning against it.

"I know." Abraham was feeling along the wall to the right.

"Do we have more guns? We need more guns," I said.

"Just. Wait."

"For what miracle?" I asked.

"This." He flipped a switch, and something bright flashed outside. The ferals howled.

"What's that?"

"Fire line. We rode over it on the way here." He shut the fuse box and strode to the window on the other side of me, then pulled back the curtains.

It wasn't dark out there at all.

Abraham slid the window open and knelt in front of it. He drew his rifle off his back and carefully fired a half-dozen shots. He waited a moment, glancing up away from the sight so he could get a wider view.

"I'll be right back," he said. "Don't lock the door behind me."

I moved away to let him through.

"Well, since the door no longer locks . . ." I said. He stepped out, and I caught the door so I could look outside.

The cleared area around the cabin was encircled by a thin, five-foot wall of flame. That trough we'd driven over must hold a pipe with some kind of flammable liquid pouring through it.

I caught a glimpse of movement on the other side of the fire, but it was sketchy and at a distance. Ferals did not like fire.

Good to know.

Abraham headed off to the right, making sure the inside perimeter of the fire line was feral-free.

I waited with the door open, the knife in my hand. Nothing jumped through the wall of fire; nothing approached the door. Within a short time, Abraham returned.

"So?"

"All clear," he said.

"I'd still be happier with a lock."

"I'll take care of it."

He walked into the cabin, and I shut the door behind him.

"You know how to fix a door?"

"I've been known to be handy." He walked off to the right, and I turned around to look at the interior of the place for the first time.

The cabin was clean and decorated with polished

wood, bright whites, and a smattering of blues and yellow. A proper mudroom off to the right held hooks with clean towels, scrub brushes, a deep sink, and a bench with room beneath for boots. Past that, the place opened into one big living space that centered around a living-room area with couches and chairs; low bookshelves separated the space from the wide kitchen that took up the whole of the back of the cabin.

Half walls on either side allowed some view of the beds that were situated there, and a door to my right was open enough for me to see that behind it were the shower and bathroom.

Since the entire interior of the place was in view at once, it took only seconds to confirm that it was uninhabited. Why would a place as nice and stocked as this be empty?

Foster stood by the kitchen table, taking off his weapons and stacking them one by one onto the kitchen table. Neds sat on the couch, looking exhausted. I took a few steps so I could see inside the sleeping area, and spotted Quinten's feet at the end of a bed.

Abraham came back with a metal toolbox in one hand.

"And that fire will keep the ferals out?" I asked.

"Yes."

"How long will it last?"

"The night," Abraham said.

"Of course, it won't keep out mercs or stitched, or whoever else want us dead," Left Ned groused. "Or their bullets or bombs."

"Life is full of risk, Mr. Harris." Abraham ran his hand along the doorjamb and studied the lock, then set down the toolbox and crouched to open it.

"Does someone live here?" I asked.

"Sometimes," Abraham said.

"Anyone living here now?"

"Just us."

"So this is here mostly for people who get stuck out at night?"

"Pretty much," he said.

I walked into the cabin and tried not to groan with each step. Now that my adrenaline had washed away, I was feeling every nick, tear, and bruise. But I was no longer as dizzy, and my head was feeling a little better. A good night's sleep sounded like pure heaven.

"This is nice," I said.

"Nice enough," Left Ned agreed. "For the night."

"What about the bikes? If we leave them out front, someone could take them."

"They'd have to get through the fire first," Abraham said as he removed the screws in the dead bolt.

"So I'm guessing we don't need to cover the tire tracks either?"

"No one stupid enough to follow us out here will live long enough to find them," Left Ned said. "Lot of pissed-off ferals out there. Which," he said, fixing me with a look, "you seemed more than capable of taking down."

"Not my first day in the sticks," I said.

"Did you come out of that bloody?" Left Ned asked.

Right Ned, who had been silent this whole time, closed his eyes, and I knew he was instantly asleep.

"Nothing bad," I said.

"Then I'm gonna take the first sleep shift," Left Ned said. "Wake me if we're dying."

For the first time since we left our property, I felt like maybe I could relax.

Abraham finished with the lock and tested it, then put all the tools away.

Foster had finally emptied enough weapons on the table that he could take off his jacket. He did so, draping it over the back of one of the kitchen chairs, and the weight of it was visible. The jacket was made of leather, but there must still be a lot of things he'd left in his pockets.

"Are you injured, Foster?" I asked.

He shrugged one shoulder and walked over to the woodstove, which was already set for a fire. "Tend your brother."

I couldn't see any blood on Foster, but the dark flannel of his shirt might be masking it.

Neds had claimed the couch and were lying on it, their bad shoulder tucked against the back of it, their good hand free, and gripping the gun they'd rested on their stomach.

Right Ned was already out, while Left Ned had that unfocused look that meant he was mostly awake and on watch while his brother slept.

Foster was right: Quinten did need my attention. I walked into the sleeping area.

I pulled off my duffel and slipped out of my jacket, but left my long-sleeved shirt on. It wasn't too cold in the cabin, and the woodstove would do a lot of good to heat it up soon, but I just didn't feel comfortable taking off all my gear yet.

It was all too clear to me that we were in a very small cabin in a very large woods. And if there were as many ferals out there as I'd been told there were, I didn't want to be caught without my boots on and my gun in my hand.

The bedroom section was a cozy arrangement of two cots and a double bed. Foster had set Quinten down on the double. His color was a little rosier, his breathing even, but I would feel better if he was awake.

I set down the duffel on the floor and unzipped it. My

hands were dirty with blood and soil and other things I didn't want to think about. So I went into the bathroom and washed my hands with soap and cold water until they were pink and stinging but clean. Just for good measure, I rolled up my sleeves and scrubbed up to my elbows.

Then I took care of Quinten. I removed all of his sweat- and bloodstained bandages. His head wound didn't look any better, but it didn't look any worse. If what he'd said about injuries going quickly toxic was true, I counted that as a win.

I reapplied the medicine from the tin can, rewrapped his head, and checked him for fever. He didn't feel hot to the touch. And when I shook him a little and called his name, he answered with a sleepy "Hmm."

That was a good sign.

"Where?" he breathed, opening his eyes long enough to focus on my face.

"We're safe," I told him. "You hit your head."

"Tired."

"You can go back to sleep, but I'll wake you in a bit. Rest. You need it." I squeezed his hand gently, checked his leg, and reapplied medicine and wrap. Then I settled the blanket over him as he fell back to sleep.

"Is he well?" Abraham asked from behind me.

I turned. The words all tumbled to a stop behind my teeth.

He had taken off his shirt and stood in the doorway of the bedroom, wearing nothing but his breeches and boots.

I couldn't help but be disappointed to see that he had no tattoos on his body, no clock with keys for hands. This, then, was not the Abraham of the timeway who had called me love.

Still, this Abraham was something to look at. Muscles

that were hard before were ripped and chiseled beneath a patchwork of tanned skin. He'd always had scars and stitches, and his chest, stomach, and hip bones were criss-crossed with a new array of them, the heavy black thread used to sew him together pulled so tight through his flesh, it left ridges.

He was a man stitched of bits of other bodies. Maybe it should be frightening or ugly.

But it was neither. He was strength, survival. He was raw and alive.

And I wanted him.

"Matilda?" he asked, his voice low. "Is your brother well?"

He took a step, and the slash across his stomach shifted, blood oozing from it.

That broke the spell.

"He's not bleeding," I said, pointing at his wound and noting the cluster of bullet holes he'd recently acquired. "Let me stitch you up."

"I'm fine. There's tea, if you want it."

"You're bleeding," I said. "That's not fine."

He looked down at his stomach, then pressed fingers alongside it, which just made his wound seep more.

"Stop that," I said. I pointed at the cot. "Lie down. It will be easier for me."

"This isn't worth your concern."

"I say it is. Lie down." When he still didn't move: "Now, hotshot."

"I am not accustomed to taking orders," he said in a low rumble.

"Well, get used to it, stud. Move."

His mouth twitched up at that, and a fire caught in his eyes. He finally walked over to the nearest cot and eased down onto it with a sigh.

I walked out of the room and pulled a bucket of water from the mudroom, found some clean cloths, and then took that back to the bedroom.

Abraham was staring at the ceiling.

"I need to clean that out and see if there are any bullets left in you. Unless you want to shower first?"

"It's fine."

I looked around for a chair and decided the crate at the end of one of the cots would work. I tipped it over, gathered my supplies, and sat next to Abraham.

"This is going to be cold."

"No," he said, still staring at the ceiling. "It won't be."

I dredged the washcloth in the water, wrung it out, and gently drew it along the outer edge of his wound.

He didn't flinch, although his skin goose bumped.

"Cold?" I asked.

"Not that I feel."

I bit my bottom lip, pulling the wound open a little with the cloth. "I need to clean inside of this slash. And I'll need to stitch it."

"Matilda."

I glanced down into his eyes.

"I don't feel it. Do what needs to be done."

"When I touch you, you'll feel it. Maybe there are rubber gloves I could put on."

"No." He reached out and gently wrapped his fingers around my wrist. His eyes dilated, then narrowed. I knew what skin-on-skin contact with me did to him. All the pain from those bruises, scrapes, and other assorted wounds was now clamoring through his nervous system.

"I want to feel this. Even if it is only pain."

"That is messed up. You know that, right?"

He smiled. "Then take my mind off the pain," he said. "Tell me about you."

"Long, boring saga." I slipped my hand free of his and set the cloth at the bottom of his wound. I held open the skin with one hand and squeezed water though the cut with the other.

Abraham inhaled sharply, held his breath a moment, then exhaled.

"I doubt it's boring," he said as I continued to sluice water through the wound.

"Well, you heard the time-travel part, and that's probably the most interesting thing about me." I finished with the water, and picked up the tin with the balm.

"That's an event," he said. "Interesting, but it's not you. Tell me about you."

"Seems like this isn't the kind of world where a woman should be offering up intimate details about herself to a mercenary."

"So you're naturally suspicious," he said. "Go on."

"I guess so, yes. Ever since I can remember, I was told to stay hidden. Told the world wasn't a safe place for a thing like me."

"You're not a thing."

"I know. But I'm not exactly human either."

"Most humans aren't all that human," he said. "What do you do in your free time? Do you have any hobbies?"

I stopped spreading the balm and grinned down at him. "Really? That's the sort of thing you want me to bore you with?"

"It is exactly the kind of thing I want to hear."

"All right. But you will be snoring before I get through two sentences." I pushed the balm down a little deeper into the bottom edge of his cut, and he grunted.

"I doubt that."

"Why? You think the pain will keep you awake?"

"No," he said. "You will."

I shook my head. "Hobbies?" I plucked up a curved needle and a length of thread from Evelyn's kit. I pulled the thread through the balm a few times, thinking. "I like to read. We never had a lot of books on the farm, but back . . . well, back when I came from, there was a book exchange through all the House Brown people, so I got my hands on a fair share of words. I'm also a crack computer hacker and can data-mine like a demon. That's fun."

I threaded the needle and pressed my fingers gently alongside both edges of the wound.

"You know computers?"

"I knew them. They were pretty commonplace in my time. Everyone had one."

"That is a skill that could come in very handy, Matilda."

"If the programming is the same or similar to what I know," I said, "maybe. Otherwise, it's just another thing about me that doesn't fit in with this world."

He didn't say anything, and I was glad. I didn't want to have to defend how much I felt like I was outside, looking in at my own life. I didn't want to explain things to him I wasn't even ready to face yet.

"Food," I continued. "I make a mad berry-pear jam that will win any contest in the country. Oh, and I am very good with knives."

"Cooking knives?"

"Killing knives."

His eyebrows notched upward. "So that wasn't beginner's luck out there with the ferals."

"Not at all. They roamed the property edges at home, and every week or so, I'd have to take a few down and feed them to the lizard. Didn't like to waste bullets or mess up the meat with tranquilizers. So it was sort of a hands-on proposition."

"Which is why you thought it was such a good idea to take those on bare-handed?"

"I wasn't bare-handed, and it was a good idea. They're dead. We're not. So . . ." I tugged on the thread a little and made eye contact. "Win."

"Are there any other unexpectedly dangerous things a man should know about you?"

"I'm smart." I stitched up the wound as gently and quickly as I could. "Some people have underestimated me, and that didn't work out well for them. I'm deadly determined. When there's a thing I know must be done, I see it through, no matter what. And I believe in the basic decency of people."

"Some would say that's naive. The only thing people care about in this world is their own skin. Their own survival."

"Is that what you think?" I asked. "That even humans aren't human?"

"It seems to prove out time and time again."

"So, why are you coming with us to House Earth? You could walk away right now. Quinten can't stop you. I wouldn't. We can deal with our matters at House Earth alone. It seems like you're doing this for the good of others."

"I made an agreement with your brother. That I would give him the information I know in exchange for what he knows," he nodded, "and what you know about Slater. This is self-serving."

"Because you're interested in killing Slater?"

"Because I'm interested in you."

My hands stilled. Hell, everything in me stilled. There were two ways to take that. Either he meant it to be romantic and was telling me he'd fallen head over heels for me the moment he'd stepped into my kitchen—something I found very hard to believe—or he was doing what any good mercenary should do: say anything necessary to obtain the goal and get paid for it.

"Why?" I asked, finishing up the last stitches and setting an knot.

I turned, my hand hovering over Evelyn's medical kit. She had plenty of sharp scalpels in that kit. Things I could use to hurt him if I needed to. Things I could use to defend myself. I picked up the small scissors instead to cut the thread.

"You intrigue me."

"Not sure how to take that." I snipped the thread.

"Any way you want."

"All right. I'm going to take it that I don't know you very well, Abraham."

"That's not what you've been telling me."

I probed one of the bullet holes, and his stomach muscles tightened. I'd need to get the slugs out. I picked up a pair of thin, delicate tongs with cupped ends not coincidentally about the size of a bullet. I slathered that with some of the balm before using it to extract the bullets.

"I don't know *this* you," I said.

"Am I that different from the man you knew?"

No. Not all that different. Harder, angrier, certainly more suspicious. But those were his beautiful hazel eyes, that was his voice that made my heart stutter. He even smelled the same, a delicious mix of spice and soap.

I liked to think there was still kindness in him. A moral core that meant he would stand for the good of others, no matter the cost to himself. But he was a mercenary, and that job description wasn't exactly suitable for the noble-minded. Still, he was doing right by his promise to Quinten. He was holding to his word of making sure we got to House Earth in one piece.

"I don't know. It's complicated."

"You told me that before. Care to explain?"

"Some things about you are the same," I said. "I want to hope that you are the man I knew." I paused, lost for a moment in the memories of what we'd had. Wondering if the smiling, tattooed Abraham in the other timeway might be the man I loved. If somehow in that time, we had found a way to be together, to build a life where neither of us had to carry guns to survive.

"But I can't," I said. "I can't hope. You are different. I guess we all are. And that's just the way of it. Now that you know I can cook, kill, and crack computer code, it's time for you to tell me a few things."

"Like what?"

"Like why you really came out to my farm." I paused, studied his face. "You wanted to bring us in for the bounty on our heads, didn't you?"

"Sallyo isn't the kind of person who shares her take," he said. "She was the one hired to bring you in. Well, her and a few others. I did not hunt you down to drag you in to Slater."

"All right. So when you say you are here now because of me . . . how am I supposed to take that?"

His gaze was steady, but his expression had closed down so that I couldn't guess whatever emotion he was guarding. "Any way you want to."

"I want the truth. Why are you with us? Why are you with me?"

He didn't answer. Not for a long moment. But I refused to look away and give him an easy out of this conversation.

"You hate Slater," he finally said slowly. "I hate Slater. Between the two of us, our resources, I believe we can remove him from the world. And I believe it will be a much better world without him."

Great. He thought of me as his killing buddy. Someone useful for getting a job done. "Did someone offer you a lot of money to kill Slater?"

"I don't talk about my personal business."

I raised an eyebrow. That sounded like a yes to me. Who would have put a hit out on Slater? Who were his enemies in this time?

"Since I'm the person patching up your gut, I think you owe me more than vagaries."

"There's no money on Slater's head," he said.

I didn't believe that.

"But that doesn't mean I don't have reasons for wanting him dead."

"Mercenaries freelance?" I asked. "For free?"

"It's personal, Matilda. And that's all you're going to get out of me on the subject."

"Noted. So, how did you know I hated Slater before you'd even met me?"

"Other than the fact that you tried to stop him from killing me in the jail? That you fought him and risked getting shot when you were just a child?"

I tilted my head, considering that. "That was a long time ago. Anyone would have tried to stop Slater from killing you after they saw he had killed the sheriff. Basic human decency, and all that."

"Hmm," he said.

"So why find me?"

"If I say because you told me to, you're not going to buy it, are you?"

"I think a man like you wouldn't listen to the crazy talk of an eight-year-old girl you met three hundred years ago."

"An eight-year-old girl who foretold the future?"

"Even then."

He smiled, just one corner of his mouth quirking up.

He really needed to stop doing that, since it just made me want to kiss him.

"There might be a business deal I thought you'd be interested in."

Wow. What do you know? He could tell the truth.

"What business deal?"

"It involves galvanized."

"Don't tell me you want to start a union."

"No. Not exactly. There are . . . deals in place that I'd like us all to be a part of. Things that will allow for galvanized to be expunged of their crimes and offered other options."

"You want galvanized to go legitimate? Can that even happen? Un-mercenary yourselves? From what I've seen, people are pretty reluctant to trust you."

"Not you," he said. "You trusted me from the moment you saw me."

I held up my wrist. "Stitched. Ergo, one of you. Also, I know you . . . kind of. Mostly. So I'm not the best example for your cause."

"You've never killed a man."

He said it like that meant something. Like it was rare and important.

"So?"

"You are the proof that we can live. That we read books, make jam. That we can believe in human decency and can be healers, not just warriors. You are proof that we are human."

Sure, he sounded sincere. But there was something more he was holding back. I may not have known him for a long time in my past life, but I knew enough to sense when he still wasn't being completely truthful.

"Who do you want to prove our humanity to? I thought you were pretty happy being a mercenary."

He must have expected a different question. Maybe thought I'd swoon over his pretty words and puppy-follow him where ever he wanted me to go.

But if our recent bouts of getting shot at and almost killed and getting jumped by mutant beasts had taught me anything, it was that this world was just as dangerous and full of deadly surprises as mine had been. Asking the right questions was tantamount to survival.

Nine days until the bombs started falling. Eight, by the time we reached House Earth . . . if we got there.

Time was ticking down, and the weight of its passage made my heart race.

But it appeared Abraham had other goals in mind.

"Important people who can make a difference," he said. "House Earth already accepts you as one of theirs, don't they?"

"Honestly, I have no idea."

"It's a start," he said. "A way for people to understand us."

I dug into the supplies for a clean cloth, then slathered it with the balm. At least he was being mostly honest. I would have hated it more if he tried to string me along.

"I don't think holding me up as proof of anything will change anyone's mind. You change people's minds by doing things." I pressed the cloth against his wound and unwound a strip of cloth to secure it into place. "By doing good things."

"Do you really believe that?" he asked.

"Yes. Why?"

"It's . . . I don't know. It's kind of sweet."

"Sweet?"

He grunted as I tightened the knot with a little more force than strictly required.

"Ouch," he noted.

I repacked the supplies so I could take them out with me to check on Foster then stood.

"Am I sensing your displeasure?" Abraham sat, his shoulder dropping so his muscular arm could fall to cover his newly bandaged wound.

"You are sensing my willingness to leave you to put on your shirt while I go take care of Foster. Also?" I pointed at him. "I am not going to be your little doll to parade around in front of people so that you can broker deals. Do you understand me, Abraham? I'm not your new toy, not your bargaining chip, not your way out of a bad situation you got yourself into and have had hundreds of years to get yourself out of."

He stood, his arm dropping away from his injury. That rakish smile of his flashed, and he stepped right up to within an inch of me. He wrapped his hands gently around my upper arms. "I feel I owe you an apology. Maybe I can apologize somewhere more private?"

Oh, that is a dirty, dirty trick.

He was going to kiss me.

He was going to do it to shut me up. Maybe to convince me to take his side, to make me swoon.

He was going to kiss me because he thought I was sweet. Because he had always liked it when I stood up, pushed back, and put him in his place.

Nope. Not happening. It was going to be me who kissed him.

For my own reasons.

I stepped into him, slipping my arms up so I could place my hands on either side of his face. His hands stroked down my back, his left pressing my hips even closer as I stood on tiptoe and slanted my mouth to his.

I was kissing him because I missed him. Because I loved him. Because he was the man I wanted and could never have again. I was kissing him because I needed to feel him again. Needed to taste him again. The real him, here in this real time of ours.

He stilled and held his breath, surprised and maybe overwhelmed with the wave of sensation.

If he was surprised about my move, he quickly got over it. His lips, hot upon my needful mouth, moved against mine with more tenderness than I'd expected.

He bit my bottom lip gently, and I licked the corner of his mouth, my tongue flicking out to touch the edge of his stitches there and then retreating back so I could dip into his mouth and finally, finally taste him.

If he'd been tender before, that one move ignited a fire in him. He shifted his grip, bending to stroke his hand over my butt.

I was teetering on one tiptoe, breasts, stomach, hips, and thigh pressed against the hard muscles of his chest, stomach, hips. He slipped one hand up, and I thought for a moment that he was going to lift me and then lay me on the cot. Instead his palm stroked along the side of my breast, and I made a soft, hungry sound.

He pulled his mouth away from mine and pressed his lips once, gently, to my throat. A shiver of pure pleasure pooled under his mouth, spreading over my neck and trickling down my breasts. Then he just as gently bit me.

"Abraham," I said. "Please."

He lifted his torturous lips from my neck and gazed

down at me, hazel eyes holding an animal intensity. "Yes?" he whispered.

"Kiss me," I whispered. "Just for the me that I am. Just for this now."

That slash of a smile pulled at his lips: rakish delight. "For this you. Forever."

He lowered his mouth to mine and kissed me with intent, as if it were the first and last time we would ever touch. The contact was fire on fire.

I was swallowed whole, lost, every inch of me straining for his touch, his caress.

His arms tightened around me, a strength, a rock in the storm that rolled inside me.

Quinten made a small sound, a whimper of pain.

And that was all it took to bring me back to this here. This now.

To whom I was with. The man I had loved. The man who was no longer that man.

I pulled away, though he reached for me, his lips begging me not to stop what I had started. What we had started. I pressed my lips together and shook my head. "I can't," I breathed.

I was lying. I knew it.

He knew it.

And we both knew this lie had to be our truth for now.

"I know," he said.

He loosened his grip, lowering me back to my own feet, giving me up inch by inch, as if savoring the warmth of me. As if it would be the last time we would ever touch. And it might be.

I didn't know if we could ever become something more. My past expectations of who he was would only mess with how I saw him now.

If I was smart, I'd be content with this one kiss, cut my losses, and move forward.

But I wasn't. Not at all.

"You should get some rest," I said, refusing to hold his burning gaze. I turned away, dizzy with him, aching for him. I was doing the right thing. The logical thing. Wasn't I?

"I need to check on Foster."

He didn't say anything, but his silence crouched between us, a weight of unfulfilled promises.

I squared my shoulders and walked out to the other room. I did not look back.

Foster stood at the stove, stirring a pot. From the rich, sweet smell, I knew what he was cooking. Hot cocoa.

"Foster," I said. "I've checked everyone else. I need to see to your wounds too."

"Yes." He pulled the small pot away from the hottest part of the woodstove.

He poured the cocoa expertly into two cups, turned, and offered me one.

I took it, and the warmth of the cocoa seeped into my hands, bringing with it a sense of comfort I hadn't felt in a long time.

"A toast," he rumbled.

I shifted the grip on my cup and raised it a bit. "To surviving the day?"

"To you. You saved," he said. "Saved our lives."

I raised my cup, the knot of emotion in my throat choking off my words. When all this was over—if I survived—I was going to carve out a little time without the threat of assassins trying to kill me, injured family members needing tending, or my heart being so achingly confused by a man I apparently couldn't stop loving. In any time.

I was going to sit on my front porch and watch the clouds go by for days.

"To our lives," I said.

I sipped the chocolate and took that moment with Foster to enjoy the rich, simple pleasure. It did a surprising amount of good to my mood.

Then I set the cup on the table. "You know, I never could have done it without you," I said. "You believed in the crazy story of a very young girl. If you hadn't . . ." I shook my head. "You are the one who saved the world, Foster, not me. Thank you." I reached over, touched his hand gently.

He smiled, his eyes fatherly and kind.

"You were lost. Alone and cold. In the rain. The dark graveyard. I had lost. Everything. Family. Children. There you were. Shining light. So alive." He paused, took a drink of his cocoa.

I didn't think I'd ever heard him speak so much all at one time. In the time I was from, speech was hard for him. The experiments he had suffered had left lasting damage. It was comforting to know he was less damaged in this time.

"Many years I have remembered," he said. "You saved me. I am proud. Of you, Matilda Case."

The knot in my throat was back. It had been years since anyone had told me they were proud of me. The last person to tell me so had been my father, back when I was very young.

"We make a good team, is all," I said, pushing away the tears before they had a chance to fall. "Let me take a look at your injuries, okay? We'll need to be in as good a shape as possible. I think we have a world to save. Again."

He shrugged out of his shirts. Looked like I was going to be digging out a few bullets.

Foster drank cocoa while I unpacked my medical supplies once again.

10

Listen, Matilda. You have a problem. I think I have a solution. But finding you is more than impossible. Which doesn't mean I'm not going to do it anyway.

— W.Y.

"Matilda?" Quinten whispered.

"Right here," I said from the bunk next to him. Abraham had decided to sleep where he could see the front door, and Foster had bedded down by the back door.

I'd thought I'd wake up every hour or so to check on Quinten, but from the shadows in the room, I could tell it was almost morning outside. I'd fallen into bed after tending Foster and hadn't woken once.

"Where are we?" he whispered.

I pushed off the blanket and got out of bed. I'd finally given in and taken off my boots, but I was still wearing my pants and T-shirt.

"We're in a cabin near the House Earth compound." I nudged a wooden crate with my foot, then sat next to Quinten's bed so he could see me.

"Why?"

"Do you remember the mercs shooting at us? Or the bus crashing?"

He frowned. "Yes," he said. "What time is it? What day is it? Is everyone still alive? Gloria?"

"It's the next morning; we've just spent the night here. Everyone is alive as far as I know. We all survived the crash, and we didn't use the radio to try to contact House Earth, though I guess this cabin might have one."

"Injuries?" he asked.

"None of us got out of it without a few bumps and breaks. You cracked your head and gouged your thigh. Neds dislocated a shoulder, and Abraham and Foster have holes in them."

"And you?" he asked.

I decided not to bring up the feral attack. "Just a bump on the head. Made me dizzy for a while, but I'm good as gold now. Before you try sitting up, I'll want to take another look at your cuts, okay? See if I need to put any more balm on them."

"Balm?" he asked.

"The stuff in the tin can. In the medical supplies."

"My medical supplies?" he asked, startled. "You didn't get into my medical supplies, did you? Tell me you didn't get into my medical supplies."

"Settle down. Neds gave me the balm and the thread I—well, Evelyn—had on hand. What's so troublesome in your medical supplies?"

"Nothing," he said, relieved. "Just . . . nothing."

"You're lying, and I'm offended that you'd think I wouldn't notice." I reached over to unwrap the bandage on his head. "Tell me what's got you so worked up."

"Just . . . things you shouldn't handle. Poisons."

"You packed poisons? Putting aside I'd love to know

why you think you should travel with them, I'm going to ask you this question first: don't you think I know how to handle a poison? I'm not stupid."

"It's . . . It doesn't appear to be poisonous. A dust. You might think it was a powder."

"Does this poisonous powder have a name?"

"Shelley dust."

My hand stilled. "You have Shelley dust?"

"Do you know what that is?"

"The only compound that can burn out a galvanized's stitches? Of course I know what it is. I thought only heads of Houses had it."

"What? No. No one has it," he said. "I saw some old references to the mixture and experimented with making some up. For the beasts I make, not for you."

"Thanks for that. I didn't expect you were plotting to kill me." It was dark enough in the room, I didn't think I'd be able to see his wound. So I stood and found the small flint striker on the nightstand next to his bed and lit the oil lamp there, turning the wick up high enough to light the room. Since the room was only divided from the rest of the cabin by short walls, I knew everyone else would know we were awake.

Quinten and I had been talking softly, but the cabin was too small for real privacy.

"I wasn't. Although." He glanced up at me.

I raised one eyebrow at his guilty look. "You packed it in case you needed to take Abraham or Foster out, didn't you?"

"They're galvanized, Matilda. Dangerous."

"So you've been telling me. Well, I want you to know that they saved all our lives back there. Pulled us all out of the bus and then took on the mercenaries, killed them, and stole their vehicles so we could find cover for the night. Not the sort of behavior I'd expect out of someone set on seeing us buried."

"Actions can be deceiving," Quinten said in his typical stubborn fashion.

"Sure. But it would have been a lot easier for them to drag us in like prisoners yesterday, since all of us were injured and easy to overpower if they'd put their minds to it. I may not know exactly what end goal either of them have in mind, but right now, they're on our side. Mostly."

I carefully lifted the pad of cotton and took a good, close look at the swelling and stitches. He was no longer bleeding, and while the wound was still swollen, it didn't look nearly as bad as it had a few hours ago.

"I think this is healing nicely," I said. "How much does it hurt?"

"Enough," he said.

"Do you want painkillers? Or are you going to macho your way through this one to prove something?"

His eyes settled on my face. "You have a lot to say about everything, don't you, Matilda?"

I gave him a quick smile. "Oh, you have no idea. And before you tell me that Evelyn never would have said such a thing. . . . Fine. Maybe you're right. But I can guarantee she was thinking those things. Because you are stubborn and ridiculous, for a man who's also supposed to be a genius."

"Supposed to be?"

"Well, I've heard you say it over and over again, but what genius thing have you done lately?"

He dropped his voice to a whisper. "Other than find a cure for the plague?"

"Untested cure," I reminded him.

"It will work."

"Good. Then take some painkiller so we can get on the road. This world's not saving itself, you know. I'll get you some water." I stood. "Think you could hold down a little food?"

"Yes."

I turned and walked out.

Neds were awake and wet-headed, so they'd taken the time to shower. The idea of a nice hot shower filled me with envy.

"Morning, boys," I said. "Use up all the hot water?"

"There ain't no hot water," Right Ned said. "Plenty of cold still available, though. Help yourself."

"Mmm. Might have to pass on that." I walked over to the sink near the woodstove. The cabin was roomy, but small enough that the woodstove, which someone— likely Foster or Abraham—had kept stoked did a good job chasing the chill out of the air. I found a cup on a shelf, rinsed it out, and filled it with water.

Then I checked the cupboards for food. Everything was canned provisions. I found a tin of crackers, and decided that would have to do for breakfast.

"Where are Foster and Abraham?" I asked Neds.

"Out," Left Ned said.

"Because . . . ?" I prompted.

"Said something about checking the bikes," Right Ned said.

"We believe them?"

"Thought you did," Right Ned said.

I glanced at the back door. Wondered if they were really out there doing repairs, or if they were doing something else, like radioing to tell someone they had us and were bringing us in. No, if there was one thing I absolutely trusted in Abraham, it was his anger and need for revenge.

He wanted Slater dead. And he wanted our help. Or maybe he wanted to trade our trust with House Earth for something he thought would end Slater.

We had that much in common: the driving need for one man's death.

It was a weird way to start a relationship.

Well, that and that kiss last night.

"Matilda?" Right Ned asked. "Are you listening?"

"Sure," I said. "Sorry. Just a little tired. What with the crashing and shooting and stabbing and all."

Neds pushed up off where he was sitting on the couch. "Let me see if I can brew some tea. There must be some leaves here somewhere."

My mouth watered and my whole body went tingly with the promise of hot, rich tea. "You don't need to bother yourself."

He stopped, and they both stared at me. "I'll make tea," Right Ned said. "Maybe after you fix up your brother, you'll take a moment to stop tending to the needs of every person around you and tend to yourself a little, Matilda. You're wounded too."

"Yeah, but I don't whine about it as much as the rest of you."

"Ha!" Left Ned crowed.

Right Ned gave me half a grin that looked like it hurt a little. The swollen eye was spectacularly black now, and the side of his face was sort of an off-yellow mixed with red and green. "Go take him the crackers. There will be tea waiting when you get back."

So I went.

Quinten was sitting on the edge of the bed, both feet over the side, staring at his boots like he was not looking forward to the pain it was going to take to try to put them on his feet.

"Neds are making tea," I said, handing him the water.

"I heard."

"Where are the painkillers?" I asked.

"In my bag. Not the case. We still have my case, don't we?"

"Yes. Abraham made sure to drag it out of the bus."

"Good. Good. I'll have to thank him for that."

I opened Quinten's bag and surveyed the jars and tins. "Which one is painkiller?"

"The red bottle."

I plucked up the bottle, unscrewed the cap, and shook two capsules onto my palm. "Two?"

"Better start with one. I'd like to be awake by the time we reach the compound. Where, exactly, did you say this cabin is located?"

"I don't know the markers. We're a couple hours' ride outside the compound, though, if that helps any."

He swallowed some water, tossed the pill in his mouth, and drank the glass dry.

"Let's get something in your stomach for that." I handed him the cracker tin, and he pulled out a butter wafer and bit it in half.

"Are you going to keep the painkillers down?" I asked.

"Yes."

"Don't try to put your boots on. I'd hate for you to fall over and hit your head. Again. We have a limited supply of bandages."

"Go get your tea," he said with a slight wave. "I'm going to sit here until the hammers in my head stop bashing at my skull."

I put a second pill down on the nightstand. "Just in case those hammers don't stop swinging."

I walked out again.

"Shower this way?" I pointed to the right.

Neds were at the stove. They had water on to boil and were pouring a can of something that smelled like soup into a pot. Left Ned glanced up. "Yep. Towels and soap too."

Good enough. The toilet was in a separate small room with a sink. The shower was its own little closet, and looked like it could double for a sauna if all the right things were hooked up to it. Cedar walls, floor, ceiling. A simple shower head with one faucet.

An oil lamp was hooked on the wall, and I found the striker hanging next to it. I lit that, and wished the soft yellow light would warm the air.

Cold water; cold room. I was so not looking forward to this, but I needed to wash the stink and dirt off more than I hated the idea of cold.

This was one time when I wished I had the limited sense of sensation, like most other galvanized.

I shut the door and locked it, then took my time getting out of my clothes. One, because I had a head injury and didn't want to fall over or pass out. Two, because I was sore, and wanted to really pay attention to where my injuries might be.

There was a mirror on the wall, large enough I could see myself from head to waist. And there were hooks set behind the door for my clothes.

I got naked, then stood in front of the mirror. I had a small bruise at the edge of my jaw that was purple lined in red. A much, much bigger bruise covered one side of my chest and my shoulder. I knew I'd hit that more than once in the tumble down the hillside. Several small, shallow cuts crossed my torso.

The worst of my wounds seemed to be the tear in the line of stitching under my breast. I'd have to sew that up for sure, before it infected.

I leaned in toward the mirror to try to get a good look at it. The thread was torn out along my rib cage too.

That was going to be a damned awkward place to try to self-sew. I wasn't even sure I could get the right angle on it.

Which meant I'd need to ask someone to stitch me up.

My brother? My not-lover? Foster? Neds?

Who did I want to be naked in front of?

None of them right now. But this was no time to be worried about a little nudity.

I checked my legs—bruised in various places—then turned and tried to get a good look at my back.

My butt was bruised, especially the left cheek. No wonder the bike ride had been so uncomfortable.

I couldn't see all of my back, but didn't feel any cuts splitting as I twisted and craned.

Good enough. And since I couldn't put off the cold water any longer, I thought hot thoughts—yes, they were all of Abraham, and he was all naked—then turned on the faucet, got in, and dunked.

I yelped from the cold and from the scrape on my head that felt even colder than the rest of me. I turned off the water and shivered as I worked soap over my goose-prickly body.

I was shaking pretty hard by the time I'd gotten sudsy. Turned the water back on and rinsed off for as long as I could stand it. Turned the water off, took a couple hard breaths, and turned it back on again.

My teeth were chattering by the time I stepped out from the shower. I grabbed a towel off the shelf and wrapped it around my shivering body. Then I took another towel—maybe a waste of a clean towel, but I couldn't bring myself to take off the towel on my body yet—and carefully twisted water out of my hair. I patted the towel down my shoulders, arms, and legs.

I glanced at my dirty clothes, and just couldn't make myself put them on again. I had a change of clothes in my duffel, which I'd forgotten to bring into the bathroom with me.

No problem. I gathered up the dirty clothes, and with the towel still wrapped around me, I stepped out into the main room.

Neds glanced over from the stove and didn't seem at all worried about my state of undress. "Food when you're ready," Left Ned said. "If you don't mind soup for breakfast."

"Also, tea," Right Ned said.

"Smells amazing. I'll be right out."

I walked into the sleeping area, and Quinten still sat on the side of the bed. "How was the water?"

"Any colder, and I'd have to chip it out of the pipes with an ice pick," I said. "But I feel better. I can heat some on the stove for you, if you want."

"No. We don't have time. And they have warm showers at the compound."

"Now you tell me," I said.

He smiled slightly and raised his hand toward his hair, but stopped halfway and rubbed at his forehead instead.

"How's the pain?"

"Better," he said.

"Are you feeling up for some stitching?"

"For whom?"

"Me."

"You're hurt?"

"Just tore some stitches." I slipped the towel down and turned, angling my arm so my breast was covered and so he could see the unstitched bit along my ribs. "Not too bad, but I know that broken stitches can mean me breaking. And I'd rather not have to find a new set of ribs."

Yes, I said it like it was a common thing. But the truth was, I'd never actually come apart since the day my brother had implanted my mind into Evelyn's body. Well, mostly Evelyn's body. She was the one who had had bits taken off and put back on during her three-hundred-year coma.

And as long as my stitches were solid and replaced every now and then if they broke, my body parts—we hoped—wouldn't need to be replaced for a long time. Maybe even an hundred years.

Quinten held up his hand, which shook terribly.

"I can do it," he said.

"Would Neds be better at it?" I asked, eyeing that tremble in his fingers.

"Maybe. Left Ned has a good hand for it."

"So, his right hand? That arm's in a sling."

"I think he could do it."

"Do what?" Abraham asked as he walked into the bedroom area.

I pulled the towel back up and turned.

He stopped dead in his tracks. His eyes widened, then narrowed as a slight smile twitched at the corner of his mouth.

It didn't take a genius to know what he was thinking.

"Apologies. I thought you'd be dressed."

"How good are you at stitching?" I asked.

"Why?" he asked cautiously.

"No," Quinten said.

"I need some repair work."

"Are you hurt?" he asked.

"Matilda," Quinten warned.

"Just tore a few stitches. Are you any good with your hands?"

Abraham's gaze flicked up to meet my eyes, his mouth

doing that crooked-smile thing again. "I am extraordinary with my hands."

"So you can you sew?"

"Oh," he said like he didn't know what I'd been talking about. "Yes. A man doesn't go through three hundred years of being a patchwork body without knowing how to thread a needle."

"I don't want him anywhere near you," Quinten said. "I can do it."

"You need to save your strength for when we get to the compound," I said. "We'll do it here, and you can supervise. If both of you would turn around while I get my pants on, we'll stitch me up, then that will be that."

"You trust him that much?" Quinten asked.

I turned to face him. "This is a medical necessity, not a date. You'll be right here to make sure he does it right."

I don't know what he saw in my expression. But whatever it was, he swore softly and averted his eyes. "Fine," he said. "You're right."

I glanced at Abraham. He had his back turned, both hands in his back pockets, elbows stuck out as if he had all the time in the world to wait.

"Thank you," I said. "Just give me a second." I dug in my duffel, and stepped into clean underwear and denim pants. I thought about putting on a bra, but the stitching would have to be done under the edge of it, and that didn't make any sense. I did pull out a soft undershirt and held that across my chest for modesty's sake.

"Okay. Let's get this done."

Quinten tipped his head back up. "Let me see it." He motioned me over to him.

I walked over and turned again so he could get a better look. He pressed his fingertips along the edge of the seam. His hand was warm, and although the tremor was noticeable, he seemed to retain good control.

"We'll need the small clamp. Abraham, that should be in the medical case she carries in her duffel."

Abraham turned around, scanned the room. I pointed at Evelyn's wooden box, which I'd left on the cot.

"Thread?" Abraham asked.

"Should be in the box. Also, we'll want the scale jelly," Quinten said. "And the needles."

Abraham gathered up all of that. "Will you be okay standing?" Quinten asked me.

"Yes." At least I thought I would be. I was pretty sure having a needle and thread pulled through my skin was not going to be the most pleasant experience I'd ever been through. But I was hoping the scale jelly would numb it a bit.

"We don't have ice," Abraham said.

"We won't need it," Quinten said.

"She feels pain."

Quinten glanced up at Abraham as he walked over with all the necessary items in his one hand and Evelyn's case in the other. "The scale jelly will help with that."

"Is that the balm you used on me?" he asked.

"Yes," I said.

"What's it made of?"

"Secret family recipe," Quinten said, before I could tell Abraham it was basically boiled lizard scales.

Abraham walked around in front of me and placed everything on the nightstand. "Let me get the light." He brought the oil lamp, while Quinten unpacked the needle, thread, and cotton pads from Evelyn's box.

I had used medical thread on Quinten. But he pulled out a bobbin with the silver life thread—*Filum Vitae*—

that held me, and other stitched things like me, together the best.

"Drag the thread through the balm, then spread the balm on her skin before you begin," Quinten directed.

Abraham had been alive for much longer than Quinten. I was sure he had stitched up himself and others a million more times than Quinten ever had. To my surprise, he didn't argue or complain. He did just as Quinten asked.

It was odd to see them working together. I kind of liked it.

I kind of liked being the thing that brought a truce between them, no matter how temporary that may be.

Abraham placed one hand on my bare shoulder.

"Are you ready?" he asked.

"I'm not made of glass, Seventh. The sooner we get this done, the sooner we'll be on the road."

"True." He gave me a curious look, then knelt beside me.

Oh. I hadn't really thought that through. Of course he'd be at a better angle to sew from there. Still, he was close enough I could feel the heat radiating off his body, could feel the warmth of his exhalation against the bare skin of my stomach.

"Seventh?" he asked, dredging the thread through the balm, threading the needle, and then setting it all on the cotton cloth.

"What?"

"You called me Seventh."

"Oh. Right. Sorry."

He dipped his fingers into the balm, releasing the scent of lemon and licorice.

"Any reason why?"

"Old story. Uninteresting."

"Don't you know by now just how interested I am in such things?"

I inhaled, exhaled. "You are persistent. I'll give you that."

"Turn just a bit." He stroked the edge of my hip to show me which way he wanted me to move, the heel of his hand resting a moment too long, an inch too intimately.

I arched an eyebrow and looked down at him.

He glanced up at me. Pure innocence in his expression.

"Seventh?" he asked again.

I shifted my stance. "In the world I remember, the galvanized were addressed in the order of their reawakening after the Wings of Mercury experiment. You were awakened the seventh out of thirteen."

"Who was one?" he asked.

"Foster."

He smeared the balm over my stitches, and every inch of my skin went goose bumpy. "That's still true," he said.

I shivered as he moved upward, his fingers pausing beneath the curve of my breast.

Abraham looked up. "Does it hurt too much?"

"No," I said as he drew his hand away. "It's good. Warm."

"It should numb it too," Quinten said. "You'll want to clamp the widest break there on her ribs, Abraham," he said. "And stitch between the broken stitches before you remove the old thread."

Abraham picked up the small clamp. "Who was thirteenth to wake?" he asked.

"Me."

"And now you're the tenth."

"I guess so."

"How long do I need to wait for the numbing to kick in?" he asked Quinten.

"A few more seconds," Quinten said.

"Who are they?" I asked.

"Who are who?" Abraham said, his hand resting casually on the side of my hip. It was a more proper place for his hand. And though he looked a question at me, I didn't tell him to move it away.

"The ten galvanized," I said.

"You know four: you, me, Foster, Slater."

"Who else?"

"Dolores, Clara, Vance, Wila, Buck, January."

I rolled the list of names through my head. That meant Loy, Obedience, and Helen were all dead. I hadn't known any of them for very long, but it still tugged at my heart. Loy was a warm, joking, kind man who always tried to see the funny side of things. Obedience had been slim and slight, but her spirit was a bright joy.

And Helen. Well, Helen had been the woman who shot Oscar Gray in the head and killed him in front of millions, framing the other galvanized for murder.

I wouldn't miss her. A small, dark part of my heart was glad Slater had killed her.

One less murderer to deal with.

"Matilda?"

I realized I'd drifted off. It was hard to separate that in my experience, my mind, it had been only a few days since I'd seen my friend and ex-head of House Gray, Oscar Gray, killed. Abraham had been his galvanized, and Oscar's last words begged me to make sure Abraham was okay.

But for Abraham here, who hadn't lived through that betrayal, and who was watching me with lines of curiosity spreading from the edge of his crinkled eyes, those things had never happened. He—well, *we*—had never experienced that pain.

"What?" I asked.

"Is the jelly numb enough yet?" he asked.

"I think so. Try, and I'll let you know if I feel it."

Abraham picked up the clamp and held my skin together with one hand. He set the clamp with the other.

Then he picked up the needle, the balm-coated thread tucked in his palm. A sure sign that he really had done this sort of thing before. He kept his left hand spread so that his fingers were on either side of my stitching. "Take a breath," he suggested.

I inhaled. Held it.

He pushed the needle into my skin. I knew those needles were incredibly sharp and the scale jelly did a good job of masking the sensation. Even so, it wasn't exactly comfortable.

But it was fairly easy to endure.

"Numb enough?" he asked me.

"Yes. Go ahead."

"So, you knew them? All of them?" he asked as he made very quick work of the stitching.

"Briefly. I'd only just met most of them. And the others."

"Who were the three others?" he asked.

I didn't think he was really interested in people he'd never known, but small talk kept my mind off the tug and slide of thread and needle through my skin.

"A man named Loy, and two women, named Obedience and Helen. You didn't know them in this time."

"I might have. We all began living in the same town. I knew Foster before he was a galvanized. Slater too, obviously. Tell me about them."

"I'm not sure I knew them well enough to say. Loy

was fun-loving. Strong and big. He loved to laugh and gamble. He and Buck got on like brothers. Obedience was a slight woman. Pale as moonlight, and fun. Bubbly."

He tugged the thread, adjusted his fingers alongside the seam, and started again.

"You liked them?" he asked, his head tipped up, eyes focused on the curve of my ribs beside my breast. We were about to be stitching in very tender territory.

"I did. They were both nice to me. Welcoming in the new girl, and all that."

"What about Helen?"

"She was compact, strong. She wore her stitches like lacework over her body. Very pretty."

"And?"

"And she killed a man you cared for like a father. Shot him in the head. I think she would have killed you too, if she had the chance."

"Hmm. You'll need to move your hand a bit," he said.

I moved my hand, taking most of my crumpled undershirt with it. I tried to keep myself mostly covered, but it wasn't really working.

Abraham didn't give me any flirty looks or winks as he worked his way beneath my breast. If anything, he became more focused on the stitches—small, tight, quick, and more gentle.

Which was good, because every stitch stung more than the next.

"Who was the man I cared about?" he asked.

"Oscar Gray. He was . . ." I paused, sucked in a breath, and held it as he worked his way up to the very delicate skin between my breasts.

"Almost done," he said softly. "Do you need more jelly here?"

I shook my head. "I'm okay."

"Oscar?" he asked, making the last quick set of stitches.

"Your friend. He was head of House Gray. Nice man. Took me in to protect me from the other Houses using me for their profit. Which didn't go very well, since he got shot, you got filled full of Shelley dust, and we had to run for our lives while saving Quinten from being imprisoned."

He placed the last stitches. "It is an interesting life you've led, Matilda Case."

"Several interesting lives, actually," I agreed. "Is that it?"

He nodded, turned for the tiny scissors, which Quinten held out for him. "Is the tie-off all right?" he asked.

I glanced down between my breasts. He had a fine hand with thread, each of the stitches holding my skin together evenly spaced and as small as was practical. At the end of my seam, he'd crisscrossed the thread so that it created an eight-pointed star.

"You embroidered me?"

"I can take out two of the stitches and leave an X there if you want, but I thought the seam needed reinforcing. Star stitch seems to do the trick, especially in delicate areas, where the stitches are much smaller."

It was pretty. Actually, it was the first time I'd ever thought of my stitches as something that could be beautiful.

"I like it," I said.

"Let me see," Quinten asked.

He'd been quiet through most of the actual work. I turned his way, my hand covering my breast, my shirt covering my other breast.

Quinten didn't even glance at my breast. He had me slowly turn so he could inspect the stitches from my ribs to cleavage.

"This is good. Very good," he finally said.

"Thank you," Abraham said.

"Spread another thin coat of jelly and pull out the old threads; then we'll be done."

I sighed and let Abraham get busy following Quinten's orders, which he did without complaint.

After it was done and the old thread was removed, Abraham gently wiped the clean cotton over the seam one last time.

"Very nicely done, Abraham," Quinten said. "Very nicely done."

"I'm glad you approve, Mr. Case." Abraham set the last of the things down on the nightstand again and put the lid back on the tin of jelly.

He pushed up onto his feet. "How are you feeling, Matilda?" he asked.

"Other than half-naked and cold? Good."

"Good." He stood there, looking at me like maybe he could do something about both of those things.

"So, if you'd step out, I'll get dressed," I said.

"Of course." He took a step to walk past me, and I tipped my head back a bit to watch him.

A wave of dizziness slipped over me. I panicked and grabbed his arm. I didn't want this time to slip away. I didn't want him to slip away.

"Matilda?" He paused.

"Are you okay?" Quinten asked.

"I'm fine." No roses, no bells. But my concussion was getting in the way of me trying to act like everything was okay.

I let go of his arm, but Abraham was having nothing of it. He wrapped his arms around me, helping to hold my hand against my undershirt so I didn't drop it.

"Get her to the bed," Quinten said.

"Fine. I'm fine," I repeated. Neither of them was listening to me.

Abraham walked me over to the cot I'd slept in and sat me there, crouching to get a look at my eyes.

"How many fingers am I holding up?" he asked.

I counted probably three-ish, but wasn't about to bank on that.

"I just looked up too quickly," I said. "Knocked my head yesterday, remember?"

"Is that all it was?"

"Yes." I didn't want to tell him about the timeways. He wouldn't believe me anyway.

"Not the painful amount of stitching you just went through?"

"I don't hurt now, and it's done. I think it's just a dizzy spell left over from the bump on my head. If you'd give me some privacy, I'll get dressed and put on my boots. We can all eat something before we get back on those bikes and hit the road."

"Are you sure?" He bit his bottom lip and frowned. He was so sincere, it caught at my heart a moment. But then I remembered this was not the Abraham I knew. This was not my Abraham.

He had kissed me like my Abraham. He had touched me like my Abraham.

"I'm sure," I said. "Go on, now. We have people to save, remember?" I pointed at the door behind him.

"I suppose we do," he said. "But I do hope you remember you're people too."

And then he walked out of the room.

I had no idea what he meant by that.

"Are you sure you're okay?" Quinten asked.

"Cold, bruised, half-naked, and hungry. I'm gold to the gills. Thanks."

"What really just happened?"

I frowned.

"You were terrified when you grabbed his arm."

"I wasn't terrified."

"Matilda," he said, "please. What's wrong?"

I took a breath, let it out. "Do you remember me telling you about the Wings of Mercury experiment?"

"Yes."

"Do you know if any part of that machine might still be around today?"

"I haven't ever heard of it."

"Back in my time," I said, "it was our ancestor Alveré Case who built the machine."

"Our great-however-many-greats-grandfather was a time traveler?"

"No. He built a machine he thought would stop time. Instead, it broke time, or, in this reality, it just sort of bent it out of shape. But I think . . . I think there might be a piece of the machine that's still causing those timeways I told you about."

"You only told me about one timeway."

"Okay. I think there are more. I don't know how many. When I slip into them, things go a little dizzy for me. That's why I grabbed Abraham's arm. I thought I was falling out of this time, into another."

"And did you?"

"No. I was just dizzy from the bump on my head."

He looked down at his feet, and I didn't know what he was thinking.

I turned my back and shrugged into my shirt, my stitches not pulling as much as I'd expected—Abraham really was good with thread—then put on an overshirt and my sleeveless jacket.

"So, if I am to believe you," he said. "You think there's a piece of that machine that is causing the . . . timeways?"

"It's a theory." I sat on the edge of the cot and put on a soft pair of socks and my boots.

"Your theory?"

Crap. I'd hoped he wouldn't ask me that. I glanced over at him. He was watching me. I knew if I lied to him now, I'd never get him to believe me again.

"Not really. I talked to someone during one of the time slips."

"Who?"

"Slater."

Quinten pulled his head and shoulders back and inhaled a breath. He held it for a moment, studying me.

"From which time?"

"This one, I think."

"What did he say?"

I shrugged. "He wants us dead. Threatened to kill you. Promised to kill me. Told me he thought one of us had a piece of the machine and were making time fracture. The usual."

Quinten pulled his fingers through his hair and tugged carefully at the curls. "That's usual?"

"Well, he's angry and insane, and blaming us for screwing up his plans. That's the usual."

"I don't want you anywhere near him."

"You know I can't promise that. For one thing, I have no control over the time slips. For another, I plan to kill him. That's likely to be up-close work."

"We're going to kill him," he corrected.

"Even so, I'm not going to be standing on the sidelines. I'm in this, Quinten. All the way."

"I know." He didn't sound happy about it.

"I'm guessing you don't have anything—a family heirloom—that might have been handed down from Alveré Case?"

"Nothing. Absolutely nothing."

"How about the pocket watch?" It was the only thing I knew that our father had gifted specifically to Quinten, since it had been gifted specifically to our father from our grandfather, and on down the family line.

He shook his head. "I've never had one."

There went that theory.

"Well, it's hard to rely on a madman's logic," I said. "How about breakfast?"

"I suppose we should."

He had also managed to put on his boots, though he hadn't tried standing yet.

"Look at you," I said. "All booted up and ready to kick some plague ass."

He smiled. "Aren't I just?"

"Can't keep a Case down for long." I walked over to him. "Why, I've heard tales that we are nearly indestructible."

I held my hand out for him, and he took it. He stood, groaning as he did so.

"Do you believe in those tales?" he asked as I looped my arm behind his back and we walked out of the bedroom to the kitchen table, where Neds had put out a bowl of soup and hot mug of tea for all of us. "*Nearly indestructible* seems like a high bar to hit."

"Not at all," I said. "We're Cases. We set that bar."

He eased down onto a chair. "I hope so," he said. "Because what we're trying to attempt is almost impossible."

"Saving House Earth?" I asked.

"Taking out a dictator who can travel through time."

Oh. That. "Don't worry," I said. "We're hitting that bar, no matter how impossible it is."

11

I found it. A way to reach you. Now to see if I can survive it.

—W.Y.

I wasn't sure what the protocol was for crashing someone's cabin, but Neds and Quinten insisted that was what the cabin had been built for: sheltering people who might have gotten caught out when night closed in—people like us.

They also insisted that House Earth would be by to restock anything that appeared to be running low. That included wood for the stove, food, and linens, if needed. Still, I took the time to clean up the dishes, make the beds, and hang the damp towels to dry.

Then we stepped out into the morning, the sky heavy with clouds. The dampness of night hadn't burned off yet, so it was a little chilly as we got ourselves situated on the bikes. I rode behind Abraham, Quinten rode behind Foster, and Neds insisted, even one-handed, they could drive just fine.

When I'd brought up the possibility of more mercenaries lying in wait for us, while we were putting away the dry dishes and spreading the ash from the woodstove so it would cool safely, the only response I'd gotten from Neds was a box of ammunition for my handgun.

Right. So if mercenaries showed up, which they probably would, our plan of action was to shoot them before they shot us.

Gold.

The road was clear as we made our way through the forest. All of the bikes were running much more smoothly—which meant Abraham and Foster most definitely had spent the early morning getting them tuned up and in good traveling shape.

When we hit the main road, I felt like we were easy targets, out in the clear.

I kept watch for any signs of people following us or lying in wait in the wheat and oat fields that lined the road. When I spotted a farmer driving an ancient tractor out in a field, at a distance from us, I about jumped out of my skin.

Did mercenaries drive tractors?

I pointed him out to Abraham, who gave me the "okay" sign. So apparently mercenaries didn't disguise themselves as farmers. Good to know.

After an hour, we stopped under the neat rows of an apple orchard, where we picked some fruit for our lunch and refilled the bike tanks with the fuel we'd packed on the back of Foster's four-wheeler.

"How much farther to the compound?" I asked Quinten.

"We should be there in the next hour," he said. "And I think now would be a good time to switch up who's riding with whom," he added.

"Why?" I asked.

Abraham was leaning against the trunk of a tree, slicing pieces of the apple into his palm with his pocket knife. He glanced up at Quinten, studying him as if he'd just brought up a very interesting topic, then turned his gaze to me to see how I was reacting. The corner of his mouth tucked back, as if he'd just tasted something sour, but he drew an apple slice to his mouth and chewed.

"Because you and I and Neds are House Earth," Quinten said. "And they most certainly aren't." He nodded toward Abraham and Foster.

Foster was lying on his back, staring up into the apple tree's branches, munching his way through his third or maybe fourth apple, all of which he consumed—peel, stem, core, and seeds.

He didn't look dangerous. Not at all.

"So, it's safe for me to assume you aren't the only person in House Earth who thinks all galvanized are murderers and thieves?" I asked.

Quinten studied me. "Because they are, Matilda."

Foster chuckled.

"And, yes." Quinten held up one hand. "I know you've had a different experience with them—apparently with *all* the galvanized. I will admit Abraham and Foster have been . . . useful travel companions."

"They saved our lives, Quinten," I said. "Twice."

"Which is why I think you and I should be on one bike together."

"Why?"

"It is going to take both of us to talk House Earth into letting them in past the gate."

I ran my hand over the noninjured side of my head. "Will they kill them on sight?"

"Galvanized don't kill easy," Quinten said.

With Shelley dust they did. He knew that. I could see it in his eyes. And I suddenly wondered if our main objective was to get the plague cure to House Earth or get the Shelley dust to them so they could defend themselves against the galvanized murderers and thieves.

Maybe both.

"So, it's a good chance they'll get shot at?" I asked.

He nodded.

"We'll stay out of rifle range," Abraham said. "Neds will ride with me."

"Like hell I will," Left Ned said.

"Think of it as a compliment," Abraham said, cutting deep into the apple core and lifting the meat of the apple, pinched between the knife blade and his finger, to his mouth. "You're valuable. To the plan," he added.

"Being your hostage ain't no compliment, stitch," Left Ned said.

"He means that he knows we like you enough, we won't leave you with him for long," I said.

"Hostage is hostage, Matilda," Right Ned said. "I won't play that role."

"Fine," I said. "Then I'll do it."

"No," Quinten said. "You will ride with me."

"If someone has to act as a bargaining chip, it should be me," I said. "I'm the only one strong enough to hold my own against both of them, if it came down to a fight. Since I happen to be galvanized too. Not human."

Foster, still on his back, chuckled again.

Abraham's head was bent, but he smiled.

Quinten exhaled loudly. "You make everything harder than it has to be."

"Really? I'm pretty sure I just solved our problem."

"Fine," Quinten said. "We'll all ride up together, all of us in rifle range. But Matilda still rides with me."

"Great," I said. "Love the plan. I'm driving." I seated myself on the bike Abraham had been driving.

Abraham pointed with the knife. "Take the quad; it has the best engine. Foster?"

Foster pushed up, walked over to me, and held out the keys to drop into my palm. "Third sticks."

The keys fell, and the world slipped sideways into the scent of roses and the soft echo of a bell.

I stood there, my hand extended. There were no keys in my palm. There was no Foster, no apple field.

I was in a darkened auditorium, can lights set in the high ceiling casting small circles of light against dark maroon carpet. The stage was in front of me, unlit, with a huge, clear screen behind it. The chairs that filled the curve of the space were dark and uniform and empty.

"Matilda?" A man's voice said.

I spun to my left, expecting Slater.

Instead, Welton Yellow sat in a chair just a few feet behind me.

"Welton?" I said, surprised and incredibly happy to see him.

"All patched back together," he said with a strained hiss at the end of his words, as if his lungs were being powered by more than just his body.

Welton Yellow, head of House Technology, wore a thick coat and loose trousers that made him appear bulkier than I'd ever seen him. His straight brown hair was cut too short, shagging high on his forehead to make his heavy-lidded eyes even more prominent and sunken, with dark circles ringing them.

He'd never been a tanned or athletic man, but he seemed pale and fragile under the bulk of his clothes. He might be alive, but he was not well.

"I know you don't have much time," he said, "and you're probably happy to see me alive. I'll just answer the things I think you need to know. I've been tracking the time ripples since you were sucked back into time, and predicted this would be a cross point. Got that right, so gold stars for me." He smiled, and the mechanical wheeze of his breath filled the room as he continued.

"There must be a piece of the Wings of Mercury machine in the main timeway—your timeway. And, yes, I know this isn't the most viable reality, which might be a relief from your point of view, since Quinten, your grandmother, Abraham, Gloria, Neds, and Foster all died in that damn blast."

"I'm so sorry," I said, knowing how much he cared for Foster.

He gave me a sad nod. "Are they alive in your timeway?" he asked, a small hope in his eyes.

"Yes. All of them."

"Am I?"

"I don't know. It hasn't been that long for me since I've been back."

"That's fine," he said, talking fast again, as if there were a timer counting down. "It doesn't matter. I'm not very alive here either. But they're alive in your time. And we are going to keep them that way."

"What happened to you?" I asked. "Why aren't you dead? I saw Slater kill you."

He shrugged, but it was a jerky motion, as if all of his joints weren't quite working fluidly together.

"My cousin, Libra, had me . . . reconstructed. It might not have been my best idea to put an unstable woman who is very bad at saying good-bye in charge of all the technology in the world." His light tone betrayed the shadows of pain etched in his face.

"What about Oscar?" I asked.

"Dead from the gunshot. His snake of a brother, Hollis, is destroying all the good Oscar did in the world. And, before you ask, the galvanized are being permanently beheaded and imprisoned. This is not much of a world to live in right now. Not for me. Certainly not for you. I doubt it will get any better for a long time to come, not that I'll be alive to see it. But there has been no sign of Slater. I suppose that's a plus."

"He's in my timeway, trying to rule the Houses."

"Prick," he said. "Do me a favor, Matilda, dear. Cause that bastard a lot of pain before you kill him."

"I'll do everything I can to make him pay."

"You are a sweetheart." He paused a second to breathe again. "I've looked for the cause of the time slips. The Wings of Mercury machine has been destroyed in this timeway. It, or some part of it, must be in yours."

"I don't think so. Slater's looking for it too, and Quinten hasn't even heard of it."

"Well, fuck," he said. "I thought he might have it. That was the easy answer."

"Do you know the hard answer?"

"Probably. You and Slater both went back in time. Your modern minds caught in galvanized bodies. That created a loop between you. A current that you both complete. Positive and negative. Time is flowing between your immortal bodies. Until that is broken, the ripples will not stop."

"So, how do we break that current?"

"My best guess? You kill him, or he kills you." The mechanical inhalation filled the room again. "That should also put an end to the echoing, the ripples of these timeways. But it's not going to be easy."

"Nothing about this has been easy," I said. "I'll find him. I'll kill him."

"Love the sentiment, but there's a wrinkle. Whatever

is triggering the time slips won't allow either of you to kill the other."

My fingers fanned up to my collarbone where the bullet had struck me and disappeared.

"I think I've already experienced that. So, how do I kill him?"

"First you'll need to break the circuit between you before he does."

"I thought you said killing him breaks the circuit."

"No. Killing him anchors the timeway you are in—whichever one that is—as the strongest, most viable reality. The other will disappear. So you'll want to make sure you kill him in the time you want to live in."

That would be the one where my brother, grandmother, and all the rest of the people I loved were alive. But I didn't know if Welton was alive. "Welton, I'm sorry . . ."

"Hush. I just told you which reality I want to thrive. Yours. Got that?"

"Yes. So, how do I break the circuit?"

"Find the thing that was a part of the Wings of Mercury machine. The thing that has traveled in time. Break it; destroy it. *Then* kill Slater. In that order. And twist the knife a couple times for me, will you?"

"I promise I will. Do you know what part of the machine I should be looking for?"

"I have no idea. I'll keep looking. In case we meet again."

"I hope we do," I said. "Thank you, Welton."

"It's nothing." He lifted a couple fingers by way of a wave. "Tell me: is Foster okay?"

I nodded. "He's wonderful. Lying on his back, eating apples in an orchard and watching the clouds go by."

Welton grinned. "Nice."

"I'll tell him all about you once I get the chance."

His smile never wavered, even though his eyes were sad. "I'd like that. And if you get the chance . . . tell him . . . well, tell him I loved him."

I opened my mouth to make that promise, but no sound came out. The world crumbled around me, whisking away with a dizzy twist and ringing with the scent of roses.

I held my breath. Then the world stopped and I was standing in the apple orchard, Foster in front of me.

The keys hit my palm.

"Oh," he said, a frown creasing heavy lines into his face.

"It's fine." I was out of breath even though I hadn't moved. "I'm fine."

Quinten was grumbling about me driving and otherwise paying no attention to me. Abraham was watching me through narrow eyes, but said nothing. Neds were already getting on one of the bikes.

I took a few more breaths to calm myself and let my brain settle back into the here and now. If Welton was right, I had the beginning of a plan. I needed to find the piece of the Wings of Mercury machine before I could kill Slater.

Quinten finally looked over at me. "What?"

I held up my hand and pointed at my stitches to remind him I was as strong as a galvanized, which meant I was much stronger than him. "Don't make me wrestle you for the driver's seat," I said.

Besides, his color was still pale and a little green. I knew he was in a lot of pain, no matter how hard he was trying to ignore it. I hoped he was a smart enough man to know when to stow his ego.

I swung my leg over the four-wheeler, and he reluctantly got on the back.

"Ready?" I asked.

"I'll tap on your left arm and point to give you directions," he said.

"If you feel sick, tap on my right arm, and I'll pull over," I said. "We'll need to talk when we get somewhere safe."

"Everything okay?" he asked, tensing behind me.

"Yes. It can wait." I started the engine, revved it, and waited for Neds and Abraham.

To my surprise, Foster was driving, not Abraham. I gave Abraham a look, and he twitched his eyebrow up, unconcerned.

Didn't look like he cared that he wasn't in the driver's seat.

Of course, if they were in danger of getting shot at, I knew Abraham was a deadly good marksman. So maybe it made sense that he ride shotgun. Or maybe they'd done this before.

For how easily they settled in, I thought they'd done it often.

Mercenaries. Killers. Thieves.

And men I was fighting to keep alive. Welton loved Foster. Foster deserved to know that.

Abraham gave me a huge wink and another grin.

Jesus. That man made everything in me collide.

Foster started the engine, and so did Neds. We all gave each other the "okay" nod, and I guided the four-wheeler out onto the street and took off at a decent speed.

I was glad they'd given us the quad. I could tell by how Quinten was holding on that he was more fatigued than he was admitting.

He pointed straight over my left shoulder, and even

though there were no intersections or side roads to speak of, I was glad to know I was going in the right direction.

My plan was to get my brother into House Earth and take him straight to Gloria. If she was well enough, she had the medical skills to make sure he wasn't hurt more than I knew.

Internal bleeding came to mind. Something deep and pernicious I couldn't scan for.

After Gloria or another doctor checked him out, I'd tell him about the last time slip with Welton.

And then we'd need to come up with a way to stop Slater.

And the plague.

Abraham had said I was a part of House Earth, and Quinten had said that too.

I didn't point out to either of them that I was also a galvanized, which meant House Earth should be just as suspicious about me as they were about Abraham and Foster.

Although in my time, I had been an integral part of House Brown. We'd done what we could to keep the fact that I was galvanized away from most House Brown notice, not because they thought galvs were killers, but because we thought it was best if the heads of Houses didn't find out a modern galvanized existed.

We'd failed pretty spectacularly at that.

It wasn't long before the fields began looking even more tended and the road more traveled. Several vehicles were parked alongside the road, with people working the land. A few nonmotor bicycles passed us, with men and women and a few kids of various ages upon them.

Even though this wasn't my world, and in many ways it lacked the advancement that had made our lives easier, the people we passed were clean, clothed, and seemed both happy and healthy. The land supported strong crops, the air was clear, and the very real and constant presence of the Houses I'd grown up dealing with and having to avoid and hide from was missing.

Yes, there were ferals, mercenaries, plagues, and dictators who had access to bombs, but my world had been riddled with all those things and had not seemed nearly as peaceful as this world.

Maybe changing time hadn't been all bad.

Especially if what Welton had said was true.

Not only were my brother, Neds, and Abraham alive in this time, but it also appeared House Earth had profited from the change in how the world was ruled.

It made me feel a lot better about what we had done and what we had all given up to make it happen.

Quinten tapped my left shoulder and pointed to the west. I glanced that way. Beyond the swell of the field were the foothills. Nestled in the valley between two rises was a walled city.

Quinten had called it a compound, but it had to be at least a couple of square miles of buildings, roads, rooftops, trees, and fields, all enclosed by massive stone and metal walls with watchtowers set at regular intervals.

House Earth Compound Five wasn't a small sheltering of shacks or survivalists hunkering down against a threat. It was a living, bustling, thriving town.

The road swung wide toward the compound, and since Quinten wasn't telling me otherwise, I followed it. About half a mile from the wall, the road was blocked by a smaller wall, with a lighthouse-looking structure at either side of the road.

Not lighthouse—guard tower. The road was gated, and just outside that gate was another enclosed structure. That appeared to be a checkpoint or tollbooth.

I could see the movement of people with guns behind the glass windows in the lighthouse towers, and knew they had a heck of a view from up there. Could probably see people coming for miles.

Which meant they'd seen us.

And if they had radio with the other city towers along the main wall and road wall, then they had a very nice system in place for keeping people, friend or foe, just where they wanted them.

Quinten tapped on my right arm, the signal for me to stop. I slowed and brought the quad to a stop. Neds pulled up on my left, and Foster and Abraham pulled up on my right.

Quinten got off the four-wheeler and walked toward the booth, his hands causally out to either side. "Morning!" he called out, while he was still thirty feet away from the booth, which was behind the gate.

"Morning," a woman's voice answered. "What's your business today?"

I glanced up at the guard towers. Yep. A single shooter in each tower had what appeared to be very sophisticated rifles aimed at us.

Well, aimed at Foster and Abraham.

"My name is Quinten Case. I'm a farmer, a stitcher, and a friend of House Earth. I came to see Gloria Epris. We're friends. I also request an immediate meeting with the custodian."

"The custodian only sees whom he chooses."

"Tell him Quinten Case is here. He'll see me."

She paused. I flicked a glance up at the towers, half expecting to see a bullet already coming my way.

"Names of your companions, Quinten Case," she said brusquely, "and their business."

Quinten didn't step any closer, and his hands were

still away from his body and any weapon he might carry there. He half turned toward me. "That is my sister, Evelyn Case, and our farmhand and friend, Neds Harris.

"The two galvanized came to our farm in offer to help us. Foster and Abraham. I will vouch for them inside these walls, and they will be in our company at all times."

"That's all well and good, Quinten Case," she said, "but galvanized do not step beyond this gate. For any reason."

"Call the custodian," Quinten said. "He is expecting me. We'll wait." Quinten turned and strode—well, walked without weaving; that head wound needed tending again—back to us.

"You know the custodian?" Abraham asked.

"I knew him before he was the custodian."

I handed Quinten the canteen of water, which he accepted.

"Evelyn?" I asked.

He nodded while he drank, then tipped the canteen down. "Sorry. But no one here knows you as anyone else."

"Does anyone here know me at all?"

"A few people." At my look, he added, "We do have friends. Can't spend a life hidden out on our property forever."

Actually, we could. And we had. Or at least I had, back in another life.

"Not with the Grubens as neighbors," Right Ned said. "Those people talk, and all the world hears them. Terrible gossips."

Left Ned grunted in agreement.

"So, how long do we just stand out here in the open?" I asked.

"Until they call the custodian," Quinten said.

"And how long will that be?"

He swigged back water, then handed the canteen to me. I took a drink; gave it to Neds.

"Shouldn't be long. He's been waiting for me."

Abraham took his eyes off the tower guard long enough to glance at Quinten. "What business do you have with the custodian?'

"Personal business," Quinten answered.

Funny—that's the same excuse Abraham had tried to pull on me.

If I were Abraham, this is the point where I'd get nervous. Looking at the situation from his side, he was riding into a House Earth encampment on the word and reputation of a man he'd met only a couple days ago. A man he knew didn't trust him, and, for the most part, didn't like him.

Plus, it was a good bet most of the people on the other side of that wall wouldn't want anything to do with the murderous, thieving galvanized.

Once again, I wondered what was Abraham's real agenda in following us here. Seemed like an awful lot of trouble and risk to go through.

"We could always wait out here while you go in," I said.

"No," Quinten said. "We all go in together."

"Quinten Case and companions. Please approach the gate," the woman called out. We all got off our bikes and walked with them to the gate.

"Leave your bikes on the road," she said.

The woman sat in the booth between the towers, a speaker system set up so we could hear her.

I studied her through what I assumed was bulletproof glass. She wore an official-looking brown jacket with a slash of black across the arm. Her hair was steel gray and cut short, with a swing of bangs. She measured us all in turn, and I wouldn't be surprised if she wasn't writing up a report on our every move.

The gate rolled aside on tracks, and beyond it stood six heavily armored, heavily armed guards. They each wore helmets with face shields, so it was a little hard to make out features, but I'd say they were a mix of light and dark, men and women, all of them strong and very clearly there to shoot our heads off if we got too rambunctious.

I had the itch to walk toward them with my hands up, but Quinten was just making it a point to keep his hands away from his body, though he was carrying the wooden case in one hand and his duffel in the other.

Abraham and Foster looked like they did this so often, it had become boring and tedious.

So I tried to relax and follow their lead.

"Please step into the clean room," the booth woman said.

The guards surrounded us and marched us down past the booth to another concrete structure that looked blast proof. They opened the door, and we all stepped inside.

The room was lined with benches; no windows, with bare bulbs set in a row down the middle of the ceiling. There was a privacy curtain, which hung open at the far end of the room, but the only things behind it were more concrete wall and wooden bench.

I noted the benches were bolted into the floor, which was also concrete.

I'd seen jail cells with more charm.

All the guards stepped in with us, except for two, who remained outside the door.

Quinten set his case and duffel on the bench, then sat and started unlacing his boots.

Neds sat too, and started on their laces.

"Should I?"

Quinten pointed to the privacy area. "Just take off your shoes, jacket, and weapons. You can stay in your pants, socks, shirt, and bra. Unzip the duffel so they can search it."

From the way he said it, this was common practice for entering the compound. I suppose it made sense. If you lived in a walled-off compound, you'd want to keep track of what people were bringing into it.

"If I'm staying in my clothes, why do I need a privacy curtain?"

"It's standard. A female soldier will pat you down. She might require you to remove something."

Foster and Abraham hadn't moved to take anything off. I caught Abraham's gaze and raised my eyebrows. He gave me another wink.

Lord. He was either full of trouble or full of himself.

Maybe a dangerous combination of both.

I trudged over to the end of the building and pulled the curtain. Took off my jacket, which stung a little as my stitches and cuts pulled too tight, then tugged off my boots. I deposited my duffel on the bench and unholstered my revolver, which was out of bullets anyway, and the knife I kept on me.

I sat and waited.

The guards didn't say anything, but I could hear Quinten and Neds taking off their gear. The curtain hadn't closed all the way. Through the thin gap I could see Abraham. He was methodically removing his weapons and placing them down with a sort of practice eye for display. I didn't know if he was trying to impress the guards or just make sure they understood how many deadly things he had on him.

Things he could still easily use to kill them.

Not that he'd need anything more than his bare hands.

Abraham caught me watching him and slid me that crooked grin. Then something about his manner changed. He liked that I was watching him strip down.

And so he stripped down for me. I didn't know if Quinten and Neds had taken off their shirts, but Abraham did, making sure I saw his bare arms; the stretch of his wide, muscular back puzzle-pieced together with whips of black thread; the hard, carved muscles bunching across his shoulders; and as he turned, his hard chest and stomach with the bandage I had tied there.

Somehow he did it all as if it was just the way he moved, just the way he always took off his clothes when under gunpoint in a blast bunker. But he paused and flexed, catching shadow and light with a photographer's unfailing instinct, displaying his body for me.

When he bit his bottom lip and slanted me a smoldering look to make sure I was watching, I scrunched up my face and stuck my tongue out at him.

He grinned, a wicked, crooked thing, then glanced over at the sound of the door opening.

Footsteps brought a woman into my limited range of view. She was wearing the same armor as the other guards, but paused outside my curtain.

"I'm going to step in now," she said.

"Okay."

She pulled back the curtain, took a quick second to note where I was sitting and everything that I'd laid out on the bench next to me, except for my boots, which were still on the floor next to my stocking feet.

"Are you carrying any other weapons on your body?" she asked as she stepped into the small space with me.

"No."

"Please stand and face me."

I did so.

She closed the distance. "I am going to feel down your arms, legs, stomach, and under your breasts."

"All right. I'm bandaged across my rib cage."

"Understood."

She quickly and efficiently patted me down, including running the backs of her fingers beneath my breasts.

"Turn, please."

I turned. She patted me down from that angle, running her hands over my pockets.

"Step to your left."

I stepped.

"I'll be looking in your duffel now."

"Okay."

It all seemed so formal and odd. When I had known House Brown, they were more like a big, mismatched family. Odd collections of farms and cooperatives working together to help each other stay beneath the notice of the other, more powerful Houses.

This House Earth had rules in place, and armed guards the other House Brown would have never dreamed of.

She rifled through my belongings rather quickly, and didn't seem particularly surprised at any of it.

"All right, you can put your boots back on, and your jacket."

I did so as she remained right where she was, watching me.

She opened the curtain so I could see into the rest of the room. Quinten and Neds had their shirts on. But both Foster and Abraham had stripped down to their breeches, which were now beltless.

Abraham had on a sort of smile that said there was a good helping of anger simmering right beneath it.

The guards also looked a little more tense, judging by their body language.

"You are free to go, Quinten Case, Neds Harris, Evelyn Case," one of the guards said.

"What about Abraham and Foster?" I asked.

"They will remain here, under guard."

I looked at Quinten. This was his chance to say something before I jumped in and explained that that was not going to stand with me.

"That's not what I agreed to," Quinten said.

Several of the guards shifted their aim to him, and I could see the wave of tension that rolled through them.

I didn't blame them. Galvanized were damn hard to kill.

Even with bullets.

Even with a lot of bullets.

And Quinten wanted not just one, but two to walk the streets of this town.

Well, three, really.

The door opened, and a man's voice called out. "Quinten Case. What sort of trouble are you bringing to my doorstep this time?"

I knew that voice. I'd know him anywhere.

"Profitable trouble, Welton," Quinten said. "As always."

The guards moved aside to allow Welton to step forward.

He *was* alive.

And, yes, I was grinning.

Welton Yellow. I'd known him as the head of House Yellow, Technology. An all-around meddler and ultimate friend to the galvanized and my family.

He looked so healthy here. His brown hair hung over his eyebrows, under which could be seen his wickedly clever eyes. He was as pale as ever, but not sickly, with shadows collecting under his languid eyes. But instead of the yellow T-shirts I was used to him wearing, or the odd, bulky gear he'd had on in the other timeway, he wore a loose brown henley and a pair of ripped-up jeans that pooled into the tops of his work boots.

I'd never seen Welton in workman's clothes before. They suited his casually lazy persona.

And now here he was, lean, intense, ruling—though not the same House he had ruled before—and looking every bit the clever slacker while he was doing it.

"Quinten Case," he said again, even though his gaze flicked over Neds and me, then took some time to consider Abraham and Foster.

Did it linger a moment longer on Foster, his eyes taking in the massive scarring and mismatched bits of the big galvanized? Was there a slight shift in Welton's breathing? Did his eyes dilate?

Did he actually recognize Foster, who had been his best friend since he was a child in the past only I should remember?

Quinten was a genius. But so was Welton. Just as smart, and maybe even more conniving. If there was a way to remember a time that no one but I remembered, I thought maybe Welton would have discovered it, even though he was no longer a part of House Technology.

"Custodian Welton," Quinten said. "I was just explaining to your guards that my companions will be staying with me, and that I will vouch for their behavior within these walls."

"I believe introductions are in order. Who are your companions?" Welton pulled off leather gloves and then folded them in his hands once before tucking them into his belt. He had weighed us each in turn and now seemed as interested in us as if we were dirt on the bottom of his shoes.

"My sister, Evelyn Case," Quinten said, motioning my way. "Our farmhand, Neds Harris, and the galvanized, Foster and Abraham."

Welton shook his head and made a *tsk*ing sound through his teeth. "You know the rules, Quinten. No galvanized in the gates."

"Not even my sister?" Quinten asked quietly.

Welton's eyebrows hitched up higher into his hair, and he turned to look at me.

For a second, everyone in the room turned to look at me.

I was just as surprised as the rest of them that Quinten had just outed me as galvanized. So much for keeping the family secret secret.

"Evelyn, wasn't it?" Welton asked, as if we'd just met at some sort of tea social instead of under the careful observation of more than a dozen armed guards. He strolled my way. "It is *very* good to make your acquaintance."

Quinten's shoulders tightened, but he didn't look back at me. I knew he was worried whether I was going to play by the rules, if I was going to agree to go by Evelyn's name.

If I was going to let Welton and all these guards know I was galvanized.

And while I hated lying about being someone I was not, the presence of guns was enough to convince me to hold to my name preference for when my brother wouldn't get shot for my stubbornness.

"It is," I said, stepping up so close to the guards, I could smell their shaving cream and sweat.

Welton offered his hand.

I took it. His finger slipped down along the inside of my wrist and rubbed just once over the threads there.

We shook.

The guards twitched a bit, and I was kind of hoping Welton would tell them to relax, since, one, they wouldn't be able to kill me before I killed Welton now that I was in contact with him, and, two, I wasn't the one who would come out of this injured if things went bad.

"Hey, it's good to see you," I said.

He pursed his lips. "That's a cheeky greeting."

"Sorry," I said. "Very pleased to meet you, custodian, sir."

The smile he couldn't seem to keep out of his eyes quirked his lips. "You are terrible at this."

"I know. Um . . . this is probably what you want to see." I lifted up my hand and pushed my undershirt sleeve back so he could see the stitches around my wrist and elbow.

"And?" he asked.

Right. Everyone was stitched to some degree in this world. So he needed to see other, permanent stitches. I pulled my hair away from the side of my face, revealing the stitches that ran down my neck.

"And?" he asked.

"Sorry, but that's where the peep show ends. Trust me. I'm stitched. Pretty much everywhere, and pretty much permanently."

"You're his sister?"

I tipped my chin up. "Yes, I most certainly am."

"So *very* interesting. Aren't you an interesting thing?"

"If I say yes, instead of kicking you in the nuts for calling me a thing, will you let me into your compound?"

The smile spread out into a smug grin, then faded. "Quinten," he said, looking at my brother over my shoulder, "you have been keeping secrets from me. Shame. But now that I've met her, perhaps I understand why. You and Evelyn may enter."

"Not without Neds, and Foster and Abraham," Quinten said.

Welton angled his head and stared at Quinten for a long moment. "If any of this visit of yours goes wrong, you, personally, will be the one who pays."

"I'm good for it. You know that," Quinten said.

Welton waited a moment. Maybe just for the dramatic flair; maybe weighing if we, and whatever history Quinten had with him, was worth the possible trouble and danger we were bringing into this compound by dragging two galvanized mercenaries along behind us.

Three galvanized, if you counted me, and we'd made sure that Welton knew just exactly what I was.

"Stand down, gentlemen and lady," Welton said, his demeanor slipping forward a gear into something that might almost be commanding. "These fine people and their companions are now our guests."

The guards didn't seem to relax much.

Welton reached over and touched my arm. "You have *so* much to tell me, Evelyn Case. I want to know everything about you. But first, I'm afraid your brother and I have a little catching up to do."

"She'll come with us," Quinten said, sitting on the bench and carefully slotting his feet into his boots.

"Oh?" Welton glanced over at him. "I see. Please escort Mr. Harris and Abraham and Foster to a room for the night. Don't worry," he said, and cut off what I'd been about to say. "You and Quinten will be rooming right next to them this evening. Abraham, Foster"—he nodded at each—"and Neds Harris. Please get dressed and follow my guards. We will return your weapons to you when you leave the compound."

Abraham angled his simmering gaze down on Welton. "What guarantee do I have?"

"My word. That's all you'll get."

Welton held eye contact, then took my hand again.

His fingers were warm and long and callused, which made me smile, because the old Welton I'd known hadn't done a hard day's work in his life.

"Now, let's the two of us talk while we walk."

"Um, sure," I hedged. "Can I take my duffel?"

"No, no. That stays here."

"It has my change of clothes in it."

"You do understand you are my guest here, and I am at the beck and call of your comfort. A lovely new outfit for the lovely young lady, perhaps?"

"She's not interested in you, Welton," Quinten said, picking up his case and duffel, then striding forward. "She only dates men."

Welton burst out laughing. It was a deep, sort of goofy chuckle that make me smile. He dropped my hand—dropped the act of flirting with me—and turned to Quinten. He draped his arm over Quinten's shoulder. Quinten winced a little at the contact, but Welton didn't seem to notice.

"Spreading rumors again, I see," Welton said as they walked out of the building, and the rest of us followed. They headed toward the wall that surrounded the town.

"Just trying to even the score," Quinten said.

"Oh, come, now. You're not still pouting over that little miscommunication last year?"

"It wasn't a miscommunication. You were bored and decided to take it out on me."

"Well, yes, that too," Welton agreed.

I glanced behind me. Neds had lingered, allowing Foster and Abraham to step out before him. The guards threw sideline looks but walked on either side of Foster and Abraham.

Neds caught my glance, and Left Ned nodded just slightly, encouraging me to keep up with Welton and Quinten.

And since Welton seemed to be the man in charge of this place, I decided it probably was safest for all of us if I did just that.

12

*He knows. Slater knows I've reached you. Good.
I hope he comes for me.*

—W. Y.

"Finally," Welton said, shutting the huge, polished wooden door behind us. "Sit. Get comfortable. Talk."

We had taken a cab to Welton's office. Despite Welton's insistence otherwise, guards had accompanied us every step of the way through the streets of the town, and finally to the doorstep of his office building and the threshold of his office.

Right now, four guards stood outside the door, and if Welton hadn't threatened to demote them, all of them would be in the room with us.

The office was very nice. Redwood furniture padded by expensive woven-tapestry and leather upholstery, heavy velvet curtains on the three tall windows, red-and-gold wallpaper styled in tasteful patterns.

His desk was a more modern affair, minimal compared to the rest of the setting, with black wrought iron cast and twisted into a geometric design. The wrought iron work was also reflected in the shelves, which contained books, statues, framed artwork, and a couple of potted plants.

Quinten settled down in a large leather chair, so I took the couch.

"Water? Wine?" Welton asked.

"Both," Quinten said.

Welton lifted an eyebrow toward me.

"Water, please."

He moved over to a wet bar on one side of the room, poured a small glass of wine, and filled two larger glasses with water.

"Gloria told me about the bomb threat," Welton said. "What more can you tell me?"

"Nothing good," Quinten sighed.

Welton turned with a tray of glasses and gave me the water and the water and wine to Quinten.

He took a small glass of wine for himself, leaned against the edge of his desk, and held it up in a toast. "To living to see another sunrise." He sipped the wine, and so did Quinten. "Talk to me, Case."

I drank the water, grateful for how clean and cool it was.

"Someone found out I was digging in House records," Quinten said. "I don't know who, but the only ones who knew everything I was doing were you and Gloria."

"Gloria wouldn't betray you. Or us," Welton said.

"I know." Quinten leveled an accusatory stare at him.

Welton shook his head. "There is no reason for me to betray you. I wouldn't do so. Not over this. Not over ending this damn plague for good. You know how many people I've lost. Friends. Family."

"I need you to swear on your dead mother's grave that you didn't double-cross me for whatever the hell plan or scheme you have in the works, with whatever the hell House or non-House you want something from."

Welton set his wineglass down and held up one hand, pinkie and thumb tucked together in his palm. "I swear to you, on my oath, on my dead mother's grave, on our friendship. I did not tell anyone or lead anyone to the knowledge or information you were looking for or to you. Is that clear?"

Quinten studied him for a minute. "Jesus, Welton. If it's not you and not Gloria, then we have a leak in the line."

He nodded. "It's worrisome. How did you receive the information that someone knew you were looking through records?"

"Three mercenaries knocked on my kitchen door."

"They got past the dragons?"

"Lizards. And yes. Two of them are Abraham and Foster."

"Interesting. Let's get back to that. Who was the third?"

"Sallyo."

He raised eyebrows. "Impressive. The job must have been paying well for her to take it. Did you convince her to tell you who she was working for?"

"House Fire. We know that much. And then we know this." He reached into his duffel and pulled out the letter from Slater.

I was surprised he was going to share it. That single action raised Welton right back into my Very Trustworthy category.

"Slater?" Welton asked.

"Do you know him?"

"Of him. Just recently he's made a move to put himself in top position in House Fire. Seems a few of the other sub-heads of Houses have suddenly contracted the One-five plague and died, leaving him conveniently in the position to seize the reins of power. Strange that the first confirmed cases of the plague, each strain of it over the years, has come out of House Fire. I've wondered just how much of that is a coincidence and how much might be by design."

"You think someone in House Water is infecting House Fire people with the plagues?" Quentin asked.

"Quite the opposite," Welton said. "If I were a head of a minor House who also happened to be galvanized and immune to the plague, well, let's say I wouldn't dismiss the usefulness of a well-placed 'natural' death or two."

"You think Slater's behind the plague?" Quinten asked.

"He might be. Or not. I really don't know," Welton said. "He has declared martial law."

"What?" Quinten said. "Why? How?"

"He has closed House Fire and accused House Water of bombing House Earth Compound Seven last night."

All the air went out of Quinten, and he buried his head in his hands. "He didn't wait ten days. He was never planning to wait ten days."

"No. But your warning helped save hundreds," Welton said gently. "We were able to get the word out. They were preparing for attack."

"How many died?" Quinten asked.

"Twenty-one. Twice that many are hospitalized."

Quinten pulled his hands away from his face. "What kind of bomb?"

Welton's mouth set in a grim line. He twisted and picked up his wineglass again, and drained it down.

"It was a suicide bomber. A man walked into a crowded square and . . ." He flared his fingertips out, mimicking the explosion. "We have monitors for aerial attacks. We have teams who sweep the streets for remote devices. But one of our own turning House and taking us out, along with himself?" He shook his head. "We were not prepared for that, I'm afraid," he said, his voice a rough whisper.

"Jesus," Quinten said. "Jesus."

They both sat there in silence. I waited for one of them to get mad, to start making a plan of how we were going to take out Slater, but the very idea of him committing such unmitigated evil seemed to have shocked them both into silence.

But not me.

"He will set off a bomb a day, at the very minimum," I said. "You understand this is just the first, right?"

They both looked over at me, as if the couch had suddenly developed the ability to speak.

"Slater's goal is to rule all the Houses. He's worked his way up in House Fire, killed the people who stood in his way. If he thought House Fire was strong enough, he'd declare war on House Water, kill everyone who stood in his way, and take over ruling all the resources at their disposal. And along the way he'd take out House Earth. I'm assuming he wants Earth on his side to take down Water."

"But why?" Welton asked.

"For power," I said very clearly. "So he can *own* what he wants. And he wants everything. People, land, resources. Immortality."

Welton's eyes narrowed. "How do you know so much about him, Evelyn?"

"Stop," Quinten said. "It isn't that way. She's not working for him."

"You're her brother," he said. "You'd never expect your sister to be the one to betray you. But she does suddenly seem to have a very good idea of Slater's character—don't you think? Almost as if she's been around him."

"I have been around him before," I said. "This isn't the first time I've seen him do these kinds of things. He is galvanized, Welton. And so am I. We have history."

I let that hang in the air for a moment.

Welton stared at me, finally blinked. He shifted his stance a bit, and turned back to Quinten. "You told me your sister was a shut-in."

"A what?" I said.

"There were reasons why I told you that. There were reasons why I never let you meet her," he said.

"Obviously," Welton said. "And how, Quinten Case, do you explain your relation to a stitch?"

He inhaled, exhaled. "When Matilda—my flesh-and-blood sister Matilda—was very young, she got sick. She was going to die. Years before, Dad had received a very odd donation: a young girl who was in a coma."

"Donation?" I said.

"Yes."

"Do you know who donated me? Her?" I corrected.

"Dad said the only name he gave was Sanders."

Sanders. That was Foster's last name. Had he been the one who made sure I was given to my family? Had he been the one to find a way to give Evelyn living parents and a family who loved her? If so, I owed him . . . everything. I didn't want to bring it up in front of Welton. But I wanted to ask Foster later.

"We Cases had made a name in stitchery," Quinten continued. "Dad was the best—you know that."

"Until you came along," Welton added. "What did your father do with the young girl in a coma?"

"He didn't have the heart to use her for parts. And it was clear someone else had already done some rudimentary stitching on her. She appeared to be only eight years old. But Dad said during the years that he looked after her, she didn't age, nor did her body degrade. He thought that very, very odd.

"It turns out she was much older than eight. Well, her sleeping body was much older."

"How much older?" Welton asked.

"Three hundred years."

They let the silence settle between them.

"Galvanized," Welton said.

Quinten nodded.

"And then what happened?"

"When Matilda got sick, I thought . . . I thought I could transfer her thoughts, personality, and mind into the body of the sleeping girl. A sister in a coma is better than a dead sister, right?"

"Quinten . . ." Welton said quietly.

"I was young. Stupid. In a panic. Grieving. I was desperate. So I performed the procedure, transferred Matilda's personality. Except I had never tested it before. It was all wild speculation." He paused.

"Matilda passed away not long afterward. And then the girl woke. I thought I'd saved her. Saved my sister."

I spoke up because it didn't look like he was going to continue. "She woke up and she wasn't Matilda," I said. "She was Evelyn, the original girl who was born three hundred years ago. The original girl who fell into a coma."

Welton closed his eyes for a moment. "Oh, Quinten," he said.

"It was a shock," he said. "For everyone. Dad and Mom decided to raise her as if she were theirs, except she was stitched, immortal, a galvanized. There was no safe place in this world for her, except our farm. So we went to some . . . extremes to make sure she remained safe."

"But if she was in a coma, then woke and remained in hiding, how does she know Slater?" Welton asked.

"Because I'm not Evelyn any longer," I said. "I'm Matilda. And you're not going to believe this, but the same experiment from 1910 that killed all those people and made just a few people galvanized also fractured time. I've lived a life, an entire alternate life, where I was the one who woke up in Evelyn's body as Matilda. And in that life, Slater was very much alive, and very much the same vicious, power-mongering bastard that he is today.

"I know him, because in *my* life, in *my* world, he's already killed my family and all the other people I love."

Yep. Now he was paying very close attention to me. Probably trying to decide whether I was lying or not. Or if he should lock me away in a little padded room.

"She's telling the truth," Quinten said. "Or at least the only plausible thing that makes sense."

"How does *that* make sense?"

"It involves time travel," Quinten said.

"Bullshit," Welton countered.

"The Wings of Mercury experiment," I said. "It broke a piece of time, killed a bunch of people, and made the galvanized immortal. But then that piece of time winged back like a boomerang and *snick*ed into place, which would have killed even more people—billions. So Quinten and you came up with the formula for how someone could travel back in time to change the Wings of Mercury experiment. And, well, I was the one who went back."

He pressed his fingers to his mouth and stared at me. "You really believe what you're saying."

"I wish I had the luxury not to," I said. "What we need to focus on right now is how to stop Slater from bombing any more people."

"All the compounds have increased their security," Welton said. "Other than you two surrendering—which

I doubt will stop him, since he's already proven that he is more than willing to go back on his word—or killing the man, I don't know how to stop the bombs."

"So we kill the man," I said.

Welton considered me. "You do understand that he's the head of a House, don't you?"

"Yes. And that he's galvanized."

"Which was my second point. Difficult to kill an immortal creature."

"We're not immortal," I said. "We just don't die easy. The only way to end him, the only way to make sure no one else is hurt, is to shoot him in the brain. Repeatedly. Which means we either get some sniper rifles and a piece of real estate inside House Fire, or we do this up close and personal."

"We?" Welton asked. "Are you a trained assassin, Ms. Case?"

"No, I'm just pissed off. But if we need a trained assassin, there happen to be two we brought along with us."

"The galvanized."

I nodded.

"You're going to trust. . . ." He rubbed his palm over his face, pulling fingers back through his hair. "Okay, so let's assume I believe you are a strange combination of human and galvanized who just happens to also be a time traveler. And let's say I believe that you know Slater is out to destroy House Earth because he is a megalomaniacal dictator who has waited three hundred years to take over the world. Fine. Got that. Fine.

"But if you think I'm going to believe you and two other galvanized are going to kill one of your own out of the goodness of your hearts and your sentimental feelings toward humans, then you are out of your old, weird, time-traveling mind."

"Funny how you think I'm asking for your permission," I said.

"Matilda," Quinten warned.

"Matilda?" Welton said. "So you go by that name now?"

"I've always gone by that name, because it's mine. Also, it wasn't my idea to come here for your help."

"All right," Quinten said. "We don't need to fight. Welton, stop antagonizing my sister. Matilda, you don't need to get angry at him. It's a lot to swallow all at once."

I realized I'd leaned forward on the couch and set myself in a defensive position, ready to spring onto my feet if I needed to fight.

This situation we were dealing was bad enough without throwing Welton's doubting attitude into it. And it was serious enough that there wasn't any room for my attitude either.

I forced myself to sit back and take a deep breath. Calm was what we needed here. I could do calm. Maybe.

"Besides taking out Slater," Quinten said, "which we intend to do with or without your help, why we really came here was for this." He tapped his fingers on the wooden case he'd put on the chair beside him.

Welton's eyes lit. "What's in there?"

"The cure."

Welton drew his head back, and his face was very, very serious. "Don't joke about that, Quinten."

"I am not. I've gone through the last of the data, and I believe this can cure an infected plague victim."

"Gloria?" he asked.

"If I can, I want to try to save her. But this is untested. And my tests . . ." He flicked a look at me, and it was filled with a guilt I'd never seen there before. I just shook my head.

". . . my tests don't always go according to plan."

"Gloria would rather have a chance at life, no matter how uncertain, than no chance at all," Welton said. "Have you talked to her yet?"

"No. I thought I'd get your go-ahead first. If this works, we'll need to begin manufacturing. We'll need the ingredients, a lab that can handle the production, facilities to administer it."

"Done," Welton said. "Anything that I have is yours. And if there is something I don't have, I will acquire it."

Quinten nodded. "Good. I hoped you'd say that."

"How long do you think it will take before you know whether the cure is effective?"

"After I talk her into it? I'll need to filter her blood, and I'll want to do it slowly," Quinten said. "Eight hours for that. Twenty-four hours after that, we should know where we stand."

A day and a half. I hadn't realized it would take so long to see results from the cure. There was no way I was going to let my brother come with me to kill Slater when he had a chance to stay here and save the woman he loved. And I didn't want to entrust this experimental cure to anyone else. I was sure Quinten didn't either.

An uncomfortable reality settled on me. I'd need to kill Slater. Without Quinten.

Maybe that was for the best. Even though Quinten knew this world far better than I did, he was still human and injured. It would take almost nothing to kill him.

I couldn't do that. I couldn't watch him die again. It was too hard the first time.

This was my fight. This had always been my fight. And I would be the one who ended it.

13

Slater has enough power here; the Houses won't stand in his way. He's sending armed squads to kill anyone in House Brown who doesn't bow to his rule.

— *W.Y.*

It was decided that Gloria was the most pressing problem, with the clearest solution at hand. Welton called Quinten a cab, and he was sent to the hospital halfway across town to tend to her.

I offered to help. If what Abraham had said was true, I couldn't catch the plague, which would make me a great assistant. But both Quinten and Welton thought it would be better if we didn't draw any attention to the procedure.

They didn't want me there because I was galvanized, and no one trusted the galvanized.

Normally that would have made me angry, but I decided it might be for the best. I'd have a chance to talk to Abraham and Foster alone, without Quinten questioning me.

And we'd need that time to plan how we were going to kill Slater.

Two of Welton's guards silently escorted me in a car to the apartment I'd be staying in.

The sidewalks of the compound were made of level brickwork, the street a single lane of concrete. All the buildings we passed were sturdy single- and two-story structures that seemed to be warehouses. Solid wood or metal doors, glass in the windows. The street was clean of litter, except for leaves that had piled up here and there.

Not a lot of people milled about on the sidewalk and street right now, which could be chalked up to the time of day.

Anyone who needed to work the fields would have left at dawn and wouldn't be back until almost sunset.

Or it could be that no one wanted to be out if there was the possibility of a bomber in their midst.

The people I did see lingered outside buildings, a few on motorized and nonmotorized bikes, and several leaning over balconies or out windows.

The thing that immediately caught my attention was the wild array of colors everyone was wearing. In my time, you wore the color of the House you worked for, the House you were indebted to, the House that claimed you. On special occasions you could wear a splash of another color, but mostly once you worked for a House, you were required to announce that by what you wore.

But here the men, women, and children wore some sort of brown on them—shirt or trouser or skirt—but all other pieces, from hats to shoes to scarves and coats, were the color of the rainbow.

I smiled seeing this, and was even happier to see that everyone here appeared healthy and clean, just like the people I'd seen on the road.

Not that I thought this was a world without poverty or crime or sickness. But, in general, these people appeared to have more than just their necessities available to them.

House Earth, or at least this compound under Welton Yellow—I supposed he might not go by that name anymore—seemed to be thriving.

The second thing that caught my eye were all the stitched things. Little four-legged, furred chickens ran across the road in front of us like a flock of quail; bat-winged cats curled in windowsills; and a fenced-off area next to one building corralled llama-bison that looked like they could provide enough wool and meat to keep an army set for ten winters.

The cab took a side alley between two buildings and then stopped in front of a house with wooden siding that looked like it had been built around the same time as our farmhouse.

Of course, some of the similarity might also be the full fenced-off yard that encircled it, holding it oddly outside the flow of the other buildings, like an island in a sea of copycat structures.

The sign on the wooden front gate read STAY INN, which was a pretty groan-worthy pun.

The guard next to me in the back of the car opened the door and held it while I got out.

"Thanks," I said. "I got it from here."

"We'll escort you in," he said. "To make sure everything is satisfactory."

I was pretty sure he meant to make sure I didn't do anything stupid, like declare war on the inn owner.

The guard opened the gate for me as I walked through. He had impeccable manners.

"Thanks," I said as I strolled up into the house.

It was nice inside, a mix of white paint and dark wood

rubbed to a shine. The entryway opened up to show a staircase going upward on the left, a sitting room or library also to the left, and a large living area decorated with furniture taking up the rest of the space. A door directly on the other side of the room was open on what appeared to be another hallway.

A slender bird of a woman in her fifties strode into the room, her gray hair pulled up in a wave that ended in a bun on the back of her head.

She had on a pale blue silk blouse, black wide-legged slacks, and a smile. A chain with several small keys hung from the belt at her waist.

"Saul," she said to the guard. "It is so good to see you. Have you brought this lovely guest to my fine establishment?"

She folded her hands in front of her, rings on each finger throwing off glints of light.

"Poppy Stevens, this is Evelyn Case, a guest of Custodian Welton this evening," Saul said.

Poppy. Nice name.

"I believe she is to be set up in the arrangements you offered to the others of her kind."

"Her kind?" Poppy looked at me. Her eyebrows lifted, folding wrinkles across her forehead.

"The other galvanized who roomed here," I said as politely as I could. I didn't like being a kind or a type, and it grated on me that I was being treated differently just because I looked different on the outside.

Well, and also because people with similarities to me had committed crimes.

How was it fair to instantly judge me by people I'd never even met?

"Oh, yes, I see." She nodded, as if I'd just let her in on

a secret. Then she stepped over to me, her wide-heeled shoes making a schoolmarm *thunk* against the wood floor.

"Thank you, Saul," she said. "I'll see to her being set up as is appropriate. Is there anything else I can do?"

Saul hesitated. What did he want—to guard me twenty-four/seven? I sure hoped not.

"No," he said, "that's all we need at this time. Thank you, Ms. Stevens."

"Then we won't keep you from your duties any longer," she said.

Both guards took the dismissal for what it was, and left the room.

She shook her head. "They mean well," she said, "but sometimes I think the responsibilities they are given change the way they look at people. So." She pressed her hands together in a muted clap. "You're Evelyn. I'm very pleased to meet you. Come this way. I have a room set aside for you, and there will be another right next to it open for your brother."

"Thank you," I said, "but I don't want to put you out. We could share."

"Nonsense! This is going on Custodian Welton's bill, and he is a rascal of a man. It will be good for him to pay a fair price for a service for a change."

"That bad?" I asked.

"The man will negotiate the angle of the blade that kills him, given the chance."

"Still, I think I'd prefer to share a room."

"Well, then. We can make that happen too."

She strode off down the hall, comfortable in this place as if it were her own home. Which I thought it might actually be.

"The gentlemen Neds Harris are staying in this

room," she said, pointing to a door on the left of the hall. "And this will be your room."

She walked the hall, past three doors, and opened this one with another key.

The door swung inward, revealing a nice room with two neat beds separated by a nightstand with a lamp on it. Lace coverlets covered the beds, with warm blankets and pillows stacked on the foot of each.

In the middle of one of the beds was my duffel.

"Is this mine?" I asked, walking into the room.

"Yes. Just your clothing and other personal items. I was told that the weapons you were traveling with are still at the clean station and will be returned to you when you leave town."

If I was going to follow through with the plan I was making in my head, I'd need those weapons. But not yet.

This room also had a little wooden fireplace in one corner, and a stack of dry timber in a crate next to it.

But what really caught my eye was the bookshelf. A single padded chair took up the side of the room opposite the beds, and behind it was a floor-to-ceiling shelf filled with dozens of books.

"Oh," I said before I could curb my reaction. "Am I allowed to read the books?"

"Of course," she said with a chuckle. "Anything in the room is yours for the night. Will they do?" she asked. "I have other titles."

"This is lovely. Thank you. Very, very nice."

"Good. We have hot running water down the hall to your right for bathing," she said. "Towels are in the bottom drawer of the dresser. We also have indoor toilets down the hall and to your right. And, if you're curious, the two other men who arrived with Neds Harris are sharing this room." She pointed one door down. "I tried to offer them each private rooms, but they insisted they'd rather bunk together."

"Thank you for making me feel welcome," I said, really meaning it from the bottom of my heart. From the way people had given me side glances on the street and the constant presence of guards, I had begun to feel like a monster. A thing that didn't belong.

"My pleasure." She handed me a key for the room, which I slid into my pocket. "If you need anything, I'll be at the front desk. Oh," she said, and half turned. "Dinner will be served at sunset."

"Thank you."

I waited until she was down the hall and out of sight; then I walked over to Abraham and Foster's room. I knocked softly. "Abraham? It's me."

The lock turned and the door swung inward. Abraham stood there, one hand on the latch.

"Evelyn," he said, remembering to use the name Quinten had given the guards.

"Can I come in?"

He glanced past me. "Where's your brother?"

"One, he doesn't follow me around like a bodyguard—"

"Except that he does," he interrupted.

"—and, two, if you let me come in, that's what I want to talk about."

Abraham stepped aside, then shut the door behind me.

Foster sat in the chair angled in the corner of the room, reading from a hardback with scrolls of gold inlaid into it. He glanced over at me, then returned to reading.

"I'm going to lay all my cards on the table," I said, crossing my arms over my chest.

"That sounds interesting." He walked over to one of the beds and sat on the edge of it. "Please do go on."

"I want Slater dead."

"You'll get no argument from me on that."

"Which means I need someone who has been inside House Fire and who knows his schedule. I figure you know those things, or know who could give us that information."

"Sell us that information," he corrected. "Probably, yes."

"I need a hard positive out of you, Vail."

His mouth twitched at the sound of his name.

"Yes. I can get you the information on House Fire's layout and Slater's schedule. For a price."

"Can you get it in the next day?"

He sniffed. And Foster glanced over at me again.

"What are you suggesting?"

"Slater bombed one of House Earth's compounds last night. He's going to keep bombing until he gets what he wants."

"Your surrender?"

I shook my head. "He just wants me dead, because he knows I'll kill him if it's the last thing I do. No. He wants House Earth's surrender, and their resources and people. With House Earth conquered, he will have the manpower and resources to take on House Water."

"Why do you think that's his plan? Has he declared a missive to House Earth?"

"No. He's blaming the bombing on House Water."

"Are you sure House Water wasn't behind the bombing?"

"Were they?"

He paused. Chewed on the stitches at the corner of his lip. Shook his head once. "No. They are not."

"Are you working for them?" It made the most sense to me. House Fire had hired Sallyo to find me and

Quinten and to drag us in, under the threat of bombing House Earth. I was not so naive as to think House Water—whoever was running it—didn't already know what kind of a man Slater was. If I was in charge of House Water, I'd be working some serious counterintelligence.

"Why would you think I'm working for anyone but myself?" he asked.

"I never bought the coincidence of you partnering up with Sallyo when there was no money involved."

"You think so poorly of me?"

"I think you're smart and working your own angle on this. Did you or didn't you take a job for House Water?"

"I have worked for them in the past."

"Good enough. So, now I'm going to give you two very important pieces of information. And I swear, Abraham, if you betray me, I will hunt you down, shoot you, pluck out every stitch in your body, and tear you apart with my bare hands before I feed you to the first pack of ferals I can find."

"Bloody and specific. Just what I like out of my relationships."

I tried not to smile. "I like to be clear about my follow-through."

"Noted. Tell me whatever this is I'm agreeing is worth dying over."

"Quinten thinks he's found the cure for the plague."

Foster put his book back on the shelf next to his chair. "Thinks he's found it or has found it?"

"We won't know for a couple days."

"He's testing it on someone here?"

"Yes."

He inhaled, his eyes set on a medium distance, flicking as if working through all of the ramifications of that information. "That's. Massive. World changing," he said. "Does he intend to release it to the public?"

"Of course. And even if he doesn't, I will. No one should die because they can't get the medicine they need."

Foster grunted, and Abraham nodded. "What's the other very important piece of information?"

"He's created a substance that can kill galvanized."

Foster shifted forward in his chair. Abraham didn't move, but I could tell he was keenly interested in what I'd just said.

"Are you certain?"

"Yes. And I think we should use it on Slater."

"Or we could use a gun," he said.

"I'd feel better having a plan B. Slater isn't stupid. He's had three hundred years to engineer his takeover of the Houses. Hell, he was planning it for at least a hundred years before that. I think he's taken the necessary precautions against bullets."

"But this . . . substance?"

"It's called Shelley dust."

Foster made a small sound. He didn't look happy.

"Have you heard of it?" I asked. "Has it been invented before?"

"Yes," Foster breathed.

Abraham nodded. "Before the asteroid storm, before all information systems crashed and the power grids were destroyed, there was a scientist who experimented with something he dubbed Shelley dust."

"What happened to him and his information?"

"We killed him and burned his records."

Oh.

"Did he test it on anyone?" I asked.

"No." He said it in such a way that I knew Abraham

had been the one behind both killing him and burning his records. "How did Quinten get his hands on records that don't exist?"

"I don't know, but he has some of the Shelley dust in his case. And I'm going to get that before we leave."

"You seem to have set your mind on this. Where, exactly, are we going?" Abraham asked.

"To kill Slater. We'll need to break in and get our weapons. Also, we need to steal transportation."

Abraham cleared his throat and held up one finger. "Your brother is suddenly fine with us breaking House Earth's laws and stealing their things?"

"I don't know," I said. "I don't plan to tell him. He needs to stay here to make sure that plague cure works. There's too much of a chance he'll get hurt if he comes with us."

"He's already gotten hurt," Abraham said.

"Yeah, and that's all I can stand. This is my fight. Slater's angry at me. Quinten will just be collateral damage. I will not watch my brother die again. I won't. So, this is your chance. Are you coming to take out Slater with me, or am I doing this alone?"

"You aren't doing this alone," he said.

Those words, from him, meant a lot to me. "Good," I said. "We'll need to travel at night. I know that's dangerous, I know there are ferals—"

"It can be done," he said. "Though it won't be comfortable. Are we leaving tonight?"

"Yes. I don't know when Quinten is coming back, so we'll have to wait until he does, so he won't know we're gone. We'll leave while he's sleeping."

"You could drug him."

"What? No. I'm not going to poison my brother."

"Painkillers," Abraham said. "So he sleeps more heavily. Although poison isn't a bad idea either."

"I'll try the painkillers," I said. "We'll need a vehicle."

"Foster and I will take care of that. Shall we say midnight?"

"It's a date," I said.

"I wish it were," he mumbled.

I raised one eyebrow. "What?"

"I said I wish I were taking you on a date, Matilda Case."

"Revenge makes you feel all warm and romantic?"

He smiled. "You have no idea."

"All right," I said. "If we make it out of this and if we kill that bastard, I'll take you out for a celebratory coffee."

He pursed his lips and shook his head. "Dream a little bigger. We could do so much more than coffee."

"If we survive this—"

"And Slater dies," he added.

"—and Slater dies," I agreed, "I'll let you choose what we do to celebrate."

"You really do like to live dangerously, don't you?"

"Pretty much every damn day of my life." I walked to the door. "I'm trusting you on this, Abraham."

"On which part?"

"All of it. Don't let me down."

I let myself out and headed back to my room. I was twitchy and nervous. I decided to try to catch an hour of sleep before dinner. I needed to be as sharp and rested as I could be if we were going to survive the night.

14

Slater wants you dead. He wants all the galvanized dead—in every time. But he'll have to get through me to make that a reality.

—W.Y.

Dinner was a hearty serving of meat and squash and other vegetables that I didn't pay attention to, accompanied by tart rye rolls and sweet cider.

I tried to act like this was just a normal dinner, Neds and Abraham and Foster and me just enjoying our evening meal together, but my mind was turning a thousand reps a minute.

When will Quinten get home? Did it go well with Gloria? Will he go to sleep so I can steal the Shelley dust? Should I write him a note telling him not to worry? What kind of vehicle will Abraham and Foster steal? Can we get to our weapons without triggering any alarms?

And the one that terrified me: *What if this compound is next in Slater's line of bombings, and Quinten is killed? What if I never saw him again?*

"Something wrong with your mustard greens?" Right Ned asked.

I glanced up. A quick look at the table revealed that nearly everyone else had cleaned their plates, and I was sitting there holding a forkful of greens that I hadn't lifted to my mouth for I didn't know how long.

"No." I stuffed the fork in my mouth. "They're good," I said as I followed that with the rye roll. "Just drifted for a bit. Tired."

"Got something on your mind you want to share with the table?" Left Ned asked.

"Nothing no one doesn't already know."

Left Ned seemed to accept that as truth, but Right Ned narrowed the one eye that wasn't swollen from that bruise on his face. "Are you all right?" he asked.

"I really am," I really lied. "It's just been a rough ... well, an extra rough couple of days. I think I'll turn in early. Though I was sort of hoping Quinten would be here for dinner."

"Quinten visiting Gloria?" Left Ned asked.

Right. I hadn't told him anything about that.

"Yes. I was just wondering if he'd be in tonight."

"I'd guess so," Right Ned said.

I finished up my food pretty quickly. "Well, I'll see you all in the morning."

"Good night," Abraham said as he poured himself an after-dinner coffee.

Right Ned was still giving me that look. Like I wasn't behaving normally. Which, considering that he hadn't known this version of me very long, was sort of disturbing.

"What?" I asked him.

"I don't know. I just thought you'd want to talk tonight. About our upcoming travel plans."

He must mean our original plan of all going together to kill Slater. Yeah, well, that plan had changed. And just like I didn't want to see Quinten hurt, I didn't want to see Neds hurt either.

"Doesn't seem much need for talking about anything until Quinten shows up. Tell you what: when he comes in tonight, we can talk. If he stays with Gloria tonight, we'll all go see him tomorrow, early."

"All right," Right Ned drawled. Still didn't believe me, but he was willing to let it go for now.

I left the table and went right back to my room. I paced while trying to figure out what I should do, since I was definitely not tired. I decided to take stock of my supplies. I emptied my duffel on the bed and checked to make sure everything that wasn't a weapon was accounted for.

It appeared all there, even Evelyn's sewing kit and the medical supplies, including scalpels, syringes, clamps, balms, and bandages. Funny how they didn't consider a scalpel or the mix of medicines I carried weapons.

But I was thankful for that. I repacked the duffel and looked around the room for anything I could steal that might be useful. Unless I wanted to try to shove a blanket in there, I didn't think the books or framed pictures were going to help.

And, yes, I did consider stealing a couple books. They were a valuable commodity back in my time, but since I'd seen them in Foster and Abraham's room too, and Poppy had offered me additional titles, books must not be as rare here.

Which I liked. If I survived this, I was going to read every book I could get my hands on.

I was also, apparently, going to go on some kind of date with Abraham.

I frowned as I took off my boots. How had I let him talk me into that? Somehow our relationship had gotten all tangled up with our agreement to kill Slater.

Love and revenge make a heart grow fonder, I supposed.

I lay down on the bed, pulling just the coverlet over me. I didn't sleep for a long while, too busy thinking through the improbability of our very sketchy plan to kill Slater. Might be crazy to head out with only the barest idea of how we would end him. But, then, not having a plan while simultaneously rushing into a dangerous situation had never stopped me before.

Sleep eluded me, so I got up, found some stationery in a drawer, and wrote Quinten a note.

It probably wasn't a very good note, but I told him I loved him and I wanted him to stay here and save Gloria. I apologized for running off to do this without him, and promised I'd see him back on the farm as soon as I could. I also mentioned that I wasn't being kidnapped, and even if Foster or Abraham had tried to do that, I would be able to hurt them. Not just because I was strong, but because when I touched them, they regained sensation.

I tucked the letter under my pillow, intending to put it under his after he was sleeping. And then I decided to try for a few hours of shut-eye myself.

I dreamed of Abraham. The Abraham of my past. Except he was also the tattooed Abraham in the hallway who had been smiling, offering me coffee, calling me love. I dreamed we were in my bed, lace curtains shifting in the morning breeze, his arms around me, fingertips gently drawing down my shoulder.

In my dream, everything was right. Our lives. Our time. Our home. In my dream, we were right together.

Then my dream slipped away, leaving behind the faint fragrance of roses.

Quinten opened the door to the room and slipped in. There was almost no light in the hall behind him, but I could see that he was carrying both his duffel and his wooden case. He set the case on the floor and sat on the edge of the bed to untie his boots. He took off his jacket and lay down on top of his covers, pulling up one of the blankets from the bottom of the bed to cover himself.

I waited a moment. His breathing hadn't changed yet.

"Quinten?" I whispered.

"Yes?" he whispered back.

"How did it go?"

"We'll know more by morning."

"Did Gloria show any signs of improvement?"

He took several breaths before he answered, his voice burred with exhaustion. "Maybe. Her fever went down, and she was breathing easier."

"We should stay here to make sure she gets better," I said.

Again the pause, then: "I know we have to deal with Slater," he whispered. "I know that bombs are aimed at innocent people. . . ."

"Gloria is an innocent person too," I said. "Staying here is important. Making sure the cure works and that it can be manufactured is important."

He took several breaths. I thought he might be asleep. Then he whispered. "Thank you, Matilda."

I felt like pond scum for lying to him. Well, I hadn't lied about everything. Gloria was important to him, and I wanted her to have every chance to live. Quinten and his cure were her best chance. But I would not be staying with him.

I waited until his breathing went from an even rhythm to light snoring. When I was sure he was asleep, I got out of bed, put on my jacket, and slung my duffel over my shoulder, then took the note from under my pillow and set it on the nightstand next to his bed.

I knelt and as slowly and quietly as possible opened his wooden case.

He had told me the Shelley dust was very dangerous and that he didn't want me in it.

I peered at the bottles and jars and medical instruments in the case. None of it was Shelley dust.

The longer I stayed here, the higher the chance he'd see me. But I didn't want to leave without that dust. My heart was pounding so hard, I was amazed it hadn't woken Quinten up yet. Finally, my fingers caught on what I had thought was a seam in the lining of the lid, but was, in fact, a slender false drawer. I pulled that free, and three thin vials of Shelley dust clinked softly.

I glanced up at Quinten.

He hadn't stirred.

I took the vials, replaced the drawer, and latched the case, setting it in the same position as he'd left it. I wrapped the Shelley dust in a handkerchief and tucked that in my jacket pocket, then picked up my boots and very quietly left the room.

I tapped on Abraham's door with the pads of my fingers.

He opened the door. He was dressed for travel, though the lack of weapons covering every inch of his body seemed a bit out of place.

"Where's Foster?" I whispered.

"Getting a vehicle. He'll meet us in the alley. Did you get the dust?"

"Yes."

"Let me lead."

We snuck down the hallway and out the door. I cringed when the hinge creaked, but Abraham adjusted his grip on the latch and lifted the door to ease the hinge.

The cool day had turned into a cooler night, and a

cloud cover hid the moon. The night was dark, although here and there down the street a watery lantern burned.

Abraham and I jogged away from the house and down a street, where I made him wait while I put on my boots. That done, we hurried, hugging the shadows on the way to the alley.

He made a low, soft bird whistle that was answered from the end of the alley.

Foster.

We jogged down to him, and he kept walking, down another street and another. Every street we passed ticked up my worry. I had no idea what kind of alarms or sentries the compound employed. Surely they had something in place that would spot people sneaking around.

After the fifth block, Foster walked up to the driver's side of a boxy vehicle that looked like a cross between a van and a tank. The front of it was fitted with a wedge of metal that reminded me of the old cowcatchers on antique steam-engine locomotives.

He got in the van. Abraham ducked into the passenger's seat, so I took the back.

The sound of the engine roaring to life made sweat break out across my entire body, even though the night had moved on from cold to shivery cold.

"We have two choices," Abraham said while Foster navigated the streets as if he knew the place. "Stop for our weapons here and trigger the alarms, or stop somewhere a few hours from here and reprovision."

"Where is somewhere?"

"Better you don't know. But there are stashes of gear hidden in the wilds between civilizations. I know one that should be untapped."

I bit my lip, thinking it over. I liked my knives and gun. Abraham and Foster treated their weapons better than I'd seen some people treat their family members. But we needed speed and stealth.

"Let's get to that stash," I said.

"Foster," Abraham said, "take the back door."

Foster turned left and left again, and we were headed for the east end of town.

We hadn't come in this way, but I expected every road into the compound to be guarded just like the road we'd come in on.

I couldn't have been more wrong.

The gate in the wall here must have been one of the originals. No towers above it; no guard shack beside it. Just a plain metal doorway large enough to drive two buses through, side by side.

It was closed and, I assumed, locked.

I certainly didn't have the key.

Foster slowed the van and brought it to a stop. Abraham jumped out and strode to the gate. There were no lanterns here, so I couldn't see exactly what he did. There was no chance he had the key. I guessed he was going to bust the lock.

It took him a minute, two, before he tugged on the gate once, hard, then slid it to one side. He had to put his shoulder into it to make the old thing roll across the tracks, and I realized it hadn't been locked; it had been welded shut.

Foster eased the van through and then waited while Abraham set the gate back in place. I didn't know if he did that to cover our tracks or to make sure ferals didn't run wild through town. Probably both. Even though the wait was interminable, I agreed that our actions shouldn't bring any more harm to House Earth.

I already felt responsible for the bomb and the people who were dead and injured because of it. And while I knew that Slater would have bombed them even if I had decided to turn myself in, it all somehow felt like I was the one who should have stopped this, who should have stopped him a long time ago.

A lifetime ago.

Abraham swung back into the van. "Go—we're clear. I don't suppose you already found us a few weapons while you were stealing this van?" he asked Foster.

Foster grinned at Abraham like a kid. "In the back."

"Foster, my friend"—Abraham patted him on the arm—"you are the most loyal, steady, and quietly devious man I've ever met." He twisted back toward me. "Can you bring the weapons up here? We won't get far without them."

I worked my way around the one bench seat into the back of the van, while Foster drove at speed down a road that was rough and full of holes. The van swayed and bucked, and I hit my shoulder against the sidewall a couple times.

A heavy blanket lay spread across the floor and was folded over once. I pulled that back and took stock of what Foster had gotten his hands on.

He must have left the inn quite a while before we did and broken into an armory.

Machine guns, rifles, grenades, knives, machetes, and two bulky tank-and-trigger hose setups that looked like flamethrowers nestled next to three splitting mauls and a bundle of rope.

Nice haul.

I tried to add up the value of what we'd just liberated from House Earth, and decided we'd left nearly the same value in the weapons they'd taken from us.

Not exactly a fair exchange if you threw in the van, but, then, we were trying to save their lives.

That had to be worth something.

I threw the blanket back over the collection, then tucked up the ends and brought the unwieldy bundle over to the bench seat and lifted the whole thing over the back, to set on the seat itself.

"Well?" Abraham asked.

"Other than squirt guns, I think we're covered."

He braced sideways in his chair, his shoulders filling the space between the front and backseat. "Have you ever traveled at night?" he asked.

"I have. But not around ferals."

"Then I'm going to tell you what you need to do. If you follow my instructions, we'll get through this. The cache isn't far off, and we can reload there."

"We'll need to reload?" I asked, glancing down at the pile of weapons.

"Those ferals back at the cabin?" he said. "Child's play. Out here there'll be many, many more. Different types. Some with thick hides bullets have a hard time penetrating. The sound of the van's engine will call them from miles around. The night's going to be swarming with them real quick."

"All right. What's the plan?"

He unwrapped the blanket, then planted his hand on the back of the seat as the van rocked. His gaze quickly took in our inventory.

"We'll start with the automatics. I'll take the back; you'll take the front. Shoot only if you can make the shot count." He glanced at me. "This is going to be bloody."

"I can handle blood," I said. "So, shoot, but don't waste bullets. Any kill shots besides eyes?"

"Eyes are best. Next is neck. Some of the beasts have reinforced skulls, so head shot isn't always a guaranteed kill." He bent and squeezed through the space between

the seats, then around back to where I knelt, holding on
to the back of seat for stability.

He reached over the back of the seat and plucked up
one of the machine guns, two extra magazines, one rifle,
a handgun and clip, maul, machete, and one of the flamethrowers.

"Do you know how to use these things?" he asked as
he attached everything to his body. His coat was worked
with a clever set of hooks and bands all meant for carrying weapons. I suddenly wanted one.

"Nothing here I haven't seen before," I said. "Is there
a coil lighter or striker for the flamethrower?"

"Van should have a coil lighter in the dash. Don't use
the flamethrower unless you have to. We'll need it for
when we're on foot outside the van."

"Got it. Good luck," I said as I squeezed around him.
The van bucked, throwing me backward into his chest.
Abraham caught me with one hand around my waist,
and we held there a moment too long.

"Ready?" he asked, his mouth low by my ear again. I
wanted to kiss him. Wanted more. But we had a night-
time drive to survive.

I nodded, not trusting my voice, and his hand released
me, palm brushing warmth alongside my waist before
pulling away.

I made my way up into the passenger's seat and got
my breathing in order. That man did things to me. Very
nice things.

When I glanced back, Abraham had already set the
weapons he couldn't carry on the floor in the back of the
van next to him, as if he'd done it a million times before.
The back doors were fitted with slot windows that could
be opened and closed and were just the right size for the
barrel of a gun.

This vehicle had been made for exactly this sort of thing: to drive at night when ferals were attacking.

So maybe we had a good chance of getting through this alive.

"We're hot," Foster said over the growl of the engine. Abraham set the machine gun at the slotted window and scanned the darkness.

I turned with the automatic and rolled the window down a notch or two, aiming the weapon forward and bracing against the seat.

Cloud cover choked the light out of the night, but the van was equipped with low lights that gave some hint of what was in front of us. It wasn't a road so much as a rutted trail through an open field. From the glimpses of posts speeding by on either side of us, I figured this was a grazing pasture in the day.

But in the night, the entire landscape seemed to move, and all of it was made of teeth and eyes and claws.

"Shit," I breathed. They were coming right at us. Like locusts, a swarm, a herd, an undulating wall of muscle and fur stretched over twisted bone and spine. The wolflike ferals were mixed in among squat squares of muscle the size of crocboars, and furred bearlike things the size of our van that didn't appear to have heads and instead articulated like centipedes. The ferals galloped toward us so many, so fast, we'd be buried by them if we slowed down.

Gunfire interrupted my moment of shock. I pushed away the very real fear of drowning.

I aimed and made the bullets count.

Just before the leading edge of ferals hit the van, closing in on us from all sides, Foster floored it.

The van plowed through the nightmare beasts in front of us, throwing and crushing them as Foster drove right through the mass. The impact shook off the creatures that pounded against the side of the van and threw off a few that had reached the roof.

I fired until the magazine was empty. Reloaded and kept firing. The beasts kept coming.

If we ran out of bullets or fuel, or if one of the beasts hit us hard enough to tip the van or make us lose a tire, we would be torn apart, beaten, and eaten in a manner of seconds.

No matter how many rounds I went through, more and more rushed the van, falling out of trees, squirming out of tall grasses, and pouring out of shadows.

"How far to the cache?" I asked.

"Twenty miles," Foster said.

Twenty miles? I didn't think we were going to make it another twenty blocks.

"Running low on ammo," I shouted back to Abraham.

"Hold on," he said.

He scrambled up through the van and handed me two grenades.

"Not going to do a lot of good with how fast they're coming," I said.

"Flash bomb. Don't throw it in front of the van."

Like I would. He pushed his way to the back again, and I rolled down the window, pulled the pin, and chucked the flash bomb as hard as I could to the right.

I turned my head and closed my eyes. The night burned bright as a desert sun.

Beasts howled and shrieked. I opened my eyes, my vision fouled, even though I'd done my best to protect them. The ferals were losing ground, less of them following us.

I opened the door, leaned out, and heaved another grenade over the top of the van to the left. "Flash!" I yelled as I slammed back into the van and covered my eyes.

The world went white behind my eyelids.

Foster grunted, but somehow kept the van on the road.

"Will that hold them off?" I asked.

"No." Abraham strapped on the flamethrower. He kicked open the back of the van.

"I thought you said we're saving the flamethrowers."

"I lied." He swung out of the van doors. For a single horrifying moment, I thought he'd thrown himself to the beasts following us. But then I saw his boots as he heaved himself up onto the roof.

"Sonofabitch," I said. "Crazy. He's crazy."

Yes, he was galvanized. Yes, he couldn't be easily killed. But there were enough ferals out there to take him down and tear him to shreds until he was dead.

The night lit up with a blast of orange. Ferals along the side of the van backed away from the fire, blinded and burned.

A distinctive *pop* sound cracked out, and a neon pink flare exploded above us.

"A flare?" I asked Foster. "Who is he signaling?"

"Maybe friends." Foster drew a handgun from his hip, rolled down his window and shot a feral in the head. Then he flicked on the windshield wipers, scraping the thick blood and gore to the edges of the window.

Maybe friends?

"What about the weapons cache?" I asked.

"They are the cache of weapons."

"What maybe-friends is he signaling? There isn't anyone out here. No one could survive this. *We're* not going to survive this."

The corner of Foster's mouth curled up, and he glanced over at me. "Have faith, Matilda Case."

And then I heard it: the sound of engines. The sound of guns. Someone *was* out here, and they were coming our way.

15

*My personal opinion? There should be only
one reality — the reality wherein Slater is dead.*
— *W.Y.*

In my very short time traveling outside at night, I had
learned several valuable lessons.

One: ferals never stop coming. There are not enough
bullets, not enough flame, and not enough pain in the
world to turn them away when they are in a hunting
frenzy.

Two: ferals are always in a hunting frenzy.

Three: only crazy people go out in the night.

Four: Abraham Vail was absolutely insane.

He stood on the top of the van, even though I was
having a hard enough time keeping my aim steady from
the inside of the van, as we rattled down the road. He
bathed the space around us in flames, and from the bleed
of orange over black, I saw our real situation.

The dead ferals were just drawing more ferals who,
once they heard the engine and saw the motion of the
van roaring down the road, turned away from dining on
their fellow creatures to take off after us.

I don't know what combination of radiation and disaster had given rise to these beasts, but there were more mutations than I'd ever be able to wash out of the nightmares I'd be having for the rest of my nightmares.

The light from the flamethrower kept some of the more visually sensitive ferals back a bit, but as soon as the flame paused, they all rushed at us again. It was like digging a hole in the sand while the walls were collapsing in on us.

Only these holes had teeth and claws and a strong desire to kill us.

I was down to a handgun, the rope, a splitting maul, a knife, and the other flamethrower.

I leaned out the window, taking out the closest beasts I could get a clear shot at. Foster had run over so many, the windshield was covered in a mess of blood and gore the wipers couldn't clear, and bits of fur and bone and other body parts were stuck in the welds of the van. I was amazed the van was still going, but the way it was constructed kept the most vulnerable parts of the vehicle out of the ferals' reach.

The engines were coming closer, though I didn't know how adding more vehicles, which would draw more ferals, was any kind of a good idea.

My gun was out of bullets, so I grabbed the splitting maul. It was weighted, but I braced one knee against the seat of my chair and one foot on the floor, and stuck it out the window.

The speed of the car meant that when my maul hit a feral, it was a hell of a jolt, both for my arms and for the unlucky beast.

But I was strong.

And angry.

The ax cut down several ferals until it buried so deep

into one of the articulated, giant-bear ferals that I lost my grip and it was ripped out of my hand.

"So, these maybe-friends of yours?" I said as I rapidly rolled up the window. "Any idea when they're going to get here?"

"Next bend."

He sounded really sure about that.

"Are you sure about that?" I picked up the flame-thrower and grabbed for the coil lighter out of the dash-board so I could light the damn thing.

"Yes."

"Why?" I rolled the window down and sent a blast of flame out, then caught a back draft of gas and burnt fur that set me coughing.

Worth it.

"That's where the world always ends," he said.

Right. I'd somehow forgotten that Foster was just as mad-bat crazy as Abraham. I didn't know why I thought he'd want to make sense at a time like this.

Then we turned the corner.

"Foster," I said, frantically rolling up the window again.

"Yes?"

"What is that?"

"What?"

"All the nothing out there?"

"The end of the world."

And it might sound cheesy, but that was when the clouds broke enough that between the pale silver glow of the moon and the light of Abraham's flamethrower, I could see the vast nothing that we were driving peril-ously along the edge of.

It was as if something huge had punched a hole into the earth. It was a huge hole with a razor-sharp edge that seemed to fall down and down into eternity.

The memory of Quinten saying the satellites had been taken out, power grids destroyed, came back to me. The world, this world, had suffered much different disasters from the world I'd lived in. A barrage of meteors had pounded the earth, breaking the progress of civilization.

This world had died and rebuilt itself. I suppose it made sense that it would carry the scars of survival.

"How is this going to help us?" I asked.

"Look."

I saw them. Vehicles like ours only twice the size, half a dozen of them, barreling toward us, lit up as bright as Christmas lights.

Abraham, still up on the roof, let off an earsplitting whistle. It was returned once, twice, three times from the vehicles.

Ferals surrounded them too. But as I watched, all the vehicles except two went completely dark. The other two were bright as a beacon, and the swarm of beasts shifted to home in on those lights, like moths dive-bombing a fire.

Foster killed our lights, and I heard Abraham run across the top of the van before swinging down inside and slamming the doors shut behind him.

Foster slowed the van.

"What are you doing? You can't slow down—they'll bury us."

"Wait," Abraham said from where he lay on his back, panting on the floor. "Give him a minute. He knows what he's doing."

"Oh, God," I said. Which was stupid, because it wasn't like Foster or the ferals or the other vehicles out there could hear me.

The two lit vehicles were also covered with dead ferals that appeared to have been lashed down tight on purpose. It made the vehicles an irresistible combination of food, sound, and light. The other ferals—*all* the other ferals—went completely mad.

The wave of bodies smashing into our van rocked us like we were a ship in hard seas, but the impacts became fewer and fewer as the ferals abandoned our dark, quieter vehicle for the two brightly shining, noisy ones ahead.

And then those shining vehicles drove right over the end of the world and into a darkness even their light couldn't pierce.

The ferals followed them down, right over the edge of that fissure.

"Holy shit," I breathed, my heart pounding so hard, I was shaking with it. "Holy shit."

"That," Abraham said as he wiped a bloody hand over his bloody face, "is how it's done." He pounded his fist twice into the floor of the van.

He was still breathing hard and hadn't gotten up.

"Are we just sitting here?" I asked.

"Yes." Foster leaned back and pulled a canteen from the door pocket, took a drink, and handed it to me.

Okay. I had no idea what was going on.

"I have no idea what's going on," I said. I took a swig of water, which was laced with a hint of fresh mint—a surreal and pleasant luxury, considering our situation and surroundings.

"Aren't we going to go help them? Your friends in those vehicles just got chased off a cliff."

"They know what they're doing," Abraham said. "There's a road down. It's hard to see from here. About halfway, there's a nice, tight left into a tunnel with reinforced-steel doors."

"And?"

"And the ferals never have gotten the hang of that tight left. Pass me the water?"

I bent and half walked, half crawled back to him. "So they're fine?"

He tipped his head so he could watch me making my way back to him. "They're fine." He was grinning like a fool. A bloody, sooty, gorgeous fool.

"You are an idiot." I knelt next to him and held out the canteen. "The roof, Vail? What devil kind of dumb does a man have to be to do that sort of thing?"

His grin got even wider, if that was possible.

"I'm not an idiot," he said, reaching for the canteen and catching my wrist instead. "I am just a very, very good devil."

He drew the canteen toward him, even though he had only propped up on one elbow. But since he hadn't let go of my wrist, I was bending down toward him. Which was just what he wanted.

"What about Foster?" I whispered.

"He's not invited," he whispered back.

He stared straight at me, looking into me. His eyebrow quirked up in a question.

Everything in me went hot. I knew what he wanted. I wanted it too, had dreamed about it. But I was not going to get naked in front of—well, behind—Foster.

He drew my arm across his body, and I propped myself over him. He smelled like gasoline and ash and sweat and something with a deep hickory tone.

He paused, waiting. His gaze drifted to my lips and then back to my eyes.

"Victory kiss?" he whispered.

Memories flooded me of the times we had made love, that same look in his eyes as he waited to see what I would do. As he made me wait to see what he would do.

He released my wrist. I tipped my head as his wide fingers dragged up my arm, sending glorious pulses of pleasure across my skin. The anticipation of him touching me tightened my stomach and turned my mouth hot from the need to feel him in me, everywhere in me.

His fingers pushed up into my thick, heavy hair, and I tipped my head down, holding his gaze.

"One," I mouthed.

I slowly, slowly pressed my mouth against his. His tongue slid along my bottom lip, and I opened my mouth to feel him. His tongue stroked along my tongue, tangling me in aching heat.

One kiss. It was all I had agreed to. Even though I wanted more.

I lowered over him, my breasts pressing against the hard heat of his chest.

He tightened at the hot, instant sensation. He lifted and rolled, pulling me gently beneath him and lying across my body so that I could feel every hard inch of him.

I shifted to wrap one leg around the back of his thigh and tug him closer.

That had exactly the results I expected. He grinned at me and held very still. Then he gently lowered himself and pressed his mouth against the sensitive line of stitches at my neck. Teeth and tongue teased the threads that held me together, threatening to undo me in every way.

I caught my breath and couldn't breathe again, every nerve in my body paused upon the play of his tongue, lips, and teeth working across my skin.

He had never done that before. Not like that.

My lungs were still, my body unwilling to accept air, filling instead with the need for him. He shifted his mouth to my collarbone.

His mouth worked its maddening magic along the bare bits of me; then he lifted away.

"Matilda," he said, gently. "Breathe."

I opened my eyes, saw him grinning above me in the darkness. Remembered where we were.

One kiss.

I exhaled while he sweetly stroked his thumb along the underside of my jaw.

Inhaled while he kissed my forehead, then gently pressed his forehead against mine.

"As much as I would like to finish this," he said, "and the need for that is immense." He shifted his hips slightly, away from me. "We need to be moving. Before the next wave of ferals hit."

"I know," I said, trying to untangle my needs and wants and crazy cravings I couldn't seem to breathe my body out of. "Right. I know. I brought you water."

"Thank you." He hesitated, and I knew that if he did anything—if he kissed me, if he said any sweet thing—I would take his clothes off and bed the man, right here in the back of the dark van with Foster just two seats away. Ferals or no ferals.

Maybe he saw that in my expression; I didn't know. But he pulled away, my leg unwrapping from the back of his thigh as he shifted and finally sat next to me.

I sat too, avoiding his gaze while I did so.

If we were ever going to be together, this Abraham and me, it wasn't going to be in the back of a stolen van, covered in blood and guts, while we were on the run for our lives.

I pictured my bed at home in the farmhouse. Lace quilt; soft mattress. I pictured the Abraham I'd seen in the hall, happy, tattooed, naked, his body warm and clean from a hot shower, smelling of soap and sex.

That's what I wanted. Even if I couldn't have that Abraham, who had called me love.

I wanted the chance at even a portion of that dream life, that fleeting timeway.

As for his part, Abraham leaned back against the side of the van and took a long, long drink out of the canteen. I followed his lead and leaned against the other side of the van, facing him in the shared darkness, but as far away from him as I could get.

"Ready?" he called out to Foster.

Foster answered by starting the engine. That was enough to strip away any romantic feelings I was entertaining. Engines brought ferals, and we were out of ammunition.

"We're out of ammunition," I said.

Abraham nodded. "We'll go underground for the next few hours. By the time we're through the tunnels, it will be dawn."

"The tunnel over the cliff?"

"Not the same one, no. There are others."

"Does everyone know about these?"

"Only the sort of people no one wants to associate with."

"Mercenaries?"

He nodded and took another drink as the van bumped along the road, then took a tight, slow left and began an unmistakable downward descent.

"Is that who answered your flare?"

"Yes."

"So you're telling me there are mercenaries just sitting around in vehicles, waiting to see random flares go off so they can drive a bunch of ferals off the cliff?"

"Would you believe me if I said it were true?"

"No."

"But there are always a few people camped out near the tunnel entrances."

"And?"

"And some might have been expecting us."

"How?"

"While you were sleeping, Foster and I made ourselves useful."

"You radioed ahead that we were coming, didn't you?"

"Yes."

"And where are we going, exactly? I'm assuming the *cache of weapons* line you fed me was just a bunch of bullshit?"

He scrunched his face up in what almost looked like a wince. "No. Well, yes, but no. There will be weapons where we're going."

"Where are we going?"

He tipped the canteen up, swallowed, then tipped it down again. "Coal and Ice."

16

Two pieces! That's what I was missing. There might be more than one thing needed to kill Slater. Unfortunately, I have no idea what either thing could be.

—W.Y.

I spent the rest of the drive through the tunnel peppering Abraham with questions about Coal and Ice. There was no counterpart to it in my world, unless I counted Sallyo's underground black market and smuggling ring.

But Coal and Ice wasn't just a black market for goods, though Abraham cheerfully informed me that smuggling made decent money. It was primarily a loose collective of spies, thieves, and assassins looking for jobs that all funneled through one man: Binek.

I didn't know why talking about a crime lord made Abraham feel so relaxed, but I supposed it was because Coal and Ice was his home ground. It was where people like him, and even those unlike him—galvanized or not—had a common goal.

Kill or be killed, and remember to factor a ten percent profit for Coal and Ice's coffers.

The other thing Abraham seemed more than willing to share was that Binek had his ear to the ground and would have the information we needed to get into House Fire and stop Slater. If we played our hand right, he might even kick in the weapons and other equipment for free.

"Warlords don't do anything for free," I said.

He shrugged, and I noted his left shoulder looked like it still wasn't hinging quite right. I should probably offer to look at it, but after the last time I'd gotten too close to him and ended up kissing him, I decided it could wait.

If it was hurting him, he couldn't feel it anyway.

"I'm sure he'll cover his interests in the deal," Abraham said.

And, frustratingly, that was all he said. He spent the rest of the ride staring out at the darkness and nothing, until he finally closed his eyes and fell asleep, knees bent and arms resting across them like a soldier accustomed to catching z's before a mission.

The back of the van was not a comfortable place to ride. Even though the tunnel road seemed smoother than cross-country, I thought cushions and springs might be nicer for my bruised butt. So I crawled back around the bench seat and sat up by Foster.

"Hello, Matilda," he said.

"Hi," I said. "Nice driving back there, by the way."

"Thank you."

"Abraham's sleeping."

"Yes."

"Do you want me to drive? He said neither of you slept much."

"No. Rest. I will drive."

I glanced out the windows, which were filthy with blood and fluids I didn't want to think about. We were inside a tunnel. I thought it could have once been a sub-way line, but it wasn't any I was familiar with. For all I knew, it could also have been an underground access for bomb shelters or a throughway between shopping centers.

Whatever it had been built for originally, it made for a fairly smooth roadway. There were no lights, but the headlamps on the van were more than enough to light the road ahead of us and also the walls, which were set far enough to our side that I could tell this was a two-lane tunnel.

I heard the echo of at least one other engine besides ours out there. The mercenaries, or at least some of them, were following us.

"How much longer until we get there?" I asked.

"An hour. Rest. Daylight will come soon."

But I was still a little too restless to try shut-eye. "You know I lived a life in a different time than this, don't you?"

"Yes."

"You were there too in that time. You had a very dear friend. His name was Welton Yellow. You helped raise him when he was a child, and you became more than just his bodyguard. You were family to him, his best friend."

Foster remained silent. He didn't even glance my way. I didn't know if he believed me or even wanted to hear about this. But I had promised Welton I'd let Foster know he loved him. And I followed through on my promises.

"In that time, my original time, you and Welton were very close. Are you friends with Custodian Welton in this time?"

"No," he said after a moment's pause.

"The Welton I knew, Welton Yellow, was a good man.

Clever. Too curious for his own good, but he wanted what was best for people. He wanted what was best for you and did what he could to make your life better. I saw him recently. I . . . um . . . slipped over to that timeway, and he was there."

"When?"

"In the apple orchard. What I want to tell you, what he asked me to tell you, is that he loves you. Still. Even though you're not alive in that timeway. He wants what's best for you. In this timeway. I promised him I'd tell you that. Even though you're not the you you were then now."

Foster still didn't say anything.

"Did that make sense? Does any of this make sense?"

"Yes," he said.

"Good, because it confuses the hell out of me." I leaned my head against the window. "I can't kill Slater until I destroy some piece of the Wings of Mercury machine Alveré Case built. That machine didn't survive in this time, did it?"

"No," he said. "Broken, burned, buried. Nothing but ashes, like all dreams become."

I rubbed my eyes, which stung from sweat and soot.

"Well, I wish something out of that time and experiment had survived. Something of Alveré's. It'd make my life easier."

"We survived," he said.

"Yes. But we're not things. We're breathing, living people." I yawned, the events of the night finally catching up to me. "Maybe I should go rest."

"Yes," Foster said. "Rest. I will think on this."

"Thanks," I said. "Let me know if you come up with anything."

I stepped back to the bench seat, pushed the coil of

rope to the floor, tucked one of the knives into my belt, and pulled the blanket that had held all the weapons over me as I lay on my side, half curled.

I slept fitfully, waking up in a series of panicked starts as nightmares pressed bloody fingers around my sleeping mind.

After the third or fourth time, I decided I'd had enough not-sleep and kept my eyes open, listening to the echo of engines passing to our left and the hum of the tires against the road.

Also, Abraham's snoring.

Man was loud.

Finally, finally, Foster tapped the brakes, slowed, and then took a sharp turn to the right. The incline was pretty steep and pushed me into my seat.

It must have pushed Abraham too. I heard a *clunk*, a curse, and then there was no more snoring.

"Warning, next time?" he demanded sleepily.

"We are climbing," Foster said. "Abruptly."

Abraham just grunted.

The van finally leveled out, and I squinted in the pale light of morning. I didn't even think the sun was up yet, but after the thick darkness of night, and the thicker darkness of the tunnel, the predawn lightening of the sky seemed intense.

My eyes quickly adjusted, and I sat, pushing the blanket off to one side. Abraham made his way up to the front of the van, sliding around to where I sat with a quick nod to me before he settled into the front seat.

"Morning, sunshine," I said. "Sleep well?"

He gave me a grin. "Good enough. Are you ready to meet the man?"

"If meeting him will get me closer to killing Slater, then I can't wait."

The road looked like it got a fair share of traffic. The hills around here did not appear to be farmed, and there were no apple orchards or really much else. I didn't know what the main resource might be in this area, other than the wink of a rather large river that I caught a glimpse of now and again.

I was expecting Coal and Ice to be some sort of city set behind walls, and I was not wrong. Except whereas House Earth's compound felt like a place where one could build a life and raise a family, this place looked like the kind of thing one might want to remain a part of only if one liked living in a battle fortress.

The walls were thick, concrete and metal, with slits for windows useful for sniper rifles. Strangely, the front gate was wide open.

We were headed to the intelligence center for mercenaries, killers, and others who took life one bloody, illegal opportunity at a time, and they didn't even have a weapons check at the door.

"Not much for precaution, are they?" I asked as we rolled down the streets.

"Don't have to be," Abraham said.

The streets were hard-packed dirt, which must turn into a bog hole when the winter rains came. The buildings had a sense of impermanence, as if they had been put up quickly and could be abandoned at a moment's notice.

The number of saloons, bars, and other sorts of pleasure houses was boggling.

The people who walked the streets—and there were a lot of them—seemed to have taken their fashion from the same page that Abraham and Foster subscribed to.

Basically, hearty clothing, accessorized by as many weapons as one could bear to support.

That put the open-door policy into perspective. Everyone was armed; therefore it didn't matter what kind of person strolled into the town. Visitors weren't a potential danger to the town; the town was a potential danger to visitors.

Coal and Ice was also much smaller than Compound 5. I estimated it to be a half mile by a half mile in acreage, and built on a grid, so it seemed even smaller than that.

Foster pulled up to a building that could have once been a church, steeple and everything.

It was painted navy blue with deep maroon trim, the door rounded at the top and gunmetal gray.

"This is our stop," Abraham said.

"A church?" I asked.

"Binek's office. Come on in. I think you'll like him."

Abraham stepped out of the van and took the time to remove his jacket while he waited for me to get out. I didn't know why he didn't want his coat on. But then I noticed the people on the street, and more people in windows across the street, who were studying him. One after another, they looked away, stepped away, and went about their business.

And I knew why. With his jacket off and sleeves rolled up, the thick, black, distinctive stitches on his arms and wrists were very evident. Add the blood and gore that covered him, and he made for an intimidating man. No, he made for an intimidating galvanized man.

Someone who even these hardened criminals would rather not mess with.

Well, that said a lot for how the galvanized were seen here.

We walked up the stairs, and Foster opened the door, which we all strolled through.

Apparently, one didn't need reservations to meet the big man.

The interior of the building fit my assumption that this had been a church. Polished wood everywhere—walls, ceiling, floor, all of it set together in long blond and toasted brown strips. The ceiling vaulted up at a sharp angle. A set of stairs leading up to our right, double doors in front of us, and a single door to the left.

We went left.

Foster opened that door. Nothing here was locked; no people were guarding the doors.

After House Earth's security setup, it was sort of odd.

A hallway took us deeper into the building, which I realized was a lot bigger than it seemed from the outside.

Still no one here. The place had the sort of hushed reverence of silence filling it.

At the end of the hall was another door. It was open.

I shook my head at the sheer lack of locks, guards, and fear. Abraham, walking beside me, smiled. He stopped in front of the doorway and knocked on the doorframe.

"Do you have time today?" he asked.

I couldn't see into the room past the mountain of Abraham filling it, but I knew the voice that answered.

"Abraham," the man said. "Come in. Of course. Come in. Tell me how things went."

"They went well." Abraham stepped into the room. I walked in behind him.

There, sitting behind a desk covered in papers and books and rolled maps, was Oscar Gray.

I was so happy to see him, I pressed my fingertips against my lips so I wouldn't say something stupid.

"Hello," he said, looking at me through the small round glasses perched on the end of his nose. He was so much the same as how I remembered him from my timeway, I couldn't help but smile. Short, curly hair gone gray, round face, and stout build. He didn't wear the mix of jackets and scarves he'd sported in the world where we'd first met. Here he was dressed in a clean white shirt under a pinstripe vest and jacket.

If I'd never met him before, if I didn't know him from my timeway as the head of House Gray, or from this time as, apparently, the head of the Coal and Ice, I might think he was a jovial accountant or a friendly uncle.

I wanted him to be the same kindhearted man I'd met in what was only over a week ago, to my memory. But just as Abraham wasn't quite the same, nor Quinten, Welton, or even, in many ways, I myself, I tried not to hold too much hope that Oscar would be the generous man I had known.

He was, after all, the head of all the criminals, assassins, and killers for hire.

"Hello, Oscar," I said, taking my fingers away from my mouth.

"Oscar?" Abraham said. "Is that it? Is that your first name?"

"That," Oscar said shortly, "doesn't matter. I am curious as to who told you it might be."

"I just thought . . . I must have heard it from Abraham," I said.

"No," Oscar said. "You did not. He doesn't know my first name. No one knows my first name."

"Not even your parents?" I asked.

His round eyes curved into crescents as he laughed. "Really. I must know. Who told you?"

"No one," I said truthfully. "I . . . guessed."

He studied me, his eyes bright. "You must be Matilda Case," he said. "The girl who knew the future. Is this lovely young woman Matilda Case, Abraham?"

"It is indeed what she tells me, Binek." Abraham strolled over and sat in the wide leather and wood chair on one side of Oscar's cozy office. "Or should I call you Oscar?"

"You should not," he said, rising to lean across his cluttered desk and shake my hand. "So wonderful to meet you." He let go and pointed at another chair near Abraham. "Have a seat. We're all friends here." He paused, looked at Abraham. "I assume we're friends?"

He nodded once. "Close enough. Though I'd think Matilda might say we simply had similar goals."

"Ah." Oscar turned and poured a honey-colored liquor out of a cut crystal decanter into four glasses. "Well, then, you've certainly come to the right place." He glanced back at me over his glasses. "We are all about friendly, temporary alliances here."

He turned with the tray and stepped over to Abraham, who took one of the glasses.

"Tell me how it is that we at Coal and Ice can help you," he said, offering me a glass.

I wasn't one for drinking, but after the night I'd had, I could use something more than water in my belly.

"She doesn't want help from Coal and Ice," Abraham said.

"Oh?" Oscar gave the last glass to Foster, who was leaning inside the doorway, his massive bulk probably making the room even more secure than a dead-bolted door.

I looked over at Abraham. I didn't know what he was talking about. I thought we'd come here for weapons and information on how to get into House Fire. How was that *not* my wanting Coal and Ice's favor?

"This will be a personal favor. To me," he said.

"Hold on," I said.

"No." Oscar lifted a finger. "I'd like to hear what he has to say. It's not often he asks such things. Also, I assume he didn't clear this with you. No?" Oscar laughed and walked back around to the other side of the desk.

"You have always had such style, Abraham. Please go on." He sat and took a sip of his drink. Only then did Abraham and Foster drink.

Oh, right. I supposed there might be traditions to be followed here.

Or they were waiting for him to drink to prove it wasn't poison.

I took a sip. It was surprisingly mild, like an apple juice with just the hint of fermentation. Nice, actually.

"Matilda and I have a common goal," Abraham went on. "She and I will work out the price of our alliance privately. What I want from you, Binek, as a friend and a man who should also see the benefit of our success, is weapons, intelligence, and political pull."

Oscar breathed in and sat back in his chair. The laughter was gone, replaced by a steel edge that I hadn't seen in him before. "You must want something very badly to bring up my family, Abraham."

Abraham didn't say anything.

Oscar sipped his drink again. "My favors don't come lightly."

"I understand that."

"Speak," Oscar finally said.

"We intend to kill Slater, head of House Fire."

Oscar blinked, then drained his drink. "He's galvanized."

"Galvanized can be killed," Abraham said.

"Galvanized don't kill galvanized," Oscar said.

"I'm going to kill him," I said.

Both of them flicked a look my way.

"How are you planning on doing that, Ms. Case?" Oscar asked.

"A weapon has fallen into my hands that will get the job done," I said, not wanting to tell him about the Shelley dust.

"That is . . . intriguing. I understand why Abraham wants to kill him," Oscar said. "Tell me why you are interested in doing a very dangerous and very foolish thing."

As opposed to all the very safe, very smart things I've been doing lately? I thought.

But what I said was, "He killed my family and my friends. And he is even now killing innocent people I care about."

Oscar frowned.

"He's bombing House Earth," Abraham provided.

"Ah, yes," Oscar said. "He's blaming House Water for that."

"It isn't House Water. It's Slater," I said.

"I didn't say I didn't believe you. Do you have proof? Documents that might be acted upon?"

"Not with me, no." I hadn't thought of that. The letter Sallyo had delivered was proof that Slater intended to bomb the compounds. If a document like that held up in court in this time.

If they even had courts in this time.

"Killing a head of a House is punishable by death, Matilda Case," Oscar said. "Even the people who walk these streets and take these jobs that so often fall into my hands—distasteful jobs that most people have no stomach for—would think twice about killing a head of a House."

"I've thought about it more than twice," I said.

"Hmm." His lips pulled back in a tight smile. "I see

that you have. And are you willing to let this ride on Abraham's debt to me?"

"We're in this together," Abraham said.

He looked over at me.

I could say no. I could bear the cost of this, although I didn't know what Oscar would want in trade for such sensitive information, not to mention his culpability in Slater's murder. Would he ask me for my farm, my house? Would he demand servitude?

And what would he ask out of Abraham?

"We are in it together," I agreed, "but we will share the debt."

"Good," Oscar said, pointing a finger at me in approval. "I like a soul who's not afraid to carry her own burden. Tell me *exactly* what you need from me."

"Slater's schedule," Abraham said. "Any entries and exits to House Fire that have changed in the past few months since he's taken over power. Weapons: guns, preferably with silencers, scopes, but also close-range weapons. And we want your brother, Hollis, to look the other way while we take care of the thorn in his side."

I had no idea what position Hollis had in this time. Back in mine, he was in league with several other Houses and trying to dethrone Oscar from head of House Gray by killing him.

Which he'd done.

"We trust Hollis?" I asked.

Oscar laughed. "I see you must have met my brother. No, we do not trust him. But he has his price, just as any man does."

"And he's in a position to help?" I asked.

"Hollis is the head of defense for House Water," Abraham said.

"Okay?"

He gave me that crooked smile again. "He should just hold the title of consummate spy. If there's dirt to be found on anyone, Hollis has it. Which means," he added before I asked, because I still wasn't seeing how a House Water official could help us with our House Fire problem, "that he can make people, even House Fire people, step aside so we can get what we want."

"Oh," I said. "Oh." I nodded. "And how much will that cost us?"

"I'll be the one setting the rate," Oscar said. "Weapons, intel, political favor." He steepled his fingers together in front of his mouth and looked over his glasses at Abraham.

Abraham took the last swallow of his drink and returned Oscar's gaze, unconcerned. It was like watching two poker players feel each other out over a particularly large pot.

"A year's contract at half pay," Oscar started.

"Six months," Abraham countered.

"Six months, quarter pay," Oscar said.

"Done."

"And," Oscar said holding up his finger, "I want something from Matilda."

"The only thing she has is a broken-down farm in the middle of the scratch," Abraham said. "Nothing worthwhile there. Don't see you as the toiling-in-the-soil type, Binek."

Oscar wiggled his eyebrows. "I'm not interested in the farm. At the moment," he added. "Although I am impressed with the size and variety of the stitched beasts that wander your property," he said. "Which are very much worthwhile, Abraham. Never kid a kidder."

Okay, so he knew about our farm. His brother was apparently the head of defense for House Water, and king spy. It was no wonder he would know where I lived.

"Just ask," I said. "If it's a fair price and doesn't put the lives of the people I love in danger, I'll pay it."

Oscar grinned and sat forward. "*That* is how I like to do business," he declared. "Do you see how easy that is, Abraham? How an amicable exchange"—he waved his hand at himself, then me—"between two interested, honest parties can bring about such a quick and simple agreement?"

"You don't have to shove candy up my ass," Abraham said. "I've known you since you were six."

"Five," Oscar corrected. "And completely beside the point. The point is what I'm asking of you, Matilda Case."

I raised an eyebrow, waiting.

"The cure to the One-five plague," he said.

Abraham frowned. "You can't ask for things that don't exist."

"But it does exist. Doesn't it, Ms. Case?"

He waited, watching me. Abraham was watching me too. He and Foster both knew Quinten had the cure. It was nice of Abraham to try to keep that secret. It wasn't my secret to tell. It sure as hell wasn't mine to give away or promise to anyone.

If I said yes, how much danger would Quinten be in?

The way Oscar was looking at me, he could be bluffing. Quinten was one of the most careful men at covering his tracks. I doubted even superspy Hollis knew what Quinten had been gathering those medical records for. He couldn't have known that Quinten was trying to find a cure for the plague.

Unless someone ratted him out.

Maybe someone like Welton.

I thought about it. Was Welton the kind of person to stir the pot and make trouble just for fun?

Oh, hell, yes. He always had been.

And with Slater declaring martial law and the Houses under attack, would Welton have traded favors and information with Oscar? Would he have outfitted his compound with better weapons from one of the Houses, or maybe better medical supplies?

Yes. Yes. And yes.

Shit. Oscar wasn't bluffing. Oscar knew.

"I can't guarantee that," I said.

"Oh? Why not?"

"It hasn't been tested."

Oscar nodded. "Is that why your brother and you left in such a hurry to go to Compound Five?"

"He has a friend there who is ill," I said.

It didn't seem to matter if I told the truth. I suspected he already knew all this.

"And is he treating this friend?"

"Yes. He has made enough to treat one person. If it works, I will do what is in my power to make sure you also have access to the formula."

"No," Oscar said mildly. "I didn't say I also wanted access to it. I said I wanted it. The formula and all rights to distribute the cure, and charge whatever price I see fit for access to it."

The man who owned the cure would own the world. I liked Oscar. The Oscar from my time. Maybe I might even like this Oscar. Abraham certainly seemed friendly with him.

But I was not at all convinced the world should be in any one man's hands.

17

*I think I know what it is. What you need to kill
him. I must reach you before he does.*

— W.Y.

"You'll have to name another price," I said. "I can't
give you the cure."

"But that is all I want." He spread his hands, as if
helpless to change his actions.

I shook my head. "It's not mine to give. Even if I
agreed and signed a contract, there are other people who
know about it. People who knew about it before you and
already staked their claim."

"I'll buy them out."

"The answer's still no. If that's all you'll accept in pay-
ment, then I'll be going. Thanks for your time." I turned
to leave.

"Wait," he said. "Wait. Even I can be . . . flexible. Offer
me a price."

"I don't have anything you would want."

"You don't know that," he said. "Try, Matilda." His
words were deceptively encouraging.

I was getting such mixed signals from him. He had

been a good man before, and I defaulted to wanting to believe he was good still. It was messing with my ability to close this deal.

What did I have that a man like Oscar, whom I really didn't know anymore, would want?

Not the farm. The thread, the jam.

No! Jelly!

"There's a healing balm unique to my farm," I said. "Can't be reproduced anywhere else in the world. It makes wounds heal faster and keeps infection at bay. I'll make you the exclusive distributor of sixty percent of the product we manufacture."

"I'm not a man who buys snake oil, my dear."

"It's not snake oil. Ask Abraham. I put it on his gut wound."

"Is this true?" Oscar asked. "Did you get stabbed in the very short time since I've last seen you?"

Abraham stood, took a breath, and let it out. He shook his head at me. "You should have given him the unproven plague cure," he said as he pulled off his jacket. "Never offer up something of real, proven value," he said, dragging his shirt off over his head, "when you can get away with providing the fake crap that a man desires." He stripped down, then turned toward Oscar, bare chested.

"Bullet hole." He pointed to three almost healed holes in a tight configuration just below his right pec muscle. "Slash from a fall down a cliff." He pushed aside the bandaging to show the stitches across a cut that looked like it was at least a week old and healing.

"You fell down a cliff?" Oscar asked. "How clumsy of you, Abraham."

"Well, if *someone* would have canceled the contract on the Cases after I told him we were coming this way, maybe I wouldn't have had to thin Coal and Ice's ranks."

"I don't see how your poor reflexes are my fault," he said. "Also, I am not one to miss an opportunity. I knew you'd take care of the mercenaries who were on your trail. And since most of them hated you and had short-changed a few contracts with me, I'm not sorry to have lost any of those assholes. Win-win." Then he looked back at me. "Ninety percent of what you manufacture."

"Fifty," I said.

He grinned. "Are we talking a bucket or a teaspoon? How much of this balm do you make in a year?"

I thought about it. I could put up about fifty pounds of it from the one lizard I'd had back in my time. And Quinten had cobbled together three dozen lizards. Even if they yielded only half the scales, it should be a decent amount.

Still, I'd been taught to never overpromise. "I don't have my records on hand," I said, "and I haven't taken inventory. But I can safely guarantee a hundred pounds over a year's time."

"I'll want a ten-year exclusive."

"I'll give you two."

"Eight."

"Six months."

His grin was back. "Three years."

"Thirty months."

"Thirty months of ninety percent of your production?"

"Thirty months of fifty percent of our production."

He considered it for a moment, and I tried not to let him see how nervous I was about it.

"Does it work on humans?" he asked.

I pointed at Abraham. "Yes?"

"No, humans. Not galvanized."

I raised my eyebrows. "I hadn't thought you'd be such a judgmental man, considering your line of work."

He laughed and clapped his hands together. "My line of work is nothing *but* judgment, my dear Matilda. I take your answer to mean that your balm will work on those of us less long-lived?"

I'd used it on Quinten, and he'd told me he used it on his own wounds too. "Yes. It works on humans. Animals too."

"Good! Most of the people in Coal and Ice tend to be one or the other." He stood and walked around his desk again, his hand extended. "It is a true pleasure to do business with you, Ms. Case."

I shook his hand. "You too. So when do we get our guns?"

It turned out guns were the easy part of our resupply plan. Information took a little longer. Oscar invited us to stay in one of the many rooms of his building while we waited. While I thought there probably wasn't a safer place to stay than with the head of Coal and Ice, and Foster agreed to stay with a quiet grunt, Abraham refused.

"There are some things I need to pick up at my place," he said. "Matilda?"

I don't know why I was so surprised. I mean, Abraham had to actually live somewhere. It made sense that he live here, with the other killers and assassins.

I just hadn't expected him to want to take me home.

"Sure," I said, suddenly itching with curiosity. In my world, Abraham had lived with Oscar, as a personal bodyguard and advisor. And Oscar, being the head of House Gray, had lived richly and provided fine living to Abraham.

I wondered what sort of place Abraham would settle down in, given his own means.

"You're in a good mood," he said as we walked along the sidewalk and toward the north end of town.

"It's after dawn and I'm not dead yet," I said. "What's not to smile about?"

He glanced over at me. "You do know every one of these people we're passing is a thief, killer, and reprobate?"

"So?"

"Aren't you worried about how far you've fallen, Ms. Case? Why, just a few days ago, you were nothing but an honest, hardworking farm girl."

"Sure," I said. "I was that. And I was a lot more than you can ever imagine."

"A time traveler."

"That too."

"Sister, fighter, hero, healer."

"Mmm."

"Lover?"

"Are you offering or are you asking?"

He stepped around a sandwich-board sign advertising fresh fruits that was propped in the middle of the sidewalk. "It depends. Are you accepting or explaining?"

"No. Nuh-uh," I said. "No weaseling out of it. Give me a straight answer."

He kept his eyes forward. Was he searching the alley and second-story windows for assassins? Probably. But he was also trying not to look at me.

It was kind of cute.

"I just thought . . . well, back there in the van." He paused, and we let a car rumble past before crossing the street.

"Back there in the van," I prompted.

He bit at the stitches on the side of his mouth. It was a nervous habit.

I liked that I could make him nervous. Liked it a lot.

"We . . . you . . . well." He finally looked over at me. He let go of those stitches and pursed his lips into a smile. "We might just be something a lot more together than apart," he said.

"Is that you telling me you like me, Mr. Vail?"

"I did search the whole world for you."

"So you did," I said. "Are you happy with what you found?"

"Other than you do seem to attract more trouble than any woman I've ever met?"

I rolled my eyes. "Please. You can't tell me in three hundred years, you've never run into a single trouble-maker like me."

"Troublemakers, yes." He stopped. Half turned toward me. "But no one like you."

I looked up at him. At the sincerity in his eyes. At the man I could easily see myself spending the rest of my life with.

"That's really sweet," I said, meaning it. "Anyone tell you how sweet you are, Abraham?"

"Yes," he said softly, sincerely. "And you, well, you have guts in your hair."

"Really? That's how you take a compliment?" My hands flew up to my hair.

"It's . . ." He pointed toward the other side of my hair.

I combed my fingers through as much as the tangles would allow.

"That's not helping much," he said. "You sort of spread it around. Might want a bath."

"And how much is that going to cost me in this town? No, wait—let me guess. I'll have to barter for it."

"Under other circumstances, yes. But since you offered to take on half the cost of funding our hunt for Slater, I'll throw a shower in for free."

"How generous. Do I get soap with that?"

"Probably."

He walked up the three stairs onto a porch of a small, well-built house. He slipped three keys into locks, pressed something else that looked a lot like a digital keypad, and then opened the door.

"This is your place?"

He glanced at it, glanced back at me. "You sound surprised."

"Sturdy walls, solid roof, and no obvious bullet holes. Exceeds my wildest expectations."

"Might charge you for hot water if you keep that up." He strolled into the place. "Come on in."

I walked up the stairs and into Abraham's house.

Oscar's church office had a heavily polished wood interior, each thin board slatted seamlessly into the other. Abraham's home looked like a modern log cabin. A short set of stairs directly to my left led up to a loft bedroom that looked out over the living space. A stone hearth rose from floor to ceiling along the back wall, and tasteful furniture set about the room in deep burgundy and browns contrasted nicely with the wall painted pale sage, beyond which I could see a kitchen.

"Bathroom there." He pointed to the left of the kitchen to a white door. "Water will be hot, and it's plumbed. Since you don't have a change of clothes . . ."

"I'll make do with what I have in my duffel," I said.

He paused, looked at me from head to toe. "I'm getting you new clothes."

"Not necessary."

"It will take days to get the stink of feral blood out of them, including the things in your duffel. I'd rather not draw ferals to us. We're leaving today. In two hours, tops. Not enough time to wash and dry your clothes."

"I'll wear them wet."

"Tempting," he said, tipping his head sideways, "but impractical. I'll get you a new set."

I walked across the hardwood, trying to avoid getting dirt or blood on the expensive-looking throw rugs in the living room. "There is a lot left to be desired by your inability to take no for an answer," I said.

"You'll get used to it, since I'm always right."

I shook my head and walked into the bathroom.

The walls were wood painted white, and the ceiling was wood left bare. But it was the enormous lion's-foot bathtub that had me drooling.

I locked the door, then stripped out of my clothing. Abraham wasn't joking. My shirt was covered in blood and chunks of stuff I didn't want to identify. When I turned to the full-length mirror, I was a little horrified at the state of my hair.

If this was how I looked and Oscar hadn't batted an eye about doing business with me, it said a lot about his clientele.

I turned away from the mirror and opened the tap. Hot water steamed into the beautiful cast-iron tub, and I crawled into it, sluicing away the worst of the grime from my body and hair before setting the plug to let the tub fill for a good soak.

Yes, there was soap, and I intended to use it all.

I was out of the tub and wrapped in an oversized towel, using the brush I'd found in the vanity to get the tangles out of my hair. I'd done my best with my clothes, using a damp washcloth to scrape most of the gore off. They were still filthy, and as much as I hated to admit it, Abraham was right: they stank to high heaven.

I had carefully removed the three slender vials of

Shelley dust and made sure they weren't broken. Luckily, they were still intact and stoppered. I made sure to wrap them back in the handkerchief.

I worked my hair into one loose braid, then checked my stitches, bruises, and cuts to make sure nothing was going bad.

I was procrastinating, taking the time to enjoy being clean. And maybe not wanting to tell Abraham he was right. I needed a new set of clothing.

Abraham knocked on the door. "Matilda? I have a pile of clean, dry clothing in your size."

Crap.

I walked over to the door and unlocked it.

He didn't smile as he very solemnly handed me the stack of clothes. "Just in case you changed your mind," he said, eyes twinkling.

"Thank you." I took the clothes from him and shut the door in his smug face.

Abraham had a good eye for size—all the way from long-sleeved flannel outer shirt, down to pants, underwear, and bra, the clothing he'd picked out fit perfectly.

It was wonderful to be dry, clean, and warm.

I tugged on the thick socks and put my boots over that, then pulled into the jacket last and tucked the vials of Shelley dust into the inside breast pocket.

The jacket was a beautiful thing, brown leather that ended at my waist, with a couple old-time patches on it I didn't recognize. I shrugged into it and it settled over me like a protective wing. It was a little too big, but I liked it.

Might even have to talk Abraham into letting me keep it once this was done.

I took a quick look in the mirror, shook my head at how well everything fit, and stepped out of the room.

Abraham had changed too, and washed the blood out of his hair and off his face and hands.

He had two backpacks out on the table in front of the couch where he sat, and was going through the contents of one of them.

"Everything fit okay?" he asked without looking up.

"Good enough," I said. "Have we heard anything from Oscar—I mean, Binek—yet?"

"No, but I expect to any minute. No matter what you think of him, he is reliable."

"I know." I sat down across from him and looked through the second backpack.

"You know?"

"I knew him."

He finally glanced up at me. His eyes widened a bit, and one eyebrow slipped upward. "You underplayed the fit. Those look great on you."

"I do like the jacket," I said, running my fingertips down the metal zipper teeth. "Who did it belong to?"

He tipped his head. "Old history, really. A woman I was very fond of."

"Your wife?"

"No. Jealous? She was a . . . she was . . . remarkable."

"Not jealous," I said. "What war was this?" I pointed at the patch of a diamond with wings.

"World War Two. She flew in the ATA."

"World War Two. That's a long time to be keeping a jacket."

"I was very fond of her." He said it clearly. And I knew that would be the last he would talk of it.

"You might want to look through the backpack," he said, changing the subject. "This is all we'll be taking in with us to House Fire."

"You mean this plus weapons?"

"Yes."

"And Oscar's going to cover that too?"

He smiled at me using his first name.

"Binek," I corrected.

"Weapons are easy. It's the intelligence to get into House Fire that's taking time."

"And the vehicle?"

He shook his head. "No problem with that. We'll want to leave soon, though. I don't want to wade through another night of ferals."

I suppressed a shudder. I knew how to kill, and had done it many times with the ferals that roamed our land. But last night had been a bloodbath. If Abraham hadn't signaled Coal and Ice, and if the other vehicles hadn't shown up to draw the beasts off us, we would have been buried beneath the sheer mass of them.

We'd be dead.

I dug through the backpack. Fresh medical supplies, a walkie-talkie, a rope, rations, and a case of lockpicking tools.

"Ooh," I said, pulling out two very nice daggers. "I likey."

He nodded. "Those are yours, of course. Also . . ." He got up, walked across the room, and opened a cupboard.

He pulled two doors away to reveal a nook, in which hung very carefully maintained firearms. "Handgun. Preference?"

"Semiautomatic if you have one, but I'm not picky. I can handle anything."

He chose a firearm, checked the breach, then picked up a couple extra clips.

"What about the big guns?" I asked.

He chose a handgun for himself and then closed and locked the cabinet. "Too much of a chance we'll be stopped if we are carrying visible firepower."

"Stopped where? I'd like a clear idea of exactly what you think we're trying to do and how we're trying to do it."

"You're the planning type suddenly?"

"When it comes to dealing with Slater, we will need all the plan A's, B's, and Q's, R's, X's, Y's, Z's as we can. He knows us, Abraham. Knew us in a different time, and knows us in this time. And he's had three hundred years to think about how to keep himself safe from us. He's had three hundred years to try to kill us."

"He hasn't been successful," he reminded me.

"I don't know why he didn't just kill you the first day he saw you, but he only recently found out I exist. And he knows I have my memories of what he's done. Of that time we were all caught in. He knows about time travel, the way the Houses used to be ruled. He told me he wants to kill us all. Kill Quinten. Kill me."

"He told you?"

I stopped. Realized I hadn't shared the time-slip thing with him.

"It doesn't matter."

He leaned back and somehow made it look even more intimidating than if he had leaned forward and grabbed my arm.

"It matters very much. You've had contact with him? When?"

I could lie. I didn't see how that would help. "Just before we went over the cliff."

"Explain." It wasn't a question. It was a command. His hazel eyes had gone dark and closed off. As if he'd decided Oscar was right to be suspicious of me.

"There's something here in this time, some part of the Wings of Mercury machine, that is causing ripples in time. I've slipped into my original timeway and another, I think. I've seen Slater there."

"Has he seen you?"

"Yes."

"Does he know what is causing the ripples?"

I shook my head. "He thinks I have whatever it is. He thinks Quinten has it. He doesn't. Welton told me I'd have to find it and break it if I wanted to kill Slater."

"The custodian? What does he have to do with this?"

"Not the Welton from this time. Welton from my original time."

"He knows how to kill Slater?"

"He knows Slater and I are tied together because of the Wings of Mercury time-travel event. He said I wouldn't be able to kill him unless I first broke the item that is causing the time slips."

"You believe him?"

"He's a genius. He understood what little we knew about the Wings of Mercury experiment. Also, Slater shot me, but the bullet wound disappeared, so that part of his theory seems valid."

"He shot you. When you saw him in the other timeway?"

"Yes."

"I'm annoyed you didn't think this was important to mention to me."

"I haven't had a chance. Not really."

"You can't kill Slater," he began.

"I can after I break whatever is causing the time ripples."

"We have no idea what that item might be, where it might be, or who might possess it," he said. "What happens if I kill Slater?"

"He dies?"

"What happens to you?" he asked.

Oh. I hadn't thought that through. We were tied together. If Slater died, did that mean I died? "I don't know,"

I said. "But we're not going to let that stop us from killing him."

Abraham didn't say anything. His face was carefully closed down, though his eyes flickered with red: anger.

"We?" he said.

I shrugged.

"You said there were other timeways. What were they?" he asked.

"They don't matter."

"We don't leave this room, we don't leave this town, until I know."

"They might have been dreams."

He waited.

"You were in them," I said quietly. "But you were happy. And you weren't a mercenary."

"And?" he asked when I could no longer hold his gaze and looked instead at my hands.

"And you loved me."

"You think that was a dream?"

I glanced up at him. "Isn't it?"

Abraham—this Abraham—was not the sort of man who settled down in a house with lace curtains. Was he?

"It doesn't have to be."

Wait. Had he just admitted to loving me?

"You told me you believe the galvanized are human," he said. "Do you think that I'm incapable of emotions just because I lack sensation? Do you think I'm incapable of caring?"

"I don't know," I said. "Do mercenaries fall in love?"

"Very rarely," he said. "Which is why we fight so hard for it when we find it. And if you think *we* are not going to make damn sure you survive this fight with Slater, then you are very wrong about me. About us."

"Us?" I said, stupidly.

"Yes. Us." He watched my reaction: a shock of disbelief backed up by a big helping of hope.

I must not have kept it hidden very well, because he leaned back, the intensity in his eyes down to a simmer again, satisfied with himself.

"I guess," I said, clearing my throat. "I guess I didn't think. Didn't think we could even be a . . . anything until after we took care of Slater. Saved the world. . . ." My words sort of gave out, which only made him smile wider.

"The world is always in need of saving," he said. "Always. Can't let that stop you from living. Or loving."

I nodded. "I want that. I do. But first we need to find the piece of the Wings of Mercury experiment. Do you have any information on it?"

"Not personally. But I know some people we can ask."

"Okay. Well, I've told you all I know about the time slips. Your turn." I sat back and hooked the ankle of my boot over my knee. "Tell me what you know about House Fire."

"House Fire is a walled city. Not as open as Coal and Ice, not as primitive as House Earth compounds. It is a very modern, technologically advanced city."

"What kinds of defenses do they have?"

"Everything. Cameras, computers, guards, weapons, trip lines. We need Hollis to get us in. If we walk up any road, reach any gate, or tried to infiltrate through underground tunnels, including the sewer system, we would be stopped."

"I'd be more comfortable about the whole thing if we could draw Slater out," I said. "It's stupid to walk into a lion's den and fight there."

"With night coming on, and by the time we get there . . . I don't know how that's possible."

I stared at the ceiling for a moment, both to try to figure out our options and to look away from him. Sexy

Abraham was a growing force in the room. I could almost feel the heat radiating off him, the hunger barely contained.

I wanted to kiss him until he begged for mercy.

"How about you turn me in?" I asked, trying not to picture him naked. "There's a ransom on my head, right? And you're a mercenary, a bounty hunter. We can walk right up to the front gate and let Slater know we want to see him."

He thought it over for a moment or two, then leaned forward and rummaged through the backpack, resettling the contents that were already settled. There couldn't be much in the backpack to look over, and he'd probably been through it several times.

He was stalling.

"You'd trust me to do that?" he asked.

Don't make me doubt you, Abraham, I thought.

"You've proved that you'll save my life. In more than one time."

He angled a look my way. "Good to know."

"What? That you came to my rescue in the past?"

"No. That you've always attracted trouble."

"You like living in constant danger?"

"I like knowing life with you will never be boring."

He was doing it again. Talking like we were going to make it through this. Like we were going to be together. I hoped he was right, but I wasn't as sure. We had a very dangerous man to kill, and we still had no plan.

"Speaking of not boring, I don't see a downside to you turning me in to Slater so I can get close enough to kill him."

"You would be unarmed," he said, back to business again. "No gun. No knife. No Shelley dust."

"I know."

"And completely dependent on him believing I'd do it."

I paused. Searched his face. Was he trying to tell me something? "Wouldn't you? Collect on the price on my head if . . . well, if things were different?"

"Maybe. But I would never get that close to Slater and not try to kill him. It's an agreement he and I have."

"That you'll kill him the next time you see him?"

"Pretty much. Yes."

"Think you could sell him on your wanting the money?"

"I don't know."

There was a knock at the door. "That's our call." He stood and pulled on a long gray jacket, then shouldered the backpack. "Are you ready?"

"Since we've decided on exactly no plan? I'm just gold." I shrugged the backpack over one shoulder and followed him to the door.

A kid about ten years old stood there. "Binek wants to see you," he said.

Abraham dropped something into the kid's hand. I thought it looked like a half stick of dynamite. "Thanks, Cart."

The kid gave me a hard look, like he'd be willing to describe me to the local law if needed; then he took off down the street and around the corner at a jog.

Abraham shut and locked the door behind us, then started down the sidewalk. "Let's go make us a plan," he said.

18

Slater found me. He isn't shy about torture.
Libra unloaded House Technology's artillery
to get me back. I had no choice but to tell him
what he wanted to know. But only half of it.
Only half of the truth.

—W.Y.

The door to Oscar's office was closed. Abraham had been standing in front of it for a good two minutes.

"Want me to knock for you?" I asked from where I stood, leaning against the wall in the silence of the hallway.

His shoulders tightened. Then he turned around. "If his door is closed, he is not to be disturbed. I'm sure he'll see us soon. Let's find the others." He pushed past me, and I really didn't have a lot of other choices but to follow.

We crossed to the lobby area, then up the stairs on the other side of the room.

"What others?" I asked.

The stairs ended one flight up. A set of doors were closed, but I could hear the sound of voices behind them. The "others," I presumed.

Abraham straight-armed his way through the doors. The rich fragrance of food—warm bread and something sweet—reached out and wrapped around me.

"Abraham!" A woman's voice called out.

I stepped into the room of delicious smells and killed the conversation flat.

The room was a cross between a lounge and a bar, with a kitchen off to one side, booze on the other, and between those two points, an unused pool table, some couches, chairs, and tables.

Scattered around the room were the galvanized. Oh. *Those* others.

All six of them. Two men and four women. Most of them glaring at me.

Dotty, or Dolores Second, as I'd known her, was a lovely woman who appeared to be in her late forties. Her ginger-and-brown locks swung about shoulder length, fringe across her green eyes. She wore a loose orange blouse under a vest that hid at least one gun, and tailored, wide-legged slacks. She seemed more curious than angered by the sight of me, though her gaze fixed on the patch on my jacket for a long moment before she shifted her gaze to Abraham.

I don't know what she saw in his expression, but it seemed to impress her.

"My, my," she said, settling back to stare at me again.

I glanced at each person in the room. Wila Fifth, along with Vance Fourth, sat on one of the couches. They'd been a part of House Blue in my time, but that was where their similarities ended. Wila was maybe in her thirties and dusky-skinned, her heavy black dreadlocks pulled back in a massive knot to make her rounded face and cheekbones even more prominent. She had a curvy figure even under the layers of shirts and slacks she wore. If she carried a weapon, I didn't see it.

Vance was a short, trim, pale, red-haired trouble-maker, with a rifle next to his knee. He and Wila seemed to take in the sight of me with curiosity.

But January Sixth didn't. She rested in a wooden chair, the queen of ice and cool, her platinum hair cut spiky and short, her face stitched with such a precise hand, it only exaggerated her beauty as she glared at me.

So she still didn't like me. Good to know.

Off to her left was long-limbed, too-tall Clara Third. Her red hair was cut in the same single swing that made her stark, melancholy features even more masculine. She wore clothes most resembling Vance's—practical denim, long-sleeved shirt, and vest with enough pockets to hide an assortment of weapons.

The last galvanized in the room was Buck Eighth. He lounged near the pool table, wearing dark trousers and a couple of layers of shirts, all in black. He cut a striking, dangerous figure, his hair shaved down to his skull, making his intense gold-green eyes practically glow within his dark-toned skin, and giving his angular face a feral cast.

"So," Dotty asked with just the hint of a Southern accent, "who do we have here, Bram, darlin'?"

"Everyone," Abraham said, "this is Matilda Case, the tenth galvanized. Matilda, this is Dotty, Wila, January, Vance, and Buck. You know Foster."

Foster sat on a stool in front of the bar, winding a pocket watch. He glanced up at me, frowned a moment when he saw the jacket, threw that same sort of look at Abraham that Dotty had given him. This time I noticed Abraham nod ever so slightly.

Foster slipped a look to me, and his smile was warm. Then went back to winding the watch.

"Tenth?" Vance asked. "Where have you been hiding for all these years, Matilda?"

I shrugged. "I grew up on a farm. And stayed there."

"Isn't that cute?" January said. "Three hundred years on the same farm? You don't believe that crap, do you, Abraham?"

Okay, so January was the same bitter thing I remembered from my time. It was good to know some things never changed.

"I think she's lying," January said, as if I didn't have ears.

"I don't really care what you think about me, January," I said. "You can just step back and relax. I won't be here, and I won't be in any of your business, for very long."

"Good," January said.

"No." Dotty stood and walked over to me. "This isn't at all how we should welcome one of our own. Matilda, I'm Dolores—please call me Dotty. I am very pleased to make your acquaintance." She held out her hand and I shook it.

"What?" She snatched her hand away. "I felt that."

Right. I'd forgotten she didn't know I could make her feel.

"I'm sorry," I said. "I have that effect on galvanized."

She rubbed her palms together and studied me more closely. "Well, that's a surprise," she said. "Quite a big surprise. When did you happen across our Abraham here?"

"He found me, actually."

Buck *tsk*ed and shook his head. "This is the girl? *The* little future girl you used to talk about?"

"Not a little girl anymore." Abraham strode over to the bar and poured himself a glass of whiskey.

"We can see that," Vance murmured. "And we approve."

Wila slapped his arm.

"This," Abraham continued, "is apparently the future." He gulped the shot, refilled the glass, and took that down too.

Wila raised one eyebrow, looking from Abraham to me. "Lot of drinking for a man who's found the one thing he's been looking for all his life. Foster, my delight, you simply must fill me in on everything that's happened between these two."

Foster shook his head and tucked the watch away into his pocket. He looked over at Wila. "Slater," he said.

That one word stalled all the questions, all the dirty looks, all the conversation. And then everyone was looking at Foster before shifting that look to Abraham.

"Slater?" Vance said.

"Matilda and I intend to kill him." Abraham refilled his glass. "I don't suppose any of you would like to join us?"

Still the silence.

Abraham swallowed half of the shot. "Of course, I don't need to tell any of you what I will do to you if you stand in our way of killing him."

He waited, measuring their response. As far as I could tell, they gave off very little emotional cues.

"It's been a long time since you've threatened us, Abraham," Buck finally said, picking up a pool stick and testing the balance, like maybe he was getting ready for a fight. "Not sure you want to be doing it now."

Abraham downed the rest of the whiskey and set the tumbler carefully on the bar. "Don't stand in my way," he said with a hard smile, "and we won't have to find out. But if you want a part of this, the offer stands."

"I'll bite," Dotty said. "How are you going to kill him? Just getting into House Fire will be hard enough. Getting to a newly minted head of a House won't be a stroll through the daffodils."

"I didn't say I was going to tell you our plan. If you're in, you're in. If you're out, clear a wide berth."

"Is she a killer?" quiet Clara asked. It was almost more than she'd said to me all at once, in any time.

They all looked at me again.

"I know my way with weapons," I said. "And, believe me—I have a need to see him dead."

"But are you a killer?" Clara asked. The intensity behind the question gave it more weight. She wanted to know that one thing about me. Slater or no Slater.

"I've protected my family, fought ferals. But I haven't killed a man, no."

All eyes were on me again. The silence and judgment were deafening.

That seemed to mean something to all of them, just like it had meant something to Abraham.

I still didn't know how my not being a murderer would make any difference in how the world perceived and treated galvanized.

"I will help you, Abraham," Clara said solemnly.

"So will I," Vance said. "But only because I'd like to see a world without that dick Slater in it."

Buck nodded. "You know I'm a sucker for a cause. I'll do what I can."

"I'm in," Dotty said.

"Y'all know how I feel about that man," Wila said. "He should have been put out of our misery years ago. Count me in."

"Fine," January said. "I'm not going to be the only one who misses out on seeing Slater die."

"What do you need?" Buck asked.

"You to follow my orders." Abraham stepped away from the bar and paced, every inch a commander addressing his team.

"Of course we will, Bram," Dotty said. "Unless you're being a complete idiot. Otherwise, we'll stand aside and let you walk into whatever fire you set off, if that's what you want."

"Dotty," he sighed. "Following orders means doing so even if I'm being an idiot."

"I know," she said. "But I, for one, reserve the right to follow my own judgment if things go completely to hell. It's more of a promise to cover your ass than a prelude to mutiny, darlin'."

He tucked his thumbs into his belt. "Fine. We also need information. Do any of you remember what happened to the Wings of Mercury machine?"

Vance whistled. "That's digging back a ways."

"Wasn't it taken apart and destroyed?" Wila asked, frowning. "The scientist, he decided it shouldn't be replicated because it was too dangerous, or some such. He tore it down, broke it up. Or did the government confiscate it?"

"I thought there was a fire," January said. "Hot enough, metal and all the components melted."

"I remember hearing that too," Wila said. "Why the interest in that old thing, Bram?"

"There is a piece of it, or a piece of something from that experiment, that is causing ripples in time."

No one said anything. Finally Buck spoke up. "Bullshit."

"Don't care if you believe me," Abraham said. "But if any of you kept a token, an heirloom, or a piece of the Wings of Mercury machine, or know of anyone who might—a historian, a museum—I need to know now."

"Why?" Clara asked.

"Without it, we can't kill Slater."

"Are you confusing murder with daydreams again, Abraham?" Wila asked. "Slater ain't any more immortal than the rest of us. He can be killed with enough bullets to the head."

"Not without destroying the piece of the time machine," Abraham said. "He's hooked to it."

Vance shook his head. "You're not making sense. No judgment—we've all stepped off the deep end now and then, some of us more often than others." He nodded at January, and she flipped him off. "But there is no time machine, Abraham. Never was. Whatever the Wings of Mercury experiment did to us had nothing to do with time."

Abraham glanced over at me. He hadn't asked me to state my case, and from the mood in the room, I didn't think they'd believe me anyway. Still, I figured I should offer my position on this mess.

"Alveré Case, the scientist who built the machine, was my ancestor," I said. "It was built to manipulate time. It didn't produce the results he expected. But it did create a weird situation where Slater might not be able to be killed unless we make sure he's not tied into a relic from the past. A relic that was a part of the Wings of Mercury machine. If Slater can be killed"—here I held Abraham's gaze—"we're going to take that shot, even without destroying the relic. No matter the consequences."

His nostrils flared and his eyes narrowed before he went back to that stony expression.

"Oh, now, this is just too much," Dotty said. "Honey, you might think your great-granddad was a time traveler, but we've been alive for hundreds of years. Time travel isn't anything more than fairy tales. Do you understand?" Dotty looked over at Abraham. "She does understand that, doesn't she? Or is she the flighty type?"

"She's sane," Abraham said. "And she's proven to my satisfaction that what she says is true."

"You'd believe anything she says," January said. "She's your will-o'-the-wisp. Now that you've caught her, you can't believe she isn't magic. She's playing you."

"I'm not playing anyone," I said.

"Is there proof?" Clara asked.

"Yes." Foster stood. "This." He was holding the pocket watch in his hand again.

A chill washed over me as I realized it wasn't a pocket watch; it was *the* pocket watch that had been handed down from Case father to Case son.

"Is that Quinten's watch?" I asked.

"You gave it to Alveré," Foster said. "Alveré gave it to me. A gift. For the corrected formula."

"What formula?" Vance asked.

"Time," Foster breathed. "Mend time. Save billions."

I walked over to him and looked at the watch in his palm. It was worn, the shine by the watch stem rubbed off, the face scratched a bit at the edges, and the chain replaced. But that was the watch I'd carried with me back in time.

I didn't feel any different standing this close to it. I didn't feel the world shift or time slide. I didn't smell roses or hear bells. If it was causing the time slips, it was not doing so now.

"Matilda?" Abraham asked.

"That's the watch," I said. "It was Alveré's, and passed down from father to son in the Case family. I took it back with me. It was the only thing of modern time that traveled back in time with me. Maybe this is the relic." I looked over at Abraham.

He bit at the stitches on the corner of his mouth. "I don't know. Was it a part of the machine?"

"No, but I took it back with me," I said again. "It was a physical item that shifted through time. And if what Welt—" I paused. I didn't want to drag Welton into this. They didn't believe me about time travel, I didn't think they'd believe that the current custodian of House Earth was the head of House Yellow in my time. Nor that he had found a way to tell me that we needed to locate the time artifact if we were going to kill Slater.

"Well," I said instead. "Well, if what we think is true, then I don't know if anything else exists that could be the relic. Plus, if this is it, there's an easy way to test it: destroy it and kill Slater."

He didn't look convinced. "You don't know for certain that this watch is the item."

"I don't know for certain that it isn't," I said.

The others swore softly or shook their heads.

"But I will go to great lengths to see Slater dead. That"—I pointed at the watch I still hadn't been brave enough to touch—"is as good a start as any."

"It's still a gamble," he said.

"I'm not afraid of a little gamble. Are you?"

Before he could answer, there was a soft knock on the door. Oscar strolled into the room. "I thought I might find you here, Abraham, Matilda." He paused and scanned the rest of the people in the room. "Hello, everyone. I hope the day is treating you well."

"Binek," Buck, and several others, said by way of greeting.

"Abraham, I have your information," he said.

"Might as well say it here."

Oscar raised his eyebrows. "Are all of you in on Abraham and Matilda's plans?"

"They are," Abraham said.

"I see," Oscar said. "This has been some years coming, hasn't it? Far be it from me to stand in the way of revenge rightfully earned. For the things he has put you all through, I hope this retaliation is sweet and swift."

"Thank you," Abraham said.

"You will need to be at the east entrance of House Fire before sunset. There will be a contact who will meet you there and guide you in behind the wall. Once past the wall, she will take you to a building adjacent to Slater's private office and residence. That's where you'll run into problems I can't solve for you."

"Problems?" I asked.

"I can't be sure exactly where Slater will be in the building. It's fifteen floors. The entrances are under surveillance, with cameras and guards, and everything is run off an encrypted computer system of his own design. To get past the cameras and through the doors, you'll need passwords I can't obtain in a day. Maybe not in a week."

"House Earth doesn't have a week," I said. "There will be another bombing today, if there hasn't been already. I won't wait a week while innocent people die."

January scoffed. "Seriously, Abraham. Where did you dig up that sweet little hero?"

I turned to her. "We get it. You're angry. Fine. If you want to bitch, take it somewhere else. If you want to fight me, you'll have to wait until I kill this bastard. In the meantime, keep your opinions of me to yourself." I turned to Oscar. "I can hack the computer."

"What?" he asked. I wasn't sure if he was startled by my snapping at January or that I had computer skills.

"I know computers. I can hack into any system. Get me close enough—the building next to where Slater stays—and I'll black out the surveillance system, spring the locks, and pinpoint Slater."

"Where did you learn computer skills, Matilda? Your farm isn't wired."

"I learned it a long time ago. I can get us past his security." I glanced up at Abraham to see if he believed me.

He chewed on his bottom lip, his gaze steady on me. "Hollis was no help?" he asked Oscar.

"Slater changes the passwords every three minutes," Oscar said. "Seems our friend has taken his paranoia to dizzying heights."

Abraham inhaled, exhaled, and released his lip. "Matilda will handle the security."

"That's what I call a vote of confidence," Vance said. "A foolish, foolish vote of confidence."

Wila chuckled, but no one else had any comments. "I'll leave it to your decision," Oscar said. "Is there anything else you need?"

"Do you have a way to fill bullets with powder?" I asked.

"Of course," he said, almost offended.

"Give me a couple minutes, Abraham," I said. "I'll be right back."

While Oscar watched me closely, I filled six bullets with Shelley dust, and still had a small amount left over.

"Waste not, want not." Oscar handed me a medical syringe and needle. I filled the syringe with the remaining powder.

"I am more than a little curious as to what that powder might be," he said as I loaded the six bullets into the handgun, then tucked the syringe into the breast pocket of the leather coat I was wearing. "Can I assume it will kill Slater?"

"Sure," I said. "That's what I'm going to assume. If I can get close enough, anyway." I stood away from the worktable he'd taken me to in a room that looked more like a bomb shelter than the basement of a church. "Thank you for all of your help, Oscar. I mean, Mr. Binek. I hope to see you again someday."

"You will," he said. "I'll need to come out to your farm to inspect that medical balm you'll be giving me seventy percent control over."

"Fifty. Nonexclusive distribution." I smiled.

"Is that what it was?" He grinned, his eyes twinkling. "You do know this is all going to work out, don't you, Matilda?"

"Nice of you to say so."

"I am a man of some reputation. A man who never makes reckless bets. And I would stake my reputation that you and Abraham will see this through to the end. That you and he will be done with Slater once and for all."

"I hope you're right," I said, climbing the stairs. "If I don't see you again . . ."

"Which you will," he said, climbing the stairs behind me.

"But if I don't, I want you to know I appreciate how much you've always gone out of your way to help others. To help me. Even when there never was much of a reason to."

I knew he'd think I was talking about the information he'd given us in this time. While I was grateful for that, it was the other, generous-hearted Oscar from the other timeway that I wished I had one more chance to thank.

But this timeway and this Oscar were the best I could do.

"I haven't done much at all, really," he said. "We'll have time to get to know one another better. I'm sure of it."

We crossed the landing and paused there in the small private room at the top of the stairs. Just beyond this single door was the lounge where I'd last seen the galvanized.

"I will give you one piece of advice," he said. "For free."

I smiled. "I was under the impression you didn't do free."

"This isn't business," he said. "This is advice, and you may set your own value for it. Abraham and I go back a long way. Almost all my life. He has been looking for you for many years, Matilda. He has never forgotten that you saved his life. I know your hatred for Slater runs deep, and so does his. But understand, all that aside, Abraham intends to pay back your act of kindness. No matter the cost.

"He may be galvanized, but he is also a man who follows a certain set of morals. Old-fashioned in his loyalties. He is capable of great kindness and immense sacrifice. I would be very upset if he comes to harm. Any harm."

"We're walking into an enemy camp," I said. "I can't guarantee any of us are going to walk out of that in one piece."

"I wasn't talking about bullets," he said. "I was talking about you."

Those words stopped me for a moment.

"You think I want to hurt him?"

"I don't know. But my advice"—he pressed his hands together like we'd just come to an agreement—"is that you should not use the advantage he's placed in your hands for wrong. Or you and I will be on much less friendly terms."

"What advantage?" I was the one new to this world. I was the one who was having to sort through however many different timeways and versions of people and rules and threats. As far as I could tell, I was more at a disadvantage than anyone else. Plus, there was a madman who had made killing me his priority number one.

Then there was that whole thing Abraham had pointed out: if Slater died, would I die too?

"He cares for you. More than he shows."

"Did he tell you that?" I asked.

"In many ways. He went with Sallyo to find you, stayed with you, brought you here, bartered my favor for you, took you to his home. You're wearing that jacket."

I tugged at the edge of the jacket. "So this is more than him showing me common courtesy and also wanting me as his kill buddy?"

"It is much more."

"Who did it belong to?"

"That's his story to tell," he said. "Ask him someday."

"If I get a someday, I will."

The door to the room opened, and Abraham stood there. "Are you ready? We don't have much time if we're going to get there before sundown."

"Good," Oscar said. "Then I will see you on your farm, Matilda Case, if not sooner. Good luck to you." He nodded to Abraham. "Stop by for a drink when you're done, Bram."

"I'll do that," Abraham said.

I nodded to Oscar, then stepped out of the small space toward Abraham.

"Did you take care of what you needed?" Abraham asked.

"I'm ready," I said, "no matter how much time we have left."

19

Does he think I'll lay down and die? That I won't find a way to tell you everything? To save you, to save Foster?

—W.Y.

We traveled in two cars across the open terrain. After driving for over an hour on rugged roads, our tires hit smooth highway and made twice the speed. Other vehicles whizzed past us, while heavy motorized equipment trundled more slowly on the right side of the road.

It was amazing how quickly the scenery went from dirt, scrub, and wilds to tended fields with rows of produce, and rows of workers harvesting and hauling.

The longer we drove, the more populated the area became. I thought that if the borders were still to be drawn in the old-fashioned manner of my timeway, we were a good deal more east and had crossed into the boundaries of the big city and metropolitan sprawls that had existed there.

After a steady blur of fields large enough to feed countless cities, we came down over a rise, and I got my first glimpse at House Fire's impressive skyline.

Abraham hadn't been kidding when he said House Fire was far more advanced than House Earth. This city looked so much like the cities from my timeway, I couldn't help but smile at the skyscrapers that spiraled up hundreds of stories, and the bridges and roadways that looped and stitched through the neon buildings, trees, and other structures.

There were no speed tubes, but there was no lack of trains, trams, cars, and motorcycles in this bustling landscape. It was big. It was busy. It was familiar.

The two things noticeably different from my time were the lack of airplane traffic—or really any traffic in the sky at all—and the massive metal wall that stretched out for miles and miles, surrounding the city.

Cameras reflected sunlight at regular intervals along the walls, and watchtowers built with heavy glass windows that allowed clear vantages of the city and its surroundings were set at equal distance along the top of the thick wall.

"That's not a city; it's a fortress," I said from where I sat in the passenger's seat next to Abraham, who was driving.

"Both," Abraham agreed.

Foster sat in the very back of the car, which was big enough to comfortably seat six. Dotty, Vance, and January filled the other seats. I was pretty sure January had only come along to watch me fail.

The galvanized carried weapons and watched the scenery go by with the casual confidence of someone who could kill their way out of any situation and had done so often enough that it had become routine.

In a way, I couldn't be among stronger allies. I couldn't be in a safer place than surrounded by these people.

But I didn't know them well enough to truly trust

them. More than once I'd wondered if any of them would betray us, turn me in for the price on my head, or just turn Abraham and me both in to Slater for other reasons.

They'd lived three hundred years. I didn't doubt there had to be some hard feelings among them. I just hoped they all hated Slater the most.

Abraham appeared relaxed. He rested his elbow on the edge of the window, his blunt fingers propped against his temple. He chewed at the inner corner of his mouth, maybe nervous, maybe bored.

I decided to take it as nervous, since this plan—what there was of it—hinged on Hollis's arranging for someone to meet us to get us past the wall and the initial security, so we could take down the surveillance systems and pinpoint Slater.

It was making me nervous.

Foster still had the pocket watch. I had spoken to him briefly during the first part of our travel and told him not to destroy it, not to do anything other than carry it until we got inside the city and knew Slater's location. Then we'd break it, whether it was the key or not, and do our best to break Slater.

With every minute, the details of the city became clearer and clearer. But we still had a long way left to drive before we were anywhere near the entry gates of the wall.

My thoughts drifted to Quinten. He would know I was gone by now and had to be furious about it. The note I'd left explained that I was heading on to Coal and Ice with Abraham and Foster. I hadn't told him that we would be hunting Slater, since I didn't think leaving behind hard evidence of a murder plot was a good idea.

But he'd know exactly what my main priority was: stopping Slater, which meant he knew I was coming here to kill him.

I hoped Gloria was recovering. I hoped Quinten and Neds weren't doing something dumb, like trying to get to Slater before us. I rolled that over in my head, wondering if my brother—well, this brother of mine—was the sort who would leave his dying love behind and run off half-cocked to try to save me.

Crap. He just might.

But they couldn't travel in the night, so that gave me a six-hour jump on him. If he had set out to Coal and Ice at dawn, he was probably just arriving there. I hoped Oscar wouldn't let him drive through the night to House Fire.

Or there was the chance Quinten was still at House Earth, tending Gloria and making more cure for the plague, like he should be. There was a chance he hadn't found my note.

I thought there might be enough sensible people there who could talk him into staying: Neds, Gloria, Welton.

Well, Gloria and Neds were sensible people anyway.

The day was sliding into evening by the time we joined the line of cars, wagons, and other vehicles waiting to be admitted into the city, the heavy cloud cover tamping out the sun. Oscar had told us to enter through the east gate. He had said there would be someone there to meet us.

If he was wrong, if Hollis hadn't found a way around House Fire security, we were rolling toward our own prison.

Or death.

The vehicle in front of us was waved through the gate by the guard who wore a uniform of red and orange. We were next.

Two guards walked up on either side of the car, and Abraham and I rolled down our windows.

"Identification," the guard on Abraham's side asked.

Abraham pulled a tag Oscar had given us from behind the visor and handed it out the window.

The guard straightened, studied the tag for what felt like forever. "Wait here."

He turned and walked toward a door set into the wall, pulling a walkie-talkie out of his belt.

There were cameras everywhere. The guard next to my window watched us, his gaze flicking over Foster, Dotty, and January, hand casually resting on the gun he had strapped to his thigh.

I didn't say anything, and did my best not to look nervous or like a criminal. Or like a nervous criminal.

The first guard paused at the door in the wall, and it opened. Vance in the seat behind me softly whispered, "Son of a bitch."

Through that door strolled Sallyo, her dark hair pulled back to somehow make the angles of her face even sharper, her snake-slit eyes widened with heavy black eyeliner, her slacks and shirt both the military-cut uniform of burnt red and orange.

She looked like an official House Fire guard, except for the stripe of black across her shoulder and the deference the other guards paid her. Which meant she was more than a common guard.

I thought she was a mercenary, not a guard on House Fire's payroll. Now I had no idea what she was.

She stopped by Abraham's window. "Just this car?" she asked.

"And the one behind us," Abraham answered.

He didn't look surprised to see her. He didn't sound surprised.

"It looks like everyone came out to play," she said. "Isn't that nice?" She flashed her sharp teeth. "It is so good of you to respond to our invitation. Exit the vehicle and follow me."

She moved away from the door, and Abraham rolled up his window. I followed his lead.

"Tell me you're not trusting her," January said from the backseat.

"I never have," Abraham said. "But she's our contact. I don't have to trust her once she gets us in the city."

"Out in the open where everyone will see us?" Vance said, cracking his knuckles. "I hate this."

"Oh, you love it," Dotty said. "Just smile for the cameras and try to look human."

"I'd rather shoot her," Vance said.

"Don't fret," Dotty said. "You might get your chance."

We all stepped out of the car, and Abraham signaled for the others behind us to leave their car too. Then we followed Sallyo, beneath the cameras, beneath the curious gazes of at least a hundred people waiting in vehicles or moving about on the streets and sidewalks inside the city near the gate.

I should feel vulnerable, exposed.

But walking with half a dozen nearly immortal killers beside me, all of us joined in the mutual task of killing a man who had destroyed our lives and the lives of too many others, and who would only continue destroying lives, made me feel the opposite of exposed.

I felt powerful with these people. My people. It was my place to fight beside them and for them. In my own way, I was doing a lot more than killing Slater. I was avenging the lives and rights of each of these people who had been forced to be criminals in this world, and slaves in the other.

It felt right.

The sky was rapidly losing light as we made our way

down a narrow strip of sidewalk, concrete wall on one side, metal chain-link fence on the other, a metal ceiling above us.

Sallyo strode in the front of us all, like she was leading a damn parade. Six armed guards marched behind us. After three blocks, Sallyo turned and then stopped.

"I'll take them to the holding room," she said to the guards. "You are dismissed."

The guards paused. They obviously didn't think it was a good idea to leave one woman, even if she was a mutant, to try to control all the galvanized in the world.

"Dismissed," she commanded.

The guards saluted, then walked back the way we'd come.

"It's real nice of you seeing us in like this," Dotty said.

"This doesn't have anything to do with you, Dot," Sallyo said. "I'm just doing the job." She opened the door and stepped inside a room.

We all walked in after her.

The room was dark, and my eyes couldn't adjust to it quickly enough.

"Fuck," Buck, behind and to my left, breathed.

The door slammed behind us and we were plunged in total darkness.

"Down!" Abraham yelled.

A body slammed into me—maybe Vance; maybe Buck—and I tumbled to the floor, grunting as I hit hard.

Buck swore, probably feeling that fall, since he was touching me.

The room broke apart into staccato flashes of light and darkness as gunfire filled the room.

Sallyo had led us right into an ambush.

". . . bitch!" Vance yelled over the rattle of guns.

Dotty, Wila, Vance, and January threw some kind of

glow bulbs impervious to bullets that stuck where they landed. Light arced a trail up to the ceiling and the walls, and rolled across the floor, crackling with the pop of electricity snapping to life.

I was crouched on the floor, behind some kind of storage crate, trying to get my bearings on the room.

The place was big enough to park fifty cars inside; concrete floor, walls, roof. Metal stairs at the far end led up to a metal walkway that hung over the far wall and halfway out to the walls on either side of us.

I spotted dozens of soldiers up on that metal walkway, firing down at us. Most of them wore goggles—hopefully, night-vision goggles that were useless now that the room was ablaze in globe light.

The galvanized were already firing back, weapons they'd kept hidden suddenly in their hands.

Vance and January rushed the stairs, both of them yelling as Wila, Dotty, and Vance laid down suppressive fire.

"This way!" Abraham grabbed my arm and pulled me to my feet.

I ran with him. Between one step and the next, a bolt of pain lanced my shoulder.

I'd been shot. I yelled, then reached for my gun, but didn't pull it. It was loaded with the Shelley dust, and there was no way in hell I was wasting those bullets on these guards.

Abraham swore and pushed me ahead of him, twisting to fire as we ran.

It wasn't until we were nearly at the far wall that I realized Foster was pounding behind us, covering our escape.

Abraham opened a door and shoved me through it.

I stumbled, caught myself.

Other than square and enclosed, I didn't have any clue what this empty room was originally intended for.

Foster slammed the door.

"Lock it," Abraham ordered, striding my way.

Foster spread his feet, then gripped the metal handle in one hand. He twisted, and I could hear the wrenching scream of metal crushing and collapsing in his hand.

I was a strong girl. And Foster was a frighteningly strong man.

"Are you all right?" Abraham dropped a clip out of his handgun and slammed a new one into position. He handed me the gun. "You're bleeding."

"Shoulder hurts like hell. I'm fine." I took a moment to get the heft and feel of the gun.

He'd already pulled a second from somewhere under his jacket.

And I'd thought Neds carried a lot of heat.

"Why didn't you fire?" he asked, striding across the room to the metal stairs that jagged up to the second story.

"I filled the bullets with Shelley dust," I said, climbing behind him.

He stopped and glanced over his shoulder. "How many?"

I pushed at his back to make him move. Foster had destroyed the door handle, but that didn't mean there wasn't another way into this place.

"Six."

"Good." He jogged the stairs, and I jogged after him.

"Do you know where you're going?" I asked.

"Should be a control room this way."

"How do you know?"

"I was a guard here many years ago."

"You could have warned me that we were walking into an ambush."

"Didn't know. Things have changed. This way."

His knowledge of the layout was handy. Although I didn't know why we needed Oscar's info if Abraham knew his way around.

Our boots shook the metal breezeway as we jogged to the door at the end.

"What about the others?" I asked.

"They'll take care of the guards."

"And Sallyo?"

Abraham pulled the door open and lifted his handgun, aiming at something inside the room.

Not something. Someone.

"Sallyo's going to put the gun down nice and slow." He advanced into the room.

Sallyo stood all the way across the room, which was filled with the hot plastic stink of computers and wires. This was more than just the surveillance room where displays showed various video feeds, though it was that too.

It was also a computer room.

Hot damn.

Sallyo held her hands out to the side, a gun in the left.

"I'll put the gun down," she said, "but you want me on your side, Abraham."

"We tried that. You led us into an ambush."

She set the gun on the countertop next to her.

"No," he said. "Put it on the floor and kick it my way."

She rolled her eyes, slowly picked up the gun, bent, and placed it on the floor, then kicked it our way.

"Is this the kind of equipment you know?" Abraham asked me.

"It should be."

"Go ahead."

He kept the barrel of his gun pointed at Sallyo. "Step to your left," he told her.

She did so. "I knew you stitched could handle your-selves around a few trigger-happy guards, and it fulfills my contract without blowing my cover. Don't you want to know who I'm working for?" she asked. "Well, who I was working for?"

"I do not care," he said. "Sit in that chair."

She sat.

I was already at the desk in front of a rectangular screen, my fingers flying over a keyboard. Felt just like home.

"It isn't Slater," she said.

"Hollis?" Abraham guessed.

"Yes. He never has liked that you all followed his brother and refused to side with him or House Water."

"If he weren't trying to kill us, we might be persuaded to listen to his arguments," he said. "I've told him our terms for helping him fight House Fire. Galvanized will be no man's army, no man's slave. Especially not a power-hungry man like Hollis, who wants to topple his power-hungry foe."

"You could be. Army, not slaves," she clarified.

"We will not be. Not one of us."

"Don't think you speak for all the galvs, Abraham. They haven't followed your rules and word for hundreds of years. Well, except Foster, and he just doesn't have enough brains to be anything other than blindly loyal to you."

Foster raised his gun, pointed it at Sallyo's head.

"No," Abraham said. "Don't shoot her. She's not that important."

"I could be," she practically purred. "I'm always look-ing to make a new deal. I'll pave your way to a truce with Hollis and the heads of House Water and Fire. I'll stand as witness to your character and desire to lay down your killing ways."

"Hollis won't believe a mutant mercenary any more than he believes a stitched," Abraham said. "I've told him our terms."

"Clean records and free rein to walk among humans, as if you were human and not a freakish, unkillable monster? Come, now, Abraham. Even you aren't so naive that you think anyone would be foolish enough to trust the stitched."

"I'm not asking for trust," he said. "I'm asking for the chance to earn it. A chance to not be hunted, shot at, and betrayed. Any luck, Matilda?"

"The surveillance system isn't one I'm familiar with. If I trip the wrong thing, we're going to shut the entire city down."

"I don't see the downside to that."

"Slater's building is electronically locked. If we cut power, he'll be bunkered in there tighter than a tick. We won't be able to blast our way in. But if I can find the right file. . . ." I flipped through strings of data, fast, faster.

And then one secure file caught my eye. It was an executable program set on a timer, and the timer was already counting down.

I continued to scan, and set up a password breaker to work on prying open the file.

"Hollis isn't the only head of House who wants you dead if you don't follow his rules, Abraham," Sallyo said.

"Mercenaries never follow the rules. And neither do galvanized. Did you get what you wanted out of this?" he asked. "Did you get a guarantee Neds wouldn't be sent back to the asylum and experimented on?"

Neds?

Sallyo was silent a moment. "Who told you?"

"You did. I saw how you looked at him back at the farm. You walked away from a job, Sallyo. You walked away from bringing Matilda and Quinten in for damn good money. And I am sure Slater was displeased. So you went to Hollis. You went to House Water to secure safety for Neds, didn't you?"

"I did what I had to do," she said, "no matter how foolish."

"Love makes fools of us all," he agreed.

I glanced up.

Love? She loved Neds? So I was right. That was why he was so angry with her. He loved her too, but neither of them wanted to admit it.

She wasn't looking at me. Her eyes were on Abraham, a self-mocking smile curving her lips.

"And here we are," she said, "the fools."

The secure file flashed on the screen and opened, spilling out the contents while the timer still counted down.

"Oh, shit," I said.

"Did you find a way in?" Abraham asked.

"They've activated the bomb," I said. "For House Earth. Slater activated the bomb. And it's aiming at Compound Five."

20

This is it. One last push. If I can reach you, I can warn you. One last time, one last chance to make this right.

— Welton Yellow

"Can you deactivate it?" he asked.

"It's counting down. The last bomb was a suicide bomber. I don't even know if there is a remote trigger." Even as I said that, I was tearing through the program. Maybe it wasn't a trigger. Maybe it was a signal sent to tell the bomber to activate the bomb.

I could stop that.

I could try to stop that. I'd find a way to stop that.

"You need to get us into Slater's building, Matilda," Abraham said. "Now. Break those locks. He knows we're here, doesn't he, Sallyo? He knows we're coming for him."

"I'd listen to your boyfriend," Sallyo said.

I knew I had to get us in to Slater. I knew every second I wasted on the bomb was too long. I knew Slater could be on his way right now with grenade launchers and troops and plenty of things to kill us dead.

But Quinten was in Compound Five. So were Neds and Gloria and Welton. I'd watched them die to give me the chance to go back in time to change the experiment, to save the world.

And I'd be damned if I watched them die again.

"Matilda," Abraham warned.

"I will not," I said, "live in a world where my brother is dead when I have the chance to save him. Or Neds or Welton or any of you. If Slater is on his way, then that's fine with me. I can kill him here just as easily as in his own apartment. It'll save me the trouble of breaking the locks."

An explosion blew in the door. The blast threw Foster off his feet. Abraham turned toward the threat, firing at the men with blast shields who pressed through the burning metal and smoke and into the room.

"Matilda!" he yelled.

I hadn't left the desk. I was almost done breaking the code. I just needed a second, a moment more.

A bullet tore into my left arm, and I yelled.

But I had the code now. I could stop the signal to the bomber. I could stop the signal to all the bombers.

Foster and Abraham fired at the guards, but there were too many of them and too many guns.

Sallyo grabbed her gun and darted to the other door. "Get out of here," she yelled, as she fired at the guards. "There's no time."

And then, right that moment, the world went slippery and dizzy. I struggled to remain focused on the keyboard, to code in the cancelation sequence that would stop the bombing.

But the world slid away in the drenching perfume of roses.

The room around me shifted. Instead of a control center, it was a storage room, boxes piled high all around me, making the place instantly claustrophobic and horrifically silent.

Since I shifted time but remained in the same space, I suddenly realized I could time-slip myself into a wall.

And then I'd be dead.

"Matilda?" Welton's voice said from a muffled distance.

I hurried through the towering stacks of cardboard and found him, leaning against the wall, exhausted and wheezing terribly.

"Are you okay?" I asked. Then I saw the blood pooling beneath where he had his hand pressed against his stomach. "Oh, God," I said. "You're hurt. You need a doctor. Or a technician. You need to get to Libra." I walked over, my hands out so I could help support him.

"Don't," he said, his breath coming out wet. "Slater knows it's the watch you took back in time. He's planning to break it in my timeway. He wants his original timeway—this one—to remain the one true reality. If he gets the watch, your family will be dead, and all the galvanized will die in prisons. I'll be dead soon too. Slater will destroy your chance to live in a world where at least some of you could find happiness."

"You can too," I said. "You're alive in my timeway. Running House Earth instead of House Technology."

"House Earth?"

"It's like House Brown. But you've modified it a bit."

That got a small smile out of him. "Doesn't that sound like an interesting thing? I'm pleased to hear I'm thriving somewhen. Because I will not survive long here. No, don't look at me like that. Libra had her fun making me into her wind-up doll, but that's over. I'm . . . over." He paused to breathe, and the sound of mechanics deep beneath the bulky coat he wore was startling.

"I've known it for months. But I wanted . . . I wanted to take my last breath knowing that bastard wasn't going to rule. In any reality."

"He won't," I said. "I promise."

"Your grandmother," Welton said.

"She's fine. She's alive too."

"Of course she is. I have had time to study . . ." He paused to inhale, exhale, and swallow. His color had gone a ghastly gray-yellow. "Her journal," he said, his voice a little shaky. "The dates of the entries were curious. So I looked into her past, looked into her life." He paused again for breath. "She's old, Matilda. Very old. She was there. In 1910, when Alveré Case built the Wings of Mercury machine, when he triggered the experiment. She was his assistant."

"No," I said, "She couldn't have been. That would make her more than three hundred years old, and no one but galvanized live that long."

"I think you weren't the only family secret your father was trying to hide," he said with a wan smile. "She was Alveré's assistant. Lara Unger Case. I've found no record that Alveré survived all these years, but I believe she did."

"How?" I was probably the last person in this world to doubt an impossibility, but to think my grandmother was—what? Immortal? Galvanized?—was a reach, even for me.

"My theory? She was in the eye of the storm when the experiment was triggered. It . . . did something to tie her to the experiment, to lock her body into the altered times." He gave me a steady look. "There is a possibility, a small possibility, that it isn't the watch you need to destroy to set reality. It may be your grandmother."

"No," I said, a chill of fear washing over me. "Never. That's not going to happen. Tell me Slater doesn't know about her. About her being Alveré's assistant."

"He most definitely does not," he said with a little bit of heat. "I made sure of that. But I thought you should know. In case . . . well, in case."

I nodded. "That *in case* isn't going to happen. In any reality."

"Good," he said. "Foster?"

"He's well. I told him what you said."

Welton smiled, though it looked like it took some effort. "He believes in this time-travel nonsense?"

"He sort of has to. He's the one with the watch."

"Time is in . . . good . . . hands," he said, his voice going soft and distant as his eyes went yellow, glossy, and fixed. His lips moved around another word, but I couldn't hear it over the machines in his chest that blared out Klaxon alarms. He shuddered.

I grabbed for him as fell to the floor. Then the world twisted and spiraled as a distant bell rang out in rose-scented peals.

I yelled as gunfire filled the room and world. Welton was gone, and I knelt in the middle of a firefight. Foster's huge hand seemed to come out of the nowhere of smoke and noise. Too fast. This was all happening too fast. I couldn't handle the whiplash between realities.

Foster pulled me up off the floor.

The bomb!

"No!" I said, reaching for the keyboard. "I have to stop the bomb. I have to stop the bombing."

"We run," he said, his eyes glowing red with anger and probably pain, since his hand was still wrapped around my wrist and he had collected more than one new bullet hole.

"We save." I yanked out of his grip and finished coding in the command to stop the countdown.

I didn't know why I wasn't shot to pieces. Either the guards were the worst shots in the history of man, or something else was getting in the way of their killing.

"Foster!" Abraham yelled from where he was holding open the door on the far side of the room.

And that's when the madness and chaos around me snapped into shape.

The galvanized poured through the door Sallyo had opened. The room became a riot of galvanized tearing a swath through the guards. Just a couple seconds ago, the guards had been behind riot shields, firing weapons. Now they were not outnumbered, but they were definitely outpowered.

"Now," Foster yelled. "Now, Matilda."

I didn't have time to unlock Slater's security system. I didn't even have time to see how many of the galvanized were still standing. From the voices shouting directions, swearing, and laughing, it sounded like all the galvanized were still on their feet.

Foster wrapped his hand over my uninjured shoulder and quickly pushed me across the room.

I jogged slightly ahead of him while Abraham stood in the doorway, his gun drawn. "This way," he said.

We were in another long hall with metal doors uniformly spaced down either side.

"Did you shut down the locks?" Sallyo asked as she ran just ahead of us.

"Why are we following her?" I asked.

"You didn't disable the surveillance cameras," Abraham said. "She's on record for having allowed us all into the city. Slater will kill her. Well, torture her, then kill her for what she did. Even Hollis can't keep her safe. Only killing Slater will ensure her safety."

"So, we're on the same side now?"

"Apparently."

"Locks?" Sallyo asked again.

"No," I said.

"Did you take care of the bomb headed to House Brown?" Abraham asked.

"I hope so."

"Good enough. Now let's blow our way into Slater's building and hunt the bastard down."

Sallyo took us down several flights of stairs, then through a crawl space between the walls I thought might be there only for electricians. Small electricians at that.

It was a tight fit for me, and Abraham and Foster cussed and swore and both lost a layer of skin by the time we exited out into a darkened hall. Good thing they couldn't feel any of their wounds.

The hall was stone on both sides, and from the dust that covered the floor, it hadn't been used in years. The metal door at one end was shut, the other end of the hall was lost in stagnant shadows.

"We're inside his building," Sallyo said. "But I have no idea which floor he's on or what kind of weapons he has."

We needed to find Slater. And since he and I were somehow connected by time, and the watch was somehow connected to time, I thought maybe it could work as a sort of compass to find him.

"Foster," I said, "do you have the watch?"

He pressed his fingers inside his jacket and pulled out the watch.

"I think I should hold it," I said.

"Why?" Sallyo said. "What does the watch have to do with anything?"

I ignored her and turned to Abraham. "Welton told me Slater knows the watch is the key. Slater wants to break the watch in the other timeway so he can lock that in as reality. You're all dead there, and as soon as the watch is broken, he would kill me too. I'm going to try to use the watch to find him. If that doesn't work, I'm going to break it now, while we're in the right time."

"Which means Slater can kill you."

"And I can kill him."

"With the watch?" Sallyo asked.

I touched the handle of the gun. "Shelley dust–filled bullets."

"What's Shelley dust?" she asked.

I held my hand out for the watch. "The easiest way to kill a galvanized." Foster pressed the pocket watch into my palm.

The world went dizzy again and the scent of roses filled my nostrils and mouth. A great bell rang, loud and louder.

Every inch of me broke and shattered, scattering on the wind. Time, all time—images and visions of things this reality had never been, things of other realities, more than I could count—echoed out around me like a hundred movies playing at once through a hundred different round windows.

It was too much to comprehend. It was too much to contain. Even broken in a million pieces, there wasn't enough of me to withstand the storm of possibilities surrounding me.

There was only one correct timeway, only one where I knew the people I loved were alive. And sorting out that one single timeway from all the other possible times was like plucking a specific drop of water from a thundering waterfall.

I was drowning, stretched too thin, unable to breathe. Unable to exist.

Then the world snapped back into one solid focus. I gasped, filling my lungs with air I could not get enough of. I was on the floor of the dark hallway, Abraham's hand under my head, the watch held at arm's length away from me in his other hand.

For a moment—a fleeting breath—he was the happier, tattooed Abraham, his hair pulled back in a band, the concern on his face more akin to shock. Then that image blinked away and it was just Abraham, the mercenary Abraham, kneeling over me.

"Matilda?" he said. "Can you hear me? Can you hear my voice?"

I swallowed, tasted vomit and blood. My head hurt like all kinds of hell, and my skin felt like I'd been standing in a bonfire.

"Yes," I croaked, my voice raw. "I hear you."

The relief on his face was instant. "Can you sit?"

I didn't waste time or energy answering. I pushed up with his help. He was keeping the watch in his extended hand as far away from me as possible.

I found myself agreeing with that decision wholeheartedly.

"Foster." He gave Foster the watch, and the big man tucked it back into his jacket pocket.

"What happened?" I asked.

"You . . ." Abraham shook his head. "I don't know what you did. But you were in agony until I pulled the watch out of your hand. What do you remember?"

"Everything. Nothing. All the time. None of it." He helped me up to my feet.

The world stayed steady beneath me and around me. I felt like crap, but I was standing, and I was pretty sure I could walk.

"When did you and I meet?" I asked Abraham. I needed to know he was the Abraham in the reality that I wanted to thrive.

"In my recollection, we met back in the jail in 1910. More recently, at your kitchen door." He frowned. "Why do you—"

I held up my finger. "You came with Foster and Sallyo. You met my brother, Quinten, and Neds, whom we left at House Earth Compound Five, which we also might have just saved from being bombed. Is this correct?"

"Yes."

Oh, thank heaven. I really was in the right timeway. "Gold. I can't touch that watch again, so I can't break it."

"We noticed," Sallyo said.

"Someone else is going to have to take care of that," I said.

The hall filled with a light so bright, I thought I'd gone blind.

"Did you think I would let you walk into my House?" Slater's voice rolled out over the speakers. "Did you think I wouldn't know you were here? That I haven't known all along that you were here? You gravely under-estimate my intelligence, Ms. Case."

"The door!" Sallyo ran for the door at the end of the hall, but it was locked. And before Abraham or Foster could break it down, before we could pull a gun, the room was flooded with a gas that tasted like grape seeds and motor oil.

Sallyo collapsed, gasping. My vision narrowed down. The hallway tilted as I fell.

And everything went black.

21

I woke to the sound of gunfire. Again. Five measured shots rang out, impossibly close. Impossibly loud.

My head and all the rest of me hurt, but I forced my eyes open. I was chained to a wall, manacles around my wrists above me, ankles shackled, waist pinned.

It was a small, clean room. Metal walls, concrete floor. One door, locked and bolted. No windows. It was cold in here, as if the person who spent the most time in the space worked hard enough to sweat.

Abraham sat, shackled, in a chair that was bolted into the floor. He was unconscious.

Foster lay on the ground next to me, bleeding from the bullet holes in his chest. His eyes were open, fixed on some distant vision between the floor and ceiling, his breathing labored and drawn.

Slater, wearing a dark, tailored suit, stood next to Foster's prone body. The gun in his hand—my gun—was aimed at Foster's head. He must have heard us talking in the hallway. He knew exactly what those bullets held: Shelley dust.

I'd heard five shots. There was only one left.

"Don't," I said, trying to make my voice heard over the ringing in my ears. "Don't kill him."

"Ah, Matilda," Slater said, his back still toward me, his head tipped down as if he were hypnotized by the bleeding man below him. "You still think you can tell me what to do."

He turned. The shadows of the fluorescent lights revealed a madness in him that time had only cultivated.

He was not a man I'd ever thought would listen to reason. He had always been self-important, conniving, vicious.

But now I knew there was nothing I could say that would make him do anything other than exactly what he wanted. There was nothing human left of him.

"Do you have the watch?" he asked with the lullaby softness of a man just warming up to the pain he knew he was going to put a person through.

"No," I said.

"You are lying to me, Matilda Case. You have always lied to me. But your friend Welton didn't lie to me when I tore out the wires of his guts and left him bleeding on the floor. He told me about the watch. He said you must have it. So. Where is the watch?"

"I don't have it," I said again. "I don't have to have it to kill you."

"More lies. It is a wonder I don't just end you forever. Now." He lifted the gun, leveling the barrel at my head.

Galvanized can live forever. We are endlessly repairable, as long as the majority of the brain is not destroyed. But that bullet was filled with Shelley dust. One of those, in my brain, would do more harm than a dozen bullets.

It would be the end of me.

"Shoot," I said. "It won't kill me as long as the watch is intact. Nothing you can do can kill me."

The smile pulled his lips away from his teeth and tightened the corners of his eyes. He gripped the gun a little tighter, and his breathing quickened.

Shoot me, I thought. It would hurt like hell, but that would be the last of the Shelley dust bullets. If he used it on me, he couldn't use it to finish off Foster. Foster already had too many bullets working to kill him. But none of them were in his head. Maybe Foster would survive.

Slater held his breath, and I held mine.

But then slowly, slowly, he lowered the gun.

He strolled toward me in measured steps, shoes a solid *thump* against concrete. He stopped so close, I could feel his breath on my cheek as he whispered in my ear. "Do not think you can tell me what to do." He shifted the gun and shoved it up under my sternum so hard, I grunted from the pain.

"Do you feel that?" he asked. "That is your death. I will pull your guts from your body with my bare hands. And I will end your agony only when your wretched screams please me. You and I are locked in this game," he said, "locked in time together. But I will hang you by your bones and bathe in your blood."

He slammed his fist into my stomach, and I yelled as ribs cracked.

"Where—" He slammed his fist into me again: the same damn place. "Is." *Slam.* "The." *Slam.* "Watch."

I was dizzy with pain. Blood covered the back of my throat and dribbled down my chin and from my nose. He'd broken more than ribs. I was bleeding inside.

Even if I could get enough air into my tortured lungs to give him an answer, I wouldn't give the bastard the satisfaction.

"No?" he whispered close to my cheek again. "Then let's see what will loosen your tongue."

I tried to pull myself up straight, but my stomach and ribs were throbbing with pain. Bones felt like broken glass shifting around inside of me, catching and cutting.

I was strong. But, holy shit, so was he.

"Is this the thing you want, Matilda Case?" he asked.

I blinked until the sweat cleared from my eyes. I expected him to be standing over Foster again. But he was beside Abraham, one hand gripping Abraham's hair tight, yanking his head back, the other pressing the gun against his temple.

"This man, this collection of old flesh and spare parts? Is that what you will risk your life for?"

Abraham's eyes were open and fixed on me. He didn't appear to have any new injuries.

"Do you love him, Matilda?" Slater asked. Then yelled, "Do you love him?"

That was a Shelley dust bullet pointed at Abraham's head.

That would be enough to kill him.

I'd seen him almost die from Shelley dust before.

I couldn't do that again.

"No," I said.

Slater's eyes narrowed, and he bared his straight blunt teeth. "Then I could shoot him, and you wouldn't care?"

I didn't say anything. Abraham's gaze held mine.

Abraham knew I was lying. He knew I was trying to save his life.

But maybe nothing I said could.

"Slater," Abraham said.

"Shut up!" Slater yelled.

And then Slater pulled the trigger.

Abraham jerked, trying to duck the shot, but the gun was too close.

I yelled as blood sprayed back, covering the floor.

Abraham slumped sideways in the chair. Slater yelled and fired again and again, even though the chamber was empty.

There had been only six bullets. He'd unloaded five of them in Foster and the last in Abraham.

Abraham wasn't moving. The left side of his face was a mess of blood and muscle and bone.

That son of a bitch had killed him.

Rage fueled a fire in me. I yanked the cuffs, straining to break the shackles. But Slater was no fool. He knew just how much restraint was needed to keep a galvanized pinned.

This wasn't how it was going to end. I wasn't going to let Slater rule this world or any other world.

No.

Not again.

Never again.

A motion on the floor caught my gaze.

Foster shifted his hand. His eyes begged me to stay silent. In his hand was the watch. His body was full of Shelley dust, and I knew it was undoing him, dissolving his stitches, destroying his organs. But he closed his hand around the watch, asking me.

I nodded.

Yes. Yes. Yes.

He summoned the last of his strength. His massive hand was pale and shaking, his breathing ragged. Foster squeezed the watch, crushing it until metal collapsed and gears ground down.

The world swayed.

Then reality exploded and fractured into a thousand different shards, shattering me with it.

A great bell tolled like thunder, driving rose-scented rain over me and the sound of my screams. I didn't know if destroying the watch would work to change the world. I didn't know if I would be lost in this chaos of times, or if I would ever find my way home again.

But right now, all that mattered to me, the only thing I wanted, was to kill Slater.

In this timeway—for however long it lasted—in this brief space between time, I was free, the shackles gone.

A thousand views of the room, the world, spun around me: broken, bloody, empty, rubble, burning, torn. A thousand different times slipped past me like spinning disks.

I didn't even try to make sense of them.

Slater was the only other fixed point. And he was the only thing I was fixed on. He stood across the room, his back toward me.

He turned.

I pulled the syringe out of the breast pocket of the leather jacket Abraham had given me, tucking it into my palm. My movements were nightmarishly slow; every action I took seemed to fill a thousand years.

I ran for Slater. I ran to end him. To kill him. Now and finally.

Each step was a struggle, as if time dragged against me, pulling like gravity, as reality shattered and shattered again, dragging me toward the bell that echoed its own peal, a cacophony of forevers.

Slater lifted a different gun.

The watch was broken. If it was the relic, I could kill him. He could kill me.

I heard him yell as he squeezed the trigger, felt the hot agony of the bullet strike my chest. Once. Twice.

I kept running, would never stop running, anger and hatred pulsing through me.

He had killed my family. He had killed my friends. He

had destroyed my world and destroyed the only time and reality I could call home.

Abraham was bleeding, dying. Foster was breathing his last breath.

I would not abide living in any time, in any world where Slater was still alive while they were not.

Breaking the watch should have severed the circuit of time pouring between Slater and me. But maybe Welton had gotten that wrong. Maybe the circuit would be broken only when one of us was dead. Or maybe the watch wasn't the key. Maybe it was my grandmother's life.

I would never sacrifice her. I could never hurt her. This had to be the answer. This had to work.

And so I ran.

"Matilda!" A voice called out over the bell, my name echoing and repeating into a song I could not escape.

Slater must have heard it too. He turned to look at the same moment I did.

And there, standing at a distance and a simultaneous nearness my mind refused to comprehend, was a small, white-haired woman. Grandma. A great wind blew her hair behind her like a wing, and in her hands was a knitted scarf.

In my time, my reality, she had been able to stitch up bits of time into a scarf I had used to freeze time. If Welton's theory was true, her ability to do that suddenly made more sense. It wasn't the little pocket sheep that gave her time, but the fact that she had been at the very heart of the time experiment, at the crucible zero of when time had both broken and mended.

She pulled on the scarf stitches, unraveling the cloth. If that scarf was anything like the one she'd given me in my timeway, it would pause time.

"Now, my sweet," she said, her voice softened by distance and yet so near, it was startling. "Now."

Slater wasn't moving anymore. He was frozen in front of me, the gun still raised.

All time, all chaos, was frozen, still and silent. The only things moving were me and my grandmother, whose hands steadily ticked away each stitch like the second hand of a clock, the pulse of the universe captured in the thread of her life.

I ran. My feet were no longer trapped and hobbled by time. I was wings. I was freedom. I was death.

I stopped in front of Slater. Stood squarely in front of him.

"This is for Robert, whose body and life you stole." I stabbed the syringe into his carotid artery. "This is for the innocents you killed." I forced the plunger down.

Then I pulled the gun out of his hand. "And this," I said, pressing the barrel against his forehead, "is for me, you son of a bitch."

I unloaded the clip into his skull.

The bell pealed, an infinite sound that filled me with the scent of roses.

Slater convulsed and fell to his knees, dead before he hit the ground.

I spun, looking for my grandmother. Was his death her death?

She was gone, whisked away by the swirling chaos of times streaming by fast. Too fast. Just like I would be whisked away.

I threw myself toward the reality I had fought for. The reality so many had died for. Before I knew if I had reached it or not, the world drained down a great hole, and I was gone.

*   *   *

I was standing, a gun in my shackled hand. Across the small, cold room where we'd been imprisoned, Slater lay on the floor. He was not moving. He was not breathing.

A pool of blood spread in a wide circle around him. The syringe of Shelley dust was buried in his neck.

I didn't know if he was dead. Didn't know if that small amount of Shelley dust and the bullets to his brain would kill him. I strained against the shackles, afraid he'd rise again.

The bone in my left wrist snapped, and I yelled. But the shackle broke free from the concrete. I threw my weight into it, and broke the right shackle free.

I fumbled with the other restraints at my waist and feet, my broken left hand tucked against my ribs. Abraham was slumped, still chained in his chair. Foster lay unmoving on the other side of the room.

I wanted to go to them to see if they were still breathing, but I had to know that Slater was dead.

I limped over to him, the bullets, shattered ribs, and broken wrist sending shots of pain through me with every step.

I didn't have a weapon to kill him with.

But I didn't need one.

I crouched over his prone body. He lay facedown. He might be dead. Well, I intended to make sure.

I gripped the gun in my right, unbroken hand, and slammed it into his head, pounding until bone cracked, until blood and brains stained my fist.

Galvanized could be revived as long as enough of our brains remained intact.

I methodically made sure there wasn't anything left of Slater.

"Hold it right there," a man's voice said. "Put down the gun, and step away from the body."

The voice broke my grim thrall, and I blinked, suddenly aware of the gore around me.

"That," I whispered, "was for Welton and Oscar and Abraham, and all the other people you destroyed, you sick bastard."

I heard several sets of footsteps behind me. I put my hands out to my sides, stood, and turned.

The heavily armored guards carried enough firepower to take out a city block, but they were wearing dark blue uniforms, not the orange I'd seen the other guards wear.

The change of color seemed important, but I couldn't figure out why.

"Gun. Down." The guard in front repeated.

I knelt, set the gun on the floor.

I was numb, my mind still scattered across the chaos of time, skittering away from the brutal chore of Slater's death and the fear that Abraham and Foster were dead.

It would be easy to fall into the madness that pulled at me with stiff fingers.

Is Abraham dead? Is Foster?

I had fought for this world. I had fought for them.

I had lost. Too much. I didn't want to lose them now.

"Matilda Case?"

I looked up. Realized I'd been standing there in a daze for more time than I could track.

I had never met the man in front of me, but I knew instantly who he was.

Hollis Gray, Oscar's conniving, ruthless brother who had stopped at nothing, including killing his own brother, to secure his place of power among the Houses.

But that was my time. In this time, he was head of defense for House Water.

What was he doing here behind House Fire walls?

Sallyo stood behind and to the side of him, her eyes

flicking with approval over the grim spectacle surrounding us.

"Yes?" I said, my voice too quiet in the quiet of the room.

"Will you please follow me? There are some matters we need to take care of."

"I won't leave them," I said. "Foster. Abraham. I won't leave them."

Hollis looked me up from boots to scalp. I knew I was covered in blood and gore—my own and Slater's. I was shot, broken, and maybe a little crazy. But I'd saved the world.

Again.

For the last time.

The guards stood aside so that medical people could enter the room with stretchers and packs of equipment.

"We will let the doctors tend to the galvanized," he said. "And to you. Please, if this . . . event is to be handled quickly and quietly, so that peace may remain intact between the Houses, you need to come with me now."

Sallyo nodded at me, imperceptibly urging me to accept his offer.

I had never trusted Hollis in my world. Even Oscar had admitted to not trusting him in this world.

But there weren't a lot of other choices in front of me.

"Are they alive?" I asked.

Hollis glanced at one of the doctors, who was easing Abraham onto a stretcher. "Yes," the doctor said. "But they'll need to be taken to surgery immediately."

"There is nothing more you can do for them at this time, Ms. Case," Hollis said. "Let us care for them. And for you."

I nodded stiffly and watched the medical team heft Abraham and Foster out of the room, moving as quickly as they could. And then I followed, with Hollis and Sallyo and all their guards at my back.

"I want you to know that I appreciate your part in this conflict," Hollis began, once we were settled in a small but posh room halfway across the city. We'd gotten there by an underground road that had taken me to a room where a doctor stitched and bandaged me and set my hand in a splint. Hollis and Sallyo had remained with me. I asked to see Foster and Abraham, and had been told they were in surgery.

We'd left that building through a garage, driven in a car with darkened windows, and given code words at two checkpoints before we'd arrived here, at what I assumed was Hollis's office.

I was still numb, bloody, and hurting. I just wanted this to end.

"What part in what conflict?" I asked, unable to sort through the deals and double crosses from the past few days. My voice still didn't sound right in my mind. Probably because so much of me was silently screaming over Abraham's looming death.

Sallyo stood near the door as any good bodyguard should, while Hollis, in his impeccably tailored shirt, trousers, and long jacket, leaned back away from the desk he was seated behind.

"Several months ago, it came to our attention that Slater was manufacturing a new strain of the One-four plague. The new strain, One-five, was devastating in its effects and the speed at which it killed—or did much worse—to people. When the heads of the sub-Houses in House Fire began to die of the plague, we were naturally curious as to the man who seemed to benefit most from their death."

I watched him, and I heard what he was saying. Slater had been doing a terrible thing. Killing people so he could get what he wanted: power to rule.

But the numbness inside of me was spreading. I wanted to walk out of this place and never see a House or House ruler again. I wanted my farm, my brother, my grandmother. And I wanted Foster and Abraham alive.

"We did not have the proper . . ." He paused to consider his words. "Equipment to kill a galvanized. And we were uncertain who among the galvanized might align with our needs. While I apologize for the subterfuge of sending Sallyo out to your property to bring you into this, I am very pleased you were willing to take care of this urgent challenge we faced."

Urgent challenge was the nicest thing anyone had ever called Slater.

"You planned this? Me killing him?"

"I planned for Sallyo to get the letter. I had hoped Abraham would accompany her, and that if you were the woman he had been searching for, that your safety would become his priority. He was once a great leader of the galvanized, you know. A hero whom they followed."

"I know," I said quietly.

"What I am telling you, Matilda Case, is that you can walk free. I know my brother, Benik, would welcome you as a part of his unique team. I would also like to extend to you an invitation to serve House Water, if you would care to."

The only thing I cared to do right now was to go home.

"Where is my brother?" I asked.

"He sent a message to Coal and Ice."

Hollis was the head of information in this world. He undoubtedly knew what that message said.

"And?"

"He was upset by your decision to continue on to House Fire without him. He mentioned that his patient is in full remission."

Gloria was cured. That was an immense relief. Quinten really had found a cure. That would change the world. He would change the world.

"Do you know where my brother is?" I repeated.

"He is on the way here, and wishes that you remain with me until he can return home with you."

That finally pierced through the numbness and haze of my thoughts: home. "I want Abraham and Foster to come home with us too."

"Of course," he said. "Once they are stable. Sallyo, will you see to that and also take Ms. Case to a room to rest, please?"

Sallyo nodded, then opened the door and held it for me. I took that as my cue to follow her, which I did.

I didn't know how long it had taken us to fight our way to Slater, but with everything that had happened, it must be the middle of the night. That meant Quinten wouldn't be here for several hours.

"Right in here," Sallyo said, opening for me another door that was just a short way down the hall.

This room was clean, with a functionally equipped desk against one wall, a bed, and a door at the back, through which I could see the bathroom.

"Clean up if you want," she said. "I can get you some food or clothes."

"Don't," I said.

I walked into the room and straight toward the shower. I didn't care how wet I got my bandages.

"Matilda," she said. "I want you to know that I'm sorry I couldn't be more honest about this."

I stopped, then turned around. "You were a part of this, Sallyo. A part of people living. A part of people dying. I heard what you said to Abraham when I was hacking the locks. I know you saved Neds, and did so at risk to yourself. For that, I thank you. Right now, I do not want to talk about . . . any of this. Please go away and leave me alone."

She narrowed her eyes, gauging me. Then she must have thought better of pushing the tired, beat-up galvanized woman who had just killed a man. She nodded once and left the room.

I walked into the bathroom, stripped. I stood beneath the sanitized spray of hot water and wept.

The next morning, while I sat on the edge of the bed, staring at my feet and trying to figure out how I could sneak out to see Abraham, the door to my room opened in a rush.

Quinten looked like he had gotten even less sleep than I; his hair was an unruly mess, and dark circles ringed under his eyes. He ran across the room and threw his arms around me in a tight hug.

"Don't ever," he said. "Don't ever leave me like that. Don't ever throw yourself in harm's way like that. Not without me. Never without me."

I wrapped my arms around him, the warmth, the reality of him sinking in through the fog that still permeated my brain.

"I wasn't good enough," I said. "He shot them, Quinten. Abraham and Foster. I don't know if they're going to live."

He squeezed me tight. "Hush. You were more than good enough. You were remarkable. You killed Slater." He kissed me briefly on my temple, then stepped back, holding me at arm's length. "I'm going now to check in on Abraham and Foster. It's been arranged for me to use the medical facility here. You have fallen into the favor of both House Water and House Fire, Matilda, though I'll be damned how you managed it."

"I killed Slater."

"I heard about that," he said gently.

From the doorway, I heard Right Ned say, "*Everyone* heard about that."

I glanced over at him. Right Ned was smiling, and Left Ned slowly shook his head. "Show-off," he said.

"I want you to know," Quinten said, "that I will make sure Abraham and Foster recover from this. If anyone can repair them, it's me."

"It's Shelley dust."

"I know. And since I am the man who made it, I am also the man with the antidote." He searched my face. "Are you sure you're okay?"

"A few scratches. I'm fine." I stepped out of his touch and pulled on the jacket Abraham had given me, the weight of it a comfort even though my broken ribs, bullet holes, and wrist ached.

"Where are you going?" he asked.

"With you. If there's something I can do to help, stitching or something, I want to be there."

He smiled and shook his head. "You are amazing, Matilda. For a little sister, that is."

Hours later, I was there when Foster woke up. I was there when Abraham opened his eyes and said my name. I am not ashamed to admit I cried.

22

I'm not one to write my thoughts down. But a galvanized named Foster came to my office with a bottle of whiskey and told me he had a long story to tell. A story in which he and I are heroes who saved the world: he by believing in a little girl, me by never giving up on my friends, scattered across two times. I find him . . . immensely likable for a killer, or, as he insists, a hero. I think this is the beginning of a most delightful friendship.
　　　　　— Custodian Welton, House Earth

It turned out Neds hadn't been kidding when he said everyone knew I had killed Slater. And while killing the head of a House came with severe punishments, those were waived as soon as Hollis brought forth his proof that Slater had manufactured the One-five plague and killed many innocent people on his way to power.

It didn't hurt that Quinten had developed and tested the cure for the plague.

The man who owned the cure owned the world.

I thought the world was in pretty good hands.

Hollis became our most outspoken spokesman and advocate, skillfully guiding the conversation to eventually address the barbaric treatment of galvanized over the years.

He championed peace between the Houses and the House Earth compounds, and even went so far as to expunge the galvanized criminal records.

For a price. House Water, House Fire, and House Earth were willing to give the galvanized a chance to rebuild their lives. But there was community service they would need to pay forward. The galvanized would be recognized as human and would be subject to the same human rights afforded those who aligned with a House.

I think the offer was enough of a surprise to the galvanized that they had all decided they needed a little time to reflect on what they actually wanted to do with their lives and how they wanted to integrate into modern society.

No matter the pretty words they used to frame it, the galvanized were officially free to make their own way in the world.

For the first time in any world.

Which was why I was baffled that they'd all decided that my piece of land was where they wanted to settle down and think things through.

Grandma, however, was thrilled with the company.

"I've left a pot of soup on the stove, Matilda," she said as she picked up her knitting bag and a jar of sweet preserves. The early-morning light slanted soft gold through the windows of our kitchen, and when it caught her white hair, she practically glowed.

I sat at the table, drinking a cup of tea, enjoying the relative silence before anyone else was up. Grandma's mind had snapped back into place after Foster destroyed the watch. She said it was like waking up from a three-hundred-year-old dream, only to find that she hadn't been dreaming. And then she'd found herself in the timeway with Slater and me.

We'd tossed around some ideas as to why she had lived so long, and I'd shared with her Quinten Welton's theory. When the Welton of this time heard about it—because apparently there wasn't anything he didn't hear about—he'd done some digging too. The best we could come up with: standing in the eye of the storm during the original Wings of Mercury experiment had slowly drained her memories away, even as it had extended her life.

Now that time was finally, firmly in place, her years were numbered.

Which she couldn't be happier about. And at the rate she was going, she intended to fill the handful of years she had left with three hundred years' worth of living.

"Soup should be done by sunset," she said. "Talk Clara into making those beautiful biscuits she does so well."

"She's off with Dotty, Vance, and Wila, arguing over who's building the best cottage on our property."

Grandma chuckled. "It's nice to have folk around again, isn't it?" she said. "Family. Now, I won't be home until the day after tomorrow. You know how that Peter Gruben likes to talk. I think he's sweet on me."

I stood up and walked over to her. "Everyone's sweet on you," I said. "Are you sure you should be driving at your age?"

"Matilda," she said, and looked around the kitchen floor, as if she'd dropped something. A tiny blue sheep galloped around the corner of the hall to the kitchen. She bent with a groan and picked it up, tucking it expertly under her arm. "At my age, I need all the doing and being and living I can get. I won't live forever. Not anymore, my dear."

She gave me a squeeze and a kiss on the cheek.

"I'll see you soon," I said.

The sound of footsteps coming down the hall made her glance that way like a startled rabbit. She pressed one finger against her lips and giggled, then dashed out the door before anyone else showed up to get in the way of her little adventure.

I grinned and moved back to the table for my tea.

Abraham and Foster strolled into the room, moving even more smoothly than a few days ago. Their skin had finally lost the sickly greenish yellow pallor from the Shelley dust poisoning.

"Good morning," Foster said as he stepped over to the stove and poured himself some tea.

"Morning," I said.

Abraham wore a pair of denim jeans and a white V-neck T-shirt. He carried his boots in one hand. His hair was in need of a cut, swinging almost low enough on the left side to hide the spray of stitches we'd had to set from the corner of his eye to keep his face together.

The bullet had made a mess of that side of his face, but had gone straight through, along the outer edge of his skull.

As gunshots to the head went, he had been very, very lucky.

"You're up early," he said as he pulled the chair opposite of where I was standing away from the table and sat in it sideways, setting his boots on the floor.

"I'd get up at all sorts of hours for a little peace and quiet."

"Before Benik stops by?" he asked, and shoved one

foot into his boot, his hair swinging to hide the side of his face.

I wanted to draw it away from his eyes, wanted to touch him to remind myself for the millionth time that he was alive and well, but instead took a drink of my tea.

"Yes, before Oscar stops by and Welton—"

"Welton?" Foster asked happily. They'd developed a fast friendship that I figured would last a long lifetime.

"He'll be here by noon," I said, "Gloria too. This house is just a hub of activity lately."

"You don't like it?" Abraham shifted to fit his heel in his boot, and the neck of his shirt opened to reveal the edge of a bandage on the left side of his chest.

"I didn't say I didn't like it. But a little alone time now and then isn't such a bad thing. What's with the bandage?"

Foster chuckled, and Abraham threw him a dirty look. "It's nothing."

"Strip, Vail. As your nurse, and landlord, I have rights to see this nothing."

He sighed, settling his wide back against the chair and studying me. He shook his head. "I was going to wait to show you."

"Oh?"

"It's nothing to worry about."

"Prove it. Show me some skin."

He grinned, then shrugged out of his T-shirt with that slow ripple of muscles that made me lose my breath.

"It's not healed yet, but since you insist."

He peeled back the adhesive tape and removed the square of cotton.

A tattoo of a watch with keys for hands spread across his left pec muscle. Below it were the words *In somnis veritas*.

"Why?" I breathed.

I had never told him about the tattoo I had seen from the timeway I could not choose. And for a moment, I panicked, wondering if time was about to go wrong again, even though there hadn't been ripples for months. Not since we broke that watch and killed Slater.

"You told me you had a dream," he said. "That I was happy, that you were happy." He shrugged and lowered his voice. "You told me in that dream, I loved you." He was holding my gaze with his, asking me questions I had wanted to answer for months.

"In somnis veritas?" I asked.

"'In dreams there is truth.' Don't you agree?"

I wanted that. I wanted him. We had both fought so hard for a chance at this crazy, happy life with these people we loved. We had fought to mend time, save the innocent, and change the world.

We had done all that and, in doing so, we had won so much more.

We had won a life. We had won a chance to live it together.

"I do," I said. "Although I think reality is going to be better than any dream."

"That's a pretty bold claim, Ms. Case," he said. He stood and walked around the table to me. "I believe it might take years for us to prove that theory." His hand slid around my waist; the other tangled up in my hair, his thumb stroking the edge of my cheek.

I stood on my tiptoe and pressed against him so close, my lips were brushing his. "Luckily for us, we have all the time in the world."

Also Available
From National Bestselling Author
Devon Monk

HOUSE IMMORTAL
A House Immortal Novel

Matilda Case isn't like most folk. In fact, she's unique in the world, the crowning achievement of her father's experiments—a girl pieced together from spare parts. Or so she believes until Abraham Seventh shows up at her door, stitched with life thread just like her and insisting that enemies are coming to kill them all. Now, Tilly must fight to protect secrets that are hidden within the very seams of her being—secrets her enemies are willing to tear her apart piece-by-piece to get...

"Original and intriguing...with the kickass heroine, powerful near immortal beings, fun sidekicks, and original world, *House Immortal* will definitely appeal."
—All Things Urban Fantasy

Available wherever books are sold or at
penguin.com

facebook.com/acerocbooks

R0195

R0184

31192020835284